MAN WITH A GUN

Most of the top floor of the fourteen-storey brick fortress at One Police Plaza was occupied by the Police Commissioner and the many clerks and secretaries, all of whom wore guns, who served him. The PC exerted a substantial presence that could be felt throughout the building.

On afternoons when he went home early, as he did that Friday, this news swept outward along the corridors, downward through the floors. It moved like a rumour. No one knew how it moved so quickly. Other clerks, who also wore guns, stuck their heads into the offices of other commanders.

'The PC has left the building.'

Each seemed anxious to be first to impart such important information. Behind big desks middle-aged men with stars on their shoulders nodded curtly, as if they barely heard, though they did.

'The 'PC has left the building.'

The news dropped through the floors faster than the PC's descending elevator. The cop on duty in the subterranean garage heard it even before he saw him striding toward his car in which the engine was already running. To the commanders remaining behind, headquarters seemed suddenly lighter. The whole building seemed lighter, as if some oppressive weight had been lifted off.

MAN WITH A GUN

Robert Daley

ARROW BOOKS

Arrow Books Limited
62-65 Chandos Place, London WC2N 4NW

An imprint of Century Hutchinson Limited

London Melbourne Sydney Auckland
Johannesburg and agencies throughout
the world

First published in Great Britain
by Hutchinson 1988
Arrow edition 1988

Printed and bound in Great Britain by
Anchor Brendon Limited, Tiptree, Essex

ISBN 0 09 955190 X

One

THE PURPOSE OF THE MEETING WAS TO EMBARRASS THE Chief of Patrol so that he would want to resign. His services were no longer required. To fire him outright might have provoked comment, stories in the newspapers, which, in the police world, were always to be avoided if possible. One did these things by indirection, or almost so. This time it took about an hour. The only one not immediately aware of what was happening was Keefe, the new Deputy Commissioner, who was still unfamiliar with police tribal rites, though he caught on soon enough.

Keefe had conferred with the Police Commissioner two days before. They had worked out the meeting's agenda. This PC had taken office promising to put in place new priorities and new techniques, and he appeared to be doing it, which was why Keefe had agreed to serve him. The agenda was solid, and there was nothing on it about embarrassing anyone.

The Chief of Patrol, Keefe knew, was in direct command of all seventy-five precincts, and of the seventeen thousand uniformed men who patrolled New York in cars or on foot. Technically he was responsible for all acts of incompetence, corruption or outright criminality committed by any of them, so there were many ways and places he could be nailed, if that were a superior's object. But the PC had said nothing about it to Keefe.

The Chief of Patrol was named O'Brien. He came to the conference table in uniform and at the height of his powers, so to speak. He was a big man – most high ranking cops were big men, Keefe had noted. Most had Irish names too. O'Brien had a somewhat overbearing manner, as perhaps befitted both his weight and his station, and he spoke with a lower-class accent, the New York street accent of his

1

boyhood. Most high-ranking cops had accents just like him, and this had surprised Keefe too. Outsiders might have thought O'Brien uneducated, which he was not, or even stupid, which he certainly was not. He had a law degree and had been admitted to the New York Bar, though of course he did not practise. He had held his job and rank for nine years under three different police commissioners, and his principal flaw now was that he had not been appointed by this one. Neither had the Chief of Operations, who was named Kilcoyne, the only uniformed officer who outranked him. They were the last two such incumbents and they sat side by side at the far end of the table. So Kilcoyne, once he saw what was happening, must have been very worried; but in his case the axe did not fall.

Both these men were in their fifties. With the exception of Keefe, every commander in the room was more or less the same age and all had known each other for years, in some cases since their days in the Police Academy together, or since they first went out onto the street as patrolmen. They had known O'Brien's smile much longer than Keefe. The man had the habit of smiling most of the time, often to the surpassing irritation of subordinates. He could smile when handing out routine assignments. He could smile at men while disciplining them, he could smile when in a rage. His fellow commanders watched that smile now, watched it get increasingly sticky, like drying paint, and as the meeting progressed most of them could not watch it any more.

In Keefe's brief experience all these executive conferences began similarly. The conference room at police head-quarters was on the fourteenth floor, adjacent to the PC's office, and directly underneath the heliport on which his helicopter sometimes waited. There were two doors into it, one for him and one for them. The sixteen commanders entered separately. Except for Keefe and Gold, the Chief of Detectives, all were in uniform. They wore gold braid on their caps, and between two and four stars on their shoulders, and all commanded some important segment of the department.

The conference table had already been prepared. There

were yellow legal pads and sharpened pencils in front of each chair, and these middle-aged men, all but one dressed identically, all armed, stood around chatting, waiting. They were not nervous: as far as they knew there was nothing to be nervous about. Several times the PC's door opened and they turned expectantly. Conversation stopped. But it was not the PC yet, only one of his secretaries, a uniformed lieutenant, who glanced into the room, counted heads and withdrew. Whereupon conversation resumed.

But finally they were all there. The lieutenant stepped all the way into the room, and was followed by the PC himself, a small man wearing a brown suit with wide lapels, and a red tie with a big Windsor knot. The PC was another in a long line of Irish Catholic New York City police commissioners. His name was Egan. That is, his name was right. It was his physical appearance that always came as a surprise. His slight stature was against him. Also, his hair was thin, its colour was blonde turning to white, and his features were delicate. He looked studious, even intellectual, and when he spoke his voice was mild and his accent, unlike theirs, was neutral. His eyes were pale blue and drooped at the edges. To the city at large, and especially to the commanders assembled in this room, he did not look at all heroic. He was not a threatening figure. He did not resemble any tough cop they or the world was used to.

He took his place at the head of the table. His chair was the only one with arm rests. "Gentlemen," he said, "please be seated."

The PC's own police career had been spent principally at the Police Academy, where he had designed most of the training programs still in use. He had been considered a man of ideas. He had been, in effect, a school teacher rather than a street commander, and he always sounded like a school teacher in these meetings.

The lieutenant, a stenographer, took the chair to the PC's left. The commanders began to choose their places, doing so more or less at random, but the chair on the PC's right remained empty until he glanced over at young Keefe, patted the seat and said: "Over here, Phil."

3

As Keefe made his way in the PC's direction he was aware that eyebrows lifted all around the table. This was the second conference at which the PC had invited him to take the same chair. In the police department a man's power sometimes matched the insignia on his shoulder; sometimes it depended on how close he sat to the throne during events such at this one. Perhaps the PC was trying to exalt his new Deputy Commissioner. Or express displeasure with someone else. Perhaps he was trying to do both. Or neither. Keefe didn't know, and it annoyed him that it was something he was continually being made to think about. The men around this table spent more time protecting their turf – and their backs – than they did trying to bring department policies into sync with modern times.

In any case, Keefe did not immediately recognize the purpose of the meeting at all. Neither did anyone else, including the Chief of Patrol. He sat at the far end of the table wearing his permanent smile, and when Keefe happened to glance in his direction he got back a friendly wink.

First on the agenda was a report on the monthly crime statistics from the Chief of Planning, who sat halfway along on Keefe's side of the table. He had with him a pile of computer print-outs, and this pile diminished in thickness as it passed from hand to hand around the table. Meanwhile eyeglasses had come out and were perched on noses. Originally all these men had been selected as cops at least in part because of visual acuity, but that was long ago. Keefe was the only man present who could still read in poor light.

The Chief of Planning spoke in a flat voice, and the headings as he enumerated them closely resembled the litanies Keefe had recited as a boy in parochial school. Rapes were up, murders down slightly. Not a litany of the saints, a litany of sins. Armed robbery, always announced to the press as the key indicator of crime, was down slightly. Auto thefts were up for the month, nearly ten thousand cars. Dutifully the assembled police commanders pretended to study the rows of figures, from time to time peering out over their half-glasses to see what else might be required of them.

They were interrupted by the PC's voice: "Any comments, gentlemen?"

The sixteen print-outs went down onto the table where they were placed carefully on top of the sixteen yellow pads. Sixteen pairs of half-glasses came off noses and were carefully folded, but no one spoke until Keefe said hesitantly: "That's an awful lot of stolen cars."

He had been to a party recently where everyone was talking about their cars getting ripped off. Keefe saw car theft as a quality-of-life crime, and more important than these men seemed to think. They're too close to it, he told himself. Then he thought: what was I brought into this department for? Speak up.

Keefe added hesitantly: "Maybe we can't do much to prevent people from killing each other, but cutting up stolen cars is a business. It requires space and equipment. It requires a fixed address, for God's sake." It seemed to him that detectives ought to be able to find such people with relative ease, but he did not say so. He thought the idea might occur to one of the others, and he waited to see it take root; but apparently it did not, for no one said anything.

This was the first executive conference at which Keefe had felt confident enough to speak out at all. Every one of these men had been a cop all his adult life, whereas he was by profession a journalist. He had spent most of the last ten years as a foreign correspondent, much of it reporting on the various coups, wars and assassinations in the Middle East. Although his apprenticeship in law enforcement was only a few months old he knew as much of violence and irrationality as they did, and more of the world, or so he had convinced himself. He had a right to speak. Was it not his job, at least in part, to broaden the insularity of these men?

Nonetheless he was not totally sure of himself, and by temperament he was a man unwilling to throw his weight around. "In terms of auto theft, maybe we could be doing more," he concluded lamely.

He was not trying to cricitize any one man in particular, and did not at first realize he had, but others did at once. Grand larceny auto was the province of the auto squad, and so it seemed to them that Keefe had at least implied criticism of Chief of Detectives Gold to whom the squad reported. As the silence continued – as the PC allowed it to continue – men began to stir, and a few threw furtive glances in the direction of the PC, who only stared impassively at his hands. Chief Gold, meanwhile, had begun to fidget almost imperceptibly. Gold had been a New York cop as long as any of the rest, thirty-two years, but he was not part of the Irish Catholic mainstream, much less of the traditional Irish Catholic hierarchy, and he had been Chief of Detectives for only three weeks. He was short and stocky and wore a diamond ring on the little finger of his left hand. It was rare for men such as Gold to reach the top of the department, particularly in so sensitive a job, and it had occasioned much surprise when the PC appointed him.

For a few seconds more the table was silent, while Keefe's words were studied and calculations made. Was Keefe voicing thoughts of his own, ad-libbing, so to speak? If it was crime – and only crime – that was at issue here, then these men were the experts, not him. His comments could be politely refuted and after that ignored. But if he was speaking on behalf of the PC then Gold's career was in jeopardy, and to come to his defence could entail great risk. As these men saw it, discretion – meaning silence – had just been imposed on all of them.

The first to speak was Gold himself. He managed a carefree chuckle, and turned towards Keefe: "Auto theft is a manpower problem, Commissioner. My detectives are spread too thin. The auto squad has only twenty-five detectives to cover the whole city."

Smiles came on all around as the other men realized what Gold himself had realized a moment before. The PC did not appear to support Keefe's comments, and in addition Gold had been appointed so recently that the PC's own prestige was, for the time being, tied to him.

"It's a pity you didn't mention rape instead of auto theft, Commissioner," added Gold. "My men caught the Queens Delivery Man this morning."

Having successfully changed the subject, Gold began describing the arrest of the Delivery Man. He was chortling.

6

"Twenty-one women he rapes the past two months. I'm going crazy. My men are staked out all over Queens. Today he finally picks on the wrong broad." He paused dramatically. "He made her put it in her mouth like he always does, and she bit him. Victims very rarely bite the rapist. They're too scared. In my experience I've never heard of it before. But this one bit him. Bit him? She changed his plans for him. That broad has strong teeth. She sent him to the hospital for reconstructive surgery." Everyone was laughing; even the PC's face, Keefe noted, wore a smile. Gold beamed expansively. He had converted a momentary fright into a personal triumph. "You never heard such screams. My men came running from all over and we grabbed him. The intended victim shows no sympathy whatsoever. She is about five feet tall. Remorse is unknown to her. 'I don't know what's in that thing,' she tells me, 'but I distinctly heard something crack.'"

The laughter took a long time to die down. Some of the men were wiping tears from their eyes.

Gold turned to Keefe. "About auto theft, Commissioner: your idea has occurred to all of us at one time or another, but I just can't afford to assign additional men to that one crime. Get the mayor to put up money for a hundred more detectives and I can promise you some results. Otherwise –"

It was the standard answer, and Keefe was annoyed. All around the table voices rose in support of Gold. There was a deplorable tendency among civilians to single out one crime or another, they said. Commanders began to speak bitterly about the press. The press often highlighted one particular crime, trying to make the department look bad, and demanded police action, when the department simply didn't have enough men or enough resources.

The commanders showed impressive solidarity on the subject of the press – they despised it – and of course Keefe himself, until not long ago, had been a member of the press.

It was Keefe's turn to stare down at his hands.

At the opposite end of the table sat Chief O'Brien, still unsuspecting, still smiling. He said to Keefe: "It's the old finger in the dike syndrome, Commissioner." In this way he defended, somewhat late, his colleague, Gold. "You plug one hole here, another bursts open there."

The PC turned to the lieutenant at his side. "What's next?"

It was the Chief of Traffic's turn, and he reported on a new midtown tow-away program; he was followed by the Chief of Intelligence who announced progress in his drive to register informants, especially those highly sensitive, super-secret informants who had never been registered in the past.

Discussions on these topics having died out, the Chief of Personnel described his interviews – apparently fruitless – with members of the Buckner Commission. This commission was investigating alleged police brutality to prisoners. Its existence stemmed from two well publicized atrocities – both prisoners had died – that predated the PC's own appointment, but its findings would be released in a few months, well into his tenure, and might smear both his department and himself. The Chief of Personnel had spies trying to find out what the commission had uncovered, without much success so far, according to his report today.

"What's next on the agenda, Lieutenant?"

The lieutenant said, "Possible measures to eliminate cooping during the midnight to eight A.M. tours."

Cooping: sleeping on the job. The PC had not even brought up the matter himself; the lieutenant did. No one therefore recognized it immediately as an attack on Chief O'Brien. The intended victim went on smiling, and the other men pretended to look thoughtful, as if as fascinated by this topic as by the ones that had preceded it. No one was as yet caught by surprise, least of all Keefe who, when helping to formulate the agenda in the Police Commissioner's office earlier, had sensed no sinister intentions on the PC's part. Cops in radio cars late at night tended to park in dark corners and go to sleep. What to do about it? To Keefe, cooping was a potential scandal that should be dealt with harshly, and he had recommended that certain steps be taken starting tonight, in secret. He had recommended that these steps not be brought up for discussion at this meeting at all, so his first reaction now was disappointment that he had been at least partially overruled. The secret was out, and opposition to his ideas would probably form.

Chief of Patrol O'Brien, smiling, said: "Cooping is a perennial problem. I've fought it and fought it, but nothing we try seems to do much good. Short of putting a sergeant in every radio car in the city every night, I don't see what else we can do." He paused, and his smile broadened. "Sergeants tend to fall asleep too, by the way. Was anyone here ever a sergeant?"

Everyone laughed.

"It's a physical thing," commented Chief Gold. Since Chief O'Brien, however belatedly, had stood up for him a moment ago, he would return the favour. "At a certain hour of the night a man's eyes begin to close."

"Blame the PBA," suggested Chief of Operations Kilcoyne, who was not only the senior officer present but also the biggest of them, 6 feet 5 inches tall, with snow white hair and often a booming laugh. A moment ago – "Was anyone here ever a sergeant?" – it was his laugh that had rung out louder than all the others. He said now: "If we could assign men to work that tour permanently they'd get in the habit of staying awake all night. But the PBA won't let us. The result is that men work the midnight tour only every third week, and they're physically not able to stay awake."

Other voices chimed in advancing much the same argument. Instead of watching the Police Commissioner, whose eyes had become more and more hooded, they were playing to each other. The PC's fingers began to tap impatiently on his knee.

The Chief of Patrol smiled and said: "Admit it, we've all had problems staying awake in radio cars in the middle of the night. All of us."

Well, Keefe, the outsider, had never fallen asleep in a radio car. Nor had the PC, apparently. His expression had hardened.

"Not good enough," he said. This brought conversation to a stop. His glance moved from face to face, and few men met his eyes. Sobered, they waited to hear whatever he might have on his mind.

Even Keefe was surprised at the gravity with which the PC apparently meant to address this subject and this group now. When they were preparing the agenda together earlier the man had treated cooping almost humorously. Cops had been sleeping during the quiet hours, the PC had told him, ever since radio motor patrol was invented, and before that they had slept in hallways, heated if they could find them, or even in doorways, standing up like a horse in case the sergeant should come by trying to catch them.

The PC and Keefe had both had a good chuckle, and Egan had explained to Keefe why all previous efforts to stamp out, or at least reduce, cooping had been frustrated – because in the past the police leadership had always failed to communicate to the cops on patrol their determination that cooping must end. As a matter of fact, most times they had been unable to communicate any decision at all on any subject to the cops in the street, since the means of communication did not exist. It was one of the weaknesses of the police world. The city was too big, and there were too many cops, all working different days, different hours. How did one reach them all? Not on the radio, for they were never all on the radio at once. To pin up notices on seventy-five precinct bulletin boards did not work. Cops were men who rarely read bulletin boards, and did not believe what they saw there anyway. They were men of action, who believed only in concrete acts as reported in the *Daily News* – they did, at least, read the *Daily News*.

All right then, Keefe had said to the PC, on this cooping matter we'll reach them via the *Daily News*. We will send out cops from Internal Affairs to catch them sleeping in their cars in the night. We will not only discipline the cops we catch, we'll sack their precinct commanders as being responsible as well. You'll announce it at a press conference. It will make a big story in the *Daily News* – and elsewhere – and cops will believe you're serious.

This had won a smile and a nodding head from the PC. The two men had beamed at each other. The PC was rapidly becoming Keefe's hero. Was he not a man of ideas – ideals too – who was willing to try things, to shake up the stodgy and traditional police world? And did he not appear to listen to the ideas of his new Deputy Commissioner on matters such as this one? It was all very flattering. It was downright irresistible.

Now in the conference room Keefe heard the PC announce that this time he would not be satisfied just to catch a few cops cooping. "Responsibility goes all the way up, or else the word is meaningless," he said. "In precincts where flagrant cooping is discovered, those commanders will be relieved of their commands."

This was a second disappointment for Keefe, who had advised him not to announce such details in advance. He's spoiled the whole thing, Keefe thought. Can he really believe that not one of these men will warn anybody? Keefe had not yet glanced in the direction of the Chief of Patrol at the far end of the table, the quality of whose smile had begun to change.

"And I don't intend to stop at the precinct level," the PC threatened, but here his tone became pleasant, almost friendly, which made this new threat sound particularly ominous. "Let the word go out that I mean to hold officers on all levels accountable for the conduct of their subordinates." His manner had become almost jocular, though it was demotions and firings he was promising, and a sudden heavy silence fell upon the room.

"You might ask yourselves," the PC continued, "how high up does this responsibility go? My answer: as high as necessary. Even into headquarters." The silence had become so leaden that Keefe at last realised what was happening – had happened. He's taken the stars off O'Brien's shoulders. The Chief of Patrol is out. And perhaps Chief of Operations Kilcoyne's booming laugh will no longer be heard around this table either.

"Accountability," the PC said in the same falsely jocular tone. "That's what I'm talking about." He glanced at his watch, and stood up. "I see I'm running a bit late. I've talked to Deputy Commissioner Keefe about this. I'll leave him in charge. He'll let me have your recommendations." Giving a grin and a half-wave all around, he turned and went back through the door into his own office.

He isn't even going to preside at the execution himself, Keefe thought. He sticks me with it.

For a time all eyes seemed fixed on the PC's empty chair. Then they shifted to Keefe. No one immediately looked at

O'Brien, who cleared his throat harshly and said: "What's he got in mind?"

It was at this point that Keefe first looked into the disintegrating smile, and a wave of pity came over him. O'Brien, so far as he knew, had done nothing wrong. Keefe had never even heard the PC criticise him in private. But O'Brien was surely out. Furthermore, Keefe realised, glancing around, all the rest of them had understood it long before he had, and he asked himself how they could have caught on so fast.

The answer must be that they had witnessed such charades many times in the past.

Keefe said: "The plan is to hit fourteen or fifteen precincts tonight." To Chief Sheridan, who headed Internal Affairs, Keefe said: "Is that the number, Chief?"

Sheridan was another big, beefy, red-faced man. He had a toothy grin, which he flashed around the table. If there were to be a sacrificial victim here, he was not it. Although almost all cops considered themselves outsiders as far as the rest of the world was concerned, cops who worked in Internal Affairs were outsiders even among their own. Sheridan had lived such a life a long time.

He said now: "Fourteen more tonight."

"Fourteen more?" said Keefe, surprised. Immediately he wished he had been able to keep the surprise out of his voice; but he was still not used to hiding his cards in these high level police poker games.

"In addition to the fourteen I hit last night."

So the PC was way ahead of me all along, Keefe reflected, and he was beset by conflicting emotions: admiration for the careful precautions to assure that the plan, Keefe's plan, would not be thwarted by these men; and disappointment at such duplicity. The PC apparently trusted no one, not even Keefe.

The Chief of Patrol said nothing. That his men had been investigated last night without his knowledge was already a tremendous loss of face. He no longer seemed able to meet the eyes of his colleagues. Once heads had begun to roll out in the precincts it would be shown that he was unable to protect his men on any level at all, and his loss of face would be total. From then on he would not be able to command. He would have to resign.

From the other side of the table the Chief of Detectives growled: "You hit fourteen precincts. So what did you find?" There was no fear in Gold's voice, and no regret either. Gold himself was not threatened, and O'Brien could not be saved. From one moment to the next O'Brien had become a former colleague, a former friend. Gold had already written him off.

"To answer your question," said the Chief from Internal Affairs, his face still creased by the toothy grin, "I found rather a large number of our stalwart heroes in the coop. It averaged out to about three cars per precinct. In one precinct there were seven out of seven."

Keefe, apparently more surprised than the others, was trying to hide it. "– Leaving that precinct totally unprotected," he muttered. "If the press ever got hold of such a thing, do you realise what they would do to us?" He was amazed to hear himself say this. A few months ago he would have killed to break a story like this, and here he was about to lead a conspiracy to conceal it.

"Sounds like a big coop," chortled Chief Gold.

"A disused fire house," Chief Sheridan said. "One of the cops had a key, which apparently he made available to all his buddies even when he himself was not on duty."

"Can you imagine if there was a fire?" inquired Gold. "The firemen would let the building burn. They wouldn't know that half the cops in the precinct were inside sleeping in their cars."

Around the table everyone was laughing, with the exception of the Chief of Patrol, whose smile nonetheless remained in place. Part of it did anyway. Even Chief of Operations Kilcoyne laughed, though not heartily. He seemed to believe he had escaped, but he could not be entirely sure. As the department's only four-star chief he had overall command of all the others, but no direct command of patrol. He was not a target here. Probably he wasn't.

Chief Gold said: "Worst case of cooping I ever heard was this lush. Thirty years a cop. Cooped every day or night. Never did an honest tour's work his entire career. Finally they put him in mounted. Times Square in the middle of the day. Figured he couldn't coop there. What would he do with the horse, right? Wrong. First day on the job he finds a bar has a cellar. You pull up the two steel doors in the sidewalk, and a staircase goes down into the cellar. The horse seems willing, so he rides it down the stairs and ties it to the furnace. Then he goes upstairs into the bar for a few drinks and some television. Finally it comes time to ride back to the stable and sign out. But when he pulls up the steel doors to get his horse out, it's lying on the floor. It had kicked over a duct and died of carbon monoxide poisoning, or some goddam thing. It's lying there dead. Now the old cop is in a panic. How is he going to explain this back at the stable? Inspiration! He calls up a friend who has a truck. They will tow the horse up the stairs onto the sidewalk, and the old cop will report that his horse died of heart failure while on patrol. The horse died a hero's death. An inspector's funeral for the horse. He goes back inside and has a few more while waiting for the tow truck. Finally it comes. They back it up to the curb, and start trying to coax the horse up the stairs. It weighs two thousand pounds. The traffic is stalled for blocks in all directions. People are calling up headquarters complaining. Every superior offficer in the area is ordered to get over there, find out what the hell is going on. About ten of them push through the enormous crowd that has gathered. They can't believe their eyes. A dead police horse is coming up out of the cellar on a winch, and a drunken cop is cheering it on."

Chief Sheridan, the executioner, began to talk about a radio car patrolman who was a famous ladies' man. "If some lady caught his eye, his partner would drive the rest of the tour alone. One day he's up on a rooftop. Some broad is bouncing up and down on his lap when this guy comes out onto the roof. The cop's pants and gun belt are hanging on a clothesline and the guy grabs them and runs off down the fire escape."

"How did he explain it when he signed out?" said Gold. "Was it easier to explain than the horse?"

One of their number was in desperate trouble, reflected Keefe, and they were all laughing. They were making jokes at somebody's funeral.

The Chief of Patrol said: "Which precinct was that where you found seven out of seven cars in the coop?"

The Chief from Internal Affairs said: "That's for me to know and you to find out."

The Chief of Patrol started to say something, perhaps to ask which precincts would be hit tonight, but apparently he changed his mind. He peered out over the table, his stiff smile focused on nothing.

I'm looking at a man smiling with his throat cut, Keefe thought. I've never seen that before: it's not something a reporter normally sees. Every day in this job I see things I never saw before.

"Do any of you have any other suggestions about how to handle this cooping problem?" he said.

In his mind he was trying to justify this apparent cruelty of the PC. But how else did you get rid of incumbents like the Chief of Patrol, or Chief of Operations Kilcoyne, both of whom, after so many years, perhaps had powerful friends? From the PC's point of view the only safe way was to humiliate one or the other until he resigned. That's what was happening here. It was neat, almost surgical. No blood on the floor. The Chief of Patrol first because he was easier; the white-haired Kilcoyne either later or perhaps not all. The cop liked Kilcoyne, called him "Mr Straight Arrow". If he stayed he would seem a link with tradition during whatever additional changes were coming. Probably he could stay, provided he realized after today that his four stars were more or less meaningless – that henceforth all power resided with the PC.

"So how many precinct commanders will be sacked?" asked O'Brien who, despite everything, was still showing teeth.

"That remains to be seen," answered Keefe. He isn't asking about precinct commanders, Keefe realized, he's asking about himself, and I don't have any information I can give him.

Abruptly he pushed back from the table. "If there's nothing else, then let's bring this meeting to an end."

All the men stood up, and some remained near the table chatting with each other. The Chief of Patrol, head down but smiling to the end, went out and started down the hall, the door slamming behind him.

About an hour later Keefe was called into the PC's office. The Chief of Patrol, he noted at once, was standing at the window looking out at the East River and Brooklyn across the way. He was smoking nervously.

"Chief O'Brien has decided to retire," the PC said. "Isn't that right, Dan?"

O'Brien turned from the window and nodded his head. He was not smiling now.

The PC said: "I want you to prepare a statement for my signature praising Chief O'Brien's thirty years of dedicated police service. Is that what it is, Dan, thirty?"

"Thirty-two," said O'Brien.

The PC and Keefe, sitting on opposite sides of the big desk, worked out the wording of the statement, while O'Brien remained at the window, smoking. When the draft was finished O'Brien read it and nodded his approval. He then asked to be excused.

This request brought the PC from behind his desk and he put his hand out. After a momentary hesitation, O'Brien shook it.

When he had gone out, Keefe looked up from the statement and said: "What did he do?"

"Nothing. I meant every word in that statement I just dictated to you."

"Then why –"

"I could feel he wasn't a wholehearted member of the new team. He stood for the old-fashioned way of doing things."

"I see."

"Thanks for your help on this, Phil."

Keefe walked to the door.

"Oh, one other thing," the PC said. "Chief Sheridan won't be hitting those precincts tonight. I've decided to cancel it, to put this cooping matter on the back burner. So we won't be holding a press conference about it either."

Keefe wondered if these were the conditions on which O'Brien had agreed to resign. He wondered if the suppression of cooping had ever been among the PC's concerns.

"Let's give Dan O'Brien a chance to get well away first, shall we? We'll go after cooping another time."

Two

THIS SENT KEEFE BACK TO HIS OWN OFFICE WHERE HE stood at the window and brooded about power. He was trying to apply what he had already known – not very much – to what he was now learning: not the so-called repressive power that cops applied in the streets, but power as wielded by the men who inhabited his floor and the one above it. Power over other men's lives; power to manipulate major forces.

He had never considered the subject much in the past. Some journalists had power, or imagined they did. Certain critics could make or break careers in the arts. Political reporters could sometimes influence elections. But foreign correspondents were far removed from this sort of thing. Until now power had never pertained to Keefe personally. He had never had any, nor much wanted any, and the closest he ever got was when sitting across the desk from an official or executive during an interview.

Until now. He had heard all the clichés. Power was like a beautiful woman, delightful to hold, even more delightful to fondle. It was sometimes a sword, more often a club – if you had it you bludgeoned other people with it. It was

17

indiscriminate. You bludgeoned people who got in your way, and also people who didn't.

This was the raw, ugly side – pushing people around who couldn't push back. This side Keefe had always avoided in the past and had avoided in this new job so far. But power had its seductive side as well. It caressed whoever stood too close to it, and it caressed him in intimate places. It seduced by degrees. There were always perks that went with it. The perks were like foreplay. They were fun. For instance, there was a car assigned to him around the clock, with two detectives alternating to drive it. That was fun. It was fun that everyone smiled at him all the time, as if with genuine fondness – and seemed grateful if he smiled back. But the fact that people tended to admire any whim that he might express was annoying.

Keefe had grown up in New York during the 1960s, a time when almost an entire generation had rebelled against power, especially as exemplified by its own blundering government. In protest the boys had let their hair and beards grow out, the girls had become "liberated". Both sexes had sat around bonfires made of draft cards and sworn that they would not be corrupted by power, not then, not ever. Keefe himself had worn his hair only moderately long, had never been a hippie, and by the time he got out of college the war was ending. Nonetheless, basically he had subscribed to the same ideals as his contemporaries, and many of these ideals he carried with him still. He could never have gone to work for an arms manufacturer, for instance, or a chemical company, could never have devoted himself to climbing some corporate ladder. His first job was working for a relief organisation in the north-east of Brazil. There were other areas where a man could operate more or less alone, according to a well defined code of ethics that was partly prescribed but mostly his own, and journalism was one of them. Keefe had got a job with a newspaper in Boston, then with one in New York which, very quickly, had sent him overseas.

And then, at a time when the new PC was trying to "round out his team", as he put it, another man Keefe scarcely knew, an aide to the mayor, had suggested Keefe's name to him, and the PC, whom Keefe did not know at all, had apparently leaped at the idea. To this day Keefe was not sure why. He had just come back to New York. As a journalist he had some prestige, and his integrity was unquestioned. He had quit his paper to write a book, and was therefore available. He may have seemed an imaginative choice to the PC, who had had seven deputy commissionerships to fill, for according to the city charter the department was supposed to be adminsitered and controlled by civilians, not by cops. Certainly it was true that government officials at this level and most others were often obliged to appoint men they did not know personally.

Perhaps by appointing Keefe the PC thought he was buying instant credibility with the press and therefore with the city. Was that the principal reason?

Keefe's own motives were equally obscure, even to himself. He was not sure why he had allowed the PC to interview him three times, or why he had accepted the appointment when it came. Was it because he felt flattered that the man seemed to want him so much? Perhaps it was a sense of duty arising out of that original youthful idealism. Was not New York, the city of his birth, as worthy of his devotion as north-east Brazil? Did it not have as many problems? And he did like to count himself as one of the good guys, and a good guy who refused to do public service on such a level as this could not call himself a good guy any longer.

Or perhaps he was merely bored. The book had come out to nice reviews but few sales – no new career there. He was tired of living out of suitcases, and he did not know what to do next. Perhaps he was merely searching for excitement, for a new direction to his life? The one thing certain was that he had not come into the police department to wield power. The idea had never crossed his mind, though it did now. He had just seen it wielded up close, and it was as ugly a thing to watch as he had always supposed. But he had learned something else today, too. He had looked down a table at men who supposedly had power but who either didn't have it after all or were afraid to use it – career policemen who took what was done to them and never looked up. The fear around that table had amazed him. The PC's other deputy commissioners, civilians all, each with a particular area of responsibility and expertise – budget, personnel, legal and so forth – had power, and they didn't use it either. They held the same rank Keefe did, and got the same paycheck – about the same as a three-star chief – but he rarely saw any of them. They moved in and out of headquarters every day and never made a peep.

Keefe stood at his window and continued to brood. There was power in this building that was not being used. There was a power vacuum. What did he mean to do about it, if anything?

He had no answer to this question and presently he moved away from the window, sat at his desk and began to respond to his accumulated phone messages. A deputy mayor had called, and the leader of a community group in the Park Slope section of Brooklyn, and the president of the Bar Association. For unknown reasons, he seemed to have become the conduit by which such people communicated with the PC and with the department as a whole; and mostly what they communicated was complaints. He responded to more complaints now. A certain field commander in the Bronx was "insensitive". The PC had failed to reply to a speaking invitation. A demonstration was being arranged to protest against the consolidation of two Bronx precincts into one. Keefe, making his calls, found himself dealing with the bruised egos of men he did not know, had never heard of until a few weeks ago. Why him? The only answer he could come to was that the PC was difficult to reach, he himself was available, and there seemed to be no one else.

Later he had himself driven back to his East Side apartment. Sharon, who was one of the producers of an afternoon soap opera, came home shortly afterwards, and he told her about his day. "The games men play to give each other heart attacks," she commented.

Often her perceptions were extremely acute, and this one made him smile. But presently she said:

"Has it ever occurred to you that since you took this job you talk of nothing else?"

He was immediately discomforted. "Well, not exactly, no."

"One could easily get the impression that you care more about the police department than about certain other things."

"Other things?"

"Us, for instance."

"Sharon –"

But she got up and went into the kitchen and began to prepare dinner, because tonight it was her turn. They thought of their relationship as thoroughly modern – different from that of their parents in big ways and small, one of them being that they shared the household chores equally. Keefe went in and stood beside her while she cooked, and he carried the plates to the table, but they ate mostly in silence.

Standing up from the table, he got ready to go back out. He apologized to her for it, even asked her permission, but she only shrugged, cracked open her attaché case and, with her stocking feet tucked under her on the sofa, began to pore over papers.

"You're sure you don't mind?" he said, hesitating in the doorway, but she shook her head, annoyed at him obviously, and did not even look up. He went out and down the stairs, stepped outside into the warm night and breathed deeply, as if he were about to begin a sporting event. He had kept the car waiting at the curb. The light was on inside, and Detective Murphy, one of his two drivers, was reading the evening paper on the steering wheel. As he approached the car Murphy got out and came around to the passenger side like an old-world servant to open the door for him.

"Where to, Commissioner?" Murphy had placed the paper on the seat between them and now started the engine.

Keefe ordered himself to be driven up to Harlem to the Thirty-Second Precinct station house, having selected one among the seventy-five at random, and as they moved through the streets he switched the radio to the Sixth

21

Division frequency to pick up the Harlem calls. None was particularly lurid yet. It was perhaps too early.

There was a power vacuum at the top of the police department: this was the one certainty that had lodged in Keefe's brain today. There was a power vacuum, and he felt himself being drawn into it, and he did not know enough about the department to make confident decisions on any subject at all. This was why, for the first time as a deputy police commissioner, he was on his way to Harlem. He meant to go out into the city with cops, see what it was they did, talk to them, and perhaps learn something. He realized he would have to do this repeatedly if it was to do any good, visit many different precincts, give to it two or three nights a week – however many Sharon would put up with. He also knew he was not going to meet colleagues from head-quarters "out in the field", as the euphemism had it. Although every single commander had started his career as a patrolman it was rare that any one of them went back to the streets. Not if he could help it. It was to be avoided at any cost apparently, and Keefe, having observed such an odd phenomenon, sometimes wondered if their principal reason was not snobbishness. These men, of noble rank now, did not want to be reminded, or remind others, of their former low station. Did lords mingle with footmen? Headquarters, it seemed to Keefe, had deliberately isolated itself from the men in the precincts. Orders flowed downward. Information did not flow in any direction at all. The very least he was hoping for, if he made these nightly forays out into the city, was to start information flowing again, if only via himself.

Night. A Harlem side street. Police vehicles parked along both curbs. A row of low buildings, all of them old, most of them defaced, some perhaps abandoned. In the middle was the station house. It was as old as the rest, though in better repair. Detective Murphy doubleparked in front, and Keefe got out and approached the door. He showed his shield to the cop on security duty there – a formality – and got a reaction he was not prepared for. The cop did a doubletake, then jumped into the station house ahead of Keefe.

"Atten – shun!" he called out.

In the big muster room there were five or six cops standing or moving through. All sprang rigidly to attention. They stood there frozen, all facing in different directions. Keefe did not want this. "At ease, at ease," he said and was relieved when whatever movement or conversation he had interrupted was resumed. He stepped behind the big desk and signed the blotter. By the time he had finished, a lieutenant was standing beside him, looking anxious. Keefe attempted to put this man at his ease also. No, there was nothing special he wanted, he had come for no specific purpose. He just wanted to look around.

"Look around?" the lieutenant said anxiously.

"Yes, look around."

From the inside the station house looked even older than he had supposed, dating from 1900 or before. High ceiling. Board floor – he could hear the footsteps of everyone. Back then Harlem was one of the swankiest parts of the city and police problems here were probably small. Not now. At this hour in this precinct there were thirty to forty cops on duty, all but a handful out on patrol.

He went up the steep staircase to the detective squad room on the second floor, the lieutenant trailing behind him. He did not need or want this either.

There were six detectives in the squad room, two of whom were on the phone, and two prisoners, one of whom sat on the floor of the cage with his eyes closed, his chin on his chest, drooling into his lap. At the fingerprint desk a burly detective in shirtsleeves was rolling the forefinger of the other prisoner across an ink pad. All six detectives were white. The two prisoners were black.

"Was there anything I could show you, Commissioner?" inquired the nervous lieutenant. "This is Commissioner Keefe," he announced to the room at large.

Of the two detectives on the telephone one, Keefe judged, was working on a case; he ignored Keefe completely. The other was probably talking to a woman, for he looked as embarrassed as a schoolboy, immediately hung up, and grinned nervously.

The other detectives had accorded Keefe a quick, brief

23

study. Cops were reputed to make their minds up fast: he could believe it. They seemed to be expressing mild curiosity rather than interest. The detective fingerprinting the prisoner shot Keefe a brief nod, then went on with what he was doing. The others began to talk loudly to each other as if Keefe were not even in the room.

It was not going to be easy. Leaning his rump against an unoccupied desk, Keefe attempted to engage the men in conversation. After a time they began to thaw, and to answer his questions. Or, rather, they began to put forth the answers they imagined he was looking for. Later, two of them prepared to go out on a burglary run, and Keefe asked permission to accompany them.

"Of course," one of them said.

Keefe frowned. Stupid question. What other answer could the man have made?

He got into their car. He followed them into a reeking tenement only a few blocks away. He followed them up three flights of stairs. Inside was a chocolate-brown young woman with a naked baby on her hip and a six-year-old half-hidden behind her. The young woman was in tears. She showed the broken window that led onto the fire escape, and the place where her TV set had been. She had only made two payments on it. She had sixteen more to go.

The detectives were good. Barring a miracle, there was no chance whatever that the TV set would be recovered, but they gave the young woman plenty of time, took down all the particulars, asked all the proper questions. They were as compassionate as any citizen could wish, and Keefe was proud of them.

Then he thought: Are they always that way, or only because I am here?

On the staircase going back down, one of them muttered: "These people have so little. It breaks your heart when something like this happens."

They drove back to the station house. As they got out of the car, one of the detectives said: "What exactly was you looking for, Commissioner?" He was about forty-five, and sounded worried. His name, Keefe remembered, was

24

O'Halloran. "I mean, was there a complaint, or something?"

The next night Keefe took Sharon out to dinner. She was cheerful and he tried to explain to her some of the new ideas taking root in his head. He couldn't tell if she understood him or not.

During the following weeks he ventured into many more precincts. He went unannounced, having decided not to present himself at the station house first. Instead he instructed his driver to cruise through the streets. They would respond to whatever calls came over the radio. Some nights he saw and learned little. Whatever precinct he had chosen was quiet. Other nights something would happen and Keefe, watching, was almost always surprised.

He watched two cops push their way through a crowd that had gathered on a street corner. Inside the crowd an old man lay writhing on the sidewalk.

"Stroke," diagnosed one of the cops, who couldn't have been more than twenty-three. He lifted his radio to his mouth and called in an ambulance even as he went to his knees beside the victim. While his partner kept the crowd back, the young cop knelt there and held the old man's hand until the ambulance came. He held it for twenty minutes, making repeated calls for the ambulance to hurry. After that the two young men sat in their car with the light on filling out the aided card. Then they went on to the next assignment.

A signal 10–13 – Assist Police Officer – came over the radio. It attracted every car within earshot, Keefe's among them. Cars came from all directions, sirens wailing. They came at great speed. It was always that way, Keefe knew. The risk to themselves and to other traffic was enormous. Often there had been terrible crashes. The address given was a restaurant. Cops doubleparked in the streets, they drove up onto the sidewalks, and some of them rushed the door with their guns out.

There was no police officer in trouble. The 10–13 had been called in by the proprietor who was inside struggling with one of his patrons, a grotesquely fat little man whose trousers sported an eighteen inch zipper and whose red wig was too small for his head. Everyone else in the restaurant was standing up, some with napkins to their mouths, leaning forward, watching avidly.

"Arrest him, officers, he won't pay his check," screamed the proprietor. "Handcuff him, he's trying to escape."

All the guns went back into the holsters, even as a sergeant came through the door and pushed through the crowd of uniforms. "Whadda ya got?" he demanded importantly. "Where's the cop in trouble?"

The proprietor had let go of the fat man, who didn't seem to want to escape at all. "He comes in here," the proprietor explained in an aggrieved voice. "He orders the appetizer, he orders the special, he orders wine, he orders coffee, he orders dessert. I give him the check and he won't pay."

"I'm sorry," said the fat man. "I have no money, you see. I wish I did. He deserves to be paid. It was a very splendid dinner. Splendid."

"Arrest him, officers. Do your duty. Lock him up."

"What?" said the sergeant, incredulously. "What? You called in a 10–13 because of a dinner check?"

"Forty-eight dollars," said the fat man. "His prices are quite reasonable."

The sergeant's face was four inches from the proprietor's. "You called in a 10–13 because of a dinner check?"

"Don't you shout at me," shouted the proprietor, "I'm not the criminal here. He's the criminal here. Do something."

"Do you realise what a 10–13 is?"

"All I know is, it gets you guys here in a hurry."

"In a hurry?" sputtered the sergeant. "In a hurry?"

"Otherwise you'd take your own sweet time. Admit it."

All the surrounding cops were angry, but they let the sergeant handle it. "You scumbag," the sergeant screamed. He was livid. The 10–13 was the most sacred call of all. He was making a speech about it and cursing the proprietor at the same time.

"It was delicious," the little fat man interrupted.

The sergeant, red in the face, stared at him.

"The turkey with giblet gravy. I heartily recommend it. The place I ate in last night was not nearly as good."

"Shut him up, somebody," the sergeant said.

"The clams casino," the fat man piped up. "I had that to start."

Red-faced, the sergeant attempted to resume his impassioned speech. Cops had been killed racing to 10–13s. To trifle with the 10–13 was to endanger the life of every cop in the city and –

"Delicious." The fat man smacked his lips. "You could bring your wives here. It's that kind of place."

"Shut him up," the sergeant ordered. "Somebody."

"It's worth every penny."

"Every penny?" roared the proprietor, and he flung himself on the little fat man, only to be dragged off by cops. But he came away clutching the too-small red wig. "I'll just hold this baby until he pays his check," he said.

"My rug, my rug," wailed the fat man, now completely bald. Darting forward he sank his teeth in the properietor's hand. The proprietor began running in circles. The fat man, attached to him by his teeth, waddled along in his wake, and six cops struggled to separate them. At last this was accomplished. The fat man's teeth were pried loose and the two men were dragged to opposite sides of the restaurant's cash desk.

"He stole my rug," screamed the fat man.

"He bit me," said the proprietor, wringing his injured hand. "Assault with a deadly weapon. Assault with a deadly weapon."

"Jesus," said the sergeant, backing toward the door. His rage was entirely gone. Even his righteous indignation was gone. This restaurant, he decided, was no place for a sergeant. His chin had begun to quiver, but he must have decided laughter would only make matters worse. "You guys handle it," he snarled, then turned and strode out of the restaurant.

The other cops began to drift away also, until only the first pair to arrive was left. By default it was their case now. Keefe left them to it.

Usually it was midnight before he got home. Sharon would be already in bed and either asleep, or pretending to be. Sometimes at breakfast Keefe would attempt to describe for her his experiences of the night before, especially the amusing ones. Sometimes she smiled. But there was increasing tension between them.

Three Saturdays in a row phone calls woke Keefe – and Sharon with him – in the middle of the night. Six people mowed down in a Harlem social club; a bomb explosion in the press room of the *New York Times*; a cop shot to death. Cars were sent to pick him up. However much he might try to keep his weekends free, technically Keefe was on duty twenty-four hours a day, and his office always knew where he was. Once he and Sharon were asleep in a friend's house at Long Beach. He got into a Nassau County police car which raced him to the city limits where an NYPD car was already waiting. Of course similar calls had forced other men out of bed also. At the crime scene, or disaster scene, he would confer with the PC and Chief of Detectives Gold, and sometimes Chief of Operations Kilcoyne. There was usually someone from the mayor's office – if it was bad enough, the mayor himself came. A small circle of important men stood in dim light contemplating the result of some grim event, usually a corpse or corpses on the floor. They watched cops cleaning up, and decided what to do next, which orders to give, what to tell the city. It was drama of the most heady kind, and Keefe was a part of it, and by the time he got home he would be too stimulated to go back to bed. Nonetheless, he came to dread Saturday nights. If asleep in a strange room he sometimes could not find the phone at first. After that he would try to dress soundlessly in the dark, knowing very well that Sharon lay awake now too. Once she muttered icily from the direction of the bed: "I myself am not married to the police department. In fact, I am not even married to you."

He went into a dark alley behind two cops. They were both about thirty. One was tall, one short. On the sidewalk the tall one had been talking about a bowling tournament. He had just won another trophy, he said.

According to the radio call, someone was supposed to be lying in this alley dead, or perhaps sick or drunk. It had to be checked out. The alley led between two tenements. Both cops carried long-barrelled flashlights. The beams played over the rubble underfoot.

"Watch out you don't step in something in here," the tall cop cautioned Keefe, aiming his beam in deeper. Light played over piles of garbage, over disused appliances. The end of the alley was blocked off. They would have to go all the way in. From either side the tenement walls seemed to lean in on top of them, compressing the stench, compressing darkness.

"A perfect place to ambush cops," the short cop muttered.

There were broken stoves in here, old furniture – perfect cover. It made the hair rise up on the back of Keefe's neck. The two cops followed their long flashlights. He followed their backs. He was safer than they were. As they moved in deeper he sensed them becoming increasingly tense. The beams of light moved more jerkily.

When they reached the end of the alley, everyone relaxed. The flashlights painted the walls with broad strokes.

"False alarm," the tall cop said.

"The last time I went into an alley like this," the short cop commented, "somebody took a shot at me."

"I had bowling that night," said his partner.

"What happened?" said Keefe.

"He went over the back fence. I never even saw him."

"You couldn't find your flashlight in time," said the tall cop. "He dropped his flashlight, Commissioner. He was lying face down in the garbage."

"You wouldn't think it was so funny if you'd been there."

They turned back toward the street. Near the entrance to the alley the short cop's flashlight shone on a plastic bag stuffed with garbage.

"There's your body," he said. From the street it might have looked like that to whoever phoned in the alarm. The cop kicked it with a sudden vicious rage. The plastic split and garbage flew. He was breathing hard. "Now it's not a body any more," he said, and strode out onto the sidewalk.

As Keefe's car drove away the short cop's voice came on the radio. "That body in the alley job," he began, "that job is a 10-90, Central. Unfounded." His voice was entirely calm.

"Where to, Commissioner?" said Detective Murphy.

Before Keefe could answer, Central came back on with an address. "Report of a man with a gun on the roof. Which car responding?"

This is Sector Boy, Central," came a voice from across the precinct. "We'll take that job."

It was a middle-class apartment building, eight storeys high. Keefe and two cops rode the elevator up. These cops too became increasingly tense, and as they reached the roof door their hands went to their guns.

The first cop slowly pushed the door open. When nothing happened, he jumped out onto the roof, gun drawn. The second cop followed, then came Keefe, who let the door close silently behind him. At moments like this he felt terrifically alive. He seemed to hear and see and smell more acutely than ever. He was in the grip of an emotion that was almost a compulsion: the overpowering curiosity of the professional journalist. He had gone into dangerous places before, sometimes on assignment, sometimes by choice. Until a year or so ago he had been covering the civil war in Lebanon. He had been every day as careful as he could be, but if it had been necessary to take a few risks to get his story, he had taken them.

There was no clear view of the roof. The three men peered about in the darkness. Chimneys, air-conditioning ducts, a water tower obstructed the view. With their guns poking out in front, the cops moved out from the protection of the doorhousing. Keefe followed.

As they crept around there came a sudden noise, as of chair legs scraping. It made them complete their movement with a rush. There was no man with a gun. Instead they came upon an elderly gentleman sitting in a camp chair.

With their fingers quivering on their triggers they very nearly shot him.

He did not immediately see them, or so he pretended. He had his head tilted back and with a telescope pressed to his eye he was examining the heavens. The telescope was as long as a rifle barrel, perhaps longer. He had set up his camp chair next to the parapet. Keefe had the impression that he had swivelled the chair around only a moment before – away from the parapet and the lighted buildings across the street. His telescope was pointed straight up, and he appeared to be in rapt contemplation of the stars directly over his head.

The guns went back into the holsters, and the two cops crossed their arms over their chests.

Slowly, the man brought the telescope down. Only then did he appear to notice them. He did not react to Keefe in civilian clothes, only to the uniforms. Glancing nervously from one cop to the other he said: "Good evening, officers."

"You got any identification, mister?" growled the first cop.

"Identification, officer? Yes of course. Certainly. What seems to be the trouble?" He shut down the telescope, but it was still about a foot long. He got to his feet and tried to shove it into a trouser pocket, but about half of it protruded. He kept pushing on it with one hand while fumbling through his billfold with the other. "What sort of identification would you prefer? My American Express Gold Card? Would that be satisfactory, officers?"

The first cop took the billfold from him. Under the beam of his partner's flashlight he fanned out cards. He found and studied the old man's driving licence.

"Is that sufficient identification, officers? You will note that I am a resident of this building. I have a perfect right to be up here."

"Come up here often, do you, mister?"

"Often?"

"Like every night, maybe?"

"I'm an astronomer," the man said. "It's a hobby with me."

"I see."

"Do you know anything about the stars, officer?"

"No. Do you?"

The man licked his lips. "The Big Dipper, the Little Dipper, the North Star – you name it."

"What star was you studying just now, if you don't mind my asking?"

The man was blinking nervously. "Well, did you ever hear of the Milky Way?"

"Tell me about it."

"The stars, officer. Where would we be without them?"

"Do you ever," the first cop said, "admire anything else from up here besides the stars?"

"Let me see that thing," the second cop said, plucking the telescope from the man's pocket. Extending it to full length, he peered over the parapet at the apartment house across the street. The barrel moved from window to window in a series of jerks. "Jesus," the cop said, "this is some powerful telescope."

After a moment he handed it to Keefe.

"It brings everything up real close, doesn't it?" Keefe said.

The old man was disappointed in them. "You men are not astronomers."

"Tell me about Arcturus," the cop said. "Tell me about Orion and Cetus."

The two cops were suddenly all business. "Why don't we escort you down to your apartment," the first one said, "before you get too excited and fall off the roof?"

"That won't be necessary," the old man said huffily.

"Yes, it will." Folding the camp chair, the cop used it to nudge the astronomer along ahead of him. The other cop carried the telescope. When they had reached the door-housing, the first cop looked over the lock. "It's a spring lock," he muttered. "You got a key to this thing?" he asked the old man.

"As a matter of fact I do."

"Let me see it, if you don't mind."

The cop peered at the key for a moment, then hurled it out into the night. When everyone was inside the housing, he slammed the door to the roof, then tried the handle a few times. The door would no longer open. "You can give him back his telescope now," he told his partner.

After seeing the astronomer to his flat, the two cops descended to the basement where they rang the super's doorbell. Although the super turned out to be a Hispanic with little English, nonetheless they made him understand that the door to the roof was to be kept locked at night. The second cop, who had some Spanish, had taken over. He kept saying: "*Comprende, amigo*? The next time they found that door open, they were going to arrest the super, they threatened.

"Do you think he'll keep it locked?" Keefe asked when they were out on the sidewalk again. There were trees on this street with a breeze blowing through them.

"Maybe. Maybe we'll come back and check up on it too, from time to time, if we ever get a slow enough night."

Three

MOST OF THE TOP FLOOR OF THE FOURTEEN-STOREY brick fortress at One Police Plaza was occupied by the Police Commissioner and the many clerks and secretaries, all of whom wore guns, who served him. The PC exerted a substantial presence that could be felt throughout the building.

On afternoons when he went home early, as he did that Friday, this news swept outward along the corridors, downward through the floors. It moved like a rumour. No one knew how it moved so quickly. Other clerks, who also wore guns, stuck their heads into the offices of other commanders.

"The PC has left the building."

Each seemed anxious to be first to impart such important information. Behind big desks middle-aged men with stars on their shoulders nodded curtly, as if they barely heard; though they did.

"The PC has left the building."

The news dropped through the floors faster than the PC's descending elevator. The cop on duty in the subterranean garage heard it even before he saw him striding toward his car – in which the engine was already running. To the commanders remaining behind, headquarters seemed suddenly lighter. The whole building seemed lighter, as if some oppressive weight had been lifted off.

It was Sergeant Rainey who stuck his head into Keefe's office. Keefe had one captain and five sergeants on his immediate staff, and about thirty-five men in all – he was not even sure what each man did, and meant to check into this when he had time. "The PC has left the building," Sergeant Rainey said.

"The who?" said Keefe.

Keefe was aware of this particular police department ritual, and was amused by it. It seemed almost religious, like the *Ite missa est* at the end of the Latin Mass of his boyhood. Police headquarters was like the Catholic Church. The god-figure was the PC. Nobody dared to go home until he did. It must be awful to work here if it's your career, Keefe reflected. His own career was something else, he felt, though he was not sure exactly what at the moment.

Still, he felt good today. His offices were on the thirteenth floor. The sun was shining in his windows, warming the back of his head, the back of his hands. It fell across his desk, on which lay memos from subordinate commanders, the draft of a speech the PC was supposed to make, reports of yesterday's unusual crimes and instructions from the PC about personnel. The police department, Keefe had learned, generated lots of paper.

He began stuffing his briefcase; he would do his homework over the weekend. All over the building other commanders were probably doing the same. The working week was over. To Sergeant Rainey he said: "Ask Detective Murphy to get the car out."

Rainey shook his head. "I sent him home," he said, which was true. "His wife was sick," he added, which was not.

Keefe stopped stuffing the briefcase and stared a moment at Rainey.

"I'll drive you home, if you like," said Rainey. He wore a dark blue suit. He was tall and heavyset and also, almost alone among headquarters cops, he wore a beard. He was older than Keefe. His hair was still black but his beard was grey.

"I was going up to my place in Connecticut," said Keefe hesitantly. Sharon, driving his Porsche, was probably there already. His unmarked police car certainly could not be garaged out of state overnight. It wasn't even supposed to be driven out of state unless on official business. However, driving a few miles into another state and then out again was the sort of private use to which everybody put these cars. The PC himself probably did it.

"It'll be a nice drive in the country for me," said Rainey, who needed a car tonight and had decided on Keefe's. Driving him to Connecticut seemed a small price to pay.

Keefe said almost apologetically, "It's too nice a day to take the train."

It was by then about a quarter to five. Keefe stepped out into his outer office among the clerks and secretaries who worked for him. The night duty sergeant, Brady, had come in and sat at the telephone console.

"I'll be at my place in Connecticut," Keefe told him.

"Right, sir," Brady said. "I hope I won't have to bother you."

Keefe hoped so too. This weekend, he had promised himself, he would devote entirely to Sharon. But the streets would have to stay calm. No major robberies or riots, no cops shot. For two days let there be nothing to oblige him to come racing back into the city.

He went down in the elevator into the garage, and Rainey drove him up the ramp out of the gloom into the sunlight. Keefe was still not used to being driven around by others, and most times was even slightly embarrassed. The bearded sergeant steered on to the FDR Drive and they started north, passing under the first of the East River bridges. Keefe had his briefcase open. If he got the homework done now he would have more time for Sharon later. The Drive was clotted with traffic, the usual Friday afternoon exodus from the city, and for a time he watched the second bridge come slowly toward them.

Rainey said: "Another week of crime and degradation is over, eh, Commissioner?"

"Unless something heavy comes down." If he were awakened again in the middle of the night, Sharon might – But he tried to force himself to stop worrying about it.

On the river a small freighter was driving uptown, same as them, but making better time. Now it was abreast of them, cleaving the water, now it forged ahead, leaving a wake. Across the river there were warehouses, and behind them the low buildings of Queens. The radio at Keefe's feet was tuned to the city-wide band but the voices that came over it were calm, relatively speaking. The city was calm. When he looked up from his reading the first bridges were behind them, traffic was moving better, and the Drive was sweeping around the hump in the island that was the Ninth Precinct. Keefe knew many of the precincts now, especially the important ones. "Important" meant violent. Two months ago he had known by number only the precinct in which he had grown up.

He began to imagine himself riding the subway instead of this car. He wriggled out of his suit coat, leaned over the backrest and laid it on the back seat. Packed into a subway he would be soaked in sweat, breathing the sour air of bodies, the grimy air of the stations. The subways were his heritage yet here he was being driven home by a chauffeur; he was an aristocrat in his own city.

Tonight was going to be hot here in the city. In the high-crime precincts the poor were going to spill out of doors. Again Keefe began to worry about it. Onto the fire escapes, onto the streets – people everywhere. He had seen it. People drunk and rowdy, or stoned and comatose; people merely milling around, people jiving to the music of the massive portable radios that they carried on their shoulders or stood against building walls: ghetto-blasters; boom-boxes; third-world attaché cases. Music blaring from all over. Tempers that got shorter and shorter. Fights over insults; it made no difference whether they were real or imagined. Fights over women. Guns or knives that appeared as if by magic. And stick-ups, principally of liquor stores. At least one or two of these stick-ups and one or more of these assaults would result in corpses – none of them important corpses, if he was lucky. Tomorrow night, Saturday night, would be worse. Seven or eight murders in all was a likely total for a summer weekend in New York. Cops all over the city would have their guns out, would have their hands full.

The police department had been an education to Keefe. Over and over he had been forced to see his city differently, to confront questions most men sought to avoid. Who was that corpse on the sidewalk? What is it like to live in a slum – and to die there in violence? What is death? Why are we all here?

However, Keefe wanted – needed – this weekend free.

Ahead now was the Triboro Bridge, in appearance the most fragile of all the great New York bridges. Its fine spidery lines soared from Manhattan across to Queens, which was as vast as a separate city and did not resemble Manhattan at all. Keefe studied the Triboro for a time. Under it sailed a Circle excursion liner, its open decks crowded with tourists. In Rome tourists went to the Sistine Chapel; in New York they rode boats around Manhattan Island, though what they ought to be clamouring to see were crime scenes. In the European capitals where he had worked, Keefe had always been conscious of the tourists, himself among them, and had never felt other than alien, vulnerable, exposed, vaguely uneasy. He felt quite the opposite now. These days the aristocrat moved through the streets of New York in his own private police car. The crazy thing was that it felt right to him. This was the place where he had been born: he was back where he belonged.

Sergeant Rainey steered up the ramp and they started across the Triboro Bridge. At the tollgate Rainey held up the police plate and they went through without paying. Then they were driving up through the Bronx on an eight-lane highway bounded on both sides by chain link fences. Keefe closed his briefcase and dropped it to the floor beside his soft Italian shoes. He must have dozed then, for the next thing he knew they were driving through Westchester County. The towns were spaced wider apart, there were

37

patches of forest to each side of the thruway, and presently they crossed into Connecticut. The traffic was thick but moving fast, and they came up on a flatbed truck that bore no identifying marks of any kind except for its licence plate. On it were lashed down three Cadillac front ends, what car thieves referred to as "nose clips".

"Jesus," said Keefe. He had sat bolt upright. "Look at that." They were glossy, shining, without a scratch or dent on any of them.

The two men glanced at each other, and Rainey started to chuckle. Keefe knew he had been a sergeant on patrol in Harlem for more than twenty years. He was an experienced policeman.

"What do we do?" Keefe asked.

"Well, we could tail him, see where he goes."

Keefe thought of Sharon waiting for him ahead. "He might be going to Hartford. Boston, even."

"You could get on the radio, Commissioner; call for help."

"We're probably out of range." Since Keefe could still hear radio calls coming in, this was obviously not true.

"Central could alert the Connecticut State Police."

Keefe did not want to do it. His transmission would be picked up not only by Central but by every radio car within range. Press and TV reporters monitored the city-wide band as well. He would have to give his name and rank. It would look to one and all like the new Deputy Commissioner was trying to play cop. The news would sweep through the department, maybe the city. Suppose this truck, and its driver were innocent. Men would laugh at him. Maybe they wouldn't, but it was a chance he did not wish to take.

On the other hand, ten thousand cars had been stolen last month off the streets of the city, the one crime where, he believed, the department could have a major impact. He was sure of it.

"Pull up alongside him," Keefe said. "Slowly. There, that's enough." They had come almost abreast of the truck's cab, which allowed Keefe to study the profile of the driver, a big freckle-faced man with reddish hair. He was alone in the cab. "Hold it right there," Keefe said, and he looked at Rainey for advice.

"We can't pull him over," Rainey said.

Keefe knew this. They were in Connecticut, where they had no jurisdiction. Nor was Keefe sure he had enough "probable cause" to stop the truck in any case.

He shook his head again, thinking of Sharon. "Drop back a little. Let's get his plate number." He jotted it down on a scratch pad from his briefcase. The truck was doing about sixty-five miles an hour. Apart from its licence plate it still bore no identification markings of any kind, no name or logo even on the door, nothing. And the three front-ends strapped down on its bed were indubitably nose clips. It was inconceivable to Keefe that this truck and its freight were legitimate; but he did not know where his responsibility lay.

They were coming up to Keefe's exit.

"What do you want to do, Commissioner?" Rainey said. "I'll do anything you want."

Of course he would. So would any cop lower in rank than himself – and all twenty-seven thousand of them were. To be handed from one day to the next such deference on such an enormous scale had amazed Keefe. The high-ranking headquarters officers especially had seemed at all times anxious to curry favor with him, according him much more power and influence than he had ever supposed he had.

Rainey grinned out over the wheel. He looked anxious not so much to please a superior as to get moving on a case, if you could call this a case. Rainey looked eager to behave like a cop. Tail the truck. Call in help. Possibly make an arrest.

Keefe's exit was upon them. Tail the truck where? Call in who? On what authority? Suppose the truck was legitimate? "I'm not a cop," Keefe said.

"That shield you have is real, though," said Rainey.

"Turn off here," said Keefe.

"Certainly, Commissioner."

Was Rainey voicing disappointment or criticism? Keefe chose to ignore him, and they moved north on a two-lane road. There were woods to each side of them with, here and there, half-concealed houses. Having fished the department directory out of his briefcase, Keefe was busy turning pages.

"Who's the commander of the auto squad?" It was a New York truck and eventually it would come back there.

"Lieutenant Craighead."

Keefe had closed the directory over his finger. "What do you know about him?"

"A flamboyant and ambitious young officer. Sucks up to every cop of higher rank."

"Nothing rare about that. So does everyone else I've met so far – captains, inspectors, chiefs." But Keefe was pleased with Rainey, the only man on his staff who ever gave him a straight opinion on anything. The officer who sat outside his door certainly didn't. His name was Captain Fallon. He was nearing sixty, and he spoke mostly in platitudes. He brought even the most routine decisions to Keefe for approval.

They rolled along under trees. Behind them on the turnpike the flat bed truck with its three nose clips was still moving unchallenged to wherever it was headed, and Keefe was annoyed with himself.

The road was narrow, rarely straight; they were rolling through heavily-wooded country. The trees were high, the foliage dense. The road was in shade, and it was cool finally, though this did not help Keefe's mood. Nor Rainey's either, apparently, for about twenty minutes passed during which neither spoke. At last Keefe began to give directions, turning Rainey on to a winding dirt road that plunged downhill. A cottage came into view, then just beyond it part of a lake. When they had pulled to a stop Keefe stared down past the house at the lake and did not immediately get out of the car, contemplating for the first time still another problem connected with his job and rank. Rainey, who was both an older man and only a sergeant, now faced the long drive back to the city alone. Should he be invited into the house first, or what?

Keefe said: "How about coming in for a beer or something, Ed?"

It was the first time he had ever called him anything except sergeant, though that part of it was okay. But did deputy commissioners invite sergeants in for beers?

Evidently Rainey entertained similar misgivings, for he declined the invitation.

Keefe decided that good manners took precedence over rank. He said: "For Christ's sake, Ed, come on in."

Both men got out of the car. Keefe was carrying his attaché case, and they walked without speaking down the path toward the house. As soon as the screen door had slammed behind them, Sharon's voice called out from the kitchen: "Wait till you see what I have for you."

Keefe had no idea what this might mean. She was not expecting Rainey and he had lived with her long enough to know that she did not like surprises. "I have Sergeant Rainey with me," he said loudly. "I thought we could all sit on the porch and have a beer."

But Sharon had already popped out of the kitchen. She was wearing a bikini, and drying her hands on a towel. Her smile vanished. He walked over and kissed her on the cheek, then said: "Sharon, this is Sergeant Rainey."

She shook hands. "It's nice to see you, Sergeant." She looked neither happy nor unhappy. There was no expression on her face at all that Keefe could read.

He opened the fridge and fished out three beers. He put them on a tray, together with three glasses. Sharon, standing in the kitchen doorway in her bikini, said: "Two will be enough."

"You're not having any?"

Rainey said: "Do you have something besides beer, Commissioner? A coke, maybe?"

"Would you like something stronger?" Keefe offered. "Gin and tonic? Scotch?"

"A coke would be fine, if you have it."

"Sure you don't want anything?" Keefe said to Sharon. He had found a coke in the fridge.

"You two sit down and enjoy yourselves, while I get dressed."

Sharon had a southern accent. When she was displeased with him the accent got thicker than usual. It had become, Keefe decided, quite thick now.

Sergeant Rainey had gone through on to the porch. He

41

was looking out over the railing at the lake. "Nice," he said when Keefe came out. He was pretending that he had noted no tension between Keefe and Sharon; Keefe recognized this and appreciated it. He handed Rainey his glass.

He said: "You're married, aren't you, Ed?" They sat down in deck chairs. "How many kids do you have?"

During their few minutes on the porch Sharon did not reappear. Rainey drank his coke quickly and stood up. Keefe walked him back to the car.

The unmarked New York City police car went grinding up the Connecticut hill, and Keefe went back into the house, to find Sharon in the bedroom. Still wearing the bikini, she was lying on the bed leafing through a magazine. She said: "You don't have to invite your chauffeur into the house, darling. I mean, I wasn't expecting him."

Keefe pulled his tie off and began unbuttoning his shirt.

"I don't like to meet strange men wearing only a bikini."

Keefe said nothing.

"I mean, suppose I had had nothing on at all?"

Keefe decided to try a friendly smirk. "That would have made you the talk of the police department, I should think."

Now stripped to the waist, he stood grinning down on her, and at last a tentative smile came on to her face. Not long ago he had wanted very much to marry her, but he had said nothing at the time, waiting to be sure first, and lately the idea of marriage had not seemed such a good one. Now she patted the place beside her on the bed. "Sit down."

Keefe could not be sure how much her invitation included. He stared down at her long slim legs, her rather emphatic bosom. In a bikini almost all of her was on display. He was eager enough, but did not wish to appear so unless she was, and said:

"Just let me make a phone call first."

The phone was beside the bed; he dialed the number of the auto squad and asked for Lieutenant Craighead. Having been put on hold, he sat with the phone at his ear, and gave Sharon a wink and an exaggerated leer.

She had closed the magazine. "Want to go for a swim?"

When he nodded, she rose, went to the bureau, withdrew his swimming trunks from a drawer and tossed them toward him. Holding the phone between shoulder and ear, he wriggled out of his trousers, which he arranged neatly on the bed. Awkwardly he got his shoes off, then his socks. Sharon watched him. He was standing barefoot in his shorts before Craighead at last came on the line.

"You're working late," Keefe told him cordially, but did not wait for any small-talk in exchange. "I got a licence number I want you to check out." He watched Sharon who was dragging a comb through her hair, and was so brief to Craighead he was almost curt. "Get back to me as soon as you can."

As he hung up, Sharon walked out of the room. The invitation, whatever it was, had been withdrawn. Keefe shrugged and stepped into his trunks.

She was standing on the dock gazing out over the lake. The sun had just dropped behind the wooded hills opposite, but it was still a very hot late afternoon. Keefe stood beside her with his hand riding above her hip in the indentation that was her waist. There were houses to either side with docks and sometimes floats out front; another dozen houses lay half-hidden in the trees on the far shore.

"Last one in is a rotten egg," said Keefe, and he whacked her softly on the thin fabric over her bottom and plunged in.

There was the shock of the cold, and then he was gliding through the depths feeling the grime of the city wash off his body, and his uncertainty about Sharon as well. When he had swum out a little he turned, and watched her swimming towards him. For a time the two of them bobbed side by side looking back toward Keefe's cottage. He did not know what she might be thinking, but when he listened he could still hear her voice calling out to him from the kitchen less than half an hour ago:

"Wait till you see what I've got for you."

The afternoon, together with whatever possibilities the weekend might have offered, seemed to have gone downhill since then, although scarcely an additional word had been spoken by either of them.

"So what is it you've got for me?" he said lightly. He reached out through the water and put a hand on her cold, silken back.

"This bikini, for one thing."

They were both treading water. "It's nice."

"You've never seen me in a bikini before, right?"

"You've certainly got the figure for it."

"I thought you'd like it."

"I do."

Even so, a new bikini didn't seem sufficiently important to make her call out to him as soon as he came in the door.

"And I've got some nice things for supper, too."

"Better still."

"And the third thing, I'll show you later."

By this time Police Commissioner Timothy J. Egan was at the hospital where he was being held up at the front desk by an officious nurse or secretary or whatever she was. She had grey hair and eye-glasses hanging from a string. According to her, visiting hours were over.

"I think my office made special arrangements," said Egan mildly.

"I'm sorry," she said. "There's nothing I can do." She busied herself with some papers.

Egan might have flashed his shield and strode past her, but he did not do so. For one thing, the hospital was big, and he did not know what floor he wanted, nor which elevator to take. For another it made him uncomfortable to stand on his rank in a civilian situation. In his own world he knew well enough how to command; now that he was PC a lifted eyebrow was usually enough. But this was not his own world.

"Perhaps you could ask someone," he suggested. He gave his name a second time.

With bad grace the woman picked up her telephone and spoke into it. As she listened her expression changed, and once she had hung up she was all smiles.

On the eighth floor Egan got off the elevator and found himself facing a labyrinth of corridors. He saw a nurse's desk and began to ask directions, only to be told – again – that visiting hours were over.

He was still trying to explain himself when John Jr. came up to the desk and in an angry voice identified him to the nurses. The group of them became immediately flustered. Egan turned away and accompanied the young man down the corridor.

"How's the patient?" he inquired with a heartiness he did not feel.

"He's dying, Uncle Tim," Johnny said.

This was only what Egan had feared and, in some sense, had known. "Nonsense," he said with the same false cheerfulness. "I talked to him on the phone an hour ago. He said he'd be out of here in a week."

"I spoke to the doctor, Uncle Tim."

Egan was not Johnny's uncle, but the two families had been so close for so long that the boy had called him uncle from the time he learned to talk.

"Does he know?" Egan said.

"He pretends he doesn't."

"Does your mother know?"

"The doctor told her too."

Egan's expression did not change, but inwardly he cursed the doctor. "He should have told John, not your mother," he muttered. First Deputy Commissioner John Gaffney stood 6 feet 2 and, at least before this happened, he had weighed 220 pounds. He had always prided himself on his toughness; whereas his wife was a flighty little thing, and not tough at all. Egan did not see how she would be able to handle the news. He resolved to send his wife over to comfort her tonight.

They had come to the room.

"The nurse is in there with him now," Johnny said. He was biting his lip and looked as if he were about to cry.

They waited in the hall. Presently a nurse came out. Whatever she was carrying was covered by a towel. Egan hated to think what was under that towel. He and Johnny went into the room. Approaching the bed, Egan was smiling. "How's it going, big guy?" he called out. Egan himself stood only five-eight. He had barely made it into the Police Academy, for in those days there was a minimum height requirement. He had always envied John Gaffney his size.

They shook hands. "The chemotherapy is working," Gaffney said. "The reason I can tell is that it's so unpleasant." He laughed.

He didn't in truth look too bad. He had not lost too much weight yet. He had lost a good deal of hair, though: whole tufts of black Irish hair were missing.

There were tubes in each of his outstretched arms.

"I'll be back in a little while, Dad," John Jr. said. He went out.

Egan laid his hand on top of Gaffney's. It seemed the thing to do; nonetheless it felt strange to him. He had shaken hands with John Gaffney plenty of times, and as kids they had wrestled and scuffled often enough. Otherwise, despite their closeness, there had been no previous physical contact between them of any kind. After a moment Egan became self-conscious about this contact and he took his hand away, then pulled a chair up to the bed.

"So what's the treatment like?" He could not think of what else to say. He was trying to adjust to the impending double loss of his best friend and his First Deputy Commissioner, and trying to smile at the same time.

"Not so bad," said Gaffney. His voice was still gruff, Egan noted. His friend talked like a mobster – one of those Mafia guys with gravel in their throats. "It isn't anything I can't stand," Gaffney said. He gave a mild chuckle.

Egan saw that the drug was dripping into his friend's right arm from a bottle that hung above the bed. The tube planted in Gaffney's left arm ended in a clamp that closed it off.

The nurse re-entered the room carrying a test kit of some kind. She opened the clamp and Gaffney's blood ran out into a vial out of the test kit. Egan watched in silence.

"They do blood counts a lot," said Gaffney. "To make sure the drug doesn't kill off too many of my white corpuscles. Or maybe it's my red ones." His voice trailed off. "I never can remember. Which is it, nurse?"

The nurse had clamped off the tube and had put a plastic stopper in the vial. "You don't have to worry about that," she replied pleasantly. "You let us worry about that." She gave him a smile and went out of the room.

"It seems like every five minutes they're taking these blood counts," Gaffney apologised.

"I guess nobody tells you much," said Egan. He was trying to sense what his First Deputy might know or guess about his condition.

"You know hospitals."

"I saw the doctor outside," said Egan, still probing. "He said you would be back to work in a month."

Gaffney's face lit up. "Did he say that?"

Egan nodded, already ashamed of the lie. His own smile was difficult to keep in place, and Gaffney's soon faded.

"Meanwhile, the side-effects are not too nice," his friend said.

"Your hair will grow back," said Egan hastily. "You'll have as much hair as you ever had."

"At first I'll have to wear a wig to work. Won't that be something? Me, of all people." After a moment Gaffney added: "I don't mind the hair. I can live without the hair. It's the vomiting that drives me up the wall."

"Vomiting?"

"The drug is pretty strong. It makes me vomit a lot. I can't control it. Sometimes it's pretty violent. I feel so – so helpless."

Egan again reached out and took his friend's hand. Gaffney did not withdraw it.

"So tell me about the department," said Gaffney brightly.

"Well, the Chief of Patrol is gone."

"Hey, that's great."

Egan nodded. "He put his papers in."

"So who are you going to appoint?"

Egan shook his head. "He's got vacation time coming, and after that terminal leave. It'll be a couple of months before the line opens up."

They began to discuss the qualities of the two-star chiefs who might succeed to the job. Finally Gaffney said: "Finnegan. He's the one you should appoint."

Egan had no intention of appointing Finnegan. "All right," he told his deputy. "If he's your choice, then he's mine too." It was not a promise he would have to keep. His First Deputy would not last long enough to know whether he had kept it or not.

"You could appoint Finnegan acting Chief of Patrol in the interim," Gaffney suggested.

"I'd rather not," said Egan. "I don't like blurring these lines of command. I'd rather try to work out something else."

Gaffney did not insist. The hand under Egan's had gone limp. Egan wondered if he might be tired enough to want to sleep.

"So how is young Keefe working out?" said Gaffney after a time.

"He's eager," responded Egan. "He seems somewhat, well, idealistic."

"That's good."

Although Egan disagreed with this judgment, he said nothing. To him idealism was a quality that existed only in conjunction with inexperience and ignorance.

"It means you can get plenty of work out of him, was all I meant," commented Gaffney. "In the NYPD all those cynics will eat him alive."

Idealism, Egan thought, was sometimes useful. Most times it was impractical or even dangerous. In a tight situation people never expected idealistic motives to prevail. They found idealism entirely unpredictable – and if it prevailed they were outraged. But Egan's First Deputy seemed to be tiring fast, so he voiced none of these thoughts.

Gaffney said: "It sounds like he can give you some support in my absence."

Egan nodded. He was outnumbered in the police hierarchy by men married to the status quo who would see his plans as threats and who would sabotage him if possible. He needed whatever support he could get, and if no one else was available then he would use Keefe.

"Watch out for him, though," Gaffney advised.

Egan made no reply.

Gaffney managed another smile. "Hey, don't look so glum. I'm going to lick this thing. I'll be back before you know it. We have work to do, you and I. Throw the rascals out. Take the department over completely."

Egan nodded once more. This had been his hope from the begining, but without Gaffney it would be harder.

The sick man's face suddenly darkened, and he seemed to have trouble catching his breath. His left hand began to squeeze convulsively on the signal module lying near it. The TV set on the wall popped on. Then the stations began to change spasmodically. Egan had jumped to his feet, and was already calling out "Nurse!" – when the woman hurried in through the door carrying a bedpan. By then the First Deputy Commissioner had begun to vomit. Egan, aghast, backed towards the door. The nurse had her arm under Gaffney's head, and was trying to thrust the bedpan close enough to his chin to catch the flow.

Egan stood in the corridor for what seemed a long time. Through the open door came the convulsive sounds of his friend.

The nurse came out carrying the bedpan under another towel. "He's very tired," she said. She looked weary herself. "I think you'd better go."

He nodded at her, but went back inside. He decided he would wait until someone from the family came. He sat down beside the bed and held Gaffney's hand. Neither man spoke. He needs my support, Egan told himself, but all I can think of is how much I need his. He could not even hire a replacement. To replace Gaffney would be to remove from him all hope, and probably all of his courage as well. It would be to tell him he was doomed. Besides, the family needed the money. The First Deputy Commissioner line would have to stay vacant, however long it took, until John Gaffney died.

Four

SERGEANT RAINEY, DRIVING KEEFE'S CAR DOWN
Broadway, turned into Seventy-Fourth Street, a street of
low brownstones, their stoops pushed out half-way to the
curb. Cars were parked bumper to bumper along each side
under the typically scraggly, half-dead New York trees. He
slid into the only open space on the block, in front of a fire
hydrant naturally, about three doors down from the
building. By now it was dusk, but the city to which he had
returned felt no cooler than the one he had left. His shirt and
trouser legs came unstuck from the seat and he got out and
stood beside the car plucking the cloth away from his body.
Air conditioners protruded from windows up and down the
street and when he listened he could hear them humming.
His coat was slung over his shoulder. He eyeballed the street
in both directions. This was habit. He had only one way of
looking at streets. He looked for the split second advance
warning that would make a cop act or react, that might save
his life. But tonight there were only empty parked cars, and
nearly empty sidewalks. The lamp lights had come on. This
particular street was quiet. For the moment it looked as safe
as any street in this city ever got.

After checking that the official plate could be seen in the
windshield, Rainey locked the car. By now it ought to be
back in its official slot in the police garage, and he knew this.
He risked disciplinary action, not only for himself but
possibly for Commissioner Keefe as well. But Keefe would
never know, no one watched these cars very closely, and
tonight he needed a car. Despite the heat he put his suit
jacket on, and tightened his tie.

He crossed the sidewalk and went into the school: it
wasn't a school, it was a four-storey West Side brownstone.

He went up three flights of stairs and through a door whose brass plaque bore the words: *The F. Hyman Effrat School of Acting*. Inside was a single vast room. At some time in the past the interior walls had been removed and the space had been converted into a studio. It had mirrored walls and a hip-high barre all around. The first time Rainey had gone in there the place had shocked him. To see himself reflected in all directions had shocked him. He was too old and he was wrongly dressed. Everyone else was young and wearing what the theatre world counted as work clothes. The boys were all in shorts, the girls in leotards. The would-be actors paid the would-be actresses absolutely no attention. They were focused completely on themselves even though some of the girls" leotards were skin tight. They must all be fags, Rainey thought. You could see everything, for Chrissake. What was he doing here? The answer was that he had seen an ad in the papers. He was curious about acting, always had been; and he thought it might be a place where he could meet girls much younger than himself, and perhaps pick one up. Though uncomfortable that first night, he had decided to bluff it through, to play the role of the distinguished older man. It was not long before the others had accepted him as such. And that was his most important realization of all, that the theater had a reality of its own. The reality of the streets did not pertain here. Reality was not family disputes, stick-ups, bodies on the floor. In the theater reality was whatever you wanted it to be.

Tonight as always the studio was brightly lit, and almost cold from the air conditioning. At first glance it seemed to contain a hundred or more people, but Rainey knew it did not. It contained thirteen including himself and the ex-actor F. Hyman Effrat. All the rest were images reflected in mirrors.

The class had not yet started. Girls in their tight leotards were stationed here and there around the walls, either stretching or examining themselves in the mirrors. The boys – it was impossible to think of such creatures as men – were mostly doing the same. As a tough young cop Rainey had often been summoned to intervene in homosexual disputes.

He had sometimes subdued the disputants with more force than was necessary.

Among the students one girl in particular interested Rainey. She stood at the mirror on one leg, her other foot up over her head, her chin pressed against her knee. Her name was Flora Bernstein; she was an extremely supple girl, and what she was doing gave Rainey back pains. It also made him want to stroke the underside of that upstretched leg.

F. Hyman Effrat, clapping his hands loudly, called the class to order. The students moved toward the two rows of chairs that faced a chalk line on the floor. The room had just become a theater. The chairs were the orchestra. Beyond the chalk line was the stage.

"Sit here," said Rainey, patting the chair next to him as Flora Bernstein approached. She did as she was told. Her behind came down almost on his hand and she flashed him her big-toothed smile as well. "I have a car tonight," Rainey whispered to her, "in case you'd like to go anywhere after."

"That would be very interesting," said Flora.

F. Hyman on the stage brought them up to date on the continuing saga of Conchita Moskowitz, a Jewish girl from Puerto Rico recently arrived in New York. Conchita Moskowitz was a figment of F. Hyman's imagination. She was a character in a play for which the students invented and acted out new scenes each week. Conchita was beset by problems. Various evil fiends were trying to prevent her from getting a job, or from saving her money, and certain among them were trying to deflower her. But all this time she remained a nice Jewish girl with a Spanish accent.

The idea of a Jewish Puerto Rican was offensive to Rainey. Jews wanted everyone to be Jewish. Even the evil fiends, according to F. Hyman, were supposed to be Jewish. Why? The police world had been Rainey's for all of his adult life. In it Jews were rare. There were few enough Jewish cops, and the street criminals were blacks and Puerto Ricans, not Jews. In the police department the pervading ethos was Irish Catholic. Non-Catholics – the Jewish officers especially – tried to conform. Rainey himself was part of the majority. Meanwhile, the city itself had a Jewish mayor and an enormous Jewish population. Jews dominated entire industries, the theater being just one of them. Everyone in this room except himself was Jewish, unless they were a fag. Once outside the department Rainey became part of an ethnic minority, and he did not like it.

Tonight it was Flora Bernstein who assumed the role of Conchita, and he watched her.

She was about twenty-four years old. She had very short, almost kinky, blonde hair, and muscular shoulders and legs. When they studied plays, she had sometimes asked his advice on how the playwright had meant something to be played.

Now she exuded great energy, and great confidence. He could not take his eyes off her.

After the class, Rainey went down the stairs with Flora. She had wrapped a skirt around her leotard, had put on a boy's summerweight sportcoat over that, and she carried a rather large imitation leather handbag slung over her shoulder. During his youth, girls had always been a segregated, unknown sex to Rainey. But now as he descended the stairs, there was nothing frightening about Flora. He had two daughters about her age. He had more knowledge of Flora than she had of him.

"What would you like to do?" Flora was two steps below him so he spoke to the top of her descending head. "How about going to get a hamburger?" Rainey was hungry. There was a place nearby that was frequented by cops from the local precinct. He would be comfortable there.

"Let's go listen to some music," suggested Flora, giving him a flash of teeth.

They went down the front stoop, and along the sidewalk under the trees until they got to Commissioner Keefe's car. Rainey unlocked the door for Flora and she got in. He walked around to the driver's side.

He had already noted a police radio car doubleparked some distance ahead. Even as he unlocked the door, he saw two cops get out and stride back towards him.

One of them said: "That's a fire hydrant there."

"Yeah," Rainey said, "and?"

"You're parked beside it."

Rainey looked at him. "So?"

"Licence and registration, please."

Rainey said: "Are you crazy? This is a department car."

"What department car?" said the cop. He might have noted the official plate in the windshield, but he was too stupid. Instead he attempted to peer into the well of the car itself, no doubt trying to discern the police radio under the dashboard. But it was too dark.

Rainey said: "Every bad guy in the city would make this car in a second, but not you. Are you blind or something?"

The cop was beginning to be embarrassed, which made him stubborn. "Who are you?" he said truculantly.

"I'm on the job, same as you."

Rainey noted that Flora was leaning across the seat and peering out at him. She would be wondering about the delay. Her image of him was perhaps being damaged, and he became annoyed.

But the cop was annoyed too. His partner had come up, and stood about six feet away, the heel of his hand on his gun butt. The first cop said: "Can I see your shield and ID, please?"

Rainey fished his shield case out of his back pocket, and broke it open. The first cop had his memo book out, and he punched his ballpoint to expose the nib. His partner had come closer. Both peered down at Rainey's shield, and the partner read off Rainey's name and shield number while the first cop copied both into his memo book.

"Satisfied?" said Rainey.

"Where do you work, Sarge?"

Rainey told him. This information went into the memo book too, after which the cop pointed into the car with his ballpoint. "Who's she?"

Rainey got angry. "That you don't have to know. Now get the hell out of my way."

He got into the car, started the engine, pulled out of the parking place and around the parked radio car. He drove out towards Broadway.

Flora said: "What was all that about?"

"Nothing."

Flora accepted this reply. "Isn't Professor Effrat a wonderful teacher?" she said presently.

Rainey stared out over the steering wheel. "How about getting that hamburger?"

"I ate before acting class. I have to watch my figure."

"I see." It appeared Rainey was not going to get any dinner.

"What I was really hoping we would do is go to a club." She named it and gave the address. Rainey nodded, though he had never been there.

It turned out to be a disco called Kaleidoscope, and was half a block from the river in the Thirties. The noise assaulted his ears a good twenty paces from the entrance, bursting out the door with a rush like a blast of superheated air. Inside the foyer it only became more focused, reverberating off the walls. Rainey stepped to the ticket window, and pushed across a fifty dollar bill. He expected change, but did not get any. When he glanced over at Flora he saw that she was admiring the posters that hung on the walls around the foyer. To her he must seem an older man, and therefore rich. But Rainey was a police sergeant. The cost of these tickets, and of the drinks inside which would be equally expensive, was going to have to come out of his wife's allowance. He was used to her berating him. For years she had taken every cent he brought home. It was time he spent some of it on himself. In any case, she now had a job of her own. Let her use her own money for a change.

As if she were a felon under arrest, he took Flora by the arm, moving her through the heavy drapes into the disco proper. It was a vast skating rink of a room – it must once have been a warehouse – and was absolutely crammed with people. The noise level had gone up still higher. There was an explosion of light as well, strobes flashing on and off, lights that cascaded down from ten or a dozen dangling, whirling kaleidoscopes, light that dazzled, that blinded. After five minutes his eyeballs felt seared.

Rainey was pulling Flora along by the arm but the place was so full it was almost impossible to get through to where

55

there were presumably tables. When they got there all of them were, of course, taken. Beside him Flora wore a goofy smile on her face. She seemed enthralled. Crowds like this were in violation of the fire laws obviously. He ought to go back out to the ticket window and arrest that stick-up man behind it. When he sniffed the air his nostrils sucked up the sweet odour of marijuana. So the drug laws were being violated too. Even better. He could arrest everybody.

But Flora took his hand and squeezed it, and when he looked down at her she rose up on tiptoes and kissed him on the right cheekbone.

"I'm having a very good time," she shouted.

A table became vacant – Flora lunged for it. One second she was beside him, and the next she was sitting down at the minuscule table and holding on to the second chair with a death grip. She had both hands locked on its backrest and her ankles crossed around one of its legs. Another woman was trying to wrench the chair away from her.

Rainey raced over and sat down on it, and the woman slunk off. He and Flora sat together in a storm of thunder and lightning.

"Do you like it?" he heard Flora shout.

"Love it," he shouted back. As the sound waves battered his body, he lifted the tiny placard that stood on the tiny table, and read the prices of the drinks. Jesus, he thought, and put the placard back down again.

When the drinks came, Flora raised her glass to toast him. She smiled deep into his eyes, and when the toast was over she hooked her fingers in his beard, pulled his head close, and kissed him on the cheekbone again. She had dimples in her cheeks and in her chin.

Rainey decided he was falling in love.

For more than two hours he sat locked inside the bombardment, inside the blinding muzzle flashes. He sat with a fixed smile on his face, from time to time trying to engage in shouted conversation with his date. He kept sipping Pepsi Cola until his lips felt stuck to his teeth. For Flora he squeezed out a third rye and ginger.

At last they were out on the street again. It was past one

o'clock in the morning and the night was humid and smoggy. Nonetheless, after the crush of bodies and sweat-soaked clothing inside, the air smelled surprisingly clean. Flora clung to Rainey's arm. Unfortunately he had no place to take her – his own small house was sixty-five miles out on Long Island. In any case he couldn't take her there. Lately he had been sleeping in the spare room at his sister's apartment – he couldn't take her there either. He had no cash left to hire a hotel room, and was over the limit on his one credit card. Her place then.

"Where do you live?" He had settled himself behind the wheel of Keefe's car.

He might have guessed her answer: at the extreme southern edge of Brooklyn, just inside the Coney Island Beach and Amusement Park. Even at this time of night it took him almost an hour to get there. Her conversation did not make the journey easier. There was no conversation. She simply fell asleep. He turned the police radio up fairly loud, reaching over between her slightly spread knees to do so, at first hoping a diet of police calls might excite her, and after that hoping it might wake her up. It did neither.

He parked in front of the address she had given him: a two-family frame house with a wooden staircase running up one side of it. She was still asleep. The streetlight came through the windshield and illuminated the lower part of her face, especially her slightly parted lips. He leaned over her. He was so close he swallowed her next exhalation, a gust smelling of rye whisky, and her lips when his own touched them tasted of rye whisky too. The kiss lasted longer than he intended – he could not help himself – and then her arms came around his neck and she kissed him back.

For a moment after that they sat in silence.

"I would invite you in," Flora said, "but my mother will wake up the minute she hears the door opening."

Rainey said nothing.

"I've had an incredibly nice time," .said Flora. She grasped the door handle. "You're an incredibly nice man." She cracked open the door so that the light came on.

"It's awfully late," she said.

Rainey said nothing.

She hesitated. "I feel awful making you drive all the way out here. I feel I owe you something." She gave a kind of leer. "At least, like, for the car fare."

"You don't owe me anything," Rainey said. He forgot even how hungry he was. "It was a lovely evening for me too."

"Are you sure there isn't something I can do for you?" The door clicked shut and the car was dark again.

What was this supposed to mean? Was she offering to spread herself out on the back seat of this unmarked police car like some two-bit hooker? He did not want to think of her in that way. Such a result would entail, for her as much as for Rainey, a loss of dignity. Once when he was a young cop in uniform he had banged a hooker on the back seat of his radio car parked in the night in the darkest corner of a school yard. The door had hung open. The hooker's heels had dragged probably on the basketball court. His partner had walked out to the sidewalk for a smoke. He had done the same thing for the partner the next night. The hooker got nothing out of either transaction except an extra twenty-four hours" freedom.

He was not the young cop he had been then. He could wait for a better opportunity.

"We can go out again next week after the class," he suggested. I'll have to find a place where I can take her, he thought.

Her smile came full on. "Okay," she agreed. "I know another place."

"Good."

"It's even better," she said.

"Even better?"

"Better acoustics, better everything."

"I'll look forward to it," he said.

Rainey came around from his side, and together they walked up three wooden steps onto a wooden stoop. She had her key out and when she had pulled open the screen door, Rainey took the key and turned it in the lock. He pushed the door inwards into the hall, and she turned and he was again looking down into her upturned face.

"Thank you again for a very nice time," she said, and kissed him on the lips. He put his big arms around her, but she disengaged rather quickly and closed the door on him.

He was left with a whiff of her perfume that clung to his clothes, and perhaps with lipstick on his mouth. He almost danced down the three steps and back to Keefe's car. This mood held for most of the long drive back to the police garage, where he left the car.

Rainey walked up the ramp and back out into the night where, in the light of a street lamp, he stopped to count what change he had left. There was not nearly enough for a taxi, and his sister lived in the Chelsea section of the city – he had about a two mile walk ahead of him. He put his hands in his pockets and started out.

In his sister's flat, he laid his gun on the top of the bureau, put on his pyjamas, and went into the bathroom. With a washcloth he rubbed the lipstick off his face. Back in the small room his sister let him use he got into the bed where he lay awake with his hands behind his head. For a time he thought about Flora. Then he thought about his life, about the suddenly expanding future.

Five

AFTER RAINEY DROVE AWAY, AFTER THEIR SWIM IN THE lake, Keefe and Sharon ate dinner by candlelight on the porch while the night got dark and the insects banged against the screen. There was a tablecloth and on it lay delicacies only: tacos stuffed with lobster, foie gras, half a cold, lacquered duck each. Such a feast as this seemed odd to Keefe. Obviously Sharon had spent a good deal of money, even to the bottle of Dom Perignon which she had brought forth. He supposed she had procured this stuff ready-made at Zabars, the famous specialty delicatessen, while driving up Broadway in his car on her way up here.

Sharon was no gourmet. She had learned about foie gras and such from riding Pan Am first class back and forth to Los Angeles; despite her relative youth, she was fairly important in the world of soap operas, and she went there often enough. Keefe himself had learned about them as a foreign correspondent in various cities abroad. In any case, she was spoiling him, and he wondered why. As he sipped his wine and breathed in the hot humid night he even felt the first faint sense of foreboding. There was something here he did not understand.

"Why the champagne?" he asked presently. It was the most neutral question he could think of.

"My boss gave it to me." She added no further explanation, and Keefe, for reasons he could not name, chose not to press for one.

The candles burned down. The flames shone in Sharon's big dark eyes each time she leaned forward to keep his glass and his plate full. Tonight she was as loving a wife as any husband could wish; only she was not his wife, and he was not her husband. Her conversation was bright and witty, and never lagged. She spoke mostly of the plot of her soap opera, an interminable story involving an almost infinite number of abnormal people. She poked fun at it, laughing at its silliness, occasionally making him laugh too. She was as vivacious as a hostess at a dinner party, though she was not the hostess here. She was, if anything, his honoured guest.

When dinner was over they did the dishes together, Sharon washing, Keefe drying. In this summer cottage, which had been in his family since he was a boy, there was no dish-washing machine. When they were finished they walked down and stood on the dock in the night, Keefe's arm encircling her shoulder, her hand resting on the small of his back. Through the trees they could see the lights of other houses, none of them too close. Keefe pulled her to him and kissed her.

"It sure is a hot night," she murmured, her forehead in the crook of his neck.

"It will be difficult sleeping."

"Want to take another swim?"

Their wet bathing suits were draped over deck chairs nearby, together with the damp towels they had used earlier. "I hate putting on clammy trunks," Keefe said. He reached out and felt them.

Sharon gave a muffled laugh. "You're so proper," she said. "It's dark enough, isn't it? Do you really think anybody would see us?"

She was wearing a sundress which she slipped over her head. Under it she wore only panties which she stepped out of, having first kicked away her sandals. He watched her dive off the dock into the black water. She swam part-way back in and stood up on the bottom. What little light there was gleamed on bare skin. Her arms were spread invitingly.

Keefe stripped and plunged in after her, and they swam out toward the nearest float. A little later he was standing in chest-deep water when she swam over, locked her legs around his waist and gave him a wet kiss. Keefe glanced hurriedly around to see if anyone was standing out on any of the docks. There was no one, so he kissed her back.

"Ouch," she said when the kiss ended. "I think a mosquito got me." She slid down his body until her shoulders were under water, then pulled his head close and kissed him again. The kiss lasted even longer. "Now you're poking me," she told him.

"Every adolescent's dream," Keefe said. "Making love in the water."

"It's not possible," said Sharon. "Believe me, I know."

Keefe held her against him. "How do you know?"

"Didn't you ever try it? I did."

"Who with?"

"Not with you."

They were kissing and nuzzling each other.

"Willie Franklin," he said.

"I never went to bed with Willie Franklin."

"We're not talking about bed, we're talking about underwater."

"Willie Franklin was never my boyfriend."

"Jerry Hawkins. He was your boyfriend."

61

She was laughing. "Jerry who?"

"It was Bill Curran, then. He was your boyfriend too."

"I won't tell you."

"It was him," said Keefe. He had never met any of these young men but he knew a good deal about them, and he wondered how many other young men would one day learn about him. A lover's deepest secrets, his most intimate behaviour, was likely to become an open book to his, or her, successors.

"That's who it was," said Keefe. But Sharon was giggling and squirming against him, and he was losing interest in Curran or Hawkins or whoever it may have been.

"Come on," she said, and took his hand. Half-swimming, half-wading, she dragged him toward the shore.

Beyond the dock was a short stretch of lawn on which could be made out the shapes of chairs. Underfoot the lawn was more weeds than grass. Having grasped one of the damp towels, Sharon dried Keefe's body. Then he began to dry hers. But when he had got the towel behind her, he pulled her tight against him.

"On the lawn," he said.

But Sharon laughed and broke away from him. "Too many mosquitos."

"I'll protect you from them like a tent."

"I'm a girl who likes her comfort." With one hand she scooped up their clothes and dragged Keefe toward the house with the other. She was giggling, perhaps in anticipation. Naked and barefoot they went through the dark house. Beside the bed they stood in the dark, two cool damp bodies pressed against each other, kissing. Then Sharon sat down on the bed and drew Keefe down on top of her.

About twenty minutes later the moon came out from behind clouds, sending a shaft of pale light through the window and across the bed. It illuminated Sharon's hair upon the pillow, and fell across her face and one breast, both faintly damp with sweat, so that Keefe reared up from where he was. He didn't want to make love to her at that moment, only to look at her, drink her in with his eyes. It was as if he had only just recognized what he now blurted out, the greatest truth of his life.

"I could look at you forever."

His emotion was more intense than any he had ever felt, and he might have said much more, except that Sharon interrupted him.

"That's just the trouble," she said. "You can't."

And that's how it ends, thought Keefe. Without warning. *Pow!* Right between the eyes. He felt he knew the rest before she spoke.

"The show has moved to Los Angeles," she murmured, and she reached up and stroked his face.

So that's what the Dom Perignon was all about, thought Keefe. "And you're going with it?"

"I have to."

In a movie, thought Keefe, the director would cut the scene off right here. The dramatic point has been made. All the rest is awkwardness, words only – clumsy ones. It is people trying to extricate themselves from the tightest of spots with as little loss of dignity as possible. Any director would bring on the car chase, because the rest of the scene in this bedroom was almost certain to end in the humiliation of the hero.

Such thoughts as these were rushing through Keefe's head because as yet he felt no pain. His towering emotion of a moment ago had vanished, and in its place was – nothing. No emotion at all. This was akin, he realised, to a man's reaction to physical trauma. Part of his being had been numbed. The true pain always came later, tomorrow for instance. He was in for it tomorrow.

He extricated himself from between her legs and lay down beside her. At once she snuggled into the crook of his arm and suddenly, for reasons he could not discern, he found that he felt closer to her than at any time since she had first moved in with him.

He said: "How long have you known about this?"

"I saw it coming."

"You saw it coming?"

"I didn't want it to happen, Phil."

"When did you decide?"

He wanted to ask her why she had never told him, but he didn't. They might have talked it out. He felt the bitterness creep into his mind, but he was trying, and so far succeeding, he believed, to keep it out of his voice. She could have warned him.

"I only gave them my answer this afternoon."

Maybe. He said: "And your boss was so pleased that he gave you that bottle of Dom Perignon."

"Yes."

"Did he give you the lobster and foie gras too?"

"I wanted to make tonight nice for you," she said. "I still do."

"Did he?"

"No."

She shifted position slightly. Her hip moved against his, the nape of her neck shifted on his shoulder. He was extremely conscious of her hot body on his, and his hand, as if of its own accord, began to stroke her skin.

"You said you had three things for me, the bikini and the dinner. What was the third thing?"

"A new nightgown. It's the sheerest gossamer. You can see right through it. Would you like me to put it on?"

Keefe gave a laugh, the best one of which he was capable at that moment. With the hand that had been stroking her forearm he patted a breast. "I prefer you like this."

But to his surprise he felt the pain coming on. He stared up at the dark ceiling, and it came both sooner and stronger than he had expected.

"You could stay," he said, trying to keep his voice neutral. I'm certainly not going to beg her, he told himself.

"They're making me a supervising producer."

He thought about his next words for some time before he spoke them. I'm not begging her, he assured himself. I hope she won't see it as begging. "We could get married," he said. He was amazed at how weak this sounded, how futile.

There was a silence during which she perhaps considered telling him that his offer amounted to too little too late. If she had given such a speech now it might not have made him feel better, but he could not have blamed her.

Instead she said: "Some marriage that would be. You here, me there."

They began to discuss bi-coastal relationships. There were more and more of them these days, he said. They never worked, he added. That wasn't necessarily true, she said. The network might pay her airline tickets, he said, but the police department would certainly not pay his.

He remembered the time just before he had accepted the appointment as Deputy Commissioner, when he had been so sick; she had taken time off from work and had nursed him for three days. He had almost asked her to marry him then; instead he had convinced himself that gratitude was the wrong motive for such an important step. He had felt another rush of love for her after she had studied the manuscript of his only book so far, because she had read it so carefully and had offered such intelligent suggestions. Love. How about the night he had made love to her for the first time. How excited he had been then – or even tonight, for that matter.

I didn't ask her to marry me, he thought, because her career was so important to her, more important than me, I was sure. It would have sounded like I was trying to own her.

He said: "When are you leaving?"

"I have to be there Monday."

He said only: "So soon?"

"That's part of the reason I wanted tonight to be so nice for you. We only have tonight and tomorrow. I have to catch the plane on Sunday."

He felt the pain descend into the region of his pride. How abject do you wish to seem to her? he asked himself.

"What will you do with your apartment?" he asked aloud, a neutral subject. Although she had not lived in it for months, she had not sold it either, one of the many hedges against the future that had been denied women in the past – women belonging to generations before his own. Women in the past had been dependent upon men, which she was not, however much he might wish the contrary right now.

"I'll just leave it empty," she replied. "Maybe I'll sublet it eventually."

So she was still hedging.

Keefe was thinking about all those past generations of men and women whose lives had been based on permanence. People had pretended to permanence. They had pretended so hard that for most of them illusion became reality. Men lived and died with one job, one wife, one house. Those people had had it easy. Permanence required only faith, but faith no longer existed. People didn't believe in it, and therefore couldn't have it.

He knew very well that once she got on that plane on Sunday their relationship was over. She would meet someone else, or he would. They both would – they would have to. A male-female relationship, a love-sex relationship lasting many months, had no more viability than certain childhood friendships he remembered once the other kid had moved away.

Raising herself up on one elbow, she peered down at him in the moonlight. "Hey, don't be so glum, it's not the end of the world." She kissed him, a long, open-mouthed kiss. "I do like you an awful lot," she said when it ended, and her hands slid down his body. "What were we doing when we were so rudely interrupted?" Again she giggled.

His physical reactions to her remained the same. In that respect he was unchanged. He had no control over it. It was just his mind that was different. He heard her groaning, felt her thrusting. The bed made as much noise as she did, but from his throat came no sound. "Fuck me, Phil," she begged at a certain point, her voice half-croak, half-gasp. Her mother in a similar situation might have said to her father: "Make love to me, Jim," or whatever his name was. Or perhaps at so intimate a moment she would not have dared say anything at all.

"Fuck me harder," groaned Sharon.

So he did, but it wasn't what he had hoped for. It wasn't anything very much at all.

The next day they lolled about in the sun, went for a canoe ride and swam. He wanted to shout at her, change her plans with kisses. He did neither. Pride would not let him. His performance was a masterpiece of restraint.

Perhaps a display of passion was what she wanted; as the day passed she grew increasingly somber, but her jaw became set and she said nothing either. That night they slept together in the same bed, possibly for the last time. Sunday morning they made love again, also possibly for the last time, but with pretended casualness, like former lovers meeting after several years and winding up in bed for want of any reason not to. Again Keefe's emotion nearly burst forth. He had the feeling she was trying to make it burst forth, perhaps so as to ridicule him. Again he controlled himself.

It remained only to drive her to Kennedy Airport. There was no need to stop at her apartment or his for any luggage, he learned, for she had thought of all that in advance; her suitcases were already in the trunk of his Porsche. They had a brief fight when he discovered them there. He finally did shout at her, and she shouted back. Her name was Sharon Russell, not Sharon Keefe, she told him. He hadn't wanted to get married and she had to go where her job took her, didn't she? Well, didn't she?

The ride to the airport was mostly silent. He walked her through the terminal as far as the security gate, where they exchanged a brief kiss, both of them smiling, as if goodbye were an amusing event.

"We'll talk on the phone," Sharon said. She looked bleak. "And we'll see each other soon." She was standing on the other side of the security archway. Keefe grinned at her as if he were happy, and waved. Her hand luggage came off the X-ray belt and she lifted it and started down the long corridor away from him. She did not look back. She was wearing high heels, he noted. After a moment he turned and walked outside to his car. It was not yet noon on a Sunday, he was alone in New York, and he could think of nothing to do with the rest of the day.

Six

MONDAY MORNING AT HEADQUARTERS. KEEFE GOT off the elevator and went into his offices. The night duty sergeant was gone, and the day staff was there, two policewomen and about a dozen men, most of them drinking coffee from mugs. Keefe stopped at the desk of Captain Fallon. "Anything?" he asked.

"PC's not in yet," his chief of staff reported, as if this were the only detail that concerned either of them.

Keefe frowned. "And the city?"

"City's quiet, Sir."

"That's good."

Fallon handed over a sheaf of reports of unusual crimes that had occurred over the weekend – about twenty of them, judging from the thickness of the pile.

"Any juicy ones?"

"I didn't look through them, Sir. I thought you'd like to do that."

"I see." Fallon must have been a young cop once, but it was difficult to visualize it. He was without humor, without imagination. He came in at eight A.M. and left at five P.M., the dedicated file clerk. If Keefe asked his opinion on something he most often didn't have one.

Keefe hung up his jacket, loosened his tie, and began to page through the unusuals.

"Lieutenant Craighead is here from the auto squad, Sir." It was Fallon in his doorway.

"Send him in," Keefe said. He decided against asking Fallon to sit in on this meeting. "Send Sergeant Rainey in too, please."

A moment later Craighead came through the door. "You really hit the jackpot, Commissioner," he began with an ebullience that, this early on a Monday morning, seemed misplaced. Then Keefe realized it was not that at all but thinly disguised obsequiousness. "When you tail a truck, Boss, that's some truck."

Keefe did not like to be called boss.

Sergeant Rainey had entered behind Craighead, who was still talking.

"That was Hot Harry Hamish's truck you spotted, Boss. Biggest car thief in the city."

"Sergeant Rainey and I tailed him into Connecticut with a load."

"We thought he was retired. You certainly proved us wrong."

Craighead pulled some papers out of a briefcase. "Here's his sheet."

There were two pages stapled together. Hamish's prior arrests filled all of one sheet and most of the second.

"What are you trying to do, Boss? Teach us our business?"

Keefe put the sheet down. "You got a photo of him there?"

Craighead handed across several. Rainey came around the desk and looked at them over Keefe's shoulder.

"What do you think, Ed?"

Rainey nodded. "That's the guy, I would say. Wouldn't you?"

"I think so, yes."

Lieutenant Craighead said: "What happens is, some guy bangs up his Cadillac. He takes it to a body shop, right? He needs a new front end. The cheapest front end is, Hot Harry sends men out to steal the same model car, he cuts it up and ships the necessary piece to the body and fender guy, who is supposedly a legitimate businessman. The rest of the pieces he keeps on inventory."

Keefe was staring down at Hamish's photo. "The body and fender guy is as guilty as he is."

"So what else is new? People ask why we recover so few stolen cars. That's the reason."

"If you know so much about this guy," Keefe said, "why is he still out there?"

"He can afford very good lawyers. Hey, Boss, you're

uncanny. When you take an interest, you really go straight to the top."

"When do you arrest him?" said Keefe.

"It's your case, Boss. Tell me what you want to do."

"It's not my case, and I wish you wouldn't call me Boss." Keefe thought about it for a moment, then said: "I want you to handle it in the normal way."

"In the normal way we wouldn't even get to it for a while, we've got such a backlog."

"Is he or is he not the biggest car thief in the city?"

"Sure. I told you he was."

"Then put some men on the case."

"How many men. Name a number."

Lieutenant Craighead looked about forty – older than Keefe, who was thirty-four and who, as always, found it difficult to use his rank when he didn't have the age – or, now, the experience – to go with it. He said: "You put enough men on that case to find the guy and the yard where he's working, and when you've done that you come back to me and we'll decide what to do next."

When Lieutenant Craighead had gone out, Keefe paced his office muttering: "You're uncanny, Boss. It's your case, Boss."

Rainey, watching him, said: "You shouldn't get upset when people call you Boss, Commissioner. That's a time-honored title in the police department."

"I'm tired of being flattered by everybody around here. Why did he tell me it was my case?"

"He thought maybe you'd like to make the arrests yourself. Headquarters bosses often like to make spectacular arrests themselves."

Captain Fallon stuck his head in the doorway. "The PC's in." He seemed proud of this information. "He'd like to see you, Commissioner."

"What about?"

"His secretary didn't say."

"Did you ask him?"

"I didn't, Sir."

"Next time perhaps you could ask him."

Keefe gave a curt nod to Rainey and went out past Fallon, up the stairs and down the hall. He went in past the clerks at their desks, and stopped in front of the PC's chief secretary, a deputy inspector in uniform. The PC's door was closed, but it opened almost at once and out came Chief Kilcoyne, also in uniform, four gleaming stars on each shoulder, and Chief of Detectives Gold who wore a blue pin-striped suit and black shoes with tassels on them. Both men said good morning to him.

"You're lucky, Commissioner," Gold added with a smile, "For a Monday morning he's in exceptionally good humor."

Kilcoyne evidently thought this remark funny, for he threw back his snow-white hair and gave his booming laugh.

Keefe peered in at the PC, who was standing at his desk on the phone, while the other two went out into the hall. He watched their backs for a moment. Neither was laughing.

The PC beckoned Keefe forward and sat down behind his desk. He was in shirtsleeves.

"To get top management moving again is so difficult," he said. "That's the first job when you take over an organization like this department. You can't do anything until you do that."

The PC had not summoned him merely to make such an observation, Keefe knew, and he waited to learn what the purpose of this interview might be.

"I've just been talking to Chief Kilcoyne and Chief Gold," the PC began. He took a roll of wintergreen lifesavers out of his pocket, thumbed off the top one and sucked it thoughtfully. Keefe glanced around the office. It was just a plain, government office, except for the PC's old oak desk which supposedly had once been used by Teddy Roosevelt, who went from behind it to the governor's mansion, then very quickly to the White House. There was a framed oil portrait of Roosevelt on one of the walls. There was a telephone console on the desk, and the walls were institutional green. A civilian executive who headed a company with as many employees as the NYPD – and as enormous a budget – would have far more luxurious offices, including probably oriental carpets on the floor and Impressionist paintings on the walls.

"I've asked Chief Kilcoyne to take on the additional job of acting Chief of Patrol for the time being," the PC said. "In addition to his own duties, of course. To ease the burden on him somewhat, I've asked the Chief of Detectives to report directly to me." He nodded at Keefe, who nodded back.

Keefe was trying to read this news as the rest of the department would read it. The Chief of Operations had just been demoted. The PC had left him Patrol, which had been part of his command already, but had stripped him of the detective bureau. At the same time the PC had brought Gold's three thousand detectives under his own direct control. All power, it seemed to Keefe, had now been consolidated in this one room. This was a big, big thing. Headquarters – the entire department as well – was going to be stunned. He wondered how the press would react. If he were writing the story it would be front-page; but the editors had no experience in police politics and might not see it that way.

"About Chief Kilcoyne," the PC said suddenly. "He's one of the finest men in this department. He'll work long hours for you, he'll work weekends. He's totally trustworthy, one of the most honourable men you'll ever meet."

Keefe waited.

"The men admire him. He's got the ribbons. He speaks their language."

Another long pause. "I think it was good of him to take on the extra duties as acting Chief of Patrol, don't you?"

Keefe gave a brief nod.

"But I don't think it's something we want to make public, do you?"

Keefe said: "Well, the press is going to find out."

"But if we don't make it public, that will mean we don't consider it all that important, don't you think?"

"Possibly."

"And if we don't think it's that important, why should they?"

"You may be right."

"But that isn't the way you'd do it?"

"If the press once suspects you're hiding something, or holding back, or attempting any sort of deception, then that's the story they're going to want, and they'll destroy you with it if they can. Destroy us."

"Let me think about it." There was a pause. "Have you ever met Senator Buckner?" the PC asked suddenly.

"No, I haven't."

Buckner had served two terms in the US Senate, but was not a Senator now. Perhaps that was why he had agreed to head the Commission to Investigate Alleged Police Misconduct – the so-called Buckner Brutality Commission.

The PC sucked on his lifesaver. Presently he said: "You should get to know him." There was another pause.

Which meant he wanted to know what Buckner was up to, and apparently he wanted Keefe to find out. The notion that the PC could be no more direct with him than this almost made Keefe smile.

The PC began a long rambling story about his own days as a rookie patrolman. Beating up prisoners was apparently common then, more common than now.

"We had a fellow in my first precinct," the PC said. "Used to be known as the Prince of Pain."

"And no one said anything?" said Keefe.

The PC shook his head sadly. "It wasn't done in those days. That's why I got out of that precinct so fast. There was nothing I could do."

Keefe said nothing.

"What did you decide about the memo I sent you?"

"What memo?" said Keefe.

"About one of your sergeants. What's his name? Rainey, I think."

Keefe had seen no memo. "What about him?"

"It occurred to me you might want to send him back to a precinct, not take the chance that he might embarrass you."

"Why should he embarrass me? Is there something specific I should know about?"

"Well," said the PC, "it was just a notion I had. You're free to disregard it, if you think that's the wisest course to take."

"Up to now," said Keefe after a pause, "I was under the impression he was the best man I had." He waited for the PC to explain himself, but this did not happen.

After another silence, the PC said: "You should find Buckner an interesting man. I knew him a bit when I worked for the Justice Department in Washington."

"I'll invite him to lunch."

"Good idea," said the PC, as if it were Keefe's instead of his own. Then he said: "The cops in my day used to say they never beat up a prisoner who didn't deserve it. Probably the cops today say the same. But now they suddenly are using implements – stun guns and the like – that leave marks. The stupidity of it is incredible. We've got to stop that. It's a form of corruption. It's as insidious as taking money from dope dealers. I've been talking to some of the commanders about establishing a hot line to my office so that any citizen can call to report any act of brutality, any act of excessive force at any time of the day or night. That's one of our ideas. There are others. We'll be implementing them one by one. You can tell Buckner that. Don't say it comes from me, of course."

The PC walked over to the window, and for a moment didn't speak. Turning to face Keefe, he said: "I need time."

He walked Keefe to the door, where he patted him on the shoulder. It was a rare moment of physical contact between the two men and Keefe was surprised. "Thanks for stopping by," the PC said. He stepped out into his anteroom, and peered down at the phone messages the deputy inspector had collected. He seemed already focused on other problems, as if he had already forgotten Keefe's very existence.

The memo about Rainey in Keefe's in-basket was signed: *Egan*. It suggested Rainey might prove an embarrassment. That was all. It was no more specific than Egan's comments a few minutes ago, and Keefe began to wonder what it was all about, and what to do about it.

Ambition had come relatively late to Dennis Kilcoyne,

whereas Al Gold seemed to have been born with it. They had entered the Police Academy the same year. They had taken the same promotion exams, waited their turns separately, risen in rank virtually side by side. Both had sought command of the key precincts, then the key divisions, then the key boroughs. They had worked hard to get themselves noticed, to be installed finally in offices in headquarters. Kilcoyne had always been part of the mainstream. His commanders had liked him. He had advanced easily in rank.

Gold had had to work harder. Many times he heard superior officers say in his hearing: "Let the Jewboy do it." Always he had grinned, and he had done the job indicated to the best of his ability. All of these slights still burned within him, but the fire was carefully banked now, and no one had called him Jewboy in years, at least within his hearing. Promotions up to the grade of captain had been, and still were, decided on the basis of civil service exams in which Gold had always scored better than Kilcoyne. But after the rank of Captain an officer advanced "at the pleasure of the Police Commissioner," and since then Gold had always been at least one rank behind Kilcoyne, sometimes more, and struggling to catch up.

The incumbent PC – both men thought of him most times as Tim Egan, rather than by his exalted rank – had been further back still. But at a certain point he had somehow got ahead of them both.

Entering Egan's office this morning, Gold had still been one step behind Kilcoyne; leaving it he was not so sure, and he pondered the matter even as he walked down the corridor beside the white-haired Chief of Operations. Technically Kilcoyne still outranked him, four stars to three; but did he in practice? It seemed clear that Kilcoyne was to keep his four stars, temporarily at least. It seemed equally clear that Gold had not added any. On the other hand, Gold now reported directly to the Police Commissioner. And Kilcoyne's own stature had just been diminished by the loss of Gold's three thousand detectives.

As they walked along the corridor Kilcoyne's footsteps

sounded heavy to him. He did not blame him. He had just received, by Gold's lights, one hell of a blow.

"What did he want to do that for?" Gold said.

"It's his prerogative, Al," said Kilcoyne. It was Kilcoyne's prerogative to call subordinates by their first names.

Gold said carefully: "He's interfering with the traditional running of the department."

"He doesn't care about tradition." Kilcoyne projected, as always, immense dignity. Gold had never thought him particularly bright, but had always admired this ability which was apparent, even at the worst of times.

"Come on in a moment, Al."

Gold followed him through the rows of desks and into Kilcoyne's private office. Several of the cops looked up from their work but Gold ignored them.

"Sit down a moment, Al."

Instead of sitting, Gold walked over and peered out the window.

Kilcoyne was possibly through as a force within the department, but this was not certain. Egan might die, or be removed. He might change his mind. Or the mayor might overrule him. Perhaps Kilcoyne could call in some favors. On the other hand, he might choose to put his papers in, retire to Florida and stay there. Even then, the next mayor a year from now might call him back, appoint him the next PC. To move upwards in the police department required great care. There was no way of knowing who might later be promoted over you. It happened. Look at Tim Egan.

And so Gold, turning from the window, measured each word.

"He's listening to somebody," he said. "He has to be. Who's he listening to?"

"I don't know, Al." The Chief of Operations was straightening papers on top of his desk. After that he smoothed back his hair. These were almost the only signs Gold could see of the pressure he was under.

"Is he listening to the First Dep?" Gold said.

"The First Dep is in chemotherapy, and not worried about us any more."

"Keefe?"

"He's got no experience."

"But he's well connected at the mayor's office."

Kilcoyne toyed with a letter opener. "We don't know that for a fact."

"We know the mayor's office recommended him for the job."

"Well, that's the rumor."

"And who do we see going in as we're coming out?" Gold was still at the window. Kilcoyne had begun tapping the letter opener on his knee.

Gold came over and sat in the chair beside the desk. "I'm on your side, Chief," he said.

"I know you are, Al."

Gold said: "I want to know what you want me to do."

"I don't see where you have any choice, Al."

"I have to do what he says."

"He's the PC."

Both men continued to refer to Tim Egan as "he," as if, like some Biblical god, one could be struck dead for pronouncing his name aloud. They thought of him one way but spoke of him another.

"Anything happens you want to know about, Chief," Gold said carefully, "I'll come in here and tell you." It was a way of suggesting he would continue to report to Kilcoyne – something he had no intention of doing.

"I appreciate your support, Al." Gold had always admired Kilcoyne's voice too. That and his dignity. Even now it was the voice of command. A deep baritone. Ringing chest tones. He had once watched Kilcoyne calm a mob with it; the mob had been on the edge of riot. Gold's own voice was high-pitched and, when he got excited, somewhat squeaky. As a result he tried to speak most times – and always to subordinates – in a growl.

He stood and walked toward the door. "Don't do anything rash, Chief. Like putting your papers in. Think it over first." If the idea was not in his head already, Gold thought, it is now.

Kilcoyne frowned, but all he said was: "I appreciate your advice."

Gold was satisfied. His performance had sounded sincere

to him, and he went out through the desks of the anteroom and out into the corridor, becoming more convinced as he walked that Kilcoyne was finished.

He went into his private office, closed the door and sat down in his swivel chair. There were papers on his desk requiring his attention, and commanders throughout the city awaiting decisions from him, but Gold's mind was elsewhere. The situation at the top of the department, as he saw it, had just become fluid. Most likely it would stay that way for some time. Certainly it was not going to stabilize now just because Tim Egan willed it to. Egan, it was clear, was trying to consolidate all power in his own person. If he succeeded he'd be unassailable. But he might fail. Opposition might begin to form. Politicians might begin to snipe at him just to get their names in the papers. There might be critical editorials. Within the department men who owed their rank or influence to Kilcoyne might begin to resist the PC's orders in many small ways.

What was Gold's own position to be? There were going to be questions asked him, discussions into which he would be drawn, calls from the press. It was a tricky situation. He would have to react with great care. He must appear to be above the struggle, a man of control. If major opposition to Egan developed, he must present himself as the element of stability everyone was looking for, solid value, the viable alternative, the possible next PC. He began to rehearse answers to questions that had not been asked, that might never be asked. Questions from politicians, from the press. He would defend Kilcoyne, but not praise him. He would express loyalty to the PC, but at the same time allow questioners to suspect his disapproval. Opportunity was near. His time had perhaps come.

His door opened, and his chief secretary, a detective captain, peered in. "Lieutenant Craighead from the auto squad is here, Chief. He won't tell me what it is."

"Did you ask him? What are you, a captain? I thought captains outranked lieutenants."

It was Gold's habit to make subordinates wait, not

78

because he liked to, but to enhance his stature in their eyes. Authority was a trick like any other. To the captain who still hung in the doorway, he said: "You got something else on your mind?"

The captain came in and handed over some phone messages. "Fourth district burglary called." Gold glanced down and it was the message on top. "They're ready to make their arrests in that Park Avenue jewelry case. They want instructions."

It was a case that had interested Gold previously, not now. Nonetheless, in his head he reviewed the facts. A rich woman had been stuck-up in her Park Avenue penthouse by two men. They had taken about five million dollars in jewels. The jewels had been in her safe. The men killed her dog, and tortured her maid in front of her until she divulged the combination. The crime had happened a month ago. It had made headlines then and would again now that detectives working for him had the thing broken. Perhaps he should call a press conference. He could use the case to get his name and photo on television and into the papers – he had done it often enough in the past – but now an idea came to him. The case might prove more valuable still if employed in a different way. The captain was still beside Gold's desk. "All right, get out of here," he told him.

The door shut. Gold's idea involved Deputy Commissioner Keefe, and he mulled it over.

Finally his mind reverted to the waiting Lieutenant Craighead. The trouble with making subordinates wait was that they wound up leaning over the shoulders of his clerks, reading reports that they weren't supposed to see. He had best get rid of Craighead. He pressed the button on his console.

"Send the lieutenant in here."

Lieutenant Craighead came through the door, advanced to within two paces of Gold's desk and stood there grinning. The grin faded fast as Gold fixed him with a baleful stare. "It's about a certain case," Craighead said hesitantly. "I've just come from Commissioner Keefe's office," he added hurriedly.

If Keefe was meddling in criminal cases, Gold wanted to know about it and he glanced up sharply – a mistake, for it made Craighead's confident grin come back on. "Do you know the name Hot Harry Hamish, Chief?"

Gold did not, and the only name that interested him here was Keefe's. "Get your finger out of your ass," he said, "I don't have all day." He busied himself with papers on his desk as if only half-listening.

Harry Hamish, it appeared, had delivered a load of nose clips into Connecticut. Tailed by Keefe. Craighead's grin had again faded and he was speaking ever more hurriedly. When he had come to the end of the story, Gold said: "What's your point?"

"Commissioner Keefe seems to have taken over the case."

"He's a deputy commissioner. You got any objections?"

"Not at all, Chief. I just thought you'd like to know."

"Maybe I already knew."

"I didn't think about that, Chief."

"You don't think about much, do you?"

Craighead, distinctly uncomfortable now, fell silent.

Gold said: "What were his specific orders to you?"

"To put some men on it, and keep him informed."

Everybody wants to break cases, Gold thought, become an instant hero. These deputy commissioners came in with their romantic ideas of detective work, and they were the worst. He said: "How many men?"

"He left that up to me."

Gold was thinking it out carefully. He said: "Put a lot on it. In fact, I want you to make it your number one priority."

"Right, Chief. Do I report to him or to you?" Despite himself, Gold felt a tinge of admiration for the subordinate officer. He sees this thing clearly, Gold thought. He's being as careful as I am. He's making sure he guessed right. Such qualities would bring Craighead to headquarters before long, and one day perhaps to this very desk.

Gold said: "The auto squad is a very cushy detail, as I understand it, is that right?"

"It's a good detail, Chief."

"It's nine-to-five work, and most weekends off. There's a

80

lot of lieutenants in this department would like to have that detail, wouldn't you say?"

"Right, Chief."

"You develop any information," Gold said, "you tell me first. Then you tell him. Do I make myself clear?"

When Lieutenant Craighead had gone out, Gold continued to brood. The First Deputy Commissioner was dying. The Chief of Patrol was out. The Chief of Operations had just been humiliated. Egan was unsupported. The result was obvious – the way to the throne was wide open. No one stood in Gold's way except – except who? Deputy Commissioner Keefe? That was ridiculous. The inexperienced Keefe was not Egan's bulwark, though Egan perhaps thought of him that way. He was his most glaring weakness, and it was a weakness Gold thought he could exploit. Beginning when? Beginning now, he thought, and he again pushed the button on his telephone. "Ask Deputy Commissioner Keefe if he could step in here when he gets a chance."

Any meeting between the two should properly take place in Keefe's office, not Gold's. If Keefe did not come, this would identify him as more dangerous than Gold had supposed. But he was betting that the naïve Keefe, who seemed impatient with a good many department ceremonies, would not stand on this one. If he did come, it would be a tacit acknowledgement of Gold's age and experience. He would be submitting to Gold's authority.

So he waited for his telephone to sound.

"Commissioner Keefe will be along in about ten minutes, Chief."

Gold expelled a lungful of air. Then he went to get the relevant files out.

By the time Keefe was announced, Gold's confidence had again waned. Coming around the desk he said nervously, almost apologetically: "There's something I want you to see." But he saw immediately that the protocol aspects had passed over Keefe's head. "I need your help, Commissioner. I need to ask you a favour."

And so began Gold's seduction of the one man who

81

perhaps blocked his way. He had the pictures ready. As he began to describe the Park Avenue robbery, he spread them out on his desk for Keefe to look at. "This is what the items look like. Five million bucks. This is the broad. Nice-looking piece for her age, wouldn't you say? I think she's forty-six. This is the apartment. There's the dead dog on the rug. They shoved a bread knife down its throat. You can just see the handle."

Keefe, studying the pictures, said nothing. He's going to go for it, Gold thought.

"Thing is, Commissioner, my detectives are stymied. They can't find out who this broad is. She's got an accent. They can't question her too hard, or she might just take off." Gold eyed Keefe carefully. "Thing is, they think she might be involved herself."

So far as Gold knew, his detectives thought no such thing. "Maybe she set the whole thing up to collect on the insurance," Gold said, and again he watched for Keefe's reaction, if any. "We checked her out as well as we could, Commissioner. Our own intelligence division has nothing. The FBI never heard of her. We got no way of finding out who she is, unless you would be willing to help us." If he wants to break cases, Gold thought, I'll give him more than he can handle.

"What do you want me to do?" inquired Keefe.

As he saw Keefe taking the bait, Gold began to get excited, and he cautioned himself to bring the timbre of his voice down, to project total authority. "She's a society broad. The chances are that the papers, especially your old paper, have a juicy file on her in their morgue. If I called up for information they'd laugh at me. But you're one of them. You could get that information. You could help my detectives break this case." The case was already broken, Gold knew. Only a dumb civilian would believe that a rich society broad would actually set up a robbery of this kind in order to collect insurance. Outside the pages of mystery novels such things did not happen. It was too risky. It required too much knowledge, and too much nerve. Most of all, it required underworld contacts that ordinary people, especially rich society women, just did not have.

"The department would owe you an enormous debt, if you could do it, Commissioner," Gold said ingratiatingly. This was arrant flattery, but Gold was confident that Keefe, who thought he was dealing with a criminal case, was not looking for it and would not see it.

"If I can help," Keefe said, "I'd be glad to."

"I wouldn't ask," Gold said apologetically, "except it looks like it's the only way we're going to break the case."

Gold scribbled the woman's name and address on his memo pad, tore off the sheet and handed it across the desk. Then he got up and walked Keefe to the door. But there was one more point the Chief of Detectives wished to make: that there could be no secrets from the Chief of Detectives. As he gripped the doorknob he said cooly: "By the way, Commissioner, I've been talking to Lieutenant Craighead. He tells me that he's working on a case for you." He saw that Keefe looked impressed, or perhaps only surprised, and this pleased him. It would give him something else to think about: "If there's any co-operation you need at this end, just let me know."

He showed Keefe out, and once the door had slammed he stood in the centre of his office, rubbing his hands together. There were two roles every American male had dreamed of playing since adolescence. The great lover was one, and the crime-buster was the other. It had not been within Gold's power to accord Keefe the first of these roles, Don Juan, but he was pretty sure he had just delivered the second of them, Dick Tracy.

Seven

KEEFE HAD WORKED FOR TWO NEWSPAPERS; THE ONE in Boston where he had started out and the one in New York which he always thought of as "his" paper, because it was while working for it abroad that he had achieved his first major successes as a journalist, even a certain notoriety. Now, on behalf of Chief Gold, he phoned a man named Seymour Becker, the paper's executive editor. They had first met almost ten years ago and Keefe had once had dinner in Becker's house in Budapest when Becker was bureau chief there.

Becker, Keefe was aware, was courted by men of wealth and influence, by political figures of the first rank. His opinions were known in Washington, and even the White House sometimes sought to change them. He was difficult to contact, but everyone, Keefe had found, was quick to accept calls from police headquarters.

"Phil, good to hear your voice."

All newspapers kept morgue files on every individual whose name had ever appeared in their pages. Becker's own paper would have a thick file on Chief Gold's Park Avenue robbery victim.

"How's the lovely Sharon?" Becker inquired. "How can I help you?" His tone was warm, or seemed to be, though just the slightest bit crisp.

"About a month ago a society woman was robbed of jewels at gunpoint in her Park Avenue penthouse," Keefe said. "Do you remember?"

"No," said Becker sharply.

Fair enough, thought Keefe. Becker was not interested in crime; he was interested in the Washington–New York power axis, and his own place in it. "They shoved a bread knife down her dog's throat," Keefe said.

"Vaguely," said Becker.

"I don't suppose you know the woman, by any chance?"

"No."

"Neither do we."

"We?" Becker said. "Meaning?"

Keefe had made a mistake. He should have identified himself with the paper for this man, not with the police department. "The detective division is all over me," Keefe said.

"Go on."

Keefe began to describe the several police intelligence files he had glanced into out of curiosity, how skimpy they were, how absurdly inadequate.

"You want access to our files?" Becker interrupted, and all the warmth, whether real or imagined, had gone out of his voice.

Keefe tried to sound confident, even cheery. "If you want to investigate someone, a newspaper morgue is the place to start, not the police intelligence files. The reporters have the juicy material, not the cops."

"Absolutely not," said Becker.

"I haven't even asked you for anything yet."

"You want access to our files," Becker said. "No."

"Oh," said Keefe, taken aback. "It doesn't seem like very much to ask."

"You want me to say it plainer?"

Keefe found he was licking dry lips. "The press spends money on their files," he said falsely cheerily. "They pay large staffs to keep them up to date, unlike this or any other police department. That's because police departments have little money to spend. They try to get by on a few patrolmen who keep changing all the time."

"Did you ever hear of the first amendment to the Constitution of the United States?" said Becker, and Keefe pictured him, the most important newspaper editor in the country, perhaps: short, portly, balding, self-important, fifty-four years old. In Budapest he had been worried about where his career was going. But that was in another life. Now when he spoke even presidents listened, for he could possibly bring them to their knees if he chose. Or, rather, his newspaper could. Maybe it couldn't, but they weren't sure and did not want to take the chance.

Keefe thought: any one of my friends among the reporters could have got me the information, but I had to call the man at the top. Why did I do that? The answer: because I knew I could. I became impressed with my new importance.

"The first amendment guarantees freedom of the press, in case you hadn't noticed," stated Becker and he began a speech on the subject.

The reaction was almost a knee jerk. I should have predicted it, Keefe thought, as he tried to decide what to say next. According to the press and the civil liberties groups, the public worried itself to death about information supposedly contained in police files. There were constant demands that such files be destroyed altogether, or at least that individual files be destroyed whenever someone was acquitted in court or not prosecuted at all. The department was constantly defending itself from lawsuits along these lines. Keefe gave a silent wry laugh. Such suits ought to be directed against the press, not the police. Day by day, year by year, press morgue files on individuals grew ever more swollen and the information they contained was likely to be derogatory in the extreme, often inaccurate, and almost always unproven. There had never been a request Keefe knew of, much less a lawsuit, to destroy such files.

"All we're trying to find out is who the woman is," Keefe interrupted.

"Our morgue files are closed to the police. That's our right under the first amendment."

"Well," Keefe said after a moment, "I don't know where else I can get the information I need."

"That's a police problem. It's not mine."

"I see."

"And if you try to subpoena our files, I'll fight you through every court in the country." He rang off.

Keefe sat tapping his fingers on the desktop beside the phone. Then he got up and went and stood at the window. Then he sat down at the desk again and resumed tapping.

That night he cooked supper for himself at home – a small fried steak, and vegetables heated up out of cans. The more he thought about Becker the angrier he got. He ate alone at the coffee table in the living room while watching the news. After that he went out to shop for groceries, and to do his laundry. He walked through dark streets with his laundry in a pillowcase over his shoulder, Becker still on his mind. The arrogance of the man and of men like him was astonishing. There was a coin-operated laundry on Lexington Avenue. That's where Sharon used to go, Keefe believed, but he wasn't sure of its exact location and so walked several blocks out of his way before he finally doubled back and found it. The laundry and shopping for food had been her jobs, the vacuuming his.

The notion that the rights of the press were supreme was ingrained in men such as Becker. What about the rights of other citizens to defend themselves against crime? That was in the constitution too. Did no one else have rights but the press? The coin laundry was a storefront. It was long and narrow, extending deep into the building. There was a row of machines the length of one wall and a row of benches the length of the other. Becker had stood on one principle, freedom of the press, and rejected another, his civic duty. He hadn't even considered it. Was the concept of civic duty as worthless as all that?

Half a dozen women of various ages sat opposite the machines, waiting. Most were reading something. A few studied him a moment before glancing back at their possessions which tossed wetly against the glass. Freedom of the press had to be defended, sure – but to the exclusion of all other freedoms? To self-proclaimed liberals like Becker the police were the enemy. Keefe too had been, and believed he still was, a liberal. He was for individual rights and against authoritarianism, but he had learnt something in recent weeks: the police were the people too. He carried the plump pillowcase down the row, looking for an empty machine. The noise was considerable. It was Becker who had chosen to turn his request for help into a police vs. press confrontation; it was Becker who had made him feel foolish.

The air smelled wetly soapy; it felt almost clammy and dank on his bare arms. In the back were the dryers; some were turning and clicking. It was suffocatingly hot there, and the benches were vacant. Anyone waiting was doing so up front. The conflict was in Becker's head. He had pronounced the law according to Becker – the morgue was closed to Keefe – and ordered Keefe to obey it, and this he had no intention of doing. Becker was not going to keep him out of that morgue.

After spilling the contents of his pillowcase on to the floor in front of the last washer in the row, which was the only one empty, he paused to read the directions printed on the sign on the wall, and a woman came over to him off one of the benches and said:

"Need some help?"

She was about his age and wore corduroy pants and a blouse. She was slim and heavily made-up and smiling in a friendly way.

"First you put your stuff into the machine." With her shoe she nudged the pile at his feet, and she seemed to him to be studying it at the same time.

He did so, and slammed the door on it. "Now put the coins in," she said.

He pushed them into the slot and heard the noise as the machine came on and the tank began to fill up.

"Now put your soap in here – careful, not too much. Very good. You'll be all-pro at this in no time. Now the water softener."

"What water softener?" said Keefe.

"You don't have any? I'll lend you some of mine." She poured some in, and they stood watching the water level rise against the glass. Then she said: "Are you going through a divorce, or what?"

When Keefe looked startled, she gave him a grin and jerked her chin in the direction of the machine. "There aren't any female garments in there."

"Oh, I see," said Keefe.

"There's a man shortage, haven't you heard? A single girl's got to keep her eyes open at all times. A laundromat is a good place."

Keefe smiled.

"So are you?"

"No, I'm not even married." Then he frowned, for this might have seemed a come-on.

"And from the look of things not at present living with anyone either," she said, and grinned at him.

"My girlfriend's gone to California," Keefe said hastily.

"If it was me, I wouldn't go off and leave you with no clean clothes."

"She left unexpectedly."

"Maybe she's not coming back."

"Tomorrow," said Keefe. "I think she'll be back tomorrow."

"But you can't be sure."

Keefe laughed. "I'm sure."

"Rats," the woman said. "I never have any luck. What's your name? If you have any errands to do, I'll watch your laundry until you get back."

So he went off to the supermarket wishing all contacts with fellow human beings could be as pleasant as this one. Had the woman really been trying to pick him up? It didn't seem possible.

As he crossed Lexington Avenue through the cars, his mind reverted of its own accord to Becker and to the missing information that was vital to Chief Gold's case.

In the supermarket he pushed his cart down alleys so narrow that two carts coming in opposite directions could barely get by each other. He bought hamburger meat, and a quart of milk. He bought packages of frozen vegetables, and a package of English muffins. He would go into that morgue himself, he decided.

He got on the check-out line, and a young woman wheeled her cart up behind him, peered down into his basket, and remarked:

"You guys who live alone don't really live, do you? You camp out."

For the second time that evening Keefe was startled. "How do you know I live alone?"

"I don't see anything in your cart that a woman would have sent you out to buy," she said, and grinned at him.

"Oh." Keefe gazed down on his purchases.

"Was your divorce messy? My divorce was messy." She blinked her eyes at him.

My God, Keefe thought. Twice in one night. If I told Sharon she wouldn't believe it. "I'm just alone for a few days," he said.

He pushed his cart up level with the cash register and got money out of his billfold. A few minutes later he was crossing Lexington Avenue again, the bag of groceries in his arms.

In the coin laundry the other woman was still there. "I put your things into that dryer there," she told him. "You owe me seventy-five cents."

"That's awfully nice of you," Keefe said, and meant it. He handed over three quarters.

"That's me, I guess," she said. "I'm nice. Everybody says so, so it must be true."

"I'll be here a while longer," she told him when he had slung his hot pillowcase over his shoulder, and said good night. "The next person through that door might be the attractive man I've been waiting for all my life."

Earlier Keefe had ordered his department car to stand by tonight. It was waiting for him when he came downstairs again an hour later. Detective Rodriguez, his other driver, was behind the wheel.

They started out. To Keefe, visiting precincts was better than sitting in his apartment alone, either mooning about Sharon or cursing Becker. Rodriguez drove into Central Park at Seventy-Second Street, and steered north on the Drive under the trees. Over the radio came a signal 10-21. This meant a past burglary, and was nothing to get excited about. The address given was Harlem. A particular sector car was ordered to investigate. Detective Rodriguez continued to move north through the park at a sedate speed in the heavy traffic, while Keefe waited for a call that would engage his interest. Within two blocks Central came back on again, changing the 10-21 past burglary to a 10-20 past robbery. People dialed the police emergency number and were so excited or distraught they didn't know what day it was, much less what crimes they were phoning in. Burglary and robbery were not the same. It all sorted itself out eventually. The police operator sought to make sense of whatever garbled message he heard in his earphones, and either he sorted it out or the cops did when they got there.

Keefe's car came out of the park at 110th Street. Within a block or two Harlem was all around him. If you were interested in police work, Harlem was the place. It had more of everything – more aided cases, more stick-ups, more murders.

Suddenly Central's voice was back on the air, and this time it was tense: "Change that 10-20 past robbery. That's now a 10-30 armed robbery in progress." A second car was ordered to respond, and caution was advised, but there was no acknowledgement from the first two cops who had been dispatched, though an anxious Central kept demanding one. Were they already out of their car? Keefe wondered. They were perhaps walking into a storm of bullets.

He said to Detective Rodriguez, "Step on it."

An excited Central came on again: "Report of shots fired. Use extreme caution. Report of shots fired at this time."

Then, a few seconds later: "Signal 10–13, assist police officer." On a high ascending note the same signal was repeated: "Signal 10–13. Assist police officer."

The two cops have been fired on, Keefe thought.

The air was rushing in the open windows. With it came the high-pitched wail of the first of the oncoming sirens. Soon there were many sirens, and they were approaching from several directions. Rodriguez had clapped the magnetic red light on the roof, turned on his own siren, and swerved out into the oncoming traffic.

"Signal 10–13," said Central. "Report of shots fired confirmed. Report of shots fired confirmed. Use extreme caution."

There was a gun battle in progress up there, Keefe thought. He was gripping the seat with both hands. The physical excitement was exceedingly pleasant. So was the intellectual excitement – his journalist's overpowering curiosity was about to be satisfied.

Only seconds had passed since the first radio call, but already many radio cars had reached the site, and Rodriguez, slewing around the corner, nearly slammed into one that was parked sideways across the entrance to the side street, its roof lights flashing. Two cops were trying to hold back an already considerable crowd. Halfway into the side street, Keefe saw as he jumped out, was parked another blue and white, and it was perhaps under fire, for cops on their knees had sought cover behind it, their guns pointing out across its hood at the building opposite. Keefe showed his shield to the two cops whose car Rodriguez had nearly struck. "What's happening?" he cried.

"They're firing shots from the roof down on to the

street," the cop replied in a shrill voice. This information was so dramatic as to cause Keefe to hover there indecisively. He had heard no shots as he approached, and he heard none now. The panicky cop beside him was perhaps only purveying rumor. Furthermore, the idea of shots being fired conflicted with the evidence of Keefe's own eyes. It was a street of low tenements with shops at sidewalk level. In neighborhoods like this, shops stayed open late, and most of these were open. Furthermore, shopkeepers stood in the doorways gawking. If there had been shots flying around, Keefe reasoned, they would be inside lying on the floor behind the counters. Still, the sight of several cops pointing revolvers across the hood of a stalled police car was alarming.

A man came out of one of the doorways, spotted Keefe and ran towards him. "This way, Commissioner," he called.

It was Sergeant Rainey, and Keefe wondered for a moment what he was doing in this neighbourhood at this hour. The big man with the neat grey beard still wore the business suit he had worn in the office that day, though with his sergeant's shield on its lapel.

Keefe cried: "I understand they're firing shots down into the street."

"Negative," said Rainey calmly. He had Keefe by the arm. Two blacks had tried to stick up a finance company office halfway down the block, Rainey explained. The first cops on the scene thought they were investigating a past burglary, but walked in on men with guns. Rainey's calmness was itself calming. "One of the perpetrators starts shooting. He lived to get off one shot. The first cop emptied his whole goddamn piece."

"Is the cop all right?"

"I got him sitting in a chair in the grocery next door. He's still trembling. The second perpetrator ran up the stairs. He's still up there someplace."

Keefe peered up at the rooftop. "If he gets onto the roof he really will fire shots down. Or he'll take off over the buildings and we'll never find him."

"He can't get onto the roof," Rainey said. "I already

checked that out. They got bars on the door up there. On all the windows too. Naturally – it's a finance company. God help them if there's ever a fire."

Keefe peered across at the cops crouched behind the radio car. "Why are those men crouching there?"

"Who the hell knows?" said Rainey. "Hey, you guys, over here. Fast." When all four men had holstered their weapons and come shambling forward, he led them into the finance company.

It looked like the branch office of a bank. There were desks, a counter, a walk-in safe. There were three employees, all middle-aged, all white, all still frightened. There was a body on the floor. The employees" eyes flitted this way and that, never coming to rest on the corpse, but always returning to it.

Keefe leaned over the body: a black teenager lying on his stomach, as if sleeping. There was blood on the dirty tee-shirt. The face and arms had already gone from black to bloodless grey.

There was a cop watching the staircase where Rainey had placed him. He was very tense. He had his gun pressed to his chest, barrel pointed at the underside of his chin. He said to Rainey in a low voice: "The perpetrator is still up there, Sarge."

"Congratulations," Rainey told him. "You're doing great so far."

Rainey looked sure of himself, and extremely happy. He's been in situations like this before, Keefe thought. He loves this.

"Let's go root him out," Rainey said, and started up the stairs. The five cops followed, guns in hand. Over his shoulder Rainey said: "Wait here, Commissioner, we'll be right back."

Ignoring him, Keefe started up the stairs behind them. He would stay out of the way, but he was not going to miss this. Except during firearms training, he had never had his gun out before. He had no intention of shooting anybody, he told himself as he drew it. The situation would not arise. Then why was it out? he wondered briefly.

On the landing, Rainey looked surprised to see him

93

there. "Commissioner –" he said, and hesitated. Then he seemed to shrug, as the cops collected around him. "We'll do this one floor at a time," he told them, and gave instructions. One cop was to guard the staircase: "Your job is to isolate this floor."

"Isolate the floor, Sarge?" Was he dense, Keefe wondered, or only scared?

"If he tries to come down the stairs, be sure to let us know."

"How should I do that, Sarge? Let you know?"

Rainey pretended to think about it. "Well," he said, "try snapping your fingers real loud."

One gunman was dead and another loose in the building, but Sergeant Rainey was making jokes.

"Supposing you don't hear, Sarge?"

Rainey thought about this, too. "Build a fire and send smoke signals. Either that or you might just arrest him."

They were standing in a vestibule facing a door that was closed and locked, for Rainey had tried the handle. Extracting a credit card from his wallet, he forced it into the doorjam, and there was a click as he slid the bolt back. He pushed the door open an inch, making no sound, then gave the door a violent kick. It bounced off the wall behind it. Rainey and everyone else had flattened themselves to one side. The gunman, if he was in there, did not respond. Now Rainey led the way into the corridor. There were offices to each side. Gesturing to the cop beside him to search the office on the left, he himself jumped into the one on the right. The two following cops took the next two offices. This left Keefe and the remaining cop eyeing each other nervously in the corridor.

Keefe's finger was still outside the trigger guard, as he had been taught, a precaution against accidents: his principal fear was that he might trip and accidentally shoot someone. When the cop beside him darted suddenly into the third office on the left it became Keefe's job to check out the third one on the right. He had to do it, he told himself. The alternative was to show all these cops he was afraid. He was worried about making a mistake, about his lack of

94

training. He was worried about getting shot. Nonetheless, he stepped into the office.

The perpetrator was in there.

He was crouched almost in a foetal position underneath the desk. He was in the kneehole behind the panel and Keefe couldn't see him. He could see only his sneakers and his kneecaps.

Keefe was terribly shocked. What was he supposed to do now? His heart began to pound. To fire at him through the panel was out of the question. Well, then, what sort of shouted order would bring the youth – he assumed this one matched his dead colleague downstairs – out of the kneehole, hands in the air? Or maybe Keefe could run out into the hall and get help? But no, in his absence, the perpetrator might decide to make a fight for it, and the next officer through the door might get shot in the face. If only he could signal his predicament to Rainey. But how?

Then he remembered Rainey's joking instructions to the cop guarding the staircase, and he stuck his arm out into the hall and began snapping his fingers as loudly as he could. It felt ludicrous even as he did it, and all of them would no doubt laugh heartily later, but it was the only solution he could think of.

To his intense relief, Rainey appeared promptly.

Rainey said: "Ho, ho, ho. What have we here?"

Two quick steps, and he was at the desk. Grasping its edge he tipped it onto its face to reveal the failed stick-up man. As Keefe had guessed, he was only about eighteen – a scared boy. Though the desk was off him now, he remained in his crouched position, his eyes tightly closed. His hands were clasped on top of his head. One of them still contained a silver Saturday Night Special, but he had no intention of using it now, if in fact he ever had, and Rainey twisted it free of his hands.

"On your feet."

The room had filled up with uniforms. The youth was so frightened as he stood up that his head began jerking spasmodically. Without being ordered, he went and spread-eagled himself against the wall, the suspect's classic pose.

"You don't even have to tell him," commented Rainey. "Would you say this one's been arrested before, Commissioner?"

Keefe too was suffering an attack of nerves. "Maybe so," he said.

"Maybe not, either," said Rainey, patting the boy down. "In this community, kids see so many arrests that by the time they're ten they know just what to do." He searched the boy from the soles of his sneakers to the roots of his afro hairdo. He was extremely quick about it, and extremely rough. The entire procedure couldn't have taken more than five seconds.

The boy's jeans, Keefe noted, were soaking wet, and there was liquid running down over his sneakers. He had had quite an evening. So had Keefe.

"Who wants to take the collar?" Rainey demanded.

"I'll take it," one of the cops said. He was the partner of the cop who had killed the boy downstairs. "It will look better if we take the collar."

"He's all yours," said Rainey.

On the street floor the three employees still stood nervously. The room was full of cops, with more still coming through the door. "It's over," Rainey told everybody. "You can go back on patrol." He began to shoo them out even as the medical examiner and some detectives crowded their way in.

Keefe's emotions were bubbling, and there seemed so many that he could sort nothing out. Around him were the cops with whom he had gone upstairs. A few minutes ago they had been a group of scared young men. Now they were all laughing and talking loudly. Cops, Keefe thought, were men who talked in loud voices that sometimes trembled slightly. Their guns sometimes trembled slightly too. They operated out of fear much of the time, or else out of bravado, which was fear's other name. Once again the difference between him and them was not bravery, but responsibility. They had had to take action, whereas he could have turned around and gone home. It made a difference in the way danger was perceived. Yet he imagined he felt the same as they did right this minute – weak all through his body.

He and Rainey stood in the street. "Your first stick-up, Commissioner?"

Keefe admitted it.

"What are your impressions?"

Whatever Keefe answered would sound silly. He managed a grin and said: "I don't know yet. Ask me tomorrow." But he brooded about it. "Not your first, I gather," he said. Rainey had shown no fear at all, Nor did he show any reaction now that Keefe could see.

"I've had a few."

They had started up the street toward Keefe's car. The wooden barriers were up. There were about ten cops at the barriers holding back the crowd.

He said to Rainey: "What were you doing in this neighborhood at this time of night?"

"I belong to this theatrical group. We're putting on some scenes in a gymnasium near here." He glanced at his watch. "We're part of the mayor's ghetto arts program." Rainey had begun looking around. "I was with someone," he said. "She doesn't seem to have waited." Then, as if to avoid further questioning, he said: "You didn't have to get involved just now, Commissioner. Why did you?"

"I happened to be there," Keefe said, trying to explain it as much to himself as to Rainey. He tried to laugh. "I wanted to see how it came out."

"Well," said Rainey thoughtfully, "they don't see much of the headquarters brass up here. It would make the job so much easier if they did. I don't mean every day, but once in a while wouldn't hurt."

"Can I give you a lift some place?" Keefe asked.

"Thanks, but the gymnasium is two blocks away, and I need a few minutes to go over my lines in my head."

They had just shared an important experience – important at any rate to Keefe, and he wanted to prolong it. He said: "I'd like to see you act sometime."

Rainey's manner seemed to become distant. "Anytime, Commissioner, just say the word."

They had reached Keefe's car. "Well," he said, "if I can't give you a lift, I guess I'll be going." But he hesitated. The sharing was already over. He was trying to keep it alive a few seconds longer, which was impossible.

"Good night, Commissioner."

Detective Rodriguez got in on his side, started the engine, and backed carefully out through the crowd. "Where to now, Commissioner?"

Keefe had no desire to chase down any more radio calls tonight. He remembered the PC's memo about Rainey that still lay in his desk drawer. He thought: the PC wants me to get rid of this guy. "Home, I guess," he said.

Eight

HOWEVER CALM RAINEY MAY HAVE SEEMED TO KEEFE, he was not calm at all. In a few minutes he was to declaim lines from Shakespeare from a stage, and as he walked down dark streets toward the gymnasium ahead he knew he ought to be trying to remember what they were, but instead he replayed in his head his own conduct. Keefe had just seen him with a gun in his hand, enjoying what amounted to untidy pleasures. It was likely that in the last thirty minutes Keefe had come to perceive him as reckless, or even brainless, no different from thousands of other ordinary street cops. He did not know he had won Keefe's admiration. He feared he had lost it.

As a young cop Rainey had usually tried to impress the wrong people, and he knew this now. He had tried to impress prisoners, and he had tried to impress other cops, and principally he had tried to impress them with how tough he was. But he no longer consorted with such people. Instead he had learned to project himself as a man of education – in the last several years he had gone back to school and now had a BA degree and almost a Masters –

who was also an armed officer of the law; and as an actor whose usual arena was more real and more violent than the stage. In the cultural circles that he now frequented he had sought acceptance and been accepted. By now this new self-image was vital to Rainey. To get caught in tonight's stick-up had been bad luck. It was even worse luck that by sheer accident his boss, Keefe, had happened by.

He worried about the reports that would go forward. He did not need to be mentioned in any such reports, which was why he had been so anxious to get away from there before the detectives arrived and started taking down names. The detectives would not have his name, but they would hear about the sergeant who had taken command and they could find it out easily enough. How conscientious would they be? If his name began to circulate through headquarters, old rumors would circulate. Men who had forgotten about him would become aware of him again, and there would be pressure to send him back to a precinct. He doubted Keefe would resist such pressure. Why should he, having seen what he just saw? In uniform in a radio car it would be impossible to maintain or project the man he now believed himself to be. His sophisticated new friends would drop away, as would his new life. Back on the street he would be exposed again to the sordidness all cops regularly saw: blood, corpses, violence, one tragedy after another. A forty-six-year-old cop was no more able to go on absorbing such sordidness than a forty-six-year-old boxer could go on absorbing punches.

As he walked along the dark street Rainey was thinking as much as possible in generalities such as these. Tonight's stick up was a specific, though. He had enjoyed himself, and his joy was what he specifically feared Keefe had noted. But why shouldn't he have enjoyed himself? He knew very well that the perpetrator whom they eventually found under the desk was not going to come out shooting. Perpetrators very rarely did. They heard the noise of all those cops, and they crapped their pants, and all inclination to come out shooting left them. It did happen from time to time, but it was very rare.

The trouble was, Keefe would not have known this. He would have seen only the apparent danger, and the apparent reckless behavior of the forty-six-year-old man in the dark business suit.

At least at the end out by the barriers he had got a chance to mention the acting. As Rainey saw it, Keefe could not possibly be impressed with him as a cop, not after tonight, but the conversation about acting might save him. He had seen something in Keefe's eyes: that Rainey knew about acting and about the theatre had certainly surprised him.

He was still mulling it over when he came to the school yard which was blocked off from the sidewalk by a chainlink fence. He found the gate, went into the yard and crossed the basketball lines towards the back of the building. There was supposed to be a door there, and he looked for it. He'd been thinking of it as the stage door for most of the day.

Inside there was a short flight of stairs, and beyond that more lights, and he came out onto what he suddenly realised was the stage. He was in a combination auditorium-gymnasium. On stage were all his colleagues from the school. There was no curtain, and he glanced out at the audience. Green canvas had been rolled out over the basketball court to protect it, and the rows of folding chairs had been set down over that. The backboards had been hoisted upwards and lay against the ceiling.

The rows of chairs extended to the back of the gym, seats for a thousand people, but only the rows down front were filled – mostly with middle-aged adults. Less than a hundred people in all, racially they seemed divided down the middle, one half black, the other half Hispanic. Rainey wasted little thought on them. Actors were supposed to be nervous before performances, but he was not. These people did not scare him, not in police confrontations, not now.

Flora noticed him and hurried over. F. Hyman was close behind her, and behind him came all the others. Obviously Flora had spread the word, and all were waiting to hear a description of his exploits inside the finance company.

"Thank God you're all right," said Flora, virtually

100

flinging herself into his arms. "If anything had happened to you, I would never have forgiven myself." She covered his face with kisses. In the street, hearing the shots, he had told her to run, and she ran. Then he ran. He had had his gun out and was sprinting for the building. That was probably the last she had seen of him. Now her embrace grew ever more theatrical, her declamation more emphatic: "Oh, thank God," she said. "Thank God."

F. Hyman by contrast spoke in stage whispers. He said: "You're late."

"A situation developed."

"We were afraid you wouldn't get here."

"It was one I had to take care of."

"Flora said she heard shots," said F. Hyman.

"Yeah."

F. Hyman waited for him to say more, so he didn't. Finally F. Hyman said: "I don't know what we would have done about the show."

"Were they really shots?" Flora asked him.

Rainey disengaged himself. "Yeah."

"Was it a stick up, or what?" demanded one of the other actors excitedly.

"Yes, a stick up."

"What happened?"

"It was unsuccessful."

"Is that all you have to say?" said Flora.

"It'll be in the paper," said Rainey. He decided to add nothing.

F. Hyman had been a worried man since the moment of Flora's breathless arrival at the school, or so Rainey supposed: worried about his show, not about his principal actor. For him the subject of shoot outs had by now more than exhausted itself. "Are you ready for your performance?" he asked Rainey.

Rainey nodded.

"Well, then, take your places everybody, and I'll make the announcement."

On came a beaming smile. F. Hyman was beaming even before he turned to face the audience. Rainey saw him hold up his hands for silence – there was already silence – and the audience leaned forward intently. As tonight's finale, he now explained, his troupe was about to perform the last act of a famous play by Shakespeare called *Othello*.

"I know most of you are familiar with this play," he said, laying the flattery on thick, Rainey thought. "But for those who may not be, I will now describe the events leading up to this last scene of the play."

Rainey turned to face the wings, looking at nothing, trying to collect his lines in his head. They had rehearsed the scene in the studio the week before. The lines were all there. Rainey had a great memory, he believed – how else had he made sergeant? When studying for the promotion exam he had memorised whole pages of stuff, and had scored near the top of the class, his crowning achievement at the time, and to some extent still.

The play was about an older man, F. Hyman was saying from the stage apron, who thinks his young wife is fooling around. He is a famous general, she a rich man's daughter. He becomes insanely jealous, and resolves to strangle her in her bed.

As F. Hyman spoke, two of the fag actors were dragging a sofa out onto the stage. Rainey heard the noise and turned and watched them. They must have got it from the principal's office. He watched them set it down just behind F. Hyman.

"We ask your indulgence," the ex-actor was saying. "We ask you to pretend that this sofa is the young wife's bed. Her name is Desdemona. We ask you to pretend that you are looking at a darkened bedroom. The jealous husband, the older man, whose name is Othello, comes into the dark bedroom carrying a candle."

He looked around hopefully. "Do we have a candle?" he called out.

One of the fags had found a candle. He came over and handed it to Rainey, who held it tilted over the fag's cigarette lighter. After several seconds the wick caught. Rainey stood holding the candle, waiting.

"Okay," said F. Hyman, "now we have a candle." He

sounded excited. He had sounded excited back in his studio too the night he told Rainey that this scene was the one they would perform. "It's Harlem, right?" F. Hyman had said excitedly. "Jealous husband strangles wife – in Harlem they'll understand that. It's right down their alley, right?" This much F. Hyman had divined from reading the newspapers. It was something he knew, but didn't really know. He had never seen it. Rainey had seen it – too many times – and he didn't think a scene of jealous murder was such a good idea in Harlem at all. Or rather it was too good an idea, too close to their lives. No one else dared say boo to F. Hyman Effrat. They were in awe of him. He had an Academy Award from twenty-five years ago, and for them this was the Holy Grail. Rainey alone saw him for what he was, a failed actor. One prize does not a lifetime make. Nor one promotion either, Rainey had admitted to himself. "They're not going to get the poetry," he had told F. Hyman. "They'll get the killing part, though. They know about killing."

F. Hyman didn't understand the pressures the poor lived under. As a young cop, Rainey hadn't understood either. He'd gone into their filthy apartments, had intervened in their family disputes. He had staunched the bleeding where he could, and called for ambulances. He had subdued them, handcuffed them, arrested them, dragged them out. His principal emotion most times was disgust. Now that he was older he understood them better. Their emotions were not something to play with. He had almost told F. Hyman so back in the studio. Then he had learned that the actor chosen by F. Hyman to play Othello was none other than himself, and he had kept his mouth shut. Desdemona would be Flora – even better. He was not going to jeopardize that. What did he care if his audience went home and strangled, shot and stabbed each other? They'd been doing it since he came out of the Police Academy. Since long before that too, of course, but only twenty-three years of it that he had witnessed personally. It wasn't his job to save them. A cop's job was only to clean up afterwards. A man's home – even his rat- and roach-infested, unheated, filthy tenement – was his castle, and no cop could go in until the crime was done, and it was time to clean up. So what did Rainey care what effect his acting tonight might have on any of these people? He cared only about an audience of one. He would play to Flora only, impress her with his acting, with his declamation. She was impressed already just because F. Hyman had picked him for the title role, not realising he had chosen him probably just because of his age and his grey beard. There was no scenery or costumes, but F. Hyman would give the crowd – the eighty or ninety people out there – at least part of a situation they could recognize: a young wife, a jealous older husband. He would get the ages right at least.

Having concluded his introduction, F. Hyman Effrat went off into the wings at stage left even as Flora came out from stage right. She was wearing slippers and a flannel nightgown: Rainey could see the lines of her underwear through the cloth. Obviously she had thought to bring her own props. After stepping out of the slippers, she lay down on the sofa and composed herself. She closed her eyes dramatically.

Everyone else faded back off the stage except Rainey in his dark suit and neat grey beard holding his candle. He waited a moment, then a moment longer. As a great hush came over the audience, he crept stealthily forward until he was peering down at Flora, and in a voice meant to convey great suffering he began his first speech.

"Put out the light," he intoned, even as he blew out his candle, "and then put out the light," this time meaning the life of his presumed faithless wife.

About ten lines later the anguished husband bent down and kissed Flora's lips. "O balmy breath, that doth almost persuade justice to break her sword! One more, one more. Be thus when thou art dead, and I will kill thee, and love thee after. One more, and that the last." There was not a sound out of the audience.

As the poetry flowed from his lips Rainey realized that he knew more about playing this scene, probably, than any actor who ever played it. His predecessors had seen Othello as classical tragedy. To him it was a classic family fight, and how many of those had he intervened in as a cop? There was no way of counting. Sometimes he had arrived in time to prevent what was about to happen in this play, sometimes not. The difference between real life and this play was in the details. Real-life scenes took place most often not in the bedroom but in the kitchen, because that's where the weapons were – knives, cleavers, rolling pins, chairs. Family fights, whether fatal or not, were likely to be messy, unlike the strangulation of Desdemona, which would be bloodless. It was true that in real life the guy sometimes choked his woman to death, but almost always he knocked her around first, and you spent hours collecting blood samples off the pieces of furniture he had thrown her into.

"Who's there? Othello?"

Rainey gazed down at Flora: "Ay, Desdemona."

"Will you come to bed, my lord?"

"Have you prayed tonight, Desdemona?"

"Ay, my lord."

"If you bethink yourself of any crime unreconciled as yet to heaven and grace, solicit for it straight."

The only Othello in history with actual experience in cases of this type had never yet encountered a murder as tidy as this one was to be. Usually there were weeping kids, their mother killed by some guy probably not even their father, and the killer weeping too. It was something a cop did not forget. Once Rainey had found the mother lying on the kitchen table where the man had placed her. She lay dead amid the breadcrumbs with an empty can of catfood beside her head. Rainey had not forgotten that one. He had not forgotten any of them. The emotion lasted so long because the event for a cop lasted so long. There was so much cleaning up to do – cleaning up of all kinds. Usually it was hours before he even got out of the fatal kitchen. The kids had to be taken care of, and it was not always easy at the time of night these things usually happened to find a shelter that would take them in. Then it was back to the station house, where the paperwork continued for hours more. The worst thing was that the cop was supposed to go home afterwards and behave as if it had never happened.

"Oh banish me, my lord, but kill me not!"

Rainey could see the thin blue veins on her upper chest. "Down, strumpet."

"Kill me tomorrow; let me live tonight... but half an hour! But while I say one prayer!"

"It is too late."

The murderer clamped his fingers on the snow-white throat. Rainey leaned into it. A collective gasp went up from the audience, and he felt rather than saw certain individuals rise to their feet as if they intended to attack the stage.

He could feel Flora's pulse under his hands. The life that was in her throbbed against his thumbs. This life it was within his power now to snuff out if he so desired, so that for a moment he realized what Othello had felt, and the millions of real-life Othellos driven by their wives, or by drugs or drink, or by poverty or suffering, into a state of dementia sufficient to commit such an act, an act of rage and hopelessness and hate and love all at once.

For Rainey now all these emotions were pretended except the last of them: love. He could kill Flora Bernstein now if he so chose, cut off her breath and life forever. It would take only a few seconds: no one would think to stop him until it was over. But this would mean facing the rest of life without her and thus the possibility of killing her became so real to him, and left him so appalled, that he sprang backwards staring first at his hands, then at the body upon the sofa, then again at the traitorous hands that might have perpetrated such an act, and which for the audience had indeed done so.

F. Hyman in the wings banged something to simulate a knocking at the door, and the voice of the girl playing Desdemona's maid was heard; in a moment she came on stage and confronted Rainey – still aghast at what he had done, what he now knew he was completely capable of doing, given the proper circumstances.

All the other actors poured on stage too – Montano, Iago – and all the other fags, playing soldiers.

"For naught I did in hate, but all in honor."

Rainey was still speaking the gorgeous lines. The

murderer, he realized, was unable to shut up. This was true to life as he had seen it. They all babbled, every one. Rainey as officer of the law would try to get the Miranda out, but he was never quick enough, the formula took too long: *you have a right to remain silent –*

They talked right over it. The man that had just killed his wife wanted to talk. The difference between him and Othello was that he never spoke poetry. "She been stepping out on me, man." No poetry there. "She peddling her ass, man. She give him head, man. What I suppose to do? Tell me, man, what I suppose to do?"

There was no answer to give them, and as a result the questions themselves, for Rainey, had become insupportable. He realized he could not go back into uniform. He could not go back into a radio car on patrol. He was no longer a kid. He was not callous enough any more. He could not take suffering like that night after night.

Flora was dead, and though there was a crowd on the stage he felt alone. He stared down at his two hands, alone with what they had done, and began to declaim Othello's final speech. Flora's off-eye was open, he noted; she was watching him. Rainey had come back to himself, and was again able to stand both inside and outside the play, even as the action continued. The soldiers on stage, he realized, were the cops of their day. They had been summoned to cope with the corpse, to make their arrest, and after that no doubt their notifications.

"When in your letters you shall these unhappy deeds relate –"

What was that except notifications? Same then as now. But the cops then, Shakespeare's cops anyway, were inept at their jobs, or else Shakespeare was, for it never occurred to any of them to toss Othello for weapons. Where was their training? Did they have no Police Academy in those days? Or did Shakespeare just know nothing about cops? The first job of any cop at a crime scene like this one would be to take away all those swords and knives that had already done so much damage, and would do more.

"Then must you speak of one that loved not wisely but too

107

well," Rainey declaimed. "Of one whose hand, like the base Indian, threw a pearl away richer than all his tribe..."

Having come to the end of the speech, he yanked the fake knife out of the breast pocket of his business suit – at which point another great gasp went up from the audience – and, as per Shakespeare's stage directions, stabbed himself. The knife that he never should have had, if the cops had been on the ball.

He crawled towards the sofa. When he covered dead Flora's face with kisses she made no response, but he himself was so carried away by so many emotions – by his role, by his audience, by the nearness of Flora, perhaps even by the poetry of Shakespeare – that the only response she did make, namely the pulse in her throbbing white throat, almost unmanned him. His lines fled from him; he remembered them just in time.

"No way but this, killing myself to die upon a kiss."

Since F. Hyman had cut the final speeches of Cassio and Lodovico, the play ended there.

The people in the audience jumped to their feet applauding. Apparently they had understood the scene perfectly well, understood the actors (principally himself) very well indeed. For about thirty seconds more, Rainey remained draped across Flora's chest, holding his pose, his face between her small breasts. Then he calmly rose to his feet, helped Flora to hers, and turned and faced the crowd. Flora grinned and waved out at them. He himself remained solemn, as befitted the mood of tragedy that, as he saw it, he and Shakespeare had just created upon this stage.

They all filed into the principal's office after that, where they partook of coffee, pastries and congratulations from the officials of the school. F. Hyman Effrat was exultant. He kept patting everybody on the back and kissing people. He even kissed Rainey, a wet whiskery kiss that Rainey found unpleasant.

An hour later he stood with Flora in the darkened bedroom of an apartment in Washington Heights he had borrowed from a cop named Hennessey, once his partner, who was working the midnight to eight A.M. tour this night. Flora was in his arms. He inhaled her scent. He had found and was again nuzzling the place in her throat that had so moved him, the place that pulsed with the life that was in her.

"I had no idea you were so sensitive a man," Flora whispered into his beard, an avowal, he believed, of her love. That she loved him did not surprise him, for he remembered Othello's words from Act One: "She loved me for the dangers I had passed, and I loved her that she did pity them." This to Rainey explained everything. Tonight, it seemed to him, had been so far, and continued to be, the most poetic of his existence.

With infinite care he undressed her, savouring each removed item of clothing until she stood totally revealed. But Flora once naked did not seem to give any significance to her nakedness. She simply stood there. He was perhaps looking for girlish shyness, a virginal blush, but there was none and he was disappointed. It was as if no momentous event had just taken place, was still taking place. She merely waited for Rainey to undress himself, which now he began to do, down to his gun in its clip-on holster which he laid atop the second neat pile of clothing he was making, had made. This holster engaged her interest. Reaching for it, she slid out his .38 and weighed the steel revolver in the fingers of her right hand while holding the holster in her left, an activity that momentarily froze Rainey. Warily he watched the naked girl. The light from the street caught on the blue steel barrel. What might she attempt to do with that gun? If he could easily have killed her earlier on the sofa on stage, she was in a position to do the same to him now. But in a few seconds she lost interest in the gun, shoved it back into the holster and put the package back more or less as she had found it. Rainey, who all this time had remained still, began to move again. Finally he led her to the bed – tenderly, almost as a ballet dancer leads his partner forward to begin the dance. There was poetry inherent in such movements, he thought, inherent also in this moment. He felt that she was as aware as he was of the rightness and perfection of it, aware intuitively with the almost occult sensitivity given to women at times like this, and he placed her down upon the bed. As he hovered over her his mind was full of poetry, both Shakespeare's and his own. Lines played through his head, and he tried to select the most beautiful of them, and to bring it forth for her, but he was not quick enough, for she spoke first.

"I've balled a lot of guys," she commented, "but I've never balled an older man before."

Next to this, the lines he had been considering proved insubstantial. All poetry fled from him. It's only her way of trying to say she loves me, Rainey encouraged himself. That's the way the young speak these days.

"Admit it," Flora said, "you've been wanting to ball me since the first night I came to the class, right?"

Rainey was trying to readjust his vision of her a bit, and of himself too. He was old enough to know that poetry had no more solidity than clouds. Reality was something else. Reality was this real live girl on Hennessey's bed. He could reach out and touch her flat girl's stomach, her plump girl's breast – she was that close. This was the best that the real world had to offer, and he had only to claim it and it was his.

Rainey moved forward and claimed what he could.

Nine

THE NEXT MORNING KEEFE DECIDED TO RESOLVE THE Rainey problem.

On reaching his office, he hung his suit jacket in the closet, loosened his tie, and deposited his gun, as he did every morning, in the wide middle drawer of his desk. In shirt sleeves it would show, and to wear it in plain view through the corridors of police headquarters would have felt silly, as if he were pretending to be a cop. It went into the drawer amid the rubber bands, paperclips, and spare ballpoints already there, and on top of the PC's memo that suggested he get rid of Sergeant Rainey. This memo had lain there unanswered for too long already, and he slid it out from under the holster and read it through again.

The PC wanted Rainey sent back to a precinct, that much was clear.

The officers attached to Keefe's staff had not been chosen by him. He had inherited them all. They were scattered over the building and he was still only dimly aware of what some of them did. He had no idea why any of them had been selected for their jobs, and that included Rainey. Well, if he was going to fire him he did not need to know why, or anything else. His chief of staff, Captain Fallon, could fire him. Keefe wouldn't even have to see Rainey again.

Just then Fallon bustled into Keefe's office: "I have your morning coffee right here, Commissioner. Just the way you like it."

The cup was steaming. Keefe took it and put it down before it burned his fingers, and thanked him. At the same time he was annoyed. Fallon was a hesitant, unassertive man. From time to time Keefe needed to know how the department worked, who the personalities were, where his own best interests lay, but Fallon was no help to him. No critical word ever passed his lips – not in Keefe's presence, anyway – and when asked for advice he was careful to avoid giving it.

Now he hovered over the desk. "How's the coffee, Commissioner? Did I get the sugar right?"

The only role Fallon seemed happy with and seemed to enjoy playing was the one that engaged him at this moment: café waiter.

"Yes, it's perfect," Keefe said. "Thank you."

"Well, good," said Fallon, and he beamed with pride.

The comparison was unavoidable. How quickly Rainey had taken charge of the panicky cops last night. How calmly he had moved them into place. The competence he displayed had seemed amazing to Keefe. However, the PC wanted him to get rid of him.

Just then the condemned man appeared in his doorway. "With your permission, Commissioner, I'd like to call

111

Lieutenant Craighead for a progress report."

Keefe waited until Captain Fallon had gone out. "Perhaps I should call him myself," he suggested.

"It will be stronger if I call him." Rainey watched him as if to be certain Keefe understood. For Keefe to phone Craighead directly was to descend to his level, and his level was lieutenant.

"I'll get back to you," Rainey said. As briskly and as efficiently as that he was gone.

Which left Keefe figuratively and literally still holding the PC's memo. He opened his drawer and slid it back under his gun. Then he got up from his chair and began to pace.

His office was a bare institutional room, even more barren than the PC's, and he had not attempted to do much with it. A metal desk, a swivel chair behind it, two chairs placed in front of it, and against the far wall an imitation leather sofa. The only wall decorations were a calendar, a target from the Police Academy practice range which he had taped up like a poster, and three framed certificates. One, signed by the PC, attested to Keefe's appointment as Deputy Police Commissioner; the other two represented the two journalism prizes he had won. It was an office that belonged to the police department, not to Keefe; he had never imagined he would inhabit it for very long.

The trouble was, he did not know enough about Rainey's past to make an objective judgment. Nor did he have any convenient way of getting additional information. To send for Rainey's records would alert the entire office that there was a problem – probably it would alert all headquarters. It would cause Rainey great embarrassment which perhaps he didn't deserve. Any trust that was beginning to develop between them would be destroyed, and Rainey, even if he stayed, would henceforth be as useless to him as Fallon. Is that what he wanted?

As Keefe pondered, he became increasingly annoyed at the PC. If Egan wished him to do something, why hadn't he told him more? Whatever flaw lay buried in Rainey's past could not be all that grave, otherwise he wouldn't still be a cop at all. Probably it was just some grudge somebody held

112

against him. Keefe saw no reason why he should be a party to keeping a grudge alive.

Rainey appeared in his doorway. "Yes, Ed?" Keefe said.

Rainey took the chair beside the desk, but he studied his notes before speaking. "Craighead and his men have leaned on all their stoolies," he began. "The stoolies tell them that Hot Harry is definitely back in business, but so far they've been unable to find out where he's operating."

Keefe was thinking about Rainey, not Hot Harry.

After a pause, Rainey said: "What do you intend to do with this case, Commissioner, assuming Craighead can put it together? If I may ask."

Keefe had some ideas, but he was unwilling to bring them out just yet, especially in front of this man whose future status was uncertain. "Let's wait and see," he said, adding, after a moment, "How did your play go last night?"

"The audience seemed to like it."

Rainey had stood up and was prepared to leave. Keefe's leading question did not interest him, apparently. He seemed unwilling to indulge in personal conversation of any kind.

"I told Craighead I would call him again in two days," Rainey said.

"Good." Keefe gave him a smile. "If he does manage to find the yard Hamish is using, we'll go take a look at it, you and I, okay?"

"Any time, Commissioner," Rainey said, and went out.

If he couldn't send for Rainey's records specifically, perhaps he could send for the dossiers of every person attached to his command. But this wouldn't work either. No one would know why he had done it, or what he was looking for. Rumors would start that he was planning a purge. There would be men within his own office who would not be able to sleep at night, and the shock waves would be felt throughout the building.

Keefe the reporter had never managed a staff before, or had to weigh the effect of his decisions on the physical and emotional well-being of men who worked for him. Nor had he come into the police department to learn how to play politics. He was having to do so now, and he did not like it. He did like Rainey, who did not deserve to be sacked for unknown reasons. Keefe wanted to keep him, but to do so meant to defy the PC. How would the PC react? Was it worth taking such a chance?

He got up and began to pace again. He paced five minutes and, then, having made his decision, typed out a brief note to the PC: Rainey was doing a good job, it stated, and for the moment he intended to keep him at his post. After stuffing the original into an envelope marked personal and confidential, Keefe sent it on its way through department mails. He stapled the carbon to the PC's memo, which went back to its accustomed place in the drawer under his gun. Then he sat in his chair with his feet on the desk and his hands clasped behind his head, and tried to convince himself he had done the right thing.

Keefe's black department car crossed Times Square, proceeded into the side street and pulled to a stop in front of the paper's building. He got out and stood beside the car a minute, glancing around, tugging at the hem of his suit coat. He was self-conscious because it seemed to him he could feel the paper's power coming out through the building's walls. He had felt it before, or thought he had, but never this strongly. At certain times of day a part of the paper's power actually could be felt from here: it was the power of the mighty presses anchored to bedrock in the building's cavernous basement. It came up through the sidewalk, up through the soles of one's shoes. From inside the building it was even more noticeable. It extended upward like an electrical surge through the thirteen floors above, and it seemed to transfer itself to the men who inhabited those floors, charging them with power too.

It was this powerful paper that Keefe was now prepared to affront.

When he peered inside the glass doors he could see the security desk that controlled access to the elevator banks. Two guards. Either they would recognise him from the past, and wave him through, or he would flash his shield, mutter the word "police" at them, and keep walking. The magic word: it opened, he had found, any door.

The guards were not his problem. His problem was the editors, particularly Becker.

If I get caught in there, he thought, it will be a real mess.

Finally he told himself that there were no constitutional issues involved here at all. Becker was being ridiculous. To forbid him access to his own paper was stupid. There was no reason why he should not walk right in.

He checked his watch: four P.M. The executive news conference was about to begin. At this very instant Becker's secretary was no doubt closing the door on Becker and ten or a dozen of his top editors. It was at this meeting that they would decide which stories landed on the front page tomorrow, which others would be downplayed or held over for another day. Keefe had sat in on a few of these news conferences in the past. They began precisely at four P.M., and ended precisely at four-thirty. Newspapers worked strictly according to the clock. The hour of the executive news conference was as immutable as the start of each night's press run. Keefe had half an hour to get in and out of the building.

He pushed through the revolving door, and approached the security desk.

One of the two guards, recognizing him, flashed a big smile. The man's name, Keefe remembered, was Richard.

"Hello there, Richard," he said and went past him. "How are you doing?"

He rode the elevator up to the third floor, turned left away from the newsroom, and strode down the corridor and into the morgue. At the counter he filled out a form. He had done this dozens of times in the past. Reporters were required to sign these forms, so Keefe signed this one, but made his signature illegible.

The clerk took the form away, and in a few minutes returned with a folder. Keefe took the folder into one of the cubicles, and on the counter there spread out the clippings it contained.

He worked for twenty minutes, checking his watch constantly, for he intended to be out of the building ten minutes before the news conference should end. Gold's robbery victim, it seemed, was a Dutch national. She was all over the society pages, had been for decades: marriage, children, donations to charity, penthouse remodelled by a fashionable architect. No scandals. From her late husband she had inherited an estimated hundred million dollars.

It seemed unlikely to Keefe that she was involved in any insurance scam. But that was Gold's problem. His own was to slip out of this building unseen. He carried the folder back to the counter and turned it in. He went out into the corridor to the bank of elevators. Four closed doors. A few men waiting. He pushed the down button. When the car did not come immediately, he began to fidget. He glanced nervously around, and pushed the down button a second time.

Doors parted. Several people got off. One was a tall female reporter he had known for a long time. She was almost as tall as he was. Her name was May Fondren. The others moved past Keefe. May did not.

"Oh," she said, "it's you."

However much he may have wanted to lunge into the cabin, this was impossible. He started to shake hands with May, then changed his mind and kissed her briefly. He asked her how she was.

"Is that all you can say, how am I?"

As the doors slid closed, he was not inside them, he was outside on the hallway.

"I thought you'd been sent to Bonn," he said.

"How's Sharon? Did you two get married yet?"

Keefe pushed the down button.

"Sharon's living on the West Coast." Immediately he recognized this remark as a mistake. Why did I have to tell her that? he wondered.

"Well, well, well," May said. "You've split up."

The door from the newsroom opened and people came out, and stood waiting for the elevator too.

"Not at all. Her show moved out there."

"Let's have dinner together and talk about it," May said, and she grinned at him.

The elevator doors had just parted again. "Sure," he said, "Anytime."

"Come on over to my desk, while I look at my calendar."

"Tuesday," said Keefe. "I really am in a terrific hurry."

The elevator doors had already closed. Again Keefe punched the down button.

The door from the newsroom swung open and Seymour Becker strode forth accompanied by the publisher. When he saw Keefe he looked surprised. That does it, thought Keefe.

Becker strode straight up to him. "What are you doing in this building?"

"I came to see May," said Keefe.

"I should have you prosecuted."

"I came to invite May to dinner."

Becker's thick glasses turned toward May. She gave a laugh. "Next Tuesday night," she said. "I tricked him into it."

Becker turned back to Keefe. "I don't want to see you in this building ever again, understand?" He had punched the up button. The elevator doors opened, and he and the publisher got into the elevator and the doors closed again.

May said: "What was that all about?"

The confrontation with Becker had filled Keefe with guilt. It was as if he had betrayed the newspaper ethic that had governed most of his adult life. "To Seymour," he muttered, "the real enemy of the people is the police."

"You've gone over to the enemy," said May. "Is that what he thinks?"

Becker, once he returned to his own office, would send somebody into the morgue to see if Keefe had been there. It was what Keefe would have done in his place. It was what any good reporter would do, and before becoming executive editor Becker had been a good reporter. Reporters were detectives. Reporters and detectives were the same, the best of them even to the bravery. Keefe was certain he had just ruined any future career for himself with this newspaper, and for what? To procure information for Gold that was most likely of no importance whatsoever.

The elevator doors had opened again. The down car. He stepped into the cabin.

"Stay and talk to me a moment," said May. "I'll check my calendar and –"

"I really am in a terrific hurry." He was standing in an open elevator that seemed stalled there. "I'll call you," he promised. The doors remained open.

"See you Tuesday, then," she said, nodding.

When he got back to headquarters he phoned Chief Gold and read him his notes. Gold professed to be immensely grateful. "I can't thank you enough, Boss."

Keefe went to stand at the window. It faced the East River and Brooklyn beyond. Brooklyn was a low city; very few tall buildings over there. It was late afternoon now. Brooklyn was flooded with orange light. He watched a tug come out from under the Brooklyn Bridge.

There were days when he believed he did not belong in this department, and wondered why he stayed. Bad days.

Sergeant Rainey stuck his head into the office. "The PC has left the building."

Keefe looked at him. It had been a good day for Rainey and he didn't even know it. "Have Detective Murphy get the car out."

In his flat Keefe moved through the rooms. They were just as he had left them: empty. The apartment even smelled empty. He made himself a scotch and soda and stood looking down at the street, watching the cars go by. I'm a New Yorker, he thought. I have that in common with every cop in the city. But I don't understand headquarters and may never.

It began to get dark. He walked to the back of the long narrow house. In the kitchen he whisked two eggs, diced a tomato on a board, scraped the pieces into the mix and cooked himself an omelette. He ate it standing up at the window looking out into the courtyard at all the other kitchen windows. Most were lit. He watched the backs of women preparing dinner for their families. He saw a little boy get his face slapped. He saw a man come in and grab a handful of his wife's behind, and kiss her on the neck.

118

The phone rang: it was Sharon from California. "Do you miss me? Tell me how much you miss me."

She didn't even talk it over with me first, he reminded himself. She just moved out. So despite his pleasure and excitement he kept his voice in neutral, or tried to. "Of course I miss you." She doesn't care about me, he told himself. If she did she wouldn't have done it. She had not phoned in days – nor, of course, had he.

After hesitating, Sharon said: "Well, I miss you too." He heard her begin to giggle. She was very excited about something, apparently. "So what have you been doing?" she said. "Have you found a new girlfriend yet?"

He imagined her in California, alone. All she had to do was stand there and men would flock around – had already, he was sure. Had she decided on one of them yet? "I've been busy," he said. "How about you?"

"You won't believe what's happened."

She was still giggling and talking at the same time. "Somebody got the bright idea that in addition to producing this soap opera I ought to be in it. Isn't that fantastic?"

A delegation representing the sponsor, the ad agency and the network had come on the set, apparently. She was so excited it was difficult to understand the details. Naturally she had shown them around. One of the vice-presidents from Colgate-Palmolive had commented that she ought to be in the show herself.

"The network man and the agency man fell all over themselves agreeing with him. They wrote me into the show on the spot. Today I just had a walk-on, but Monday I'm going to have lines." She began laughing.

"How old was this business tycoon? What did he look like?"

"He was very nice. He was about your age. He wanted to take me out to dinner to talk it over."

And after that? The trouble with illusions was that you could never be sure they had lost their power over you.

The silence was broken by another giggle from Sharon. "You're jealous."

"No, I'm not."

"You are so, silly. I told him no."

"Why did you do that? You should have gone with him. If you wanted to, that is."

"Well, I didn't want to."

Telephone calls were the worst illusions of all. With a telephone at your ear you imagined you could touch someone you wanted really desperately to touch, and you couldn't.

"I guess he didn't take it as a definitive answer, though," he said. Now he was just torturing himself, and he knew it.

"What's that supposed to mean?"

"He still wanted you in the show."

To Keefe her happiness sounded genuine. "I haven't acted since I was in college," she said.

In college, she once told him, she had appeared in two plays. One was *Barefoot in the Park*, and he had forgotten the other. Keefe said: "You may find the role less demanding than the last ones you played."

"I play the lawyer who defends Roland in the incest case. If the audience likes me, I may stay in the show even after the case is over – if it's ever over. I have to plead in New York's felony court."

"There is no felony court in New York."

"There is in this show."

Her giggling stopped, and she said: "You sound lonely."

"I'm fine," he said. "I just made dinner for myself and in a few minutes I'm going out."

"Where to?"

He might have invented a date with someone as exciting as she was, maybe even throw her into a state of jealousy similar to his own. But he had no desire to make her unhappy, assuming he still had that power. And, besides, he tried never to lie. "To a movie, maybe."

"I wish I was there and could go with you."

Keefe looked out of the window. There were two or more people in almost every kitchen. People who looked comfortable with each other. "I'll send you a critique," he said.

"My soap takes place in New York, you know. Maybe I'll

have to come back to do research in that felony court you have there. You can show me where it is."

"That would be nice. When would it be?"

In one of the windows a man and woman, both about Keefe's age, stood peering down on whatever was cooking on the stove – the way he had sometimes stood in this kitchen with Sharon on her nights to cook – the way he might stand with her again if she made the trip she was talking about.

"Well, not right away. It's only a possibility."

He lapsed into a disappointed silence.

"Or you could come out here."

"That's not very realistic. I do have a job."

"You could come for the weekend."

He could fly five thousand miles for a few hours that overall would not change anything and would make him feel worse when they were over. "I'm on call all weekend."

"Don't I know it."

"What's that supposed to mean?"

There was an edge to his voice, and he knew she heard it. He was immediately repentent. He did not want to start a fight.

Neither did she, apparently. "Are you enjoying the job any better?" she said.

"Sometimes I love it. Sometimes not so much."

"And tonight?"

How sensitive she was to his moods. A week ago – even ten minutes ago – he might have talked to her about his distasteful day, about Seymour Becker, about Gold. But now he could not do it.

"I think you'd better tell me."

"Tell you what?"

"Tell me why you're in such a bad mood. What went wrong?"

"Nothing went wrong."

"Yes, it did." Then she gave another laugh. "You know you want to tell me. And I want you to. Come on and tell me. Maybe I can help."

"How can you help when you're two and a half thousand miles away?"

This silenced her, to his immediate regret. "I may have done something really stupid today," he said hastily.

"You got married," she said.

They were again on the verge of a fight: his fault. He swallowed the sharp retort that had sprung to his lips and began to describe his mission on behalf of Chief Gold. "Do you remember a reporter named May Fondren?"

"A tall girl with blue eyes."

"I never noticed the color of her eyes."

"They're blue."

"Okay, they're blue. As I was getting on the elevator –"

"She always had a thing for you, too. Did you ever notice that?"

Keefe said nothing.

"All right, you're getting on the elevator and she's getting off."

"I couldn't get away from her. Finally along comes Becker."

Sharon laughed. "He caught you."

"He's liable to blackball me throughout the newspaper business. That's serious."

"What really bothers you," said Sharon, "is that he made you feel like a burglar."

"Yes."

"You burglarized secrets."

"Yes."

"Any one of which you could have bought for a quarter on the day it appeared."

This notion made him smile. "Well, I guess so."

"So they weren't very valuable secrets, were they? I'm afraid you'll have to do better than that if you want to make it as a burglar."

His gloom seemed to acquire a weight of its own as he remembered his conversation with Gold.

"When I told him over the phone what I had found out, I had the impression he wasn't the least bit interested. He didn't seem to take notes, he didn't ask any further questions. Now I feel he set me up."

"Why would he do that?"

"As a form of flattery. Make me feel I'm important to him. Make me feel fond of him in case he needs me for something."

"You're exaggerating."

"I feel like he made a fool of me. Or, rather, that he caused me to make a fool of myself. But I'm not sure, don't you see? That's the worst of it."

"I still think you're exaggerating."

"You don't know police headquarters. It's a bed of snakes."

Sharon was silent.

"Furthermore I come out of this with a dinner date with May Fondren." It was a confession he felt he had to make.

"You what?"

"I invited her to dinner as a means of trying to get away from her."

"She doesn't wash her hair too often," said Sharon. "Did you ever notice? Have a good time."

"Now who's jealous?"

"Be careful she doesn't rape you."

"Well," Keefe said, "there's no one else around looking to rape me, sorry to say."

There was a long pause. Then Sharon said: "I found an apartment."

"That must be a relief to you." But not to him. If she had an apartment then she meant to stay, and the stay could be permanent.

"It's big enough for two – if you should ever come out here, I mean." She began to describe it room by room. She had moved in yesterday, she said, and he copied down her new phone number. She had cleaned it all day. "I had to scrub the tub out before I would take a shower. And I took the shower curtain down too, it was so disgusting. I took a shower without any shower curtain." Keefe could visualize opening the bathroom door on her, no curtain and water sluicing down her body. "I got water all over everything," she said. "I had to mop it all up."

In his thoughts he tried to find an explanation for the emotion known as love. Love worked despite enormous distances. It was just as strong from two and a half thousand miles away as from the next room. It was an absolute craving. It was perhaps entirely physical or chemical in nature. It could no more be seen than magnetism could be seen, but the physical or chemical explanation was perhaps there to be discovered some day. When that happened somebody would invent a pill so that men and women could turn it on and off at will. But there was no pill yet, no pill for Keefe tonight; he would have to get through the night some other way, but he was too upset and too stubborn to admit this to Sharon.

She rang off shortly afterwards. "Love you," she said and hung up. He spent the next minutes trying to measure the weight of the words "love you". Had she spoken them too lightly? Without thought? He himself had not spoken them at all.

He went out into the night and prowled the streets with his hands in his pockets. Every place he turned he saw women. New York did not lack them. Two women coming out of a restaurant barely avoided bumping into him; he jumped back just in time. He walked on. A woman was peering into lighted shops, moving from window to window up Lexington Avenue. A blonde woman sliding onto the seat of a taxi showed him most of her thigh.

He walked east to Third. He saw women talking brightly to each other, women alone. There was one who seemed especially appealing waiting on line outside one of the first-run movie houses; even as he watched her the line began to move forward. He very nearly joined it. As he walked on he was thinking about the power of illusion again. Was it the illusion of the woman that had attracted him, or the illusion of the darkness inside? In the dark illusions became more plausible, even someone else's, even illusions ten times life-size.

Finally he decided to stroll across to the West Side. Along Central Park South big trees hung over him. He walked along the bottom edge of the Park. The row of luxury hotels and apartment buildings rose up across the street. Hansom cabs waited for fares along the curb. The horses nickered at him, jiggled their nosebags. He inhaled the moist acidic odor of their flanks. Drivers doffed top hats at him, offering him rides through the park as if he were a tourist. As a teenager he had often daydreamed of taking a date through Central Park in one of those cabs, the two of them snuggling under a rug, and getting up the nerve to kiss her to the clip-clop of the horse's hooves. He had never done it. When at last he had begun to form relationships with girls, he had found that hansom cabs were not necessary and were, besides, very expensive. But the idea, another of his illusions, had persisted; obviously he carried remnants of it in his head still, or he would not have remembered it.

He came out onto Columbus Circle. The explorer, high up on his pedestal, peered down on him. We're all explorers, he thought. Ahead is the unknown. He started up Columbus Avenue. There were restaurant tables pushed out halfway to the curb. He was in a flow of pedestrian traffic here, and it moved him along. At the outdoor tables there were more girls and women, most of them in animated conversation.

He came to a singles bar. He knew what it was, and he paused.

Of course bars had always been excellent places to find complacent women, but these new places were different: luxuriously appointed, expensive, jam-packed every night, and noisy: conversations competed with booming rock music. The centerpiece, as brightly lighted as a shrine and visible from the street, was always the bar, which was usually circular, with a number of barmen working behind it. But there were tables too almost all of them tiny, at which people dined, either before making a connection or after. Votive candles burned on each tablecloth. They were like prayers. They threw flattering light up onto faces that, because of the din, were almost always pressed close together.

Keefe, who had never gone into such a place, did so now. Three bartenders were working, all wearing red coats and sporting handlebar moustaches. There was a concealed spotlight somewhere. Its beam struck the shelves of bottles a glancing blow and bits of colored glass gleamed like jewelry.

Trying to approach the bar, Keefe forced his way through bodies. The noise was incredible. People were shouting into each other's ears.

"I'm surprised we didn't meet previously, either in Europe or Aspen, aren't you?"

"I found the Grand Canyon incomprehensible except at dawn."

Fragments of conversation were all around him as he pushed forward, fragments of lives.

Keefe reached an arm through, waved at the barman, and gave his order.

"Did I ever tell you I was Jewish, Bernice?"

"No, but –"

"You hoped, Bernice, you hoped."

A place opened up at the bar and Keefe stepped into it. His drink was set down, but before he could even look around he felt rather than saw two bodies, both women, wedge in next to him tight on either side, like Mafia hitmen sidling up to their victim. Breasts, or perhaps only arms, pressed against him. He concentrated on his glass. It contained an inch of liquid that turned milky as he poured water in, and the woman to his left said: "What kind of drink is that?"

He looked into an inappropriate smile. She was too old for him, and she wore heavily mascaraed eyelashes that she batted nervously. She was wearing a black cocktail dress and much lipstick. He had the impression also of costume jewelry, a brooch, some rings, a necklace. He could not be sure because he gave her only a glance before turning back to his glass, which he stirred with his forefinger. He did not want her to imagine he was appraising whatever it was she had to offer, for he recognized loneliness when he saw it, and this woman seemed to him as vulnerable as any he had met. His own loneliness was as nothing compared to hers.

The woman on the other side of him had not yet spoken, but he knew she was there because she was pressing against him.

"I mean, I never saw a drink that color before," the first woman said.

"It's Pernod. It's French."

"I've been to France." She smiled again, or tried to. She was certainly not a hooker. She was far too nervous for that. "The Eiffel Tower. The Right and Left Bank. You name it."

"I used to work in France. It's a nice drink, actually." He was embarrassed. He shouldn't have come in here. People get the wrong idea.

The woman said: "My name is Joyce."

Keefe did not want to be rude, nor hurt her feelings. I'm really just here out of curiosity, he wanted to tell her. I'm going home soon. Please don't misunderstand. He gave his name.

"And who do you work for now, Phil?"

This took a moment's thought. "I'm with the city."

Instant intimacy. He was talking directly into her ear, she into his. The alternative was to shout for the whole bar to hear – as some others were doing. One listened to them without wanting to.

"Why should I deny the part of me that is denying part of me?"

"I don't love her, I tolerate her."

The bar was polished oak and only slightly moist. Keefe's check lay close by his fingertips. He could throw down some bills and –

But Joyce beamed up at him. "Working for the city means great job security. Right, Phil?"

"Not exactly." On the executive floors of police headquarters nobody believed very much in job security.

Joyce sounded alarmed. "But you do have a good job."

"Oh, sure."

"I certainly am glad to hear that."

A bit more assurance had come into her smile. Evidently she believed the conversation successfully launched. Which meant it was his turn to inquire about her.

"Are you a working woman?" he asked reluctantly.

"I'm in business." She nodded several times. "Manufacturing."

The barman came over and placed her check on top of his, but Joyce quickly separated them. "He shouldn't have done that," she said apologetically. "Office furniture." This sounded like part of the same apology. "I'm with Charles Smith and Company."

"Interesting," said Keefe. He studied his drink.

The barman said: "Another round, folks?" The spotlight on the red coat was blinding.

"Not for me," said Keefe, but too late.

"I'll have one," said Joyce.

They watched the barman agitate a shaker close to his ear.

"The drinks are very expensive here," Joyce said. "Maybe you'd rather go someplace else."

"Well –"

"I know a much cheaper place, if you'd like."

Keefe said nothing.

"I could cancel my order."

The barman was pouring from the shaker into a cocktail glass.

"It's only just down the street."

The barman put the glass down in front of Joyce. "Separate checks?" he said.

"You could put it on mine," said Keefe.

Joyce said hurriedly: "Please don't feel you have to."

Keefe had become increasingly aware of the woman on his other side, who had begun nudging him. He had the impression that she stared straight ahead at the rows of bottles behind the bar, and she must have decided to make her move now or never, for suddenly she lurched into him. Since he had just lifted his glass off the bar, this sent its contents out over his hand.

"I'm so sorry," she protested. "Please stop pushing me," she said loudly over her shoulder. She was wiping Keefe's hand with a cocktail napkin, spilling even more of his drink as she did so. "Someone pushed me," she confided. "Are you married?"

She was younger than Joyce, and more buxom, with bleached blond hair and a toothy smile.

New York had more single women than single men according to articles Keefe had read. Maybe twice as many. To meet unattached men was extremely difficult, it seemed. He could believe it.

Behind him Joyce said: "Do you come in here often?" To get his attention back she had touched him tentatively on the sleeve, withdrawing her fingers almost at once.

He turned back to her. "This is the first time." He gave her a smile.

"Me too."

Although the napkin by now was sopping, the blond was still patting his hand with it. "My name is Stella."

"Glad to meet you, Stella."

"Well, are you?"

"What?"

"Married?" She was half shouting over the music. It made him glance self-consciously this way and that.

"No, I'm not."

She cocked her head at him. "I'll bet you're divorced."

Keefe studied the puddle around his glass. As if waiting for such a signal, the barman came over, lifted the glass and smoothed under it with a rag.

"No, I've never been married."

"Lot of guys never been married are gay."

"My girlfriend went to California –" said Keefe.

"I've never been married either."

I've got to get out of here, Keefe thought.

"I had a relationship with a guy, but a couple of months ago he got transferred."

At his other shoulder was Joyce's voice: "You're not, but I am."

"You're what?"

"Divorced."

Colors from the bottles bounced back onto her face. Keefe tried to appraise her age. "How long were you married?"

"Too long," Joyce said.

"First he moved out, to be honest with you," said Stella, "then he got transferred. He said he just didn't think it was there for us. He said he felt rotten about it. How did he think I felt?"

"Do you have children?" Keefe asked Joyce.

"Rotten, that's how," said Stella.

Joyce nodded. "They're with their father this week. He married again."

"You wouldn't come in here if you were gay, right?" said Stella.

Joyce said: "He knows I like to go out. He never used to take me out."

Stella said: "I don't think we would've married. I was really looking for someone taller."

"Yes," said Keefe.

"He was much shorter than you are."

Joyce leaned even closer. He could feel her breast against him. "You're lucky you're not married," she told him. "I said to him, if you want to go with a slut, then go with her. I threw him out."

"You threw him out."

"I threw him out."

Stella had been telling him something. He missed all but the end of it. "Why go all the way to Florida to get hurt when you can get hurt right here?" She too pressed closer than before. When she laughed, her breath beat against the side of his head.

"I don't live very far from here," Joyce said into his ear.

Stella said: "We could move to one of the tables and be more comfortable, if you would prefer."

"I could make us some coffee," said Joyce.

Keefe stepped back a bit from the bar so that Stella and Joyce found themselves unexpectedly face to face. "Are you ladies acquainted?" he said.

The two women glared at each other.

"I don't think I've had the pleasure," said Stella.

"Pleased to meet you, I'm sure," said Joyce.

The brilliant red coat loomed over them. "Another round, folks?"

"Please serve these ladies whatever they might like," Keefe said. He pushed money forward; he didn't even know how much.

"You're not leaving?" said Joyce.

"My God," he said. He checked his watch. "I didn't realize it was this late."

Joyce said: "What's the matter?" But there seemed real concern in her voice, and he was surprised.

"I'm late for an appointment."

"I'll bet," said Stella.

The two new cocktails were set down. The handlebar moustache, grinning pleasantly, hung over the bar. "There you are, folks."

"It's really a terrifically important appointment," said Keefe. "I really wish I could stay." He shook hands with both of them. Stella's hand was fleshy, Joyce's small and somewhat moist. Then he was outside on the sidewalk. He breathed in the cool night air. When he peered back through the window Joyce and Stella had begun talking, somewhat sadly it seemed to him, to each other.

He thought: Sharon, where are you?

Ten

SENATOR BUCKNER AND HIS IMPENDING PUBLIC HEAR-ings had headquarters off-balance. In so large a department obviously there were examples of brutality to be found, and nobody was proud of them. New York cops made more than a hundred thousand felony arrests a year, prisoners did not always come willingly, and those who got hurt charged brutality. Buckner had his agents out there. What cases were they working on? What charges would he make? If they were severe enough there were going to be commanders" heads rolling too. Whose careers would he destroy? Such questions were agonized over every day.

Keefe, however, was not afraid of Buckner, whom he now met for lunch. Why should he be? The politician was effusively friendly. He called him "Phil" several times in every sentence, and even "Phil-boy," as in, "The clams are delicious here, Phil-boy."

But on the subject of his investigation he was mute. Keefe could get almost nothing out of him.

When Keefe got back to headquarters the PC was not waiting anxiously in his office for his report. He was not at headquarters at all. Instead he was out somewhere, would not be back, and in his place was an invitation to dinner at his house at seven P.M. This was a surprise. As far as Keefe knew, no present commander had ever even visited the PC's house, much less dined there. The PC, who still had a number of small children living at home, was not a social person. He never seemed at ease on social occasions. So why had he invited Keefe tonight? He can't wait to hear my news, whatever it may be, Keefe thought. Unfortunately I don't have any.

He began trying to think what he would do in Senator Buckner's place.

Obviously a few mauled prisoners were not enough. To make a splash, Buckner would need to present cases of prisoners who had been beaten to death while in police custody. He would need to show a pattern. Many cases, then. Where would he get them?

Keefe had himself driven to the morgue where he spoke for thirty minutes to the chief medical examiner. Buckner's men had been there. They had begun studying possible cases going back ten years. They were going to reopen every case where police brutality had been alleged or even suspected. They intended to ask for court orders to exhume bodies.

Keefe came away with the paperwork on certain of these cases. He was feeling pleased with himself, and he spent the rest of the afternoon on other business, the most pressing of which was a speech the PC had asked him to look over. The PC was scheduled to make it the following week to the New York Bar Association. A draft had come in that morning. Keefe now found it bland and unfocused. This speech was potentially an important one, a chance for the PC to begin to get his ideas across to the elite of the New York legal profession, men in a position to help him put them into practice.

The department's principal speech-writer was a middle-aged lieutenant in the planning division. Keefe had met him.

He had been writing speeches – basically the same speech, he had told Keefe proudly – for every police commissioner of the last twenty years, and had rarely found it necessary even to discuss in advance the contents of these speeches with the men who would give them. He had never yet spoken to the current PC, nor did he see any need to do so.

It was upon hearing this last statement that Keefe had realized not only how afraid most cops were of the PC but also how afraid most police commissioners were of speeches. Public utterances from podiums usually seemed dangerous to them. Any police commissioner who brought attention to himself was courting trouble from the mayor, or some important politician. The lieutenant from the planning division had suited everyone fine until now.

But the present PC had announced on the day of his appointment that the department had been allowed to lie stagnant too long. He had declared that new priorities and new techniques must be put into place, and he had stated what some of them were. It had sounded, for a police commissioner, quite daring. It was what had attracted Keefe to him in the first place.

Now, months later, the PC's ideas for change kept raining down from the fourteenth floor, usually in the form of memos entitled "Executive Topics". Some memos promulgated broad concepts. Others were quite specific, as the PC sought to alter the way cops both perceived their role and performed it – from executives in headquarters to patrolmen on the street.

Unfortunately, it was difficult to inspire subordinate commanders to translate his ideas into action. Most commanders seemed to believe that the best way to hold on to power was to do nothing at all. They did not mind thwarting the PC, whose powers, particularly in terms of personnel, were limited. With the exception of his seven deputy commissioners, he could bring in no outsiders who might share his views. By law, everyone else had to be promoted from the ranks, and if he fired one commander he would be obliged to replace him with a man who probably resembled him almost exactly.

Therefore the PC could not order the acceptance of his

new ideas, or force their implementation. He could only send them out and watch to see what happened. Which, usually, was very little.

As he read and reread the leaden draft, Keefe had a new notion of his own: that it might be possible to attract support for the PC's ideas from outside the department, from the Bar Association, for instance; also from any other civic groups that the PC might be asked to address. There were tremendous possibilities here. These speeches could be used to mobilize support, to force change on the department from the outside. They ought not to be allowed to go to waste.

Keefe got out the folder containing the PC's Executive Topic memos and began copying notes into the margins of the draft, and as he worked he became increasingly annoyed at the planning division lieutenant. He isn't even bright enough to crib from these memos rather than from his own past speeches, he thought. He would speak to the PC about replacing him. Unfortunately, the replacement might be little better. He too would have to be a cop, and there was no rich pool of police literary talent.

Another notion occurred to Keefe. The criminal justice system in America was without a single recognized spokesman or leader, which was part of what was wrong with it. The PC could be the leader that the country was crying out for. He had the biggest city, the biggest department, the most new ideas, the biggest mandate for change. A few hard-hitting, well-received speeches might be all it would take.

The margins of the draft became filled with the PC's ideas couched now in Keefe's own phrases: "the criminal might be likened to a rubber ball, and the court system to a wall; we arrest the criminal and throw him up against the wall, and he bounces right back down into the street again." The police department received a disproportionate share of the criminal justice dollar, in the PC's view, and Keefe wrote this in. "This department would be willing to give up a portion of its budget if that money were used to hire additional prosecutors, additional judges."

134

The PC lived in a small brick house in the Forest Hills section of Queens. There was a plot of grass out front, plus a small bed of flowers and a small tree. A police car was parked a short way up the street under the trees, with two cops on guard inside it, for the PC received death threats regularly, and in a country and city full of armed crazies such threats had to be taken seriously. Keefe left his own car parked out front too, with Detective Murphy still behind the wheel, and walked up and rang the bell.

The door opened and the PC invited him inside. The whole family was in the vestibule to greet him, which somehow was exactly what he had expected.

"So glad you could come," said Edna Egan, a small pleasant woman in her forties. There were also two small boys who dutifully shook his hand, and the PC's middle-aged sister, Marla.

For more than an hour the PC played the role of genial host, and did not ask for any report on Buckner at all; it was as if he had forgotten that one was available. And the two men were never alone long enough for Keefe to raise the subject.

"Dinner," announced Edna Egan.

Everyone trooped into the dining room. Now we'll say grace, Keefe thought.

"Tim?" said Edna Egan.

They all bowed their heads – two small boys, two women, two men – while the PC intoned grace before meals, after which all of them, Keefe included, made the sign of the cross.

Dinner was roast beef, mashed potatoes with gravy, and frozen peas. The PC will carve, Keefe thought. The PC carved. There will be wine of some indeterminate nature, Keefe thought. There was. It was served out of a crystal decanter that may have been a long-ago wedding present only lately being put to practical use.

The dining room table was large, and the room contained twelve chairs, half of them pushed back against the wall, for the other Egan children were married or away at college. The conversation, Keefe thought, will concern absent members of the family.

"Aunt Julia missed the train."

"Since Bill died she hasn't been the same."

"Did Frankie get his cast off yet?"

There was no police talk at all.

"May I be excused?" piped up one of the boys.

"May I be excused?" echoed the other.

When the two children had disappeared Keefe said: "I had lunch with Senator Buckner today."

"Oh yes?" If the PC was interested in this subject his interest did not show.

"He told me he was going to schedule public hearings in two or three months," Keefe began.

"More coffee, anyone?" The PC lifted the pot invitingly above the tablecloth.

Buckner told me, Keefe thought, that he was going to chew up your police department and spit it out. But he said only: "He's a very impressive man."

"Yes, he is." The PC was pouring. He concentrated on it, filling now Marla's cup, now his wife's.

"Physically, I mean," said Keefe. "I mean," he explained, "everybody recognizes him."

The PC passed round the sugarbowl.

"Just as long as he knows he has our complete co-operation," the PC said.

Keefe thought: he's got to be more interested than he seems. Buckner is in a position to destroy his career.

"I'll clear the table," said Mrs. Egan.

"I'll help," said Marla.

Should I offer to help too? thought Keefe. But he answered his own question: not in this house.

"Well," said the PC, "shall we move back into the living room?"

As he followed him down the short hall Keefe thought: I'll never understand this man. Is he really this cool? Why is he trying to hide his thoughts from me?

In the living room the PC still failed to interrogate him about his news. Instead he began talking about what he called the marginal performance of so many of the men in his department. He paused to light a pipe. "We have to learn to identify marginal performance at all levels of the department, and to find methods of dealing with it." The pipe was drawing now, and he puffed on it. "Conversely, how do we identify quality performance?" He played with this idea for a time.

In its way, Keefe decided, this was a strangely intimate conversation. Never mind that nothing of a personal nature was discussed or alluded to. He sat alone with the Police Commissioner of the City of New York in the PC's own living room, and this in itself impressed him. Furthermore, the man was speaking from the heart. He was speaking earnestly, leaning forward intently.

After a time Keefe concluded that Egan simply was not interested in his lunch with Buckner, or in the additional information he had acquired. Then why did he invite me here? Keefe asked himself. He was entirely perplexed. He must have had a reason. What could it be?

Before long he took his leave, having found no way to introduce the subject of Buckner again. He got back into his car beside Detective Murphy feeling disappointed in himself, frustrated.

Behind him Timothy J. Egan stood in his doorway until Keefe's car had pulled away from the curb. The Police Commissioner of the City of New York hoped he had convinced the young man just now of the importance of the job yet to be done, and to stay and help do it. Perhaps he should have spoken this thought outright, and obtained from Keefe a commitment. But this he had been unable to do. He had been to the hospital that afternoon to see the First Deputy Commissioner. Sitting beside the bed he had outlined some of the problems he faced, and described what progress he believed he had made, but his old friend was so weak he could only nod from time to time, and indicate his understanding by tapping the back of Egan's hand.

As for Keefe's lunch with Buckner, Egan had decided at about the time that Keefe rang his doorbell that he did not want to know about it. The news, whatever it was, was certain to be bad, there was nothing he could do, and he had enough problems already. He appreciated the effort Keefe had no doubt made. He wished he had told him so.

He had never been good at revealing his emotions. Some men could give out details about themselves of the most intensely personal nature. He himself could only keep silent; he had never understood why. He was locked within himself in some way. He regretted it, but by now it was so much part of his character that he knew he could not change.

If informed of what Buckner was up to, he would perhaps feel obligated for the good of the department to try to stop him, or conduct his own investigation along similar lines, then announce his own result before Buckner's public hearings were held. But if he did any of this, Buckner would surely denounce him and possibly accuse him of crimes. Buckner would cry cover-up, or corruption, and Egan's reputation and career would be ruined. No, it was a temptation to which he had decided not to subject himself. It was better not to know.

The next night Keefe had himself driven up to Westchester to his parents' house, for his mother had invited him to dinner. It was a big brick house with a Dutch tile roof. There were plenty of fireplaces. The rooms were big with decorated ceilings and hardwood floors. His father was a partner in an investment bank. His brother and sister-in-law were present tonight. He had always been close to his brother, who was a year and a half younger and already a partner in a prestigious Wall Street law firm.

Before dinner most of the conversation was about loans and corporate mergers. Keefe's mind went off. The PC was a complex man. It was difficult to see him clearly, but Keefe had become devoted to him, and he thought he knew why. The police department, this one or any other, stood for the ultimate triumph of good over evil – idealistically speaking, that's what cops were trying for. Seen this way, law enforcement became a religion and all the major religions of the world assigned the role of chief only to God. In the New York Police Department, however, it was assigned this year to the small, apparently emotionless man on the fourteenth floor, the one with the droopy eyes and the quiet voice.

Keefe had become mesmerized by him; or rather, not so much by the man himself as by what he represented, by the magical possibilities he held out to him. When one stood too close to idealism, this was always the risk.

At the dinner table everyone wanted to know about Sharon. Both his parents had always liked her. This family is so straight, he realized, that I seem like a bohemian to them.

"I'm resigned to you two not getting married," said his mother, "but when is she coming back?"

"Oh, Mom."

"She *is* coming back?"

"Sure, Mom."

"Well, when?"

Keefe parried this question and others. He left as soon after dinner as he decently could.

Eleven

THE PC SPOKE TO THE BAR ASSOCIATION FROM THE stage of Town Hall on West Forty-Third Street. About a thousand lawyers and civic officials were present. The press and TV crews, as if consigned to outer darkness, occupied the rear rows. The PC stood at a lectern on a small podium and was bracketed by spotlights. A smaller spot on a flexible stem focused light on the pages of the speech as he read it.

Keefe stood in the dark at the top of the center aisle and listened as the PC's thoughts and ideas but Keefe's phrases were amplified to row after row. The PC read the speech from beginning to end and did not change a word.

It was not exactly a cry from the heart. He read in a monotone and displayed no emotion at all. Although his subject was crime and violence his points were thoughtful, almost intellectual, and were much stronger as a result:

"The entire world at this time is concentrated on finding new and more efficient methods of accomplishing whatever task is at hand," he said in closing, "but in our courtrooms efficiency is never mentioned. To those of us in law enforcement it is as if the word itself were unknown."

The applause started only politely, but grew and grew, while the PC gathered his pages, switched off the flexible light and stepped down from the podium. Within seconds the stage was crowded. Men surrounded him and pumped his hand. The TV crews were trying to get closer. Microphones were being thrust over heads.

For Keefe it was a heady moment.

"Is this your work?" he heard a female voice ask, and when he looked he saw to his surprise that it was May Fondren. She was holding a copy of the speech in one hand and tapping it with the other. The theatre lights had come up and she had encircled, Keefe saw with a glance, some of his best phrases. But he had broken their dinner date some weeks ago, and her presence therefore discomforted him.

"They're the PC's ideas," he told her, keeping this on a professional level for as long as possible. "And for the most part they're his words too."

May looked at him for some time in silence, letting his discomfort build. "You stood me up."

He had invented a meeting of the PC and certain top commanders, including himself, with the mayor at City Hall.

"Aren't you going to ask me if it broke my heart?"

He did not answer.

"No, it did not break my heart. I knew you were going to invent some excuse. I knew it probably even before you did."

"How could you have known that?"

"I know you." And then, after a pause: "You didn't use to stand me up."

She gazed steadily at him and it was hard to meet her eyes. He had always liked her eyes.

"Well," she said, "I certainly can't force you to have dinner with me if you don't want to. Although I don't know what you're afraid of."

Now they were both discomforted. They continued to gaze at each other for a time, and neither spoke.

"What do you hear from Sharon?" she asked him.

He felt a rise of annoyance at Sharon who had put him in the position of having to answer this question or similar ones over and over again. "Not much," he said.

She nodded absently. "Well," she said, "I have to go."

She turned to move past him. "Listen," he said hastily, "how about us going out to dinner right now?"

May waved the copy of his speech at him. "I have to go back to the office and write my story."

They were both silent.

"Ask me for tomorrow night," she said.

It made him smile. "How about tomorow night, May?"

"Okay," she said. She looked very pleased.

Lieutenant Craighead opened the door with a key. "We were lucky," he said. "Usually you have to do surveillances like this from the roof. When it rains you get soaked. When it's cold you freeze your balls off. One of the tenants always comes up and finds you there, and an hour later the whole neighborhood knows."

The three men stepped into the empty apartment in the abandoned building. Keefe saw that this had once been a luxurious place. The rooms were big, with high decorated ceilings and hardwood floors, some of them partially ripped up. The walls were stained, the window panes missing or filthy.

"Viva the South Bronx," said Rainey.

"We put the lock on the door ourselves," Craighead said. "This way, Commissioner."

The surveillance team was set up on folding chairs at the windows in the bedroom. One detective had binoculars, the other a camera with a long lens. Both men stood up as the three newcomers came into the room.

"This here is Commissioner Keefe," Craighead called out.

Keefe saw the two men glance nervously at each other. It was about eight A.M. on the morning after the PC's speech. Keefe had come here directly from home.

"Anything happening?" Craighead said.

"For the time being it's rather quiet," said one of the detectives.

"Very quiet," said his partner.

There were lunchboxes on the floor near the chairs. Both windows were open as high as they would go, but because both shades were pulled down almost all the way the room was airless and hot. The two detectives, Keefe noted, had sweated through their shirts.

"Give the Boss your binoculars," Craighead said. "Step up and take a look, Commissioner?"

Keefe sat down in one of the folding chairs and focused the binoculars. The sun was still low and threw long shadows across the junkyard. There was a high cinderblock wall all around it. The top of the wall was studded with broken glass. There was a sheet steel gate in the wall on the side below the window, and a similar gate on the opposite side that gave onto the far street. The yard occupied an entire block – wrecked cars, tires, piles of other iron junk. There were four sheds and a cinderblock building that was presumably the office. There were men working who came and went as Keefe watched.

Craighead at his shoulder said suddenly: "That's Hot Harry Hamish himself, Commissioner. Recognise him?"

Keefe moved the binoculars around.

"Next to the office," said Craighead. "The guy lighting the cigar."

"Yeah," said Keefe, "that's him." He stood up and handed the binoculars to Rainey. Rainey took the chair, worked the eyepieces briefly and began to nod his head. "That's him," he agreed.

"Well, good," said Craighead.

"All right," said Keefe. "You got a junkyard. You got Hot Harry Hamish lighting a cigar in this junkyard. What else do you have?"

"A lot, Boss," Craighead said.

"We've been sitting on this place more than a week, Commissioner," one of the detectives said.

"Night and day," said the other.

"We've got photos of cars driving into that place that don't come out," said Craighead. "We've got photos of Harry's flatbed truck coming out with noseclips on it."

"How many cars have gone in?"

"How many would you say, Fitz?" Craighead asked.

"The last three, four days, I photographed at least ten myself," said the detective named Fitz.

"Maybe he bought them," said Keefe.

"In the middle of the night, Commissioner?"

"Of course, at night you can't get pictures," said Fitz.

"At night," explained Craighead, "all we got was observations."

"It sounds like a solid case," said Rainey to Keefe.

"You bet it is," said Craighead.

Keefe was trying to think it out. "What's your next move?"

"You tell me, Boss."

Keefe shot a glance in the direction of Rainey. He was looking for help. He said: "I mean, do you bust in there, or what?"

"We could, Commissioner. We could."

Rainey came to the rescue. "You got warrants?" he said.

"We got no warrants yet." Apparently Craighead was waiting to be given orders. But this was a criminal case. Keefe was unsure what orders to give.

"Your next step, Lieutenant," said Rainey firmly, "is to get your warrants."

"This time tomorrow, I'll have my warrants,' promised Craighead to Keefe. "What then?"

Rainey said firmly: "Once you got your warrants, you bring them in and show them to me or to the Commissioner."

"And then?" persisted Craighead to Keefe.

"And then we'll see," snapped Keefe. Craighead seemed to be pressuring him to take over direction of the case. Why? He had no expertise. It made him extremely uncomfortable.

He said: "You'd hit the place about this time of day?"

"Probably. Unless you tell me different, Boss."

"How could you be sure of finding stolen cars in there?"

"They've driven five or more cars in there every night since we've been sitting on the place," said Fitz. "None of them ever came out."

"Let me know when you have your warrants," said Keefe and he turned and left the apartment.

The two cars, his own and Craighead's, were parked nose to tail two streets away. The two drivers were sitting on the fender of the lead car, smoking. Detective Murphy ran over and opened the door for Keefe, and they started back to headquarters.

In the back seat Rainey was silent.

"Will Craighead get those warrants?" Keefe said.

"I would assume so, Commissioner."

"Maybe a judge won't sign them."

"With the photos he's got, and the observations he's made, I'd be very surprised."

A plan took root in Keefe's head. When he got back to his own office he asked Rainey to step inside.

"What would you say," he began, "to the idea of inviting a busload of reporters and TV crews to watch the detectives hit that junkyard?" Being such a departure from the normal police practice of operating always in secret, such a raid would generate terrific TV time, occupy space in all the morning papers. The department would seem to be doing something about this crime that so plagued the city.

Rainey pursed his lips. "The first thing anybody here will tell you", he said cautiously, "is that it's never been done before."

"That in itself is no reason not to do it."

"It certainly could be done," said Rainey. "Why not? I don't see any reason why not. Do you?"

Did he see the possibilities as Keefe did? Or was he eager only to tell the boss what he thought he wanted to hear?

"It would raise the morale of the entire city," Keefe muttered. This was the least of the possible advantages he foresaw.

"You don't have to convince me," said Rainey.

"It would enormously enhance the prestige of the PC,

144

whether he led the raid himself or not," said Keefe, and he watched for Rainey's reaction.

"What?" said Rainey. "The PC?"

"Sure. Why not?"

Keefe supposed he shouldn't be talking this over with a sergeant, but he wanted to hear how the idea sounded.

"It would fit right in with last night's speech about chaos in the courts," conceded Rainey.

"If Craighead makes as many arrests as he says he's going to make," said Keefe, "and especially if he bags Hot Harry, the PC can point out how many times each of these men has already been arrested, but that none of them has ever done meaningful time in jail. The courts simply have not coped with this kind of crime."

"Right," said Rainey.

Keefe was much encouraged. "Okay, let's talk about the downside. What could go wrong? One of the reporters could get shot."

"That's the least of your worries," said Rainey. "Car thieves don't shoot. Any more than KGs shoot." "KGs' meant Known Gamblers. "Did you ever hear of a bookie firing shots? Narcotics-movers shoot. Truck-hijackers shoot. Car thieves do not. Why should they? The worst they're looking at is probably three months suspended."

In any case, the reporters could be held on the bus for five minutes until everything inside the junkyard was under control.

Keefe said: "Suppose the raid is a bust. This one particular day the junkyard's clean."

"You heard Craighead. A minimum of five or six cars go in there every night."

"But this one particular night, they take the night off."

"This is a thriving business, Commissioner. They can't afford to take nights off."

Keefe, leaning back in his chair, was tapping a pencil against the edge of the desk.

"There's another advantage you haven't yet mentioned, Commissioner," Rainey said. "A political advantage, you might say. The TV news will show white guys getting arrested for a change. The mayor's always making up to the black community. He'll like that idea."

It made Keefe smile. "All right, suppose the PC leads it. Am I right in supposing that it would boost his prestige with the city?"

"And with the cops," Rainey said with feeling. "Especially with the cops. A police commissioner down there with them in the streets! The cops will love it."

For Keefe this argument was the clinching one. He would present his scheme to the PC, see how he reacted to it.

The man himself, when Keefe entered his office ten minutes later, was smiling broadly. He was in shirtsleeves standing behind his chair.

"Well," he said, "that speech last night certainly attracted some notice, didn't it?" The *New York Times* had printed the entire text, and Keefe's former paper had run an editorial calling the PC a man of vision. He eyed Keefe in a fond way. "Convey my compliments to the lieutenant in the planning division."

Keefe smiled back. He saw that Egan did not need to be told who wrote the speech. "I'll do that."

Egan began to talk about baseball. The Yankees had won their sixth straight yesterday. He was so relaxed and unhurried, so obviously pleased with his deputy, that Keefe decided to bring forth all his ideas for the future.

"What would you think," he began, "about using future speeches to enunciate with the same clarity as last night your positions one by one on every major criminal justice problem?"

"Sounds good to me," said the PC, and they began to discuss the various invitations that had come in, which to accept, which topics might suit which group. Keefe meant to work up gradually to the junkyard raid. It seemed to him that the PC was in a mood to say yes to everything.

"The probable result of making such a series of speeches", Keefe said, "is that you would be seen as trying to become *de facto* leader of the law enforcement community in this city, and probably in the country as a whole."

Apparently this idea surprised the PC. He became immediately cautious, and his caution surprised Keefe.

"You would seem to be taking over the leadership," Keefe told him, "and believe me, it's yours for the taking."

But the PC did not leap at this plum.

"People would let you have it," Keefe said.

"People?"

"The papers, TV, the public in general."

"I see."

The PC moved around behind his desk, behind his chair. Chair and desk were now between him and Keefe, and he eyed him.

"The only other official of your stature," Keefe continued, "is the Director of the FBI, and he's so low-key no one even knows who he is."

The PC said nothing.

"The country cries out for a law enforcement leader," persisted Keefe. "He could be you." But the PC was no longer listening. "No wonder the system goes nowhere," Keefe added hurriedly. "There's no one in charge."

"Interesting," said the PC. He suggested Keefe put it all in a memo, and he came around from behind his desk to usher him toward the door. "Be sure to mark it confidential."

"There's one other thing I'd like to talk to you about," Keefe interjected, and he began to describe Hot Harry Hamish, the stolen car ring, Craighead's warrants. "What I'm suggesting, Commissioner, is that we bring reporters and TV crews in with us on this raid."

The PC gazed at him, so that Keefe expected him to say no to the raid. Instead he walked over to an easel on which stood a number of charts. He began to flip pages over the top until he came to the one marked "Grand Larceny – Auto".

"Here's the graph on auto thefts," he said.

"A successful raid would generate enormous publicity for the department," Keefe said.

"It would also call attention to our clearance rate. According to this graph, our clearance rate is not so hot."

"Chances are that the courts would do nothing, or next to

nothing, with the thieves we will arrest. Which, coming on the heels of your speech last night, would dramatize the failure of the courts to support this department."

The PC threw a few more sheets over the top of the easel, finally revealing the chart marked "Robbery".

"This is the crime I wish we could do something about."

Keefe found himself speaking too fast. "I was even going to suggest that you lead this raid yourself."

The PC studied him for a moment, then went back and again stood behind his chair behind his desk. Watching him, Keefe spoke of the risks of the proposed junkyard raid. He explained what they were, how he had examined and re-examined them, how minimal they appeared. But it was precisely this risk factor, he concluded, which assured a great triumph for the PC if the raid were successful.

Leaning over his desk, the PC consulted his calendar. "I see that I'm not available tomorrow."

"We could put it off till the next day," Keefe said.

The PC tapped his desk calendar with his forefinger. "I'm tied up the next day too."

"We can drop the whole idea. The detectives can make their arrests in private. We can send out a press release."

His voice had become sharp with disappointment, but the PC looked across at him and smiled. "No point in losing the value of all the good work you've done so far. You don't need me. You lead it. It will be good experience for you."

"Me?"

"You go ahead with it."

"But –"

"Sounds good to me."

Before he could protest further, Keefe found himself ushered from the room.

When Keefe had gone out Egan returned to his desk. He had visited the hospital that morning on the way into headquarters. John Gaffney had seemed a little better. He might last another month, perhaps several. Egan needed a solid law enforcement professional in John's job, a man with a big reputation, a man who thought as he did and could give him the support he needed. While waiting, he had decided this morning, it was best for him to pull back a bit. He was too vulnerable. He counted himself a political realist. He certainly could not risk a junkyard raid that might misfire, that might cause criticism even if successful.

He could not risk the run of speeches Keefe proposed either. He was appalled at Keefe's lack of delicacy. Take over the leadership, indeed. Such things had to seem to happen absolutely spontaneously, especially in an area as sensitive as the police. They could not be openly discussed beforehand. If they were, then you simply couldn't do it. Obviously Keefe did not see the matter as delicate. If he had, he would never have presented it so blatantly. He had probably discussed it with other people already. The mayor, the district attorneys would hear about it and would be furious, and they were elected officials, whereas he was only an appointed one. Egan would seem to be setting himself up independently of them. The papers might present him as an overly-ambitious police chief, a menace to the civil rights of everybody. A run of speeches was out of the question.

On the other hand, it was in Egan's interest, as he waited to appoint a new First Deputy, to build up Keefe's stature both within the city and within the department. He himself would seem more formidable as a result. Tomorrow's raid might accomplish this, if it succeeded. He saw no reason why it shouldn't.

But if it failed? It was Keefe's case. He had instigated it. Let him take the responsibility for it. Life was tough and no one got a free ride. It was sink or swim for everybody.

Keefe in his confusion went back downstairs. He moved in through his outer desks with a grim look on his face. Sergeant Rainey immediately stood up and followed him into his private office.

"What did he say, Commissioner?"

"Close the door."

Rainey did so.

"He thinks I should lead the raid, not him."

Rainey said nothing.

"If it flops," muttered Keefe, "if somebody's going to look

bad, he wants that somebody to be me." It seemed to him that the PC feared it would flop, or expected it to. "Let's go over it again. What are the chances of failure?"

Rainey shook his head. "Craighead isn't going to let that happen."

Keefe realized that Rainey too seemed to want the raid to proceed. Why?

"Whether the PC leads it or you do is immaterial to Craighead," said Rainey encouragingly. "Either one of you as he sees it can make or break his career."

"Once the raid starts Craighead isn't going to be able to control what happens."

"What are you going to do, Commissioner?"

Keefe was silent.

"You don't have much time to decide."

"I don't know yet," Keefe snapped.

"Right," said Rainey.

"I'm sorry," said Keefe. "Let me think about it."

He was left alone at his desk. If shots were fired he would be criticized for risking the lives of the reporters and TV crews even if they were still confined to the bus outside the yard. Or the detectives might uncover so little evidence that the raid would look ridiculous. It and Keefe would be derided by the media. He could be accused of playing at the role of cop, of seeking personal publicity.

The risks were truly amazing. On the other hand, it was his case. It was a good strong case. It would glorify the auto squad detectives who ought to be given their chance in the limelight, and –

The phone rang. It was Lieutenant Craighead to say he had secured his warrants. "I await your pleasure, Commissioner."

"What do you mean, you await my pleasure? Forget about me. How would you normally handle this?"

Craighead sounded slightly taken aback. "Well, I'd hit the place. And quick. You keep the place under surveillance too long, you're liable to blow the case."

To take over the raid, or not? Keefe had still not decided. "Make plans to hit the place tomorrow morning," he ordered brusquely. "I'll get back to you."

He began to study an inspections division report about wastage and inefficiency in the traffic division. Inspections audits were the responsibility of the First Deputy Commissioner. The PC had asked Keefe to take a look at this one and make recommendations. The report's findings were appalling. The midtown traffic squad still functioned according to a plan established eleven years previously, duplicating the work of meter maids and traffic wardens who had since been hired by the Department of Transportation. In Brooklyn certain school crossings were still manned by details of cops five years after the school had closed.

Keefe called for Sergeant Rainey. "All right," he told him, "reach out for Lieutenant Craighead. Get him in here."

An hour later Craighead stood in front of Keefe's desk. He was several years older than Keefe, who eyed him steadily for a moment. "You have the warrants?"

Craighead handed them across. They looked all right to Keefe but then he wasn't sure what warrants looked like.

"Sergeant," he said and held them out to Rainey who stood silently to one side. After nodding his head, Rainey handed them back to Craighead.

Keefe said: "You're going to hit that junkyard in the morning, is that correct?"

"If you say so, Commissioner."

Keefe still hesitated. Finally he said: "What would you think if we invite the press and TV crews to come along on this raid?"

It took Craighead a long time to answer. "Well, Commissioner, I'd say it's never been done before."

And he waited. If he had any professional opinion he was keeping it to himself. At the same time he seemed to be watching Keefe carefully. You don't ask him, Keefe advised himself, you tell him.

"You'll hit that junkyard at eight-thirty A.M. tomorrow. Is that the optimum time? All right then. Now let's work out the details."

Craighead unrolled his crude drawings across Keefe's desk and, as the three men leaned over them, pointed out where the detectives would approach. The bus containing the press and TV crews would follow along this street here, and would enter through this gate here.

"I'll need additional men, Boss," Craighead said as he rerolled his drawings. "For safety's sake."

"Safety's sake? I understood there was no danger."

"Well," said Craighead, "I've hit a dozen of these junkyards and never been shot at yet. But with that many journalists we don't want to take no chances."

"Get more men," said Keefe.

Craighead's maps were under his arm. "Can I have that in writing, Boss?"

Keefe turned to Sergeant Rainey. "Have Captain Fallon type up a 49 and I'll sign it."

A sharp glance came his way from Rainey, but Keefe ignored it. Fallon, a captain, was about to learn from a subordinate that plans had been hatched behind his back. It was a serious breach of protocol, of which Keefe was at least half aware. Fallon would do what he was told, and Keefe was not interested in protocol.

Rainey and Craighead went out. Through his open door, Keefe heard them dictating the letter to Fallon, who apparently typed it out himself. A few minutes later all three men trooped back in. Fallon, looking petulant, placed the paper in front of Keefe who attached his signature and handed it across to Craighead, saying: "Go make your dispositions."

Rainey and Craighead again left the office, but not Fallon.

"May I ask, Commissioner, why I wasn't informed about this?"

Keefe looked up in surprise.

"I have to learn about it from a sergeant in my command, Commissioner. Do you realize how that looks? Do you realize what the men must be saying?" Fallon looked upset enough to cry.

"I'm sorry, Captain. I didn't mean to offend you."

"My authority is totally undermined."

"No, it's not."

"Either I'm running this office, or I'm not running this office."

Keefe began to realize the enormity, by police department standards, of what he had done. "You're a captain. Of course you're running this office."

"But that's not how it looks, Commissioner, don't you see?"

Keefe held down a rising flood of impatience. "I'm new here," he said. "I don't always know how things are supposed to work. You have to make allowances for me. I think I can promise that it won't happen again." He was annoyed at himself. He sounded like a schoolboy. "Do you want to take part in the raid yourself?" he said to Fallon.

"Now?" said Fallon. "It's out of the question. It would be even worse now."

Rising from his desk Keefe ushered Fallon towards the door. The interview was over. But Fallon had a few more points to make or, rather, he wished to reiterate old ones, so that Keefe almost admired him for a moment. This was more spunk than the man had shown since Keefe's appointment to the job.

On leaving Keefe's office, Lieutenant Craighead went straight to Chief of Detectives Gold to whom he showed the order Keefe had just signed.

"So what should I do, Chief?"

After a few seconds of looking into Gold's baleful stare, Craighead dropped his eyes.

"If I was a lieutenant," said Gold, "and a deputy commissioner told me to do something, I'd do it."

"Right, Chief."

"Until such time as any such orders are countermanded."

If this remark confused Craighead, it was meant to. "Do I make myself clear?" said Gold.

"Perfectly clear, Chief."

Gold gave the order assigning additional men to Craighead, and dismissed him. Then for about five minutes he sat at his desk in silence. If the raid were allowed to proceed, and if it succeeded, then Keefe's stature within the department would be enhanced. His influence over the PC, which seemed to Gold already strong, would be enhanced also. If the raid made the TV news shows and made headlines, which Gold thought it would, then Keefe might even begin to loom as a personage to the city at large.

All of which, it seemed to Gold, would weaken his own standing. He got up from his desk and went to see Chief of Operations Kilcoyne. He virtually barged in on the higher ranking man, but then Gold no longer reported to Kilcoyne. They were virtual equals. He dropped Keefe's order onto Kilcoyne's desk and waited.

Kilcoyne was in shirt sleeves. He read the order and looked up. "What does this mean, Al?"

But his face had darkened, and Gold saw that he understood what it meant.

"I think you should have a talk with him, Chief," Gold said. He had not called him Dennis since both of them were two-star chiefs working in different boroughs more than five years ago.

Kilcoyne stood up. He was tightening his tie. "We'll go up there together, Al."

Gold shook his head. "Call him up on the phone, Chief. Tell him to come down here."

"He's a deputy commissioner, Al."

"He'll come."

Kilcoyne thought about it. He sat down again. Picking up his phone he asked to be put through to Keefe, and the connection was made.

"I wonder if you and I could have a talk, Commissioner?" Kilcoyne said. "I have Chief Gold with me."

Gold studied his fingernails.

"Well, Commissioner, I don't like to talk over the phone," Kilcoyne's voice, Gold thought, lacked authority. His words were punctuated by bits of nervous laughter. "You never know who might be listening, wouldn't you say?"

Gold had turned his chair and was staring out the window.

"He's coming," said Kilcoyne, when he had hung up. To Gold there seemed to be a note of pride in his voice.

Kilcoyne got to his feet and moved towards the coat tree. Taking his jacket off the hanger, he rubbed his sleeve over the four stars on each shoulder, as if shining them up. He gave Gold a wink as he did it. He was buttoning the jacket up the front as Keefe came in.

"Good of you to come down to my office, Phil."

Gold thought calling Keefe by his first name was a good touch. But then in the next sentence Kilcoyne ruined it. "By rights I probably should have gone to yours."

"I was on my way out anyway," Keefe said. "Just as easy for me to drop by."

Kilcoyne looked over at Gold. They exchanged what the Chief of Operations no doubt thought were meaningful glances. The rank thing seemed to have gone over Keefe's head.

"I've heard," began Kilcoyne hesitantly, "that you're planning to bring the media along on a stolen car raid tomorrow morning."

"That's right." Keefe looked surprised.

"Those are Chief Gold's detectives you're using so I thought Chief Gold should be present for this talk."

"What seems to be the trouble?" said Keefe, and it appeared to Gold he had become suddenly guarded, and much more alert.

"Far be it from me to attempt to overrule a deputy commissioner," said Kilcoyne, with what Gold considered excessive cordiality. "I can't, as a matter of fact. All I can do is talk the situation over with you. Raise some of my doubts. For instance, are you sure that this is such a good idea?"

"I don't see anything wrong with it."

To Gold, Keefe seemed sure of himself. Too sure.

"We're not bringing the newsmen into any sort of physical danger," said Keefe. "We're merely giving them a chance to watch some of our detectives in action in a positive way."

"The members of the press," said Kilcoyne, "have never been friends of this department, Phil. I suppose you realize that." He was leaning back in his chair with both hands clasped behind his white head, the perfect counterfeit of self-confidence. To Keefe he perhaps looked relaxed. To Gold, who knew him better, he looked like a man who was suddenly not sure he had chosen the right issue to take a

155

stand on, or the right moment, or the right opponent.

"The press is only out looking for dirt," he continued. "They're only looking for a cop who's doing something he shouldn't be doing."

"Exactly," responded Keefe. "Tomorrow they'll watch some cops doing what they should be doing. We're going to bust in on one of the biggest car thieves in the city and we're going to take him. If all that turns up on tomorrow night's newscasts it seems to me the department will have profited."

In the course of this speech Keefe had become, it seemed to Gold, more and more confident, and also more annoyed. Who was Kilcoyne to question his judgment?

"But will the raid turn out as you say?" said Kilcoyne. To Gold he seemed ever more uncertain. "That's what I ask myself, Phil. We've never done anything like this before. It could backfire."

"Backfire?"

Kilcoyne gave an approximation of his normal loud laugh. It sounded to Gold more like a dog barking. "Suppose there is a shooting?" Kilcoyne said. "Suppose the raid is a failure? Suppose the media decides to criticize you for this... this innovation."

Kilcoyne fell silent and for a moment Keefe was silent too. These deputy commissioners are all alike, Gold thought. They don't care about the department. They only care about themselves. They're out to make reputations at the department's expense.

"Among other things," Kilcoyne continued, "you'll be making media heroes out of these hoodlums. Have you thought about that?"

Now Keefe displayed impatience. "As a matter of fact, Chief, that idea never entered my head. I don't see how a car thief in handcuffs can appear to the country at large to be a hero."

Keefe turned suddenly to Gold. "How about you, Chief? Craighead and the others are your men. What are your feelings?"

Gold decided he had seen enough. He knew now how this interview would end, and the time had come to distance himself as much as possible from the losing side. "I'm just listening," he said. "Trying to learn something. That's what detectives do. They listen." But he had best reassure Kilcoyne as well. "I do think," he added, "that Chief Kilcoyne has made some good points."

It was less than solid support, and Kilcoyne perhaps realized it. When he turned back to Keefe, his mouth seemed tighter than before. "I remember us having lunch together, Phil, the day you joined the department. I gave you some advice, do you remember? The police are despised by the general public. You can't change that. That's just the way it is." He hesitated. Perhaps he was coming to terms still again with the public perception of policemen, himself among them. "What people think of us can't be changed. Society can't be changed, and our role can't be changed. Our role is unpopular. Now, you come in here, and you have new ideas, and some of them are good ones, I'm sure. What I'm not sure of is that this particular idea is a good one."

Keefe's impatience showed more strongly. "If policemen are despised it's because they always attempt to operate in secret. People don't know what the police are doing, and therefore they're afraid. What this department needs is to have a few windows thrown open. We work for the people of this city. They have a right to know what we're doing. If they knew who cops were and what they did, maybe they wouldn't despise them so much."

Kilcoyne was in the position of a man trying to hold a line that had already been stormed. "Let me reiterate some of my arguments, Phil, pointing out the difficulties as I see them –"

But Keefe interrupted him. "I've talked it over with the PC. The PC is in favor."

For a moment Kilcoyne and Keefe merely stared at each other. Gold, who sat to one side, was again examining his fingernails.

Then Kilcoyne said: "Oh, I see. Well, if the PC is in favor, then I'm all for it. I'm sure Chief Gold is too. Isn't that right, Al?"

But Gold said nothing.

Keefe left the office. Behind him Kilcoyne and Gold sat in silence. Kilcoyne had just further weakened his stature within the department, Gold believed. How many more such defeats could he take? One or two more, Gold thought, and he would certainly put his papers in. Keefe, on the other hand, had not been weakened at all. Perhaps the raid itself, if something unforeseen happened, would take care of that. He would wait and see.

Gold realized that Kilcoyne was staring at him with what he read as a beaten look on his face. He was practically pleading for support; but Gold was careful to continue to study his hands.

Keefe meanwhile was on his way uptown where he would pick up May Fondren for dinner. By then it was past seven, so he would be a bit late. He had been looking forward to this date all day.

Twelve

SHARON WAS SOMEWHERE ABOVE THIRTY THOUSAND feet, somewhere above probably Ohio. She was coming east at six hundred miles an hour, and she had problems. One of them was sitting next to her, and the other waited ahead, and in the hour or so before the plane landed she was trying to decide what to do about both of them.

She was riding first class, compliments of the network. She had her seat back almost to the horizontal, leg rest up, and she was wearing a black-out mask. In total darkness under the small airline blanket, she was day-dreaming about Keefe. Tonight might be very nice, but he had not called her for a while. When she got there he might not be glad to see her. This morning she had been unable to warn him she was coming. He might not be home. Or he might be with some other woman.

As for her problem close at hand, it was in fact a hand, and was more pressing. It was pressing on her thigh, small insistent squeezes under her blanket. It belonged to a

158

director named James DeForest, and although she knew various ways of coping with this sort of thing still DeForest was not a man she wanted to embarrass, much less offend.

This morning the network's executive vice-president for daytime programming had come on the set and drawn her to one side. Good news. Everyone wanted her in the show on a permanent basis. As a result they were asking her to fly to New York at once, that very day. A film crew was already at work there filming street scenes and other establishment shots. Also needed, now that Sharon was to appear regularly, were shots of her entering and leaving buildings, walking in Central Park, standing in front of landmarks – this footage too could be edited in as needed. It was Wednesday. If she could get to New York that night she could connect with the crew tomorrow and Friday. It would all be wrapped up by Friday night, and she could fly back in time to be on the set Monday morning. The executive was apologetic about the rush.

Although Sharon was willing enough to go to New York – she might be with Keefe within hours – nonetheless it was bad precedent to let herself be pushed around. She was being rushed to New York to save the network money. The crew would not have to be held over into next week. If she was being inconvenienced to save money, then she ought to get some of that money.

She had been thinking so hard about protecting her interests that she felt very little elation about the proposed trip. She kept her face a blank and negotiated hard. Approval as an actress meant approval of the physical her, of the way she moved and talked and wore clothes. It meant approval of her voice, her smile, her eyes and no young woman, no human being, is ever self-assured enough not to be gratified by such approval, not even Sharon, who had been accustomed to turning men's heads for a long time. Nonetheless, actresses came and went. They had no security and short careers. And so she made it clear that she intended to keep her title as producer, and the job itself as well; she believed she could do this if furnished one additional secretary, meaning two in all.

The executive vice-president agreed provisionally. And he went on trying to persuade her to make the trip. At last, as if reluctantly, she said she would go.

As soon as he had departed, she rushed back to her office where she spoke to her agent by phone. She outlined the contract she was hoping for.

By the time she could call Keefe it was lunch time in New York and he was out. She decided she would phone him again from her apartment on the way to the airport.

A limousine had been called. When she came out of the studio it was standing at the curb, and as she ducked into it she landed almost in DeForest's lap.

He was to accompany her to New York, it seemed, which no one had mentioned.

DeForest was quite young for a director, about her age, and he was about her size, meaning short for a man. On the set he had a kind of boisterous charm and had often made her laugh. He had been with the show for about two months, had pursued Sharon from the first day, and for a short time she had allowed herself to become involved with him. It made her miss Keefe. Almost at once she had asked herself: what did I do that for? And she had broken it off.

The limousine did not take Sharon directly home. It stopped at DeForest's place first.

"Want to come on up?" he said as he got out of the car, and he gave her an elaborate, comical leer.

Sharon smiled but declined. She had no intention of starting that up again. "I'd better get some work done while I'm waiting," she said, and opened the briefcase on her lap.

He was gone rather a long time. By the time he came out time was short. When they reached her apartment she ran inside and began throwing things into a bag. She was extremely irritated both at DeForest and at the network.

The limousine's horn had begun honking outside. She phoned Keefe, was put on hold by some sergeant, and she stood beside the bed waiting while the horn went on honking. Finally she slammed the phone down. I'll call him from the airport, she told herself, and rushed outside. She was sweating inside her dress, and she was furious.

She did not have time to phone Keefe from the airport. They almost missed the plane.

Once aloft, caviar and champagne were served. It was then that DeForest made his offer. He would become her mentor. He would teach her all she needed to know about becoming an actress, a real actress who would be in demand by all the big directors, a star.

This was no doubt only brash talk. Still, she was pleased to entertain thoughts of herself as famous.

DeForest began talking about minimalist acting. On film one could lift an eyebrow an eighth of an inch and convey extraordinary emotion. Tricks were what Sharon would have to learn. She was listening carefully.

"Let's have dinner together tonight," DeForest said. He looked boyish and sincere, obviously hopeful that their affair could be started up again. It was a problem. She wanted to encourage him professionally but not personally. She certainly didn't want to offend him.

"Oh, I can't tonight," she said.

"Tomorrow then."

Her thoughts began to form, but they were too slow. Maybe Keefe didn't want to see her. For all she knew their relationship was over. She would rather dine with DeForest than alone, whatever the ultimate consequences.

DeForest said: "I think you better slow down on the champagne, doll."

She did not like to be called doll. Looking him straight in the eye, she drained her glass.

She thought of her father, who was an associate professor of history at the University of Virginia, and who did not approve of her lifestyle. Already she was earning more money per year than he had ever earned in his life, and she wasn't thirty yet.

The champagne, or DeForest, had made her drowsy. She was tired of this ride. She wanted to think about Keefe, and it was at this point that she had asked the stewardess for the blanket and eyemask. Blindfolded, she lay back almost at the horizontal, ignoring DeForest, thinking about tonight. Her thoughts were not really sexual. She wanted to stand

and be hugged by someone taller than she was. She wanted to rest her head on a man's bare chest. She wanted to sleep all night in the same bed with someone and if she woke in the night she wanted to slide her foot across until it touched his foot. She wanted to wake up in the morning, and he would be there. Or else he would be in the kitchen making the coffee. She wanted to watch him shave. She wanted to lunch with him, walk the streets with him. She wanted to sense that whatever else he might be doing, he also loved her.

Other women, earlier women, had felt the same, she realized, and had had a word to describe it: marriage.

Did she then want to be married? The answer, she believed, was no. She was not yet ready to give up the independence she had worked so hard for. Her career was not yet solidly established. She could not drop everything and sit home and have babies. Some of her friends from college had them, and sometimes, visiting them, she had felt a bit envious; not too much. Still, she'd like to have babies some day, one at least. However it was difficult to believe it could happen to her. She couldn't really believe in her belly all swollen out, in a baby coming out of her. And suppose she didn't love it after it was born? People said all women did, but they didn't. Plenty of babies were abandoned on doorsteps, or stuffed into garbage cans. If she didn't love it her career would be over anyway, and before long she would hate the baby's father, even Keefe, she knew that well enough. This thought made her want to cry. They serve too much champagne on these planes, she thought.

She became conscious of the weight of the hand on her thigh under the blanket. How did it get there?

She went deeper into her reverie, enjoying a weekend in New York with Keefe, and she did not wish to be disturbed by DeForest's hand. She really liked Keefe an awful lot. It was the first relationship she'd ever had in which they never fought. In the others she and the guy had fought constantly, as if the only closeness came from making up afterwards. With Keefe there was a sharp word from time to time, but no making up to do at all. Instead there was this terrific closeness.

Keefe was also the first man she had ever lived with, which perhaps had something to do with it. Life was all so confusing. Unlike television, nothing was written down in scripts. No one held up cue cards to tell you what to say and do. You had to figure it out for yourself. Her parents had been no help to her. She lived in a different world from theirs. The rules had all been changed. For young people like herself, it sometimes seemed that somebody had taken down all the street signs. They were being made to find their own way without any directions.

The hand on her thigh had begun its insistent, almost imperceptible pressures. Now it's going to start to move, she thought. I'm going to have to do something about it.

Maybe she was in love with Keefe, really deeply in love, the type of love whole lives could be based upon. But how could she be sure? What she really wanted was someone to give her some answers. There had been moments of intense emotion during which she had looked to Keefe to make decisions for both of them. If he had ever said: let's get married, she might have done it. But he never had, the moment always passed, and each time she felt a coldness come over her entire body. It was like putting on a nylon slip in the early morning in an icy cold room. It seemed almost to freeze her to the spot.

When she agreed to move to California, it was because she did not know what else to do. He might have stopped her. She might have stopped herself. She thought they would phone each other every night. She had never seen California as an end to their relationship. But perhaps he had. She would know tonight.

The hand on her thigh was three or four inches above her knee, and advancing, and she felt suddenly so upset, so suddenly totally alone, that she almost did or said something rash. Instead she controlled her rage, pressed the button to straighten her seat, threw off the sleep mask and blanket and got to her feet. It took her a moment to find her handbag. She marched in the direction of the first class lavatory without looking back.

Keefe had agreed to pick up May outside the paper. She was

standing on the sidewalk wearing a white linen skirt and a green silk blouse. He kissed her on the cheek, then climbed into the back seat of the police car beside her.

He took her to the Cote Basque for dinner and at first was ill at ease. They talked about what she called his "foray into our morgue files." Seymour Becker had sent around a memo that emphasised the adversarial relationship between the press and government, she said. Henceforth all government officials were to be denied access to the physical plant of the paper unless accompanied by a staff member throughout.

"The memo did not mention you by name, darling," May said.

"That's nice."

They were sitting side by side on a banquette looking out over the dining room at the other patrons, and Keefe, though he knew it would be very expensive, ordered champagne.

"When we were in Paris," May said, "you hated champagne."

"And you hated French coffee."

They knew things about each other more intimate still, and the shy smiles they turned on each other were followed by a great shift in emotion.

"You went to India."

"I thought it would only be for a couple of weeks."

"You did good stories from there."

"By the time I got back to Paris you were in Lebanon."

"We kept missing connections all the way around."

The waiter brought the champagne, popped the cork and poured an inch into Keefe's flute. It was cold with a smoky, flinty taste, and he nodded for both glasses to be filled.

"What are we celebrating?" she said when the waiter had departed. But she looked happy.

"Being together again." Sharon had been gone a long time, and he felt his whole body stirring.

"It's good champagne."

Her hand was on the banquette between them. He put his own hand on top of it. Then the captain handed out menus, and the moment passed.

164

Peering at her menu, May said: "What's this mysterious press conference for tomorrow at dawn?"

"So you know about that too."

"There are no secrets –"

"– in newsrooms," he finished. There seemed no reason not to tell her about the raid. He was thinking of her not as a reporter but as a woman he had been in love with once. He was making one mistake after another today, but none of them felt like mistakes as he made them.

"The real reason for the secrecy is not security, it's to make sure the editors assign reporters. They don't know what it is. It could be anything. They have no choice."

For a moment May eyed him speculatively, "You better not let Becker hear you talk like that."

Keefe was relaxed. He studied May's profile. Their time in Paris had been the first foreign assignment for them both. They had shared the excitement not only of each other but of the old world as seen with new eyes.

"Does this restaurant remind you of anywhere?" Keefe said.

"That one in Paris where the woman threw her desert in the man's face."

They both laughed.

"What I remember most about Paris was how we could never find a taxi at six o'clock outside the Bureau."

"That's not what you remember most," May said.

They ate their dinner and drank their champagne, and talked about Keefe's future in journalism. "I assume there's no chance of my getting back on the paper?"

"Not while Becker's there. Do you care?"

He shook his head. "Not at the moment."

"I never understood why you took this police job."

"It's complicated."

"I'd really like to know."

So he tried to tell her. The PC was a good man, he said, a man who could make an enormous impact on law enforcement in New York and in the nation as a whole. Keefe was in a position to help him do it.

"He's your candidate," May interrupted.

Keefe frowned. "He's not a politician."

"You're not the first man to fall in love with his candidate."

"I'm not in love with him."

"If he goes onward and upward, you go with him."

"I'm not a cop. I'm there for a short time to do what I can to help. In a year or two I'll be somewhere else." The PC stood for something noble, he added, trying to convince her. So did the department itself. The fight against crime was a fight against evil. To give a year or two of his life to such a fight seemed to him worthwhile.

May gave him a fond smile. "You always were a choirboy."

"It's also a lot of fun. Every day some crazy thing happens. Some are absolutely fantastic. The police barriers are up, it's a crime scene, and I'm inside it and the reporters are outside. I'm seeing things and learning things that other reporters never even get close to."

"Now you're making me jealous," said May.

The waiter came and refilled their glasses.

"Is it really finished between you and Sharon?"

"Well, she's moved to California."

Her eyes came up. "Permanently?"

Keefe turned the stem of his glass. "It certainly seems permanent to me."

"I see," said May, and she smiled.

Keefe raised his champagne: "Here's to Seymour Becker, who won't be there forever."

"I can think of a nicer toast than that."

As soon as the plane landed Sharon hurried inside the terminal to a telephone where she dialed Keefe's apartment. There was no answer. Suddenly unsure of herself, she put down the receiver. She might have phoned his office – she knew he had men on duty around the clock. But she hated talking to those cops. No one had ever taught them how to answer a telephone properly. They were gruff and scarcely polite. She would have to explain who she was, and even then they might not tell her anything.

Besides that, DeForest was standing at her elbow, waiting impatiently, close enough to hear.

She turned away from the wall phones and went down the stairs to the baggage retrieval area. A number of limousine drivers waited, holding identifying placards against their chests. She located her own driver easily enough, but the placard he was holding bore DeForest's name, not hers, which infuriated her. She was the one this trip had been laid on for, not him; he had tagged along at the last moment, probably just to annoy her.

"Let's go," he said, when they had their bags.

"I have to make another call first."

"Make it at the hotel."

"No," she snapped, and stepped across the hall to a wall phone.

The bell rang a long time in Keefe's empty flat before she hung up.

In the limousine she tried to decide what to do. The network had reserved a room at the Sherry Netherland. She could check in there, and phone Keefe again.

Or she could go directly to their apartment – his apartment – for she still had her key. Or would this be unwise?

"Sure you won't have dinner with me?" asked DeForest beside her. It was past eight P.M. New York time.

If she went to the hotel she'd have to fend this guy off all night. She would go directly to Keefe's apartment, and take her chances when she got there.

The limousine crossed into Manhattan over the cast iron Fifty-Ninth Street Bridge. When they came to Keefe's street Sharon asked to be put down at the corner. She waited until the limousine had turned towards Fifth Avenue, then stepped into a phone booth. Again there was no answer. His house was half way down the side street. She walked along under the trees carrying her small bag, feeling sweaty and dirty after more than five hours on an airplane. When she came to the building, she stood looking up. No lights showed in the top floor windows. I'll just go in and look around, she told herself. Then I'll decide.

As soon as she had let herself into the apartment she was almost overcome by the sense of being home. It still looked the same, smelled the same. She set her bag down by the door, and proceeded through the rooms, looking, sniffing. She looked through the drawers where her own clothes had once lain, then through the closets. She found no sign that any woman had entered the apartment in her absence. She even went into the bathroom and looked through the medicine closet.

She carried her bag into the living room, sat down on the sofa and tried to decide what to do. She was home, but she was not home. In a certain sense she was an intruder. She could not, for instance, merely climb into bed and fall asleep and wait until Keefe came home. She was not his wife. She had no such right.

She went into the kitchen and found the sink full of dirty dishes. I can wash his dishes for him, she thought, and began to do it. She scrubbed the sink out with powder, dried her hands and stood looking around. It was nearly ten P.M. and he still wasn't home. That meant he was out with someone, most likely, perhaps with another woman. Would he bring her home?

She thought she knew Keefe. He was not capable of picking up some floozie. He'd have to fall in love with a woman before he brought her home, and there hadn't been time for that yet. She did not think so. She was almost sure of it.

She was feeling intensely fond of him, but perhaps she should go. She could leave a note under the telephone on the small table. He'd see it as soon as he came in. She could go to the hotel, take a shower and wait for him to call.

She realized she was also quite hungry. Postponing a decision, she went back into the kitchen and peered into the fridge. She found English muffins, cheese and a bottle of beer. She toasted the muffins, spread them with cheese, sat at the kitchen table and ate them and drank the beer.

She went to the telephone and dialed his office. The duty sergeant came on. There were several of these men and they alternated. On the telephone they all sounded alike, not

168

only ill-mannered, but also defensive. What did they have to be defensive about? It was only a telephone. This one either didn't know where Keefe was or wouldn't tell her.

Sharon hung up. The more she waited the more sticky and dirty her clothes felt on her, the more she longed for a shower. Finally she wrote on a piece of notepaper: *Guess who's taking a shower in your bathroom?* She hung this from the table under the telephone and went into the bedroom and got undressed. Naked, she walked around the apartment picking up magazines and putting them down again. But this got her nowhere. She went into the bathroom where she stood in the shower a long time washing all that mileage off her flesh. She even debated washing her hair, but she'd washed it only last night; it was okay, and besides, she hated going to bed with wet hair.

She turned the water off, towelled her body, dried her ears, wrapped the towel around herself and stepped out into the bedroom again. She picked up her wristwatch. By now it was past eleven. Where could he be? More importantly, what should she do?

Still wrapped in the towel, she walked out into the foyer and retrieved her note. She could write another one and scotchtape it to the door outside, giving him ample warning in the unlikely event that he did bring someone home.

Or she could turn the television on loudly. He'd hear it in the hallway. But that might scare him. He might imagine he'd been burgled. When you lived in New York you had thoughts like that.

If she really intended to wait here till Keefe came home, certainly she should get dressed again, just in case.

She was about to return to the bedroom to put on her clothes when she heard footsteps in the corridor. Too many footsteps. They were outside in the corridor. Approaching this very door. She was standing in the foyer six feet from the door, wet feet half-buried in the carpet, hand on the telephone table.

The key turned in the lock, and she found herself frozen there, though she wanted to run. The door was pushed inward. She stood watching Keefe and May Fondren, whom she recognized. Keefe had inserted the key and pushed the door open with one hand. The other was behind May Fondren's head. They were framed by the doorway. The kiss went on and on.

They became aware of Sharon virtually simultaneously. Both looked astonished. Keefe's astonishment even seemed to turn into delight. That was the expression around his eyes, or so Sharon chose to think. As for May, her mouth set into a line like a suture. Without a word she spun about and started back down the hall.

Keefe's attention was immediately divided. He still had not spoken. He turned from May's retreating figure back to Sharon. May's footsteps could be heard descending the stairs.

"I'll be right back," said Keefe, and he turned and hurried after her.

Sharon closed the door. In the bathroom she hung the towel on the rack, then stepped out to the bed and put her stale clothes back on again. When she was dressed she walked out into the foyer, placed her key beside the telephone and, carrying her overnight suitcase, slammed the door behind her.

Keefe meanwhile had run down the stairs. He stood with May in the street trying to flag down a cab.

"Really, Phil."

"I'm terribly sorry. I had no idea she was there."

"You told me it was over."

"I thought it was over."

"But she's waiting for you wearing only a towel, Phil."

He said nothing.

"You had to tell one of us to leave," said May. "You couldn't tell her. She was wearing only a towel, for God's sake."

A cab pulled to a stop, and May wrenched open the door. "I'm sorry," Keefe said. "Please forgive me."

"Certain things, my dear, are not forgivable."

The cab door slammed, and Keefe watched the tail lights diminish up the avenue.

Sharon and Keefe met face to face in the middle of the staircase between the second and third floors. She was on her way down. He was rushing up the other way. He said: "Where do you think you're going?"

"To my hotel."

"No, you're not."

"Please get out of my way." He was standing two steps below her with his hands on her shoulders and she could not get past. "What did you do with your girlfriend?" she said.

"I put her in a cab."

"You admit she's your girlfriend? How long was I in California? You didn't wait very long, did you? Couldn't you wait any longer?"

"She's not my girlfriend. Why didn't you tell me you were coming?"

"I seem to have ruined your evening," Sharon said. "I'm so sorry. I'm really so sorry. You bet I am."

"Come back upstairs with me."

"I'm going to my hotel." Again she tried to move past him, but he grabbed the overnight case out of her hand and started up the stairs with it.

"Give me that," she said.

"No."

He kept climbing the steps. She climbed after him. "Give me back my suitcase."

"No."

At the door to his flat she attempted to yank the bag away from him. He held on to the handle, and with his other hand opened the door. Then he pushed Sharon inside and slammed the door behind them. "Will you please sit down for a minute," he said.

She walked into the living room, sat on the sofa and looked at him with her face set like stone.

"You're being unreasonable," he said.

She looked at him.

"I took her out to dinner," Keefe said. "I told you over the

171

phone that I had to take her out to dinner."

"Can I have my suitcase back and go now?"

"No, you can't."

"You were bringing her up here to dinner. Is that it? A little midnight dinner."

"We were going to make coffee."

"Oh, I see."

Keefe was pacing back and forth in front of her.

"How many times have you seen her since I've been gone?"

"Just this once."

"Only once. You certainly work fast, don't you? Or is she an old flame? Is that it? Are you just renewing an old acquaintanceship?"

Keefe said nothing.

"Did you have a previous affair with her? I asked you that once before, if I remember correctly. I don't particularly care one way or the other, but you assured me you didn't. So if you really did, that makes you a liar. Don't lie to me this time, please."

"I don't have to answer that question," he said, "and I won't." But he looked miserable.

Sharon stood up. "Then there's nothing further to talk about, is there? May I have my suitcase back?"

Keefe said: "I'll answer your question in the morning when you calm down."

"What makes you think I'll be here in the morning?" In fact she was calming down already. She even felt a little ashamed of herself. What had brought on this sudden jealous rage? She had behaved like some housewife out of the sixties. It was a type of sexual jealousy that had no place in the life of modern young people. In fact, it should not even exist. "If I stay," Sharon said, "it's only because it's dangerous walking through the streets of this city at this hour alone. Is that understood?"

"Sure," Keefe said. He nodded glumly.

Sharon walked over and turned on the TV set. Then she sat on the couch watching with apparent interest whatever show had appeared on the screen. After a moment, Keefe picked up the suitcase and carried it into the bedroom. She heard the noise of hangers in the closet, heard him get undressed. She heard him brush his teeth. When he came out into the living room again, he was wearing pyjamas. "Are you coming to bed, or not?"

"I'm not tired. I'll come to bed when I'm tired." He nodded again, and his face looked as glum as before. He went back into the bedroom and she heard him get into bed, presumably on his side. She sat watching the television for half an hour, perhaps longer, then went into the bedroom herself. The lights were out, and Keefe appeared to be asleep. She took her suitcase into the bathroom, got undressed and put a nightgown on. When at last she got into bed, Keefe made no attempt to turn towards her. Maybe he really was asleep. There was a three hour time difference between New York and Los Angeles, and the hour was later for him than for her. She lay in the dark and considered encroaching on his side of the bed, but she didn't do it. She considered waking him up, if in fact he really was asleep, and she didn't do this either. She lay isolated on her side, stared at the familiar shadows on the ceiling, and began to berate herself. She wanted nothing so much as to hold him tight and be held tight by him, but she was too proud to make the first move. No move was made by either of them. Eventually she fell asleep.

Thirteen

RAINEY, MEANWHILE, HAD EATEN SUPPER ALONE IN A diner. He had sat on a plastic stool with his knees under the counter. The place reeked of stale grease and of the 836 orders of coffee served that day, mostly in steaming styrofoam cups. The counterman watched Rainey covertly and talked to others who came and went, not him. Noting his sombre three-piece suit, the counterman made him for a corporation executive or high-powered lawyer – more probably the lawyer because of the beard – and for this reason did not try to talk to him. He wondered why such an important man would want to eat in a dump such as this.

Rainey, for his part, ate chicken à la king and mopped up with toast. He was thinking mostly about Flora Bernstein. He drank two bottles of orange soda, for he was extremely thirsty. After leaving the diner he stepped into a candy store that was still open and bought and ate a bar of chocolate. He was developing a sweet tooth lately, which he put down to his deprived childhood in a poor neighborhood. Most of what candy he had got as a kid he had had to steal, darting into candy stores then running out again with a handful.

It was a hot summer night. He decided to go back to headquarters and phone Flora. The lights shone down through the leaves as he cut through City Hall Park. He crossed Centre Street through traffic, then strolled across Police Plaza. One couldn't make a call in comfort from the street any more. Today's telephone booths were open to the winds from the waist down. There was not even a seat to sit on. The comfortable booths with their folding doors that he remembered as a young cop had all been replaced. He remembered them fondly even though in the old days in the parts of the city where he had worked the populace had been inclined to use them as toilets or hotel rooms or garbage dumps much of the time. Or as vertical coffins. He had dragged a number of corpses out of telephone booths – people who had been stabbed or shot, or had OD'd on drugs. One time a woman had been raped in one of them standing up. Her nose was broken, she was covered with blood and she couldn't or wouldn't talk. It was impossible to get a straight story out of her. Maybe the detectives did later.

He went in past the cop on security duty and took the elevator up to the thirteenth floor. The night duty sergeant – it was Dolan tonight – was sitting at the telephone console, with his feet up, reading the *New York Post*.

Dolan put down his paper. "Is there some kind of raid on tomorrow morning?" He gestured towards his telephone console. "There have been quite a few queries. Is the boss going to lead it, or what?"

Rainey had known Dolan a long time. He told him the plan. There was no reason not to. "Anybody asks you about it tonight, you don't know a thing."

"Of course," said Dolan, nodding. Then: "Is it going to work?"

"Maybe," said Rainey.

A raid like this, both knew, was a little like sending soldiers into battle. The two men contemplated each other. Anything that could go wrong, the generals always said, usually did. Crime and war were not that different. Criminals were unpredictable, so the outcome of raids was unpredictable. But Rainey had no personal stake in tomorrow's outcome. The only career at stake was, possibly, Keefe's.

Dolan said: "I heard he went waltzing into that stick-up with you in Harlem. The way the cops up there are talking about it he's got brass balls."

"That's an exaggeration," said Rainey. He too had been surprised by Keefe's behavior, but he had chosen then as now to regard it as a fluke.

"Is he gonna last?" said Dolan.

They both had an interest in this, but how much? You never knew. The next Deputy Commissioner might come in and transfer everyone. On the other hand, each time a new man was appointed the incumbent staff could usually count on being frozen in place for months while he tried to learn everybody's name. "It depends how much support he gets from the man upstairs," said Rainey. "I got to make a call."

For privacy he went into Keefe's office, sat in Keefe's chair and dialed Flora's number. As he did so he ruminated about the following day's raid. There was something about it that had troubled him all along. He didn't know precisely what: a detail missing here or there, perhaps. He hadn't troubled to figure it out because it did not concern him. The raid was Keefe's problem, not his. Of course he hoped for success. They might all get some laughs out of it. In the past he had busted in on gamblers surrounded by numbers slips, on narcotics crews in surgical masks, on guys like Hot Harry surrounded by cut-up cars. He loved catching them red-handed. The looks on their faces. The absolute surprise.

And then the expression of absolute misery – not because they were going to jail but because they had had something nice going, nice to them, and you just disrupted it, and now would confiscate their toys. If tomorrow's raid failed there would be none of that, or little of it. But the risk of embarrassment was Keefe's, not his.

All these thoughts were fleeting ones as he listened to the buzz in his ear that matched the ringing telephone in the frame house out at Coney Island. Then the connection was made and Flora came on. He pictured her in her girlish bedroom. He had made her describe it for him. Perhaps she was lying on the bed in her slip, hair spread out on the pillow. He pictured the girlish items spotted about the room, the old teddybear, the posters of singers – the room he had never been in.

Flora's conversations tended to be extremely long. They were punctuated by long silences, and long sighs. It was like overhearing the one-sided conversations of his daughters. His feet were on Keefe's desk. The chair was tilted back as far as it would go, and he listened to her darling voice on the phone and said relatively little. Her mother wasn't home. "Too bad you're not here," she said.

"Why is that?" he said, though he hoped he knew.

"So we could ball, silly."

He liked the word now, liked to hear her say it. She worked as a stenographer in a factory a few streets away from where she lived. She went from her tawdry house into that tawdry factory every day and typed up letters having to do with heavy machinery. He wanted to take her away from all that, introduce her to beauty and the bigger world outside of Coney Island.

She had bought new shoes with the money he gave her, she told him – red, with spike heels – and also a tape by the new singing group known as the Dung Heaps. This name startled Rainey, who once again was amazed at the names these groups gave themselves, and by which they became rich and famous. Knowing Flora was opening him up to a world that was truly amazing. He was only beginning to perceive it. For years the department had restricted his movements and even his thoughts, and before that so had the Catholic Church. He had been married at twenty-one on a patrolman's salary to a girl whose three brothers were all priests. There were priests on Rainey's side of the family too. His wife had refused to practice birth control, and he had become the father of four children nearly as fast as he could pull the trigger of the off-duty revolver presently rammed into the belt of his trousers, and pressing hard, because his feet were up on the desk, into his abdomen. With the birth of each child he had had to move his family into a worse house, each one further from the city, and to live with broken furniture and hand-me-down clothes. At present his home was sixty miles out on Long Island. The commute was murderous, always had been, and once he had driven the same car, a Volkswagen Beetle, for more than eleven years. He had had to hold down full-time jobs on the side, getting only four or five hours sleep a night. Such a life had imposed intolerable strain on his self-esteem, on his ability to function at all. So from time to time he had cracked, and done wild things.

Now he was going to have all he had missed previously. He would forget the past and trust to the future, and the embodiment of this future was Flora Bernstein.

"Wait till you hear this group," she was saying enthusiastically.

As she prattled on his mind wandered. Idly he pulled open Keefe's center drawer. He was perhaps looking for a pencil with which to doodle, or a toothpick with which to pick his teeth. Instead his eye was caught by a memo lying there, because his own name was in it. He reacted as if slapped in the face. In fact there were two memos stapled together, and his own name appeared in both.

He read them, the one signed by the PC and the one signed by Keefe. Then he read them again. Keefe, whom he hardly knew, who owed him nothing, had stood up for him in front of the Police Commissioner. In this department nobody did that. The NYPD was not a democratic organisation, and the PC's word, this PC's or any other's, was never questioned.

Rainey's chest became tight and his eyes misted over, for he was a sentimental man and it seemed to him that Keefe, at great risk to himself, had saved his job for him. No one had ever stood up for him before in a crisis, or so he believed, and he was so greatly moved that he wanted to cry.

"Are you still there?" demanded Flora.

The question brought him back to reality. "Yes, of course."

"You didn't say anything for so long, I thought maybe you'd hung up."

"I could never hang up on you," Rainey said. He felt suddenly extremely rich. No Texas oil man or Arabian sheik could possibly feel richer. He had Flora and also, for the first time in his life, he had a boss who trusted and admired him. He found himself almost overcome, filled to the brim with love and benevolence. He had this girl to look after and protect, and Keefe to look after and protect as well. He made a date with Flora for the following night and broke off the conversation; he had work to do.

For a time he sat tapping a pencil on his knee. Then he picked up the telephone and dialed Lieutenant Craighead's home number.

"The Boss wants you to come in," he said. "How soon can you make it?"

"Come in?" said Craighead. "I just got home."

"How soon?"

"What do you mean how soon? What's it about?"

"He wants you here forthwith."

"I haven't even had dinner yet –"

Rainey cut him off. "Do you know what forthwith means?" In the New York Police Department the word meant instantly, and Craighead knew this.

"Let me talk to him," demanded Craighead after a pause. "Put him on. Don't I even have time to eat my dinner?"

"No."

"Can I talk to him?"

"He's in his car," lied Rainey. "He's on his way in."

Craighead was silent.

"If I were you," said Rainey, "when he gets here I'd be waiting for him."

"Can I know what it's about?"

"What the hell do you think it's about?" said Rainey. "Forthwith," he said again, and rang off.

While waiting Rainey considered all aspects of the forthcoming raid until finally he understood what it was that had been bothering him: Keefe had never taken control of the case but had left it to Craighead. Which, in Rainey's mind at least, was to court unacceptable risks. There were questions Keefe had not asked, had not known enough to ask, that he certainly should have asked, and that Rainey now had decided to ask for him just as soon as Craighead arrived. He could only hope he was not too late.

Presently the phone buzzed and Sergeant Dolan announced Lieutenant Craighead. "Send him in," said Rainey, who had remained at Keefe's desk.

Craighead appeared in the doorway. He was wearing corduroy pants, a loose shirt and canvas shoes. Seeing Rainey in Deputy Commissioner Keefe's chair, he became immediately suspicious. He said: "Where's the Boss? I don't see the Boss."

"He's not here yet," answered Rainey cooly. "Why don't you and I get started? I have some questions to ask you."

"I don't have to talk to you."

Rainey sighed. He had, of course, known this would turn into a confrontation. "You do if you want this raid to happen."

The two men stared at each other. "I've never liked you, Rainey," Craighead said.

"Mutual." Rainey was again tapping a pencil on his knee. "If I don't get the answers I want I'm authorised to stop the raid here and now," he lied. He could not stop feeling that it ought to be cancelled, no matter what. Or at least Keefe's part of it should be.

"What the hell is the matter with you?" cried Craighead. "It's set to go. We went over the whole thing this afternoon."

"The whole thing? No, we went over part of it."

Craighead had his drawings rolled up under his arm. In his exasperation he began to lay them out on the desk, weighing the corners down with Keefe's desk calendar, his telephone, the edge of a folder of memos. But Rainey, ignoring the drawings, started on the questions that had not been asked earlier.

"I want to know how you found that junkyard."

"We found it. What difference does it make how we found it?"

"As I understand it," said Rainey cooly, "you tailed this Hot Harry for weeks, and he kept shaking the tail. You put a wire on his phone and it led you nowhere. So how did you find the junkyard?"

"A stoolie told us where it was," said Craighead grudgingly.

This was usually the way cases were broken, and Rainey nodded. "Did you pay him?"

"Sure I paid him. Think some creep would just give away information like that? Without being paid?"

Now we're getting somewhere, thought Rainey. "So how much did you pay him?"

"What difference does it make how much I paid him?"

"How much?"

"Two thousand dollars."

"Jesus," said Rainey truly. surprised "Where did you get that kind of money?" It hadn't come out of any ordinary informants" fund; that much was certain.

But Craighead only stared at him. He said nothing.

"I'm waiting," Rainey said.

"The Chief of Detectives gave it to me," said Craighead grudgingly. "Satisfied?"

At last we see it, Rainey thought, that which has been invisible until now: the fine hand of the Chief of Detectives. He didn't know what this meant, but Keefe ought to be advised.

"What's in it for him?"

"How should I know?"

"Money like that, you usually have to beg for. Did he make you beg?"

"No," said Craighead. "I asked him for it and he got it out of the safe."

"And gave it to you with his own hands?"

"So what?"

"Isn't that unusual? A chief of detectives handing over informant money with his own hands."

"Yes," said Craighead. "I mean, no. I signed for it."

"And then you gave it to the stoolie?"

"Sure. Happens every day."

"Except that this time it was an unusual sum of money."

"I don't have to sit here and listen to this third degree shit," Craighead said.

"Let's go back to the beginning. You told the Chief of Detectives that Commissioner Keefe was interested in a case, and he told you to break that particular case at any cost. Keeping him informed at every step. Is that right?"

"More or less."

"What else did he tell you?"

"What is this?"

"What else did he tell you?" Rainey demanded.

"What are you hinting at?"

What was Gold up to, Rainey wondered. Was it in his interest for the raid to fail? Was he perhaps trying to drive a wedge between Keefe and the PC? Rainey knew nothing about upper-level police politics, but it was possible. Should Keefe be told? Was there some way to protect him regardless of what Gold's game might be? Rainey thought there was.

"When I was a young cop," he said, "the auto squad was a money squad. I want to know if it still is." When Craighead did not immediately answer, Rainey grinned at him. "You're in charge and should know. So what can you tell me?"

"My men are clean," hollered Craighead. He seemed genuinely angry.

"Are they?" said Rainey. He was suddenly furious with Keefe. It ought to be Keefe demanding answers to these questions, not him. He shouldn't have to protect him. He wasn't his father. But Keefe knew nothing about money squads. The PC probably never heard about money squads either. The PC was a Police Academy cop, and after that he was a headquarters cop. He was never a street cop. The PC at least knew about characters like Gold. Presumably he did. Keefe didn't even know that.

In the old days gambling and narcotics were the biggest money squads. Safe and loft, which dealt with hijacked trucks and goods, was profitable too; and so was the auto squad. Auto squad detectives, in addition to investigating complaints about individual stolen vehicles, were also obliged by law to make regular inspections of licensed used car lots and junkyards. They prowled around looking for altered plates, altered vin numbers. They demanded to see papers. If there was a discrepancy they could arrest every man present for grand larceny auto, and close the place down. Stolen cars was big business, and the businessmen involved didn't want this to happen. Occasionally detectives might follow a trail to a pier where one car or dozens waited to be loaded on to a ship to South America. It then became in everyone's interest that the ship sail on time. Some auto squad detectives became rich.

Then had come the biggest and most profound corruption investigation in the history of the department. Many cops went to jail. Stringent new controls were put in, and from one day to the next the money squad concept ceased to exist. There were thousands of cops on the street today who had never heard of money squads.

The chances are, Rainey reflected, no one today is watching the auto squad at all. Which could make tomorrow's raid from Keefe's point of view incredibly risky.

And across from Rainey stood the auto squad's commander, and he was boiling. "I'll have you in the complaint room for this, Rainey."

"Sit down," said Rainey.

"I'll have you answering charges."

"I said sit down," shouted Rainey. Craighead sat. "Good," said Rainey.

Command depended not on rank – rank was artificial. Command was in the eyes, the bearing, the voice. Craighead waited angrily.

"The reason I asked to have this chat with you," Rainey said, "is because it occurs to me somebody might be trying to set the Boss up."

"Like who?"

Like you or one of your men or Gold, thought Rainey. "Suppose," he said easily, "we bust in there tomorrow and Hot Harry is home with a cold. And there are no stolen cars on the premises either. Or else all we find are a couple of lower-ranking individuals who have been paid to take the fall. A couple of stand-in arrests for appearance's sake." Rainey eyed Craighead. "If that was to happen, I would feel my Boss had been set up, wouldn't you?"

Craighead said nothing.

"He wouldn't look too good," Rainey said, "if that was to happen. Do you agree?"

"Nobody's trying to set up anybody," said Craighead. "Something like that would be the breaks of the game."

"But you can't blame me for asking you such questions now, can you?" inquired Rainey. He slammed his hand down on the desk. "I want you to tell me that none of your detectives have friends inside that particular junkyard."

"I'll swear by my men," Craighead said.

"All right," said Rainey and his voice took on a false sweetness, "you swear by your men. And you better be right, because if you're not, I'll see that you're roasted."

"You're a sergeant. I'm not afraid of you."

Rainey smiled at him. Craighead, although obviously furious, remained glued to his chair.

"Tell you what," Rainey said, "let's figure out a way to be certain in advance that there will be stolen cars inside that junkyard when we bust in tomorrow. Let's be certain that Hot Harry is in there too, and a reasonable number of accomplices."

"How the hell can I promise any of that in advance?"

"Well," said Rainey, "as a start, I'd get all of your men together right now. I'd phone them up and tell them they have to come in, and I'd have some of them watching and photographing that junkyard all night. I'd put others on surveillance outside Hot Harry's house, wherever he lives, and I'd also watch any of his colleagues that you've managed to identify, and I would tail all of them through the streets tomorrow morning to that junkyard. And I would make certain they are all in there, and only then

183

would I give orders for the bus to drive up there loaded with press and TV guys. Do I make myself clear?"

Craighead sighed.

"You got a list of your detectives there?" inquired Rainey. "Let's go over it together, shall we? Let's make our decisions together. By the time the Boss gives his news conference tomorrow morning, I want to know for certain what's in that junkyard."

Fourteen

THE ALARM WOKE KEEFE WHO, AS HE REACHED FOR IT, was already conscious of Sharon in bed beside him. The clock had barely beeped before he pressed the stop button and sat up and looked over at her sleeping. Outside his window it was still dark, and he slipped out of bed and went into the kitchen to put on the coffee. In the bathroom he shaved and showered.

When he came back into the bedroom he was dressed in underwear and socks and carrying a single cup of coffee, his own. The light was coming up outside, and he stood looking down at Sharon, content to have her there, but uncertain what to do. Should he wake her, or only leave her a note of explanation? But if he only left a note, perhaps she would not be there when he got back.

Her sleep cycle was on Los Angeles time, he reasoned, and she looked really sound asleep, completely out of it. In addition, his department car was probably already waiting downstairs.

Just then her eyes opened, and she looked up at him, after which her arms came up and reached for him, so that he grinned and said lightly:

"Is it me you want, or only my cup of coffee?"

"You," she said.

So he set the cup down on the bedside table, and drew the

bedclothes back off her and thought: my driver is just going to have to wait.

The next ten minutes were for Keefe, and for her too, he believed, a period of intense emotion.

Finally Sharon said: "Your coffee's cold."

He took the cup out into the kitchen and came back with two hot ones. She sat up against the pillow. He sat on the edge of the bed. They drank their coffee and looked at each other.

"It's early," Sharon said.

"I have something on very early this morning."

"Yes, I noticed."

He put his cup down and she said: "What? Again?"

"I've missed you, you know," he answered. For a while neither spoke at all.

"I'll be home about six," he said, when he was dressed and about to leave. He found himself afraid to ask if she would be there. "We'll go out to dinner."

"We'll eat in," she said. "I'll do the shopping."

He went down the stairs two at a time, got into the car beside his driver – Detective Rodriguez today – and said cheerfully: "Well, Louie, what do you have to say for yourself this fine morning?"

An hour later he stood on the dais in the press room at headquarters and looked down on thirty to forty reporters and many microphones and TV cameras. Lieutenant Craighead, who had already shown his drawings and described the planned raid, stood to one side.

"What are our chances of getting shot?" one of the reporters said.

This caused a round of nervous laughter.

"We're all going to be brave about that," said Keefe at the lectern. "We're all going to take our chances on getting shot. Is there anyone here who doesn't want to get shot?"

The laughter this time seemed more nervous than before.

"We don't expect trouble," Keefe assured them. "Car thieves as a whole, do not shoot. In addition, I've asked Sergeant Rainey to hold all of you outside the yard until it is secure. No more than a minute or two, I hope."

Rainey stood in the doorway watching. Ten minutes ago he had spoken with the detectives staked out up in the Bronx. There were five men already inside the yard, he had learned, including Hot Harry himself. During the night six presumably stolen cars had gone in, most of them Cadillacs. None had reappeared. Only one potential problem: several reporters from Keefe's old paper were already on the scene. How had they found out about the location of the yard, Rainey wondered, about the raid to come? The detectives were having trouble keeping them back out of sight until the raid was ready to start.

Rainey decided not to mention this to Keefe. Nor would he mention his additional precautions last night and that morning, lest it seem he was vouching in advance for the success of the raid. He was not vouching for anything. It was a risk he did not need to take, and would not. He had done his best by Keefe. If the raid failed now, he did not mean to be blamed for it.

"On the other hand," Keefe was saying, "most of these stolen car yards are staked out with vicious dogs. The dogs are their burglar-alarm system. They can't ask the local precinct for protection, you see." There was some genuine laughter this time, and Keefe's grin broadened.

He's enjoying this, decided Rainey. For once he's making the news instead of merely reporting it.

"So if you see any dogs, don't try to pet them."

The meeting broke up, and Keefe and Craighead were driven to the site in Keefe's car. Craighead seemed excessively nervous to him, and twice as obsequious as in the past, though Keefe didn't know why. They went upstairs to the look-out apartment where two detectives still watched the yard through field glasses.

"Nothing to worry about, Boss," said Craighead at his ear. "How much you want to bet we make six to eight arrests today?"

It was as if he were afraid Keefe might cancel the raid at the last second. Keefe studied him briefly.

"I'll be happy with Hot Harry and two or three," he said. "The only thing I'm afraid of is none."

He took the glasses and peered down into the yard. He could see men moving back and forth. He watched detectives move into position in front of the steel doors. To his surprise he saw that a reporter and a photographer were with them. He recognized both men. May's work, he thought. The busload of newsmen, when they arrived, would accuse him of favouritism. What was he going to do about it? What could he do?

"Let's go down there," he told Craighead.

There wasn't time to do much. As they stepped out of the building the press bus was coming into the street.

Beside him Craighead spoke into a walkie-talkie to the detectives on the far side of the yard: "Hot Harry One to Hot Harry Two. K."

"This is Hot Harry Two, K."

Detectives nearby were trying to push the two newsmen backwards, and there was a struggle going on. The reporter was protesting loudly, and calling out Keefe's name.

Craighead said into the walkie-talkie: "This is Hot Harry One. Are you ready over there? K."

"Ready, K."

Rainey had stopped the bus about a hundred feet away. He stood in the door with newsmen trying to push past him. Others were trying to climb out the bus windows.

"Hurry," Keefe said to Craighead.

Craighead said into the walkie-talkie: "Hot Harry One to Hot Harry Two. Lights, camera, action. K."

The detectives on Keefe's side had a battering-ram. He supposed the detectives on the opposite side had too. Four men swung it into the gate at the hinges, which tore loose. Half a dozen blows and the steel doors went down with a clangor like cymbals. It couldn't have taken ten seconds. Between blows Keefe could hear frantic shouts from inside. Then the detectives spilled in, trampling the downed doors, and Keefe went with them.

A number of cutters had run out of one of the sheds. Their visors were pushed back and their torches were still flaming. Other men were sprinting down the center alley toward the far gate, which fell down in front of them, as more detectives flooded in from that direciton. The detectives' guns were out. The running men stopped, put their hands above their heads and began to back up.

Then came more of the tinny cymbal thunder as reporters and TV crews arrived. They too began running in all directions, and Keefe listened to the whirr of cameras, the excited voices.

"Arrest everybody who isn't wearing a shield or a press card," Lieutenant Craighead shouted. Looking extremely relieved, he was pointing toward a parked flatbed truck inside one of the sheds. "Is that the truck you spotted on the road, Boss? Now I ask you, Boss, is that your truck?"

Keefe was trying to take it all in. The reporters and car thieves were mixed together. It was impossible to tell which was which. The yard had become extremely noisy too, cries of amazement, cries of consternation. In his ear Craighead shouted: "There's probably more of them hiding in the office. Come on, let's go root them out."

The office was a cinderblock building with a cluttered interior. There were two old desks, two broken-down sofas, some armchairs with stuffing sticking out. There was a hotplate on the windowsill. The coffeepot on it was steaming. There were overflowing ashtrays, piles of old newspapers, and girlie centerfolds tacked to the walls.

"Hello, anybody home?" shouted Craighead. "Where's the can?" he asked rhetorically. He turned to Keefe. "When they hide, Boss, they invariably hide in the can."

There was a hallway, and some doors that Craighead began yanking open. One was a stuffed-full closet. The next was the bathroom.

Craighead stepped into it and peered up at the wall above the toilet.

"Look at this, Boss," he said.

The toilet tank was fixed to the wall about eight feet above the floor. It was connected to the toilet by a length of pipe. It was a small enough toilet tank, but on top of it was perched a man. He was balanced on it, barely.

"One slip and he flushes himself into the Hudson River," said Craighead to Keefe. "Get down off there," he ordered.

Perhaps the man started to comply. Perhaps his shift of weight was enough to break the tank away from the wall. It began to topple. The man was riding it. Keefe and Craighead jumped backwards out of the room. The man tried to grab the door, which slipped out of his grasp and slammed shut. Behind the door came the noise of crashing man and cascading water. Keefe went out into the yard laughing. Behind him he heard Craighead's voice: "Hey, are you still alive in there? Or did you drown?"

The suspects, one of them Hot Harry himself, stood in a row spreadeagled against the wall of the shed. There were detectives behind each one, patting them down for arms or contraband. The TV crews stood in a semi-circle, filming. The raid so far had gone off without a hitch, and Keefe was very pleased.

At the other end of the junkyard something caught his eye that he did not understand, and he moved toward it. A parked truck was pointed out toward the street, engine running. A detective was arguing with the driver who sat high up in the cab.

From within the truck came the driver's voice. "You get out of my way. I am late. I gotta go."

"He won't get out of the truck," explained the detective when Keefe came up. "Stand here, Commissioner, while I pull him out by the hair of his head."

Keefe looked up at the driver, a middle-aged black man, whose face broke into a grin of recognition.

"Hey, I know you," he said. "I seen you on TV. You the Commissioner."

"Get down from that truck," Keefe ordered.

"Yes, sir." The black man jumped down. He was grinning broadly, and trying to shake hands with Keefe, but the detective ran forward and slapped handcuffs onto the outstretched wrist, then yanked it around behind his back.

"You're under arrest," the detective said.

"Under arrest? What for? What I done?"

"You have a right to remain silent. Do you understand that? You have a right to –"

But the black man kept interrupting. "What I done? I pull

in here ten minutes ago to get a wheel changed. That broken wheel on my truck. Look, I gotta go, I am late."

With his hands cuffed behind him he had made his pathetic appeal partly to the detective, partly to Keefe.

"The place is full of stolen cars, Commissioner," the detective said. "The law says anybody present gets locked up."

The prisoner said: "I don't know nothing about stolen cars, Mr. Commissioner."

"That's the way the law reads, Commissioner."

The aggrieved black man was perhaps telling the truth. Keefe tended to believe him. It sounded true to him.

"I never arrested one yet didn't claim he was innocent," the detective said.

"Well –"

"They're all innocent as babes."

"Mr. Commissioner –"

The man was the detective's prisoner, not Keefe's, and possibly guilty. In any case, the law was the law. As the detective dragged him away, the man was still calling out plaintively:

"Mr. Commissioner. Please, Mr. Commissioner."

Keefe strolled past another of the sheds. He didn't know if anyone had checked it out or not. It was so dark in there he could see nothing, so he stepped inside, and a large animal came leaping at him out of the darkness. It was a mastiff at the end of a chain, which yanked it down. Its teeth missed Keefe's throat but fastened on to his trousers near the knee, and there was the sound of ripping cloth. Snarling and grinding its jaws, the beast held Keefe fast.

"Nice doggie," he said. "How about letting go of me now, Fido?"

A stick against the wall caught Keefe's eye, and he stretched for it, but unless he wanted to take his pants off he was as restricted by the length of the chain as the dog was. He took his gun out of his belt and pressed it to the growling skull.

"If you don't let go, you'll be sorry," he said aloud. I hope nobody hears me talking to this dog, he thought. He did not fire. A shot would bring everybody running. It would make headlines – comical ones. He would appear ridiculous.

Just then Sergeant Rainey entered the shed. He watched Keefe with amusement.

"Shoot the dog, Commissioner," he said.

"The yard is full of TV crews," said Keefe. "The headlines would read: Deputy Commissioner Slays Pet."

Rainey, laughing, made no move to help him.

"Just hand me that stick over there."

"What stick?" said Rainey.

"For God's sake," said Keefe. "He's already eaten through my pants. In a minute he'll start on my knee."

Rainey hefted the stick, measured his distance, and clubbed the dog across the eyebrows. He stood looking down at it. "I've laid my nightstick across many a thick skull," he commented. "But that's the first time I ever laid out a dog."

Outside in the sunlight, Keefe examined his trousers. "Thank God no one filmed that little episode," he said. "I would have been the laughing stock of the city. If anybody asks, I snagged them on something."

"Wipe some of that slobber off," said Rainey, "or no one will believe you."

They went forward.

"Okay, guys," Craighead called out to his detectives, "drive those vehicles out of here." There was a mobile crane, a pick-up truck, and Hot Harry's flatbed truck, plus the truck belonging to the black man.

"This is where we really hurt them, Boss," Craighead said. "We impound all their machinery and vehicles. They'll be out on bail by nightfall, but they are out of business, at least as long as it takes them to round up more equipment."

The prisoners were being herded out the gate, and the newsmen as well, but both processions were obliged to step aside to let the vehicles pass.

"Where he going with my truck?" the black man cried out to Keefe.

Keefe's life was about to be rearranged by this man, but he did not know it at the time. He did not reply.

"Please, Mr. Commissioner."

He did not yet know the man's name, which was Joshua L. Brown, though he would learn it soon enough and after that never forget it.

Lieutenant Craighead said: "Your truck is confiscated according to law."

But the black man was pleading with Keefe. "I don't know these other dudes. I come in here to get a wheel fixed. Mr. Commissioner —"

Keefe did not know what to say to him.

Craighead said: "If you beat the case, you get your truck back. Otherwise we keep it."

"Mr. Commissioner —"

Keefe did not have enough experience to intervene.

"That's the law, pal," said Craighead.

A detective dragged Brown out the gate, and Keefe turned to Rainey. "We may be locking up an innocent guy."

"You're not Solomon," Rainey said. "Let the courts decide. You'll make yourself crazy."

On the way back to headquarters Keefe had his driver stop at his flat, and he went upstairs to change. Sharon was not there. Her things were neatly hung and when Keefe put his head into the closet the air carried the scent of her.

His second press conference of the day began about thirty minutes later. The newsmen were seated in rows before him, and the bright television lights were on.

"This Harry Hamish, how many priors?"

Keefe gave the answer.

"How do we know this man Dickerson is his partner?"

Keefe gave the answer.

"I would like to know why your former paper was tipped off about this raid, and the rest of us weren't."

From there on the questioning turned hostile.

"I would like to know just who did the tipping-off."

"Let me get this straight," said a TV reporter named Pulisfer. "The purpose of this charade was to make the cops look good on television tonight, am I right?"

Others joined in. Keefe had manipulated the news, and therefore them. Did he seriously think that the prisoners would receive any meaningful jail time?

On scores of occasions Keefe had taken part in news conferences at which reporters had badgered a subject. Now the subject was himself. He was not used to it, and had to work hard to appear calm. "You TV people got nice footage. Maybe the detectives will look pretty good in that footage tonight. I don't see where that's so awful. We locked up nine men and recovered eleven stolen cars..Charade?" he snorted. "How can you call today a charade?"

"Those defendants will be cutting up more cars somewhere else tomorrow," insisted Pulisfer. "I'll be on the air live from the courthouse during the six o'clock news. With any luck I'll have live pictures of those thugs walking out of the courtroom free as the air."

"Should that happen," said Keefe tightly, "you'll have a dramatization of the ineffectiveness not of the police department but of the courts. It's an angle I hope you'll play up. It's an angle that will please every cop in the city – in the world."

He stepped down off the dais and walked out of the room. He left them still milling around in there. Sergeant Rainey followed him back to his own office.

"How do you think it went, Ed?"

"Great," said Rainey. But to Keefe he looked less cheerful than earlier. "Now we just have to wait to see how the press plays it up."

"Yes," said Keefe. "Exactly."

But as he sat down behind his desk and reached for the contents of his In basket he became less glum. It was true that he had used the press for his own purposes, but he didn't see where today's newsmen could do anything about it. The raid had produced the arrests and the recovered cars and they were obliged to report this. Once they had done so they could not very well confess to their audiences that they had been used. Anyway, the press was always being used. In Washington it was used by the President and his men constantly. Everywhere in the world it was used, every day. An enormous percentage of what one read in the papers and saw on TV was staged precisely for the purpose of bringing publicity to whoever staged it.

There were times enough in Keefe's experience where the

press as a group had taken what had seemed to him an honest and legitimate story and had reported it as something quite different. However, today surely he was safe.

Fifteen

ACCOMPANIED BY SERGEANT RAINEY, KEEFE HAD himself driven back up to the Bronx to watch the arraignments. On police business he went almost nowhere alone any more, but entered almost every room at the head of a delegation of greater or lesser size, and this too constituted one of the perks of his office. It made him both seem and feel more important than he was used to. But he had no sooner entertained this idea than he pushed it out, having convinced himself that he needed Rainey lest something come up that, because of his relative inexperience, he did not understand.

The courtroom was crowded with defendants, lawyers, families, arresting officers, people of all descriptions. There were TV crews out in the corridors, reporters inside the courtroom. The assistant DA who would present the case was pointed out to him. It was a young woman. She stood off to one side paging through her notes.

Prosecutors were not used to meeting reporters in arraignment court, which was only the first step in a process that might or might not lead to conviction months or even years from now. This one was about to stand in a spotlight she did not know was there, and Keefe decided he had best warn her. He was not interested in making enemies of assistant district attorneys.

He walked over and introduced himself. Her name was Anne Christianson, he learned. She wore a severe dark suit and no make-up, and her hair was pulled back into a severe bun, as if to make her appear older and plainer. Both attempts failed. She had lovely eyes, a sexy mouth and a somewhat prominent bosom. She gave him a faint smile as they shook hands, but after that, as she listened to him, her face only got darker.

When he had finished she merely stared at him in a hard-eyed way.

"So how will you handle the case?" he asked, trying to show his friendly intent.

"Just like any other, Mr Keefe," she replied coldly. "Now, if you'll excuse me –"

She walked away from him. He strode after her. "If there's anything else I can –" But he was talking to the back of her head.

Anne Christianson was twenty-six years old, a year and a half out of law school, and as a prosecutor was making little progress that she could see. She was still assigned to arraignment court when others had been promoted. She was beginning to think she would never be permitted to try a case before a jury. Professionally speaking, she had been close to despair for a long time. And now the case that Keefe had just described had had to drop into her lap. There was no time to prepare for it. She was afraid it would set her back even further.

She had always been a top student. At law school she had finished first in her class, the result being that when she applied for a job here the District Attorney had been more or less obliged to hire her. But what an ordeal it had been. During every job interview she had been subjected to an incredible third degree designed, it seemed to her, to prove her a brainless pin-up. This was true even of her final interview with the elected District Attorney of Bronx County himself, an older man who should have known better. Many of the other assistant prosecutors these days were women. It was not an all-male club like it used to be, but few other women had her looks for a handicap. Finally, however, she had been appointed and sworn in, only to find that her supervisor was an older woman – a plain, dowdy, unmarried older woman – who took an instant dislike to her, or so Anne believed. This woman had stuck her now for months in arraignment court. When she asked about her progress, the frump merely advised her to be patient. There was no recourse except for an interview with the district attorney himself, but his secretary always replied that his appointments calendar was full: try again next week.

All the assistant DAs, not just Anne, spent their days looking and hoping for the one spectacular case that would attract the notice of one of the big law firms, enabling them to go on to careers as important trial lawyers. But such cases were rare, and when they did happen were almost always taken over by older and more experienced prosecutors who always happened to be men.

Anne had just such a case now, though she didn't yet know it. Keefe had just explained it to her. He didn't know it either. Furthermore, it was a case she would find a way to carry all the way to the end, which she also did not know. Instead she perceived it only as still another setback along her career path, perhaps even a major defeat. These car thieves were going to be out on bail in an hour, which was not her fault, but would seem so to the press. In their reports she would be made to seem incompetent, possibly even ridiculous. She should have been warned about this case hours ago. Ideally she should have had time to study the evidence, to seek out the judge during a recess so as to explain to him the tightness of the case – if it was tight – and the importance of the defendants; time to explain to him about the reporters; time to get him to agree to suitably high bail, which would keep at least some of the defendants in jail at least for a few days until they raised it.

But the case had been sprung on her at the last minute. She was very upset. Although she had just met Keefe and did not even understand clearly who he was, nonetheless she was already furious at him.

When the case was called, she moved up close to the bench together with the defendants and the arresting officers. The judge – it was a man named Baum today – said: "Who represents the defendants?"

A lawyer stepped forward. Anne did not know him. "Stanley Goldberg, your honor, representing eight of the defendants who plead not guilty."

196

Judge Baum peered down on the nine prisoners, eight of them white, one black. The white men wore work clothes. They were dirty and unshaven. The black man looked respectable. "Who represents the ninth defendant?" said Baum.

"The defendant, Joshua L. Brown," said Anne, "has refused legal aid, your honor. He says he's not guilty."

Anne felt herself on stage – the only stage she had been permitted so far – a stage so crowded and noisy that no one sitting even a few rows back could hear how competent her performance might be. What was about to happen was not her fault. As for Keefe, who was at the back of the court and straining to hear, Anne had temporarily forgotten about him. She was concentrated on herself.

"This is not a trial, Mr Brown," said Judge Baum. "This is an arraignment court. You're entitled to legal representation. If you can't afford it, the court will appoint a lawyer to represent you."

Anne looked up from her notes. "The defendant has money, your honor. He was carrying more than eight hundred dollars in cash at the time of his arrest."

Joshua L. Brown advanced toward the bench. He was a tall thin man, stooped, with grey hair. "Your honor, I don't know none of these dudes. I just stopped in there to get a wheel changed. I don't know nothing about no stolen cars. Now you want to put me in jail. You want to take all my money to pay a lawyer."

"That's enough, Mr. Brown. Quiet please." Baum began banging with his gavel. "Order in the court please."

"Your honor –" said Brown.

"Stand over there," ordered Baum. "Will an officer of the court come forward to restrain this man, please?"

Two uniformed courtroom guards moved Brown to one side and stood with him there. His head was darting around, but he was silent. The other eight defendants had stood with their chins on their chests throughout, ignoring it all.

"Proceed, Mr. Goldberg," said the judge.

Goldberg was a stout, baldish, middle-aged man wearing an expensive suit. "Your honor," he began, "although it may seem on the surface that my clients have some culpability under the law, inasmuch as there were apparently stolen vehicles on the premises in which they work, nonetheless I would ask for them to be released on their own recognisance at this time on the grounds that the junkyard in question is owned by a Brooklyn company called Body and Fender Associates, Inc., and none of the defendants is a principal of that firm. They are working men, your honor. I ask that they be released without bail."

The judge peered down at Anne. "Madam District Attorney?"

Anne again looked up from her notes. "Your honor, I ask that bail be set at fifty thousand dollars each. These men are all known to the police department as professional car thieves. A number of them have been arrested up to eight times previously, and Mr. Hamish, the gentleman on the right, has fifteen previous arrests and has two other cases pending."

"Has Mr. Hamish ever been convicted of a major felony, or served any meaningful sentence?"

"No, your honor, but the evidence against him this time is so strong –"

Judge Baum interrupted her by banging his gavel. "I set bail for these defendants at five thousand dollars each."

"But your honor –" Anne protested.

Goldberg stepped forward. "Your honor, that amount seems unfairly high in light of the arguments I have previously advanced –"

Judge Baum again banged the gavel. He had disposed of scores of cases already today and had scores more to go. The courtroom was stuffed with them. So was the corridor outside. He could afford to devote less than five minutes to each case. "Five thousand dollars bail or they're remanded."

"Yes, your honor," said Goldberg, who was barely repressing a smile of triumph. He turned to his clients, some of whom were grinning, and nodded. A bondsman came down the aisle and approached the bench.

"This is a farce, Judge," Anne protested. "These men –"

The judge was huddling with the bondsman.

"Your honor, if you please," cried Anne.

But Judge Baum silenced her. "There are many other cases waiting to be heard, Madam District Attorney." Having finished with the bondsman, he turned to the black man, Joshua L. Brown, still standing to the side between the two courtroom guards. "Bring Mr. Brown forward," he said.

This was done, and Judge Baum peered down at him. "Mr. Brown, I'll enter your plea as not guilty. Bail is set at five thousand dollars. Pay up or you're remanded to jail."

"Your honor," cried Brown in an anguished voice. "I don't have no five thousand dollars. I ain't no car thief. I haul fish. That's what I was doing this morning. I was on my way to the fish market to haul fish. I had eight hundred dollars to buy fish with. Now I ain't got no money at all. You can't send me to jail, your honor, I ain't done nothing."

Judge Baum banged his gavel. "Bail is reduced to eight hundred dollars cash. Next case."

"You can't do this, Judge. I got my rights. They take my money. They take my truck. I got –"

"Order in the court," cried Judge Baum. And he banged his gavel several times more. "Guards, clear this man out of my courtroom. Next case."

In the corridor outside waited the reporters, who backed Keefe against the wall. Microphones were thrust into his face, and the floodlights came on. Rainey, he noted, stood to one side looking amused.

The reporters wanted him to denounce Judge Baum, or Assistant District Attorney Christianson, or the court system in general. He had no intention of denouncing anyone. No one asked him about Brown. They presented the same questions again and again. Was he then satisfied with the disposition of the case? Did he think that bail in such ridiculously low amounts in any way satisfied the demands of justice? Did he consider the court careless, or inefficient, or merely blind?

"I neither condone the action of the court nor criticize it. I have no comment to make on the court."

"Are we to view the arrests this morning as an exercise in futility by the police department?"

Anne Christianson came out of the courtroom. Instantly the mass of reporters abandoned Keefe and rushed to surround her. She too was pressed back against the wall, and microphones thrust at her. Keefe watched her: he had the impression she wasn't handling it well. Once he caught her eye: she glared at him furiously.

At least he himself was free to depart, and he slunk away down the corridor, hoping that no reporter would come after him. Rainey at his side was laughing.

Sixteen

ABOUT AN HOUR AFTER MAKING BAIL, JOSHUA L. Brown came back to the courthouse. He went straight to the courtroom where he had been arraigned earlier. It was as crowded and noisy as ever, but there was a different judge on the bench. He then asked for Judge Baum's chambers. Somebody gave him directions. Maybe he intended to kidnap or kill the judge, but there was no one there except a cleaning woman. Brown demanded that she produce the judge. He pulled out a gun, put it to her head, and she started screaming.

There were still people moving through the halls outside Baum's chambers. Not many, because it was now supper time, but some. They heard her screams and spread the alarm. A few cops came running. By the time they got there, Brown had barricaded himself inside Judge Baum's inner office. He was holding the cleaning woman, and demanding to see the judge. One of the cops ran down to his car and put out what Sergeant Rainey later called "this delicious emergency call" over the city-wide band. In about five minutes there were fifty people crammed into Baum's outer office and more coming, so that they began to fill up the hallway outside: cops, courtroom guards, federal agents of one stripe or another. Reporters and TV crews were close behind them.

Among the first arrivals was Rainey himself. After Brown's arraignment he had gone upstairs to talk to two former partners from long ago, now members of the Bronx District Attorney's squad. They sat around in an office for an hour or more. Rainey was to meet Flora later and had time to kill. There was a speaker attached to the wall above the desks. It was tuned to the city-wide frequency, and was open all day, though most times barely audible. Detectives in that office did not answer radio calls but did like to listen in whenever they detected in Central's transmission, or some cop's transmission, the shrill note of panic. Someone would reach over and turn the volume up loud. Tonight the "delicious" emergency call came over just as Rainey had stood up to leave. He was stretching lazily, already anticipating his date with Flora. Then he heard the radio call and started running. The two detectives ran with him.

Keefe at that moment was walking through the door of his flat. Sharon, he saw, stood close to the windows in the light that came through them. She was studying his torn trousers.

"A dog got me," he explained.

"A dog got you?"

He removed his gun from his belt, and as always felt immeasurably lighter without it. He set it down on a cabinet, then picked it up again.

"This vicious dog had me," he told Sharon. "I put this thing to its head and I couldn't pull the trigger."

"Because you were worried about how it would look in the headlines?"

"I realized I would have been unable to pull the trigger no matter what. I couldn't have shot the dog. The idea of ever shooting another human being is inconceivable to me. What do I have a gun for?"

She gave him a fond smile. "You wanted to see what carrying a gun was like."

"I don't know why I wanted to do that."

"Deep in the breast of every man," she told him, "beats the heart of a boy."

He put his arms around her. She had his torn trousers clutched in both hands between them and her forehead was

201

pressed against his throat. It was a moment of intense closeness for them both.

Keefe said: "How much time do we have?"

"I have to go back on Sunday."

"Maybe Sunday will never come." He said this with so much feeling that it made her laugh. It made him laugh too. But their laughter died out quickly.

Having withdrawn from his arms, she resumed studying the torn cloth. "Maybe a good tailor can do something, but I doubt it." She draped the trousers over the sofa.

Keefe went into the kitchen to get a bottle of wine. When he came back he switched on the TV and put the corkscrew into the bottle in almost the same motion, while Sharon began to tell him about the scenes she had shot earlier in the day. They sat together on the sofa. The TV sound came up, and his own face stared back at him. He felt himself tighten up. The TV reporter's voice – it was Pulisfer – was heard questioning him.

"Commissioner," the voice said, "wasn't this just a staged raid to make the cops look good on television tonight?"

"Wouldn't you know they'd put that in?" commented Keefe. He poured out the wine, turned to Sharon, and they clinked glasses, just as his own image disappeared abruptly. It was replaced by the startled studio anchorman who announced an unexpected live report from Pulisfer at the Bronx courthouse.

Pulisfer was standing in a corridor, and people were rushing past him. "The case of Hot Harry Hamish's car stealing ring has just taken a bizarre turn," he cried into his microphone, and he described how Joshua L. Brown, armed and apparently crazed, had barricaded himself and his hostage inside the chambers of Judge Baum.

Keefe leaped for the phone so fast he spilled his wine. He left Sharon sprawled and half-sputtering on the couch.

"Send me a radio car from the precinct immediately," he told his duty sergeant. "Reach out for Sergeant Rainey. Send my car up there too." He turned to Sharon. "I have to leave."

"Here we go again," she said.

"It's my case, don't you see?" He had grabbed his gun off the cabinet and was thrusting it into his belt. "I'll be back as soon as I can."

He came out onto the sidewalk as the police car turned into his street. He jumped into the back, the siren came on, and the car took off in a squeal of rubber.

They went up the East River Drive and onto the Triboro bridge. The cop at the wheel weaved in and out of the traffic, his siren moving cars aside. From high up on the bridge Keefe could see almost the whole city. In comparison to the crisis that waited ahead the city seemed small.

They came into the streets of the South Bronx. There were vacant lots piled high with rubble, and buildings that looked bombed out. Yankee Stadium when they passed it was all lit up, reflecting its halo against the sky, tonight's fans already gathering, an island of civilisation in a war zone. All around it the poor in their tens of thousands lived like rats. In an hour the jammed stadium would prove – what? That the American culture was alive and well, perhaps. The police car sped up the hill; above the stadium stood the multi-storey courthouse, another of the South Bronx's islands of civilization. As soon as the car stopped, Keefe jumped out and ran inside.

Everyone was moving in the direction of the judge's chambers, and the closer Keefe got the more the corridor became choked with people, most of whom seemed to be trying to push through one small door. Keefe had his shield pinned to his lapel, and was struggling to get through himself. From time to time he shouted the only question which at the moment had any meaning for him: "Who's in charge here?"

Finally he managed to squeeze inside. It was like forcing his way into a subway train at rush hour. People were packed together, and most of them had something in their hands, klieg lights or mircophones or cameras or guns. The place was brilliant with light, and overlaid with a cacophony of voices. It was incredibly hot.

There was empty space only at the front of the room near the door that led, presumably, to the judge's private office.

This door was the focus of the excitement. It was slightly ajar, and no one was standing too close to it.

"This way, Commissioner."

It was Sergeant Rainey, who beckoned him forward.

There were so many stimuli vying for Keefe's attention that his confusion was almost total. He noted the partly opened door. He could see that a filing cabinet lay on its side on the floor inside holding the door that far open and no more. He noted too that the men at the front of the room all had their guns out, but were crouched close to the walls. Some were pressed as tightly against the walls as they could get, and most now were staring at the newcomer, Keefe.

"Stand back in case he fires through the door, Commissioner," Rainey told him. "You can see him from here."

It was true. There was a mirror inside on the judge's wall. To his surprise it presented him with a single comprehensible picture of this singularly incomprehensible event, and as he looked into it time began to slow down a bit. The mirror must have been placed there so that Judge Baum could give himself the once-over on his way to court. Adjust his robes. Admire himself in his role as judge.

But the mirror held no memory of this homely image or of anything else it may have reflected in the past. At present it reflected Joshua L. Brown crouched beside Baum's desk holding a gun to the head of the terrified cleaning woman. It was about the size of an off-duty police gun, but silver. Over and above the clamor all around him, Keefe could hear the woman's whimpering, her muffled sobs. Then came Brown's voice on an angry importunate note:

"You get me that judge, or I put a bullet in this lady. Hear me out there?"

Still more men – law enforcement personnel and press – forced their way into the room. Keefe became distracted. The noise level seemed to go up and up until he could scarcely think, much less concentrate. "Is there a command post?" he shouted to Rainey. "Who's in command?"

Rainey shook his head. "I think you are, Commissioner."

Keefe rejected this idea at once. "Oh no I'm not. Where is

everybody? Where's the Chief of Operations? The Chief of Detectives? The Police Commissioner?"

"There's another time-honored police department tradition you maybe haven't learned about," shouted Rainey in his ear. "Whenever something heavy comes down, the brass tends to disappear. If somebody's going to screw up and wreck his career, let it be a sergeant."

Keefe had no intention of taking command. No one would expect him to. He was not a cop. He was not qualified.

"The next highest rank in here is lieutenant," Rainey added.

When Keefe stared at him, he held up both palms; he disclaimed responsibility. In times of crisis the department brass behaved as it behaved. It was not his fault.

Lieutenant Craighead pushed to Keefe's side. "I've got five of my men, Commissioner. What do you want us to do?"

There were certain orders that cried out to be given. The situation demanded them, orders that would be obvious, Keefe believed, to anyone. They could not wait.

"Clear the room of everyone who doesn't belong here," he ordered Craighead. He was not assuming command. Or so he believed. He was trying to re-establish order so that whoever arrived to take over would have room to operate. "Is there a phone in here?" he demanded of Craighead. He saw over the massed heads that there was. A reporter had it. The man was standing on the desk where the judge's clerk perhaps sat during the daytime, and he held the phone to his ear, keeping an open line to somewhere. "Put a cop on that phone," Keefe told Craighead. "Get the Police Commissioner in here. Get the Chief of Detectives in too. Get the Chief of Operations. Where is the hostage negotiating team?"

A man in civilian clothes thrust credentials into Keefe's face: an FBI agent. He gave his name. "I've got three men with me. What do you want us to do?"

Keefe had already taken command, though he did not know it. His intentions were invisible and were outweighed by his actions, which were not. It never occurred to him

205

that, once he had appeared to assume command, others would be glad to let him have it; that afterwards he would not be able to relinquish it because no one would take it back.

Two emergency service patrolmen lumbered in. They wore steel clothing and carried shotguns. Both had their visors up. They identified themselves: "If you want us to bust in there, Commissioner, just give the word."

Craighead's detectives had begun trying to clear the room, but the reporters resisted. They were pushing back. One of the detectives, standing on the desk, had at last wrenched the phone away from the reporter who had it. Good, thought Keefe, now he'll begin to get some commanders in here. Then he realized that the phone must have been damaged in the struggle, for the detective threw it away in disgust and jumped down off the desk. Keefe turned back to the mirror. "Has anybody even tried to talk to this guy?" he demanded of Rainey. In the mirror the hostage was babbling at times. She was whimpering constantly. There was so much noise behind Keefe that he could not really hear this, but he saw it. He was moved by the need to help her, to establish a dialogue with the gunman that a more experienced man could use later, and so called out:

"Hello in there."

At the sound of his voice the man in the mirror glanced up sharply, but he made no answer.

Keefe decided to continue. "What would you like us to do? How can we help you?"

Behind him the room had emptied out slightly. The noise level had dropped slightly. There were uniformed cops helping Craighead's men clear the room.

Craighead came up to Keefe to report. "We broke into the office next door, Commissioner. I've got a man making those calls you wanted."

In a mid-town hotel ballroom a fund-raising banquet was underway on behalf of Catholic Charities. Dinner had not yet been served, but the speeches had started.

"I look out at all you important businessmen," the

cardinal intoned into the microphone. "I look around me at the dignitaries on the dais, and I have confidence in my city, our city."

The PC sat on the dais with the mayor on one side of him and the cardinal's empty chair on the other. He was pretending to listen attentively, but a man came up and whispered in his ear, causing him to get to his feet and move behind the curtain to a telephone.

After listening for a time he said into the receiver: "Keep me informed, of course."

Making his way back to the dais he regained his place beside the mayor, turned an attentive face in the direction of the cardinal at the microphone, and again pretended to listen.

In his office at headquarters Chief Kilcoyne was about to go home. He had put on his uniform coat and had buttoned it down the front. He had adjusted his gold braided cap on his head. He was stuffing papers into a briefcase when a deputy inspector in uniform, one of his secretaries, poked his head in the door.

"They're asking for you up at the Bronx courthouse, Chief. Some nut is holding a hostage."

Kilcoyne looked up sharply. "Who's in command?"

"I spoke to a detective from the auto squad, Chief. He said Lieutenant Craighead was there, and maybe some sergeants. Commissioner Keefe is there too."

"Keefe?" said Kilcoyne. He thought for a moment. He had no way of knowing what Keefe was doing there, but hoped he had the sense to stay out of the way. He said: "Have they sent for the Hostage Negotiating Team?"

"I think so, Chief. Do you want to take the phone?"

Kilcoyne shook his head. But he also removed his cap, smoothed down his white hair, and began to unbutton his coat. "I'll wait here until this is over," he said.

There were a hundred or more people in the corridor outside the room. Some were clerks and secretaries working late being drawn now from all over the building; some were sightseers in from the street. The crowd kept changing. People got bored and went away, but they were replaced by others. The ranks of press and TV crews had swollen and were still swelling. They waited impatiently to be informed; in the meantime they interviewed each other.

"Are there two hostages, or only one?"

"I heard somebody's been shot. Can you verify that?"

There were four uniformed cops with their backs to the door. Craighead had put them there. Keefe could see them each time the door opened or closed. He could see part of the mob in the corridor as well, for the door opened and closed frequently. The cops were keeping out the civilians and the press, but were letting through law enforcement personnel without distinction, with the result that the crowd inside the room did not diminish, nor did the noise level.

There were federal agents from Alcohol, Tobacco and Firearms, and from Drug Enforcement. There was a man with a gun from the New York State Beverage Control. Each time the door opened Keefe glanced up expectantly, looking for rank, but none came.

A lieutenant from the local precinct said the precinct commander had gone home an hour ago. Keefe told him to go next door and get the precinct commander on the telephone, get him in here.

There was a Sergeant Carmichael from the Stakeout Squad. He was accompanied by two detectives carrying sniper rifles. Carmichael presented them as the two best shots in the department.

"I don't think this situation lends itself to that particular skill," said Keefe sharply.

"What's the set-up in there?" demanded Carmichael.

"Look for yourself," said Keefe.

"We got through to the Police Commissioner," interrupted one of Craighead's detectives.

"And?"

"He's not coming. He asked to be kept informed."

"How about Chief Kilcoyne?"

"I don't think he's coming either." The detective looked abashed, as if he had failed in his assignment.

"Go back to the phone," Keefe told him. He realized he

was shouting partly to be heard over all the noise, partly out of anger and frustration. "Tell Craighead to phone Chief Gold. Order him to come in here at once."

"We don't have his home number," the detective explained. "And his office won't give it to us."

Keefe had the unlisted numbers of the police hierarchy in his address book, which he thrust into the detective's hand. "It's in there. Call him. Tell him I order him to hurry."

But Gold, who lived in a Long Island suburb, and who had got up from the dinner table to take the call, decided that it was not in his best interests to hurry. After phoning for his car he resumed his place at the head of the table and finished dinner. When he went outside the car was waiting, and he walked toward it across his lawn while calmly picking his teeth.

"Where to, Chief?" inquired his driver, when he had sat down in the front seat.

"The Bronx Courthouse," said Gold. "Take your time. Nothing to be alarmed about. It's a nice night, isn't it? Look at the moon. Look at those stars."

There were no stars, no moon that the driver could see. It was not yet even fully dark. He steered down the suburban street. The Bronx Courthouse was about an hour away.

"I am waiting for that judge."

The shout jerked Keefe's head around. Stepping forward, he peered through the partly open door at the reflection in the mirror. He could see both heads. The gunbarrel was resting against the cleaning woman's cheek. Her face was soaked in sweat.

"Why don't you put that gun down, and come out here and we'll talk?" he said. Talk can't hurt, he thought. That's what hostage negotiators did. They kept talking. They kept the pressure on the gunman, and they kept the hostage's hopes alive. It was his job as he saw it to get a dialogue going and keep it going until someone came to take charge.

"How can we help you if you won't talk to us?" he called out.

"I got nothing to say to you," the answer came back. "You get that judge in here. I got plenty to say to that judge."

Keefe turned to Rainey. "Where's the judge?"

"His clerk was here before. According to the clerk he's on a plane to London."

"Beautiful."

The Stakeout Squad sergeant said to Keefe, "There are windows in that room, Commissioner. Maybe it's possible to get a shot at him from across the courtyard. All we need in our scopes is a couple of inches of head. My men don't miss."

This idea seemed appalling to Keefe. "There's a hostage in there with him, Sergeant."

The uniformed lieutenant from the precinct was back. "I spoke to the precinct commander. He'll be here as soon as he can."

Keefe was vastly relieved. "Good."

"He lives about an hour out on Long Island," apologized the lieutenant.

Everybody in the police department, it sometimes seemed to Keefe, lived an hour out on Long Island.

At his ear the Stakeout Squad sergeant hissed: "Just a couple of inches of skull, Commissioner, that's all we need."

"Tell me your name again," he said.

"Sergeant Carmichael."

"I don't think it's time to kill anybody just yet, Carmichael," he said. "Do you hear me?" He realized how much his voice had risen only from the surprised expression on Rainey's face.

"I am beginning to lose my patience," Brown cried from the other room. "I want that judge in here. You bring that judge in here or this lady is going to get a bullet in her ear."

"Let me look over the building, Commissioner," said Carmichael confidently. "I'll get back to you." He and his two sharpshooters began shouldering through the crowd to the door.

Keefe might have moved to stop them, but he was distracted by the cleaning woman's voice which now was heard for the first time. She made a short speech composed mostly of the word "please" repeated many times. Her voice descended in volume until finally it broke and disappeared completely and she began to choke audibly on her fear.

"We've got to help her," Keefe said to Rainey. But he didn't know how to do it. He said: "Who is this Brown? Do we know anything about him? Do we have a sheet on him?"

"Do you have his sheet?" said Rainey to Craighead. "The Commissioner wants his sheet."

Craighead handed over two yellow pages stapled together – Brown's sheet. Keefe read it. Rainey read it over his shoulder. Disturbing the peace, dismissed. Aggravated assault, three months" probation. Assault with a deadly weapon, no disposition. Resisting arrest, no disposition. It told very little. In no way did it explain why Brown had gathered up the neat little package which was Keefe's case and done this to it. "A man of violence?" Keefe said to Rainey. "Or a man whose gorge is up to here, and who strikes out?" It was impossible to tell. "I don't see anything about stealing cars," Keefe said. "If he was a car thief, there ought to be something on here about stealing cars, wouldn't you say, Craighead?" He eyed Craighead coldly. Craighead eyed him back the same way.

It was Craighead's neat little package of a case too, Keefe reminded himself.

"And I want my truck," came Brown's voice again. "I want to look out this window behind me and see my truck parked in that street down there."

"Where's his truck?" said Keefe.

"In the department pound in Long Island City," Craighead said. "Naturally I sent for it right away but it's still rush hour outside, Commissioner. No telling how long it will take to get here."

"Simply beautiful," said Keefe.

The burly Sergeant Carmichael was back. "Commissioner," he said, "There's a line of sight into that room from across the courtyard." His eyes looked to Keefe too bright. "You can't see him, but you can see her. All he's got to do is move his head about five inches forward, and whacko. Do you want to take a look?"

"Let's take a look," said Keefe. There was enough tragedy here already. He wanted no one shot, and Carmichael frightened him. Until someone else turned up to assume command, whatever Carmichael did was his doing. Whatever anyone did. Among his jobs here, he saw clearly, was to hold Carmichael in check. To hold everyone in check.

With Rainey and Carmichael he pushed out into the corridor through the masses of people who waited there, and the reporters among them followed him down the hall with their questions, their microphones, lights, cameras. Many knew him personally and called him by name.

"You have an obligation to tell us what's happening, Phil."

"Have you taken personal command of the situation, Phil?"

"What outcome do you anticipate, Commissioner?"

The reporters were under stress too. He had been one of them in situations like this, and sympathized, but could not stop to answer questions now.

Gradually the reporters dropped back, their attention divided between the action presumably taking place inside the judge's chambers and the three men going away from it.

The confident Carmichael was in the lead, and Rainey was talking earnestly to Keefe in a low voice:

"The Stakeout guys hide in the backs of stores that have been stuck up a lot. Next time a stick up man comes in, they yell: 'Police! Freeze!' Usually the stick up man turns toward the sound of the voice. This is considered an aggressive act, and they shoot him dead. They've killed a lot of guys. Carmichael himself is known in the department as 'the Executioner's Song'."

On the opposite side of the building they entered a darkened office whose window gave onto the courtyard. The sash was all the way up, and the two snipers knelt with rifles on the sill, and peered across the courtyard through their scopes.

"Take a look through this, Commissioner," said Carmichael.

Keefe knelt. After a moment he managed to focus the

crosshairs on the hostage. Her brown face was so drained of colour it appeared grey. Her hair was grey. She was a middle-aged woman rigid with terror. Brown's arm was around her throat under her chin, his gun was pressed into her hair. She was about the same age, Keefe judged, as his own mother.

Brown himself was hidden by the angle of the wall and not visible.

"See what I mean, Commissioner?" said Carmichael.

Keefe put the rifle down.

"All we got to do," explained Carmichael, "is make him lean forward a bit and we take off the top of his head." He was like a mechanic explaining how to free a stuck brake. You pull gently on this lever and –

And a man's skull is shattered, Keefe thought. Brains go flying all over the room. It was an unacceptable solution, at least as yet. He was not sentimental about Brown's life, but killing was a last resort. "We're not going to kill anybody if we can help it," he said. "Okay? Understood?"

"Tell your men to pack up their weapons," said Rainey.

Carmichael's response surprised Keefe. "Can I see you in private, Commissioner?"

They stepped to one side of the room. "This Sergeant Rainey, Commissioner. I don't know if he's advising you or not. You ought to know that he's got a very bad record. He was the department's big lush for years." Carmichael was almost whispering. He was also watching Keefe. "He used to beat up prisoners when in his cups. His wife too, I heard. The department chaplains had a lot of trouble with him. They were always having to go out to his house."

"Sergeant Rainey is not our problem, Carmichael."

"There were, you know, other things, as well."

"Our problem right now is that cleaning woman."

"Right, sir. Now if we can get him to move just a few inches out of that corner, my men can put him away."

"Absolutely not." Keefe tried to stare Carmichael down, the better to convince himself that the man would do nothing without orders. He turned to Rainey. "Let's go back, Ed."

In the corridor he and Rainey hurried along. "How well do you know Sergeant Carmichael?"

"He used to be a drinking buddy in the days when I drank," Rainey said. "You know about that. You must have studied my record."

Keefe wished now he had. Even so, Rainey was the only man present in whom he had any confidence. "Sergeant Carmichael doesn't like you."

"I don't work for Sergeant Carmichael."

It was said quietly, but with a barely repressed fervour, an avowal of loyalty. Keefe looked at him, and then away, his thoughts reverting to the hostage. Where were all the other commanders who ought to be here by now? He was hoping for someone who would know exactly what to do. Why was he being left to handle this alone?

The three men waded into the mob that clogged the corridor. The TV lights came on again, and they were photographed as they pushed towards the cops guarding the door. The faces of the newsmen looked hostile to Keefe. He and the two sergeants went through them into the room.

"Has he said anything more?" Keefe asked Craighead.

"The same old stuff. He wants his truck and he wants the judge. Otherwise he's gonna kill the woman."

"Your truck has been sent for," Keefe called out. He was talking to the mirror, watching for a reaction. "It will be here soon. In a few minutes you should be able to look out the window and see it parked down there."

Brown did not answer.

"Mr. Brown," Keefe called out, "that cleaning woman has nothing to do with your problem. She's just an innocent woman, and I'm afraid you've frightened her. Why don't you let her come out here? Then we can talk."

Brown still did not answer.

"We can't produce the judge, I'm afraid," Keefe said. "He's in an airplane on his way to London. Is there anyone else you would like to talk to?"

An idea came to him. "Supposing we sent a lawyer in to talk to you? He can represent you. He can see that you get a fair shake out of this." Keefe was under great strain and his

214

voice was already hoarse. The lawyer, if they could find one brave enough to go in there, would seem a neutral negotiator, and would be in relatively little danger. He could negotiate the woman's release, then his own, without bloodshed. His appearance would comfort the woman. Her terror would diminish. She would not be alone. "If we send a lawyer in there, will you let the cleaning woman go?"

Or he could send a cop in disguised as a lawyer who, if he could get the hostage out of the line of fire, might overpower Brown. But a cop might merely kill him. A lawyer was better.

After a long pause came Brown's voice. "Yeah, I'll talk to a lawyer, you send him in here."

Beside Keefe, Carmichael said: "I'm your lawyer, Commissioner." He pulled his pants leg up, and Keefe saw he was wearing an ankle holster. He lifted his leg like a dog and patted the gun significantly. Keefe glanced from Carmichael to Rainey.

"I'll go, Commissioner," said Rainey.

Keefe called over to Craighead. "Send some men into the courtrooms. See if you can find a lawyer who'll go in there." He watched Craighead pull his men to one side and begin speaking to them.

"We have sent for a lawyer, Mr. Brown," Keefe called out. "Why don't you and I talk a few moments while we're waiting?"

"I know that voice," said Brown.

"My name is Keefe."

"I know who you are," said Brown. "You're the Commissioner. I just changed my mind. I don't want no lawyer, Mr. Commissioner, I want you. You the one got me into this. You come in here, and I let this lady go."

Jesus, Keefe thought, and turned away from the mirror.

"Stall, Commissioner," Rainey advised him.

"What else do you think I've been doing?" Keefe said. "How much longer can we stall before that poor woman's mind cracks – or his does?" Where was everybody who ought to be here? He had no intention of going in there.

"You don't want to talk to me, Mr. Brown." He turned

back to the mirror. "You need a lawyer to represent you. You hear me? What you need is a lawyer."

"Don't you tell me what I need," shouted Brown. "I said get in here. You the one I want. You come in here, they listen to me. You come in here in one minute, or I put a hole in this lady's ear that goes all the way through."

"He's bluffing, Commissioner," said Sergeant Carmichael. "If he shoots her, he's got nothing left to bargain with."

"He's already got nothing left to bargain with," said Keefe. "He can't possibly imagine that we'll let him walk out of here, can he?"

Brown's voice again jerked his attention back to the mirror. "You got a clock on your side of the door, Mr. Commissioner? I got one here and the second hand is moving. You got thirty seconds, Mr. Commissioner."

Again the cleaning woman's voice was heard, and she began to plead for her life. Again the operative word was "please", repeated many times. Keefe had never heard such terror in a human voice. The woman was forgetting to breathe. Finally she ran out of air, and once again began to choke.

It made Brown laugh, not at all an insane laugh, but an angry one. "You heard the lady, Mr. Commissioner. You got twenty seconds."

"You got to go in there, Commissioner," Carmichael said. "You got no choice." He genuflected in front of the hero-to-be as if in front of a god, but it was only to hike up Keefe's trouser leg. Keefe could feel the fingers working on his bare leg as the empty holster straps were tugged tight.

"Hand me your piece, Commissioner," Carmichael said, and when Keefe only stared down at him, he repeated it: "Your piece."

Carmichael shoved it into the holster. "There you are, Commissioner. Go in there and take him out."

Carmichael, it was clear, expected him to do it. So, apparently, did most of the faces around him. Keefe's principal emotion was disbelief. How had he got to this point? But he had no intention of going through that door. There were a dozen inspectors and chiefs who ought to be here by now. Where was everybody?

The situation as it existed was his responsibility. It had flowed from decisions he had made, events he had initiated. He accepted that. It even occurred to him that all the missing inspectors and chiefs accepted it too, which was why they weren't here. They were leaving him to it, leaving him to get out of it by himself.

"You got about ten seconds, Mr. Commissioner," came Brown's voice.

About ten seconds meant he had more. He saw that clearly. He was still thinking clearly – so he told himself. There were options. He could go into that room or not. But Brown's ultimatum sounded genuine to him: Brown would shoot the woman and then probably himself: two victims, not one, a holocaust. He himself would be responsible. It was his case. The woman was totally innocent. She did not deserve to die. As for Brown, Keefe was satisfied he had been unjustly arrested. He did not deserve to die either.

Suppose Keefe went in there? Was he brave enough to try it? He could negotiate and come out again. Brown meant him no harm. He would be as safe as any lawyer. He would get the woman out, then sweet talk the gun away from Brown. His fallback position was the lethal tool strapped to his leg. But he would never use it.

There were thirty men in the room, perhaps more. All had fallen silent. This was more drama than they had expected. As they saw it, the siege was over. The police department was about to attack; its instrument was this civilian deputy commissioner who in a moment would display the quality they prized above all others – physical bravery. They recognized Keefe's symptoms: the dry lips, the blinking eyes. Most of them had experienced similar emotions often enough. They noted his suddenly too tight collar, the constricted movements of his head and neck. Bravery and fear were not incompatible.

"Are you going in there?" said Rainey. He seemed to be suffering. His voice was full of compassion.

Go in and the cleaning woman might die anyway, first her, then him. Or the other way round. After which the cops outside would mow down Brown. The only man in the room who did not want him to try it, apparently, was Rainey.

The men had crowded around. He was the focus of their concentration, which was pleasant. Frightening too. He glanced from face to face. Suppose Brown didn't want to talk? Suppose all he wanted to do was shoot?

"Remember your training," said Rainey. "If you have to go for your gun you don't shoot to wound." Now Rainey did think he should do it, apparently. "Go for the life support system, the head, the heart, the spine."

The silence was of such intensity as to communicate itself through the door to the cops on guard outside it. Heads peered in. The news, jumping instantly to the surrounding newsmen, actuated the energy stored up so tightly for so long in that hallway. The mass lurched into motion. The door was pushed inward, and newsmen broke past the now disorganized line of cops. Only about a dozen got inside before control was re-established and the door again slammed shut, but this dozen included two complete television crews. Their lights turned the room brilliantly bright, and the mini-cams began to operate, sending Keefe's picture, live, onto hundreds of thousands of television screens in the metropolitan area.

"You got two seconds, Mr. Commissioner," came Brown's voice.

The cleaning woman was weeping piteously.

"You got one second, Mr. Commissioner."

The cleaning woman screamed.

"Wait," cried Keefe. "Don't shoot, I'm coming in." He stepped forward. Shoulder first, he edged through the door. "I'm coming in," he repeated, his voice on a choked descending note. First his shoulder extruded into the room, a target, then his head, a better one. He would be shot dead instantly, or not, and his eyes began to blink as if this room were brighter than the other, which it wasn't. He could not control them. Then he was all the way into the room and still alive. The incapacitating part of his fear dropped away. It was like the moment after the gun sounded at the start of a race. The imagery in his head was all guns at this time. There

218

was, considering the job to be done, no room for fear now.

He stood just inside the door, his eyes locked onto those of Joshua L. Brown. Behind the desk, pressed into the corner, were Brown and his hostage. He and Brown simply stared at each other. Brown seemed a man trying to hold his ground, and therefore not dangerous. I'm going to get out of this okay, Keefe told himself.

The cleaning woman had begun weeping again, but there was a different quality to it. The tears rolled down her face, and they seemed to Keefe to be tears of relief, of gratitude, even though Brown's arm was still wrapped tightly around her neck, while his other hand held the gun to her head. She was speaking, or trying to. She was babbling her thanks. She was thanking principally God, though Keefe as well.

"Approach this desk, Mr. Commissioner," ordered Brown.

But Keefe, standing just inside the door, shook his head. "Let her go first."

The staring match resumed. Neither he nor Brown would drop his eyes.

In the anteroom whose safety Keefe had just left, a frantic commotion took place as Rainey, Craighead and the others struggled to eject the newsmen and TV crews once more. Keefe was aware of the great babble of voices behind him. He was aware of everything. His senses had never seemed so keen. He stood in a room where lives were at balance in a state of total silence. In the room behind him a war was going on, each side battling to defend its rights which, under the circumstances, were of negligible importance.

The press had the power to spotlight, the power to magnify, and had just done so. A commonplace hostage confrontation had just become an event. The images, the excited commentary, had gone out live onto TV screens.

"Deputy Commissioner Keefe, in an act of incredible bravery –"

In Keefe's living room Sharon stood with her fist to her mouth, mute, unbelieving.

219

Chief Kilcoyne, once he had been advised, was unbelieving too.

For most of an hour he had sat behind his desk in shirtsleeves and tie, finishing up some paperwork. He was waiting without much interest to hear what the outcome would be. There was only one hostage, who was not in any way celebrated – a cleaning woman, apparently. The hostage-taker was a petty criminal of no notoriety. Both were black, which was all to the good: no political or racial overtones. Nor were the gunman's demands in any way spectacular. As Kilcoyne understood it, the man wanted only to see the judge who had arraigned him. It was a case, to Kilcoyne's mind, that could be handled by any sergeant or lieutenant, which is what he assumed was happening. The Chief of Operations lived in a world in which whole embassies were held hostage, or airliners packed with passengers. This case in the Bronx had failed to excite him. Once, looking up from his desk, he had even wondered why he had not gone home at his usual hour. His answer: he was a conscientious man who sometimes carried conscientiousness too far. Hostage cases could be tricky, and could take unexpected turns, and so he had stayed.

As he sat poring over memos the heavy-holstered service revolver that he had carried all his adult life was partially supported by his belt, partially by the chair in which he sat. He was so used to it he was scarcely aware that it was there. Since he was white-haired and middle-aged, an outsider might have found his appearance at the same time both menacing and incongruous. On the one hand he represented the epitome of law and order. On the other he could stand as the embodiment of the western sheriff grown old in the job.

He had not been watching TV himself, for the office screen hung on the wall in his outer office, but certain of his subordinates had, and one of them now rapped on his door.

"Chief, that psycho is still barricaded in the judge's chambers. But he's got Commissioner Keefe in there now."

Kilcoyne was incredulous. *"What?"*

"It was an ultimatum, Chief. He was going to kill the hostage if Commissioner Keefe didn't go in there. So he went."

Having got to his feet, Kilcoyne yanked his jacket off the coat tree. As his fingers worked the buttons, as he found his hat and clamped it down on his head, he was at the same time issuing orders. "Have my car brought around in front. Reach out for the Chief of Detectives. He is to report to me at the Bronx Courthouse forthwith. Get me the PC on the phone."

While these things were being done, Kilcoyne stood in his doorway, eyes fixed on the TV screen. The pictures were unclear. The cameraman was being jostled. Then he understood that the press was being forced out of the room. Finally the commentator came back on and explained what little was known. So now we have two individuals hostage, not one, Kilcoyne thought. And because one of them is a deputy police commissioner, the situation has escalated beyond all reason.

His next thought was the critical one, the one he would operate on: the problem was not what it seemed – it was not Keefe being held hostage, but the department itself. Such a thought was peculiar to a man like Kilcoyne, who had been a policeman for thirty-three years, who had operated always according to a strict code of honor but who, nonetheless, had felt himself despised by most of his fellow citizens during all that time. The entire city will be watching to see how we get out of this, he told himself. *If* we get out of it. Talk about operating in a spotlight. He would have to take personal command now. There was no other possibility.

Then he realised with what passed for elation in a man of his age that this was perhaps not such a bad thing. He would take command, and with luck save the situation. As a result his own career would take a great bound forward. With a single stroke he might hope to regain all the ground he had lost recently.

"I have the PC for you, Chief."

Kilcoyne grabbed the phone. "There's a little problem developing up at the Bronx Courthouse," he began. He told what he knew, then fended off questions for which he had no answers. He could hear the confusion in the PC's voice. Egan was not going to know how to cope with a thing like this. "No, I have no details," Kilcoyne told him.

"I'm on my way up there now. I'll take personal command."

Egan began to talk about this dinner he was at. Should he himself go up to the Bronx Courthouse, as well? Apparently he was seated between the mayor and the cardinal. Politically it was a good spot to be in, Kilcoyne realized. Egan was expected to make a little speech later, he said. He intended to tell a joke. If he made any sudden departure this would certainly be noted and remarked upon.

Kilcoyne didn't care whether he came or not. Once he himself had reached the courthouse and begun to give orders bookish Tim Egan, this little man who was in the process of turning police tradition upside down, would not interfere.

Though anxious to get to his car, Kilcoyne was obliged to listen to him to the end. Finally Egan concluded that he had best leave the dinner and get up to the courthouse.

"Fine," said Kilcoyne. "I'll see you up there then."

Kilcoyne's message reached Chief Gold in his car. He was sitting beside his driver, staring impassively out the window at the darkening sky when the radio began to crackle at his feet.

"Car number four, K?" came the voice of Central.

Central's voice was emotionless. Gold's would be equally emotionless when he answered. The two parties would converse principally via symbols. Momentous events would be discussed, if they were discussed at all, in a kind of rune.

Gold took the microphone off the dashboard hook and said into it: "This is car number four, Central."

"Car number four is ordered to report to the Bronx Courthouse forthwith, K."

"Central, this is car number four, we're about thirty minutes out, K."

"Car number four, 10–4."

"10–4," Gold said into the microphone, and he hung it back up. To his driver he said: "Something's happened. Put the red light on. Use the siren when you need it. Let's go."

Seventeen

IN THE DARKENED OFFICE ACROSS THE COURTYARD THE two snipers knelt at the open window. One was peering along his rifle through the telescopic sight. The other's rifle rested on the sill while he exercised the muscles of his neck. "I get a stiff neck staring through that thing," he complained to his partner.

"There he is!" said the partner excitedly. "There he is!"

The first sniper had dived back to his own rifle. "Where? Where?"

"I just got a glimpse of him. Then he stepped back. He's not behind the desk no more. He's on the other side of the room."

Both stared through their scopes, fingers on the triggers. "How did he get there?"

"I don't know. It's a white guy. I thought he was black. If he steps forward again, I'm going to pop him."

"Hit him under the shoulder, if you can," the second sniper advised. "It's just as fatal, and much less messy." They both knew this, but in a real-life situation a shooter was tense and could forget.

The first sniper was moving his scope around. The crosshairs were searching. "You're right," he said. "Brains explode."

All the news crews had been ejected, but when Rainey looked around him the room seemed as crowded as ever. The emergency service men in armor were still there waiting, shotguns across their breasts. There were cops in uniform and cops in civilian clothes with shields pinned to their shirts. Nearly everybody had his gun out. Rainey had never seen so many naked guns in one room. Two of the FBI

223

men held the barrels against their ears, pointed at the ceiling. They looked like high school boys playing cops and robbers.

Rainey himself was in front, Sergeant Carmichael at his elbow. Through the door they watched Keefe's back. Rainey could no longer see the gunman and his hostage; Keefe's body blocked the mirror. Rainey was listening hard, but the only voice he heard was Carmichael's whispering in his ear.

"If the guy comes out of his corner less than a foot, this will all be over in a second. My guys –"

"My God," cried Rainey. "The sharpshooters don't know the Commissioner is in there."

Then came Brown's voice from inside the room: "I said approach this desk."

Rainey had already turned and was rushing toward the door. He charged out into the hall, pushing aside cameramen and reporters who got in his way. People were cursing at him but he got clear, and began sprinting down the hall. He had at least a hundred yards to run, and perhaps only seconds to run it in, he was forty-six years old and was not in particularly good shape. As he rounded the corridor he ran full tilt into two cops in uniform who tried to grab him. Perhaps they thought him a perpetrator trying to escape. He bulled through them like a fullback, and then at last had reached the door on the opposite side of the courtyard. He threw it open and was just in time to hear one sniper cry excitedly to his partner, "There he is again."

"Don't shoot!" shouted Rainey. "Don't shoot. The Commissioner's in there with him now."

The two men turned from the window. All the air seemed to go out of them, and out of him too.

"Jesus Christ," one of them cried. "Somebody might have told us." Both of them began complaining to Rainey. Nobody ever told them anything, they whined. How could they be responsible for what might happen when no one ever kept them informed for Chrissake?

Rainey went back the way he had come. He shouldered through the mob. The cops at the door let him through, and he moved up to the front as before. Only a minute or two had passed; nothing had changed.

Inside the judge's chambers Keefe still stared steadily into Brown's eyes, which finally fell. An important victory perhaps, though minor. Keefe's voice, to his relief, came out sounding controlled, firm. "You can't have two hostages," he said. "You can only have one. Her or me. Which is it going to be? I'll come over there and talk to you, but not until you let her go."

"I's the man with the gun this time, Mr. Commissioner. You going to do what I say, and exactly what I say."

"No."

The cleaning woman was babbling again, her voice rising and falling. Her face was wet with sweat and tears.

Keefe said to her: "Mr. Brown has decided to let you go. Take his arm away from around your neck. Go on, just lift his arm away from around your neck. That's right. Very good. Now step to the edge of the desk. All right, now come here. Walk very slowly. Nothing is going to happen to you."

Keefe, as he called out these instructions, never took his eyes off Brown's face. Brown himself for the first time seemed confused. After a moment he ignored the cleaning woman. His gun turned from her head until it was pointed directly at Keefe.

"One move, Mr. Commissioner, one move and you dead."

A silver revolver. Keefe recognised neither its make nor its calibre. A Saturday Night Special, perhaps. He did not know much about guns. "Take another step toward me," Keefe told the woman, who was now only a step or two away. "Now reach out and take my hand."

There was a moment during which the two outstretched hands almost met. Suddenly the cleaning woman screamed, plunged past Keefe and twisted her way through the door. Once on the other side she simply kept running, still screaming, running out past the crowd, out through the second door into the corridor. No one in the anteroom moved to stop her in time, nor anyone out in the corridor either, though of course she would have been prized as an interview subject by any of the newsmen present. But her appearance was too unexpected. She was too fast for them. Then she was gone.

Keefe sensed this from the sound of her diminishing screams. But his concentration was fixed absolutely on Joshua L. Brown, and on the gun whose muzzle hole stared at him like an eye. Having succeeded in extricating the hostage he had just realized with sudden shock that to extricate himself would be more difficult, perhaps impossible. The cleaning woman, while still in the room, had even been something of a shield for him, for she was not a fit object for Brown's rage. Keefe himself, however, was. He saw his own mortal danger so suddenly and so clearly that he was for a few seconds immobilized by absolute terror. He was unable to move except to tongue his dry lips, to blink rapidly several times.

"Close the door behind you, Mr. Commissioner."

"You want to talk?" Keefe said, trying to project the confidence he had felt only moments ago. But there was a crack in his voice. He heard it and he knew the gunman heard it. "All right, let's talk."

"I said, close it," Brown shouted. And then: "That's better. Now lock it."

Without taking his gun off Keefe, Brown edged to one side until his outstretched hand touched what he was looking for, the judge's high swivel chair. He sat down in it, and the angle of the wall was such that he was still protected, Keefe noted, from the snipers across the courtyard.

"Approach this desk, Mr. Commissioner. Your judge wants to speak to you. I the judge now."

Keefe took a step forward. Then he took another one. Brown's gun got closer. He found he could not bear to look at it. Instead his eyes ranged over the room. In front of the desk was a chair, in which Brown evidently wanted him to sit. Against the wall was a row of filing cabinets. Keefe looked them over. In his terror he was looking for possible cover – anything he might dive behind. The filing cabinets were one possibility. But he noted nothing else. Across the room was a sofa, but it was too far away and no protection

226

anyway. Keefe sat down on the chair indicated. Brown, eyeing him from behind the gun, showed no trace of madness that Keefe could perceive. He was not dealing with a crazy man but with an angry one. Brown conveyed only the awesome power of one human being who holds a gun on another. His attitude, Keefe judged, was of barely controlled violence.

"I want that judge in here. You hear me? I want my truck, and I want my eight hundred dollars. I get all those things, maybe you live a little longer."

To Keefe's relief his intense fear had begun to dissipate. "Your truck will be here in a few minutes," he said. "We've sent for it. You'll be able to look out the window and see it down there."

"That's the first smart thing you've said so far, Mr. Commissioner."

"Yes."

"I want to see the ignition keys on this desk. I want to see the eight hundred dollars on this desk. And I want the judge in here."

"The judge has nothing to do with this now. What do you want to see the judge for?"

"When I walk out that door, I want everything legal."

"You want everything legal?"

"All it takes is a piece of paper. You can do anything in this world, you got the right piece of paper. The judge, he give me the piece of paper, and I walk right out that door."

"You walk right out that door."

"I get in my truck, and I drive away, all legal."

"Tell me about your truck. That's a nice truck."

"You know how long it took me to buy that truck? Six years. Now I own it free and clear. I got my own little business going. You already caused me to lose a day's pay. I want my truck back and I'm getting mighty impatient." Somewhat calm at the beginning of this speech, Brown had begun to tremble with anger by the end of it.

"All right, calm down. Your truck will be here soon."

"And my money, and the judge."

"We'll take this one step at a time."

"We miss any of them steps, Mr. Commissioner, and I blow your head off."

This possibility seemed entirely too real. Keefe's whole body was sweating. He was soaked in sweat. "What purpose would that serve? Supposing you blow my head off – then what?"

"I go out on that statement."

"You go out on that statement."

"You wasting my time, Mr. Commissioner. I feeling this powerful urge to shoot you right now and have done with it."

In the anteroom there was no more babble of voices. Everyone was listening hard to the muffled words that came through the door. Rainey, his ear pressed against the wood, became increasingly agitated. "I've got to get in there with him," he muttered. "He shouldn't be in there alone. He doesn't have any experience for this. That psycho will kill him."

"I can have my men start firing through the window," suggested Sergeant Carmichael in a hoarse whisper. "The diversion will give the Commissioner a chance to go for his gun."

Ignoring Carmichael, Rainey shouted through the door. "This is Judge Rainey out here, Mr. Brown. They tell me you want to see Judge Baum. He's not here, but I'll be glad to take your case. My name is Judge Rainey."

Rainey's eye had fallen on a coat cupboard in a corner of the anteroom. He ran to it, and inside found a judge's robe which he put on. Wearing it, he ran back to the door. "Can you hear me in there, Mr. Brown?" he shouted. He tried the doorknob. "This is Judge Rainey. If you can just let me in, I'm sure we can straighten everything out in a jiffy."

But in his highbacked judge's chair behind Judge Baum's desk, Brown became enraged. "You cops get away from that door. Touch that door one more time and I put a bullet through Mr. Commissioner."

With that he cocked the revolver. In the sudden silence it sounded to Keefe enormously loud. It was a shocking thing to do. The gun was pointed directly at his face. It could go off even by accident. He was trying to remain absolutely

228

still, for any sudden movement might cause Brown's finger to twitch, but the sweat was trickling down his cheeks, down his nose, as well as down his back and chest, and he was afraid that any second he would sneeze, or cough, or scream, and as a result he would be shot.

He called out as loudly as he dared: "Judge Rainey, I wish you would back away from that door. You're making Mr. Brown nervous. You're making me nervous too."

Did Rainey make some reply? Keefe imagined he had said something. In any case, the door handle stopped moving.

Behind the door the distraught Rainey was again muttering to himself: "I got to get in there. He needs my help. I got to find some way to help him."

Keefe's concentration was on the gun. Brown had begun to rock almost imperceptibly back and forth in the judge's chair, and the gun was still cocked. "Mr. Brown," Keefe said, "you've got that gun cocked. The slightest pressure and it could go off. You're angry. I don't blame you. In your place I'd be angry too. I know you don't want to shoot me by accident, but with the gun cocked like that it could go off without your meaning it to go off. So why don't you uncock the gun? Please, Mr. Brown, uncock the gun."

"If this gun go off, Mr. Commissioner, it's not going to be no accident."

Keep him talking, Keefe thought. If you can keep him talking he won't shoot. "Why don't we talk about where you're coming from, Mr. Brown? Tell me about yourself. For instance, do you have any children? When and where were you born?"

But Brown continued only to rock very slightly back and forth in the judge's chair. He said nothing.

"I'm sorry about this morning," Keefe said. "I think you were done an injustice this morning. We've managed to investigate your case since then. We realize that you weren't involved in that car stealing ring. So getting your truck back, and your eight hundred dollars bail – those things are just a matter of time. If you'd just be patient a little longer. And I do wish you would uncock that gun. Maybe you could point it off to the side for a second while you uncock it, in case the hammer should slip when you're letting it down."

Suddenly Brown began to laugh. It was in no sense a maniacal laugh, only an ugly one. It was the laugh of a man of power who is unconcerned about the results of his use of that power. "You ever had a gun pointed at you before, Mr. Commissioner? You ever had your hands handcuffed behind your back? You ain't had very many experiences in your life, have you? I wouldn't be as afraid of getting shot as you are, Mr. Commissioner. I've been shot before."

"Calm down, Mr. Brown. Your truck will be here soon."

Keefe tried to force his mind to work, but it felt as sodden as his clothing. He could not think what more to say, much less do, and so became subject to another onrush of terror. The terror was such that he felt unable to bend his arms and legs. The door behind him was locked. No one could get in. No one could help him. He would have to help himself. There was a gun at his ankle, and he began trying to force the hand in his lap along his thigh, down his calf toward it. His hand proceeded in a series of jerks. His fingers began trying to raise the trouser leg.

Suddenly Brown called out: "What you doing there?"

"An itch," said Keefe. His body was again rigid. He sat straight up in his chair. "I wanted to scratch an itch."

"Next time you scratch an itch will be the last time."

Eighteen

CHIEF KILCOYNE, HAVING REACHED THE CRIMINAL Courts building, strode down the corridor toward the mass of newsmen, law enforcement officers, and curiosity seekers of all kinds who entirely choked the corridor off. To Kilcoyne they were a lump in the throat of the building, in the throat of justice itself. The Chief of Operations would have seemed imposing enough alone, for he was big, ramrod straight, and white-haired, a presence. But his importance was reinforced by the weight of his entourage. Beside him and behind him advanced a number of other officers – some captains, an inspector, even a deputy chief. All the hats wore gold braid, though none as much as his.

"Move back." Two of the captains had begun to function as ushers. "Move back, I say. Make way for Chief Kilcoyne."

Kilcoyne's voice boomed out: "Inspector, clear these people out of here. I want this corridor clear. Media people, out. A man's life is in jeopardy."

But as he moved through the mob, microphones were thrust in his face. "Chief, we're on live here," shouted a TV reporter. "My station has preempted other programming –"

Kilcoyne ignored all the microphones and the cameras. "When we get our man out of there, you can have your story." There were cops in uniform at the door. "You police officers help move these people back," he ordered, and he delegated two captains to stay behind to see that it was done.

He passed through into the anteroom where he called out: "Who's in charge here?" He expected – and got – no answer. The room had fallen silent to see this impressive man among them, this perfect picture of a commander. There was a silent sigh of relief. Kilcoyne could feel it, could almost hear it. "How long has Commissioner Keefe been in there?" he demanded.

It was Sergeant Rainey who answered. Kilcoyne didn't know him. "About thirty-five minutes, Chief."

Kilcoyne began to ask questions. Dozens of men crowded around him, but it was Rainey who answered most of them. At Kilcoyne's request, Rainey also drew a rough lay-out of the room beyond the closed door, including the filing cabinet on its side that partly blocked the doorway. He penciled in the approximate locations of the gunman, and of Keefe. Even though the door was now locked the gunman's voice was still coming from the neighborhood of the judge's desk, and Keefe's came from that direction too.

"I have men in a room across the courtyard," said Sergeant Carmichael.

Kilcoyne knew who Carmichael was. "We'll get to that," he said.

He had handled dozens of hostage situations in the past. The taking of hostages was not a new police problem, whatever the public might think. The political use of hostages was not even new. The idea itself went back to Biblical times, or before. The hostages of legend were usually captured kings, captured captains, or else famous beauties like Helen of Troy. To Kilcoyne nothing changed in the world except for designations. You could call a crime by a new name but it was always an old crime, and criminals were the oldest and least innovative persons one could imagine. By the time Kilcoyne himself had come into the department there were no more kings in the world, or at least few of them, and no more famous beauties, or at least few of them. The hostage-takers he had encountered were usually stick up men caught in the act, and trying to weasel out of it by holding a gun to the head of some terrified grocery clerk; or else they were distraught husbands, threatening to kill faithless wives. Sometimes, too, the hostages were cops who had done something stupid, and been caught by the criminal and disarmed, and that was the category facing Kilcoyne now, or so he believed. He himself had not taken command in a situation like this since the rank of captain – a long time ago – but before that he had never failed to secure the release of the hostage in question unharmed, and the capture of the hostage-taker. The secret then and now, he believed, was quickness in planning and decisiveness in execution.

By the time he had finished questioning Rainey the situation was entirely clear to him. So were his various options, and he believed he knew exactly what to do.

He began to give orders. He was avid for the action to commence. Slow down, he cautioned himself. Think it out carefully. No mistakes. "I want a battering-ram brought in here," he ordered. "Also a loudhailer."

"I can take care of the ram, Chief," said Lieutenant Craighead.

"Then do it," said Kilcoyne. He turned to another of his

232

captains. "Find some telephones and put men on them. Call for an ambulance. Get a doctor in here. And stretcher-bearers. I want to see them in this room. I want portable radios. I want bulletproof vests." He had noted the two emergency service men with shotguns: two were all he would need to make the initial assault, if there were to be an assault; but he would need cops in uniform in reserve, and he wanted them in vests. Glancing around he selected at random the cops he wanted. He sent them to stand in the corner like schoolboys. "You federal agents," he said, "thank you all for coming. We don't need you any longer. Please clear the room. You courtroom guards, thank you, and please clear the room." There was so much authority in his big voice that he was obeyed without protest. Slowly the room emptied out. "My staff, stand by," he ordered. "Sergeant Carmichael, stand by. All you other police officers wait outside in the hall. We'll call you when we need you."

Among those just dismissed was Sergeant Rainey, who came forward and said anxiously: "I work for Commissioner Keefe, Chief. I request permission to stay."

Kilcoyne now managed to put a name to the man facing him. "I know you. You're Rainey."

"Let me stay, Chief."

Kilcoyne was trying to recall what he knew about Rainey. At the same time he was about to deny his request. In a hostage situation you wanted uniformed men only, and one reason was because gunmen usually found it harder to shoot at uniforms than at men in plain clothes. But there was such urgency in Rainey's tone and in his eyes that Kilcoyne weakened. Rainey was, after all, the only one present who seemed to know what the interior of the adjoining room looked like. In addition he could take care of Keefe when this was over – drive him home, or whatever. By then Keefe would not be in good shape, even if he got out of this without a scratch.

"All right, stay," Kilcoyne said. He turned to Carmichael. "I'll take a look at that room across the courtyard now."

To his satisfaction he found the corridor outside empty

233

except for law enforcement personnel. A crime scene barrier had been placed across the top of the staircase, he noted. Behind it were the newsmen who shouted out demands for information as soon as they saw him. He ignored their clamor and walked on.

The two snipers were still crouched over their rifles. Kilcoyne had with him Rainey's drawing and he peered over the snipers' shoulders and compared it to what he could see of the room across the courtyard. It seemed accurate enough, though he couldn't see much: the windows were too small. He could see nothing of the gunman, nor of Keefe. He could see so little that he decided to withdraw the snipers. The likelihood of their getting a clear shot in advance of any action by him he judged small, and he did not want to worry about them firing into the room once his own men were in there. They represented an uncontrollable and essentially extraneous element. Furthermore, the public did not like to read about people being picked off by police snipers, and this was a consideration too. He told them to pack up their weapons and leave, and waited there until they had done so.

He then returned to the judge's anteroom where he walked over to the clerk's desk and calmly sat down. His preparations were made. He had only to wait for the gear he had ordered to arrive, and for the Police Commissioner to arrive – Chief Gold too, if he should be in time. Although Kilcoyne knew precisely which steps he meant to take and in which order, he was too wise in the ways of the police department to move in any direction at all without first seeking a consensus. For a man of his rank in a situation of this nature, consensus was a formality only, but it was an important one and over the years he himself had climbed upwards in rank over the ruined careers of men who had thought otherwise. He would present his plan to Tim Egan who would acquiesce because he was a weak man, and to Gold who would acquiesce because he was a subordinate. Only then, fully protected, would he proceed. If the results of his actions should in some way turn out calamitous, the blame would be spread three ways; in case of success, the

234

credit would be his alone. But success seemed certain. By morning the mayor would be calling a press conference at which to congratulate him publicly. The papers would be speaking of him as a possible next PC, and Egan's wishy-washy theorising of the past few months would be just about over.

On the other side of the door, Keefe knew nothing about the arrival of Chief Kilcoyne, nor about his preparations and plans. He was alone, and he was quite literally sweating it out. His face was soaked, his clothing too, and because he was immobile, unable to take any action at all on his own behalf, his fear and tension seemed to become minute by minute more extreme.

"I ain't gonna wait much longer," said the voice behind the gun. "You tell them that outside." When Keefe did not immediately comply, Brown shouted: "Tell them, I said."

Keefe complied. "Mr. Brown is becoming impatient," he said. His voice was loud enough, but not quite steady, and he was interrupted by a fit of coughing. When it stopped he continued. "He said he is not going to wait much longer."

To Brown, Keefe said: "I told you before that your truck was on its way, Mr. Brown. That's the truth. We had it in a pound in Long Island City. It was rush hour, you know. Traffic was probably pretty bad out there in Queens. I'm sure your truck will be here soon. The eight hundred dollars is no problem either. The problem is the judge, Mr. Brown. We haven't been able to locate Judge Baum. You'll have to accept another judge. Are you married, Mr. Brown? Where do you live?"

"Don't you tell me what I have to do. I am the man with the gun."

Keefe stole a glance at the clock. How long had he been locked in this room? How long before he got out of it? *If* he got out.

The Police Commissioner had reached the courthouse.

"This is an awful thing, Dennis," he said to Kilcoyne as he arrived. "Awful."

"Do you want to take command, Commissioner?" asked Kilcoyne.

Egan's answer did not surprise him. "You're the tactical expert here, Dennis. You carry on."

Kilcoyne nodded. He accepted the PC's statement at face value. His own competence was superior and Egan knew it as well as he did. He scarcely realized that the PC too was perhaps thinking politically, trying to spread any eventual blame.

"It's not just one man who's being held hostage in there," Kilcoyne told him. "It's the police department itself."

"You're right." The PC seemed to shrink before his eyes, to become, if possible, even smaller in size, and much more agitated.

"We can't permit such a situation to last much longer," said Kilcoyne. "Nor, under the circumstances, can we make any deal."

Egan nodded. His thumbnail was at his teeth and he was gnawing on it.

"The bottom line," said Kilcoyne, "is that we send an assault team in through that door. There are a few things we can try first, but that's the bottom line."

When Egan nodded at him again, Kilcoyne added: "I'm waiting for the tools now." This, to him, concluded the discussion, and the transfer of power as well.

A uniformed cop entered carrying a loudhailer. "I got it out of my radio car in the street," he explained. He stood there beaming, as if he expected congratulations.

"Thank you," Kilcoyne told him curtly. "Now, wait outside." He turned the instrument on, tapping the mouthpiece with his finger and listening for the noise. It was working. To Egan he said: "Might as well get started."

"What about the hostage negotiating team?" said Egan hurriedly.

Kilcoyne saw that Egan was losing his nerve. "It's a five-man team, Commissioner. Three of them are in Philadelphia giving a seminar to the department there. I have men trying to reach the other two, but I'm not sure that we can wait for them." He studied Egan carefully, waiting to see if he would countermand him. He himself had never believed in the hostage negotiating team anyway, though he realized that

236

most of the world these days seemed to. According to modern theory, if you just kept talking to hostage-takers long enough they would give up without bloodshed. The trouble was, the talking most times went on far too long. There were cases where it had lasted days or even weeks, with no guarantee in the end that it would work. It seemed to Kilcoyne that in fact such methods had failed as often as they had succeeded, especially in one-on-one situations like this one. The success ratio of the old method – sudden overwhelming force – was just as good, and far quicker, and action was a good deal easier on the nerves of all concerned.

"We can give the hostage negotiating team a shot at it, if they get here in time," Kilcoyne said. "But it won't hurt for me to get started with this thing." He gestured at the loudhailer in his hands. He waited a moment to see if Egan would say anything more, but he did not.

So Kilcoyne stepped close to the locked door, raised the loudhailer to his mouth, and began a speech that, in the small closed room, came out with almost explosive power.

"Brown? Listen to me, Brown. This is Chief of Operations Kilcoyne speaking. I am the highest-ranking uniformed officer in the police department. This has gone far enough. Your demands cannot and will not be met until you have released Commissioner Keefe to safety. Once that happens, we promise you your day in court."

To Keefe on the far side of the door Kilcoyne's voice had sounded no less loud. It terrified him anew, and it made Brown laugh. His laughter was not amusement but a single abrupt guffaw, an angry ironical bray. To Keefe, Brown was a bomb waiting to explode. His sudden laughter now only reinforced this impression. Kilcoyne was a bomb waiting to explode also. Events were about to be set in motion over which he, Keefe, would have no control, and his level of fear rose up and up until it seemed to reach the roof of his skull. It was like an elevator rising with so much speed as to threaten to burst out through the top of his head.

Again the voice from the loudhailer sounded through the door.

"Listen to me, Brown. You have chosen to take on the

entire New York Police Department. You can't win. We have too much fire power for you. The time has come to put that gun down, and submit to due process of law. I'm going to ask Commissioner Keefe to stand up, do an about-face, walk to the door and let himself out of the room. Once he is out of that room, you will have precisely sixty seconds in which to give yourself up." There was a dramatic pause, then the loudhailer resumed. "Now, Commissioner Keefe, stand up."

It might work, Keefe thought. Still staring into the muzzle of the gun, he rose slowly to his feet.

"Commissioner Keefe, do an about-face," the loudhailer ordered.

Though standing, Keefe found himself unable to take a step in any direction at all.

"Mr. Commissioner," Brown said, "if you do not sit down again promptly I will blow a hole in your head."

"Now, walk to the door, please, Commissioner," said the loudhailer.

Keefe slowly sat down. From his chair he called out: "Chief Kilcoyne, please let me handle this."

This reply seemed to shake Kilcoyne's confidence, for there was a long silence. Then the loudhailer sounded again. "Walk toward the door, Phil."

"Please," said Keefe in a cracked voice, "I can't."

Kilcoyne slowly lowered the loudhailer. He handed it to a cop who looked at it for a minute, then stood it up on its open mouth near the wall.

Kilcoyne meanwhile stared at the Police Commissioner. Neither spoke.

The battering-ram arrived. It was the same one used at the junkyard earlier that morning, and it was carried by two of the same detectives who had employed it then.

Chief of Detectives Gold arrived too. He had been listening to news broadcasts in his car for the last twenty miles, and he had reached the courthouse with preformed impressions that a glance at the room, at all the tense faces, in no way caused him to alter. The presence of the ram told him which way Kilcoyne intended to go; but he had already decided what his own posture was going to be.

The PC, Gold noted, stood some distance apart nibbling on his thumbnail, staring at nothing.

Gold allowed himself to be drawn off to one side by Kilcoyne, who began whispering, though nothing of what he had to say sounded secret to Gold. It was a briefing, and not a very coherent one.

"It's all over the news broadcasts," Gold interrupted him. "I know all I need to know." Not true. He knew all he wanted to know. What did he want to know more for? He was not in command here and saw no way command might devolve upon him. He wanted no responsibility of any kind for whatever might happen next. He didn't even want to know about it.

"We are damned if we do, and damned if we don't," said Kilcoyne. "This has gone on much too long. I think the time has come to go through that door."

This was only what Gold had expected from Kilcoyne. It might work or it might not. In a hostage situation, you bet on one tactic or another, and there was no sure thing. But Gold had no intention of betting on either.

"I get your thinking," he said, then added, as if encouragingly: "Hitting the door might create enough of a diversion for Keefe to escape alive." This was perhaps what Kilcoyne was thinking. On the other hand, he was perhaps thinking nothing at all except how much he wanted to save the situation and become the hero of the city.

Gold glanced around, looking for members of the hostage negotiating team. He did not see any, and when he asked Kilcoyne about it he learned that three of them were in Philadelphia, and the remaining pair had not yet been located. This information made him nod his head. "Who okayed Philadelphia?" Gold asked.

Kilcoyne jerked his head in the direction of the PC. "The Boss did."

Gold thought it over. Politically speaking, the way to handle a hostage crisis was to stay away from it – to leave it to the hostage negotiating team, a bunch of patrolmen and sergeants. It was too late for that now. Politically speaking, the PC would be in trouble tomorrow however this came out, and if anything happened to young Keefe so would

Kilcoyne. Gold in no sense wished harm to Keefe, and would have helped him if he could. However, he could not. Therefore he had one concern, and one only: to stay out of the line of command himself; to make certain that when this was over he himself was in a position to move one step further up the career ladder, possibly two.

"What's Keefe doing in there in the first place?" demanded Kilcoyne almost petulantly.

"Good question," said Gold.

"He shouldn't be in there," concurred the PC who had joined them. "What are you going to do?"

"We've waited too long already," said Kilcoyne firmly. "Every minute that passes, Brown grows more confident. He knows he's got the entire New York Police Department at a standstill out here. Psychologically, he gets stronger every minute and we get weaker. If we're gong to do it, we do it now."

The PC glanced from Kilcoyne's face to Gold's. Although Gold knew Egan was waiting to hear his advice, he kept silent.

The doctors and stretcher-bearers had come in. The three men studied them in silence. Finally the PC said to Kilcoyne: "You're the tactical expert here, Dennis." After a pause he said to Gold: "Any ideas, Al?"

"Whatever Chief Kilcoyne decides is fine with me," answered Gold, and Kilcoyne nodded his appreciation.

The bulletproof vests were brought into the room and distributed, and Kilcoyne was almost ready. But whatever was to happen would have to be documented, he realized. A deputy police commissioner was involved. Therefore he was obliged to wait for the arrival of the forensic personnel. This wait was a short one. As soon as they reported, Kilcoyne placed them to one side and picked up the loudhailer.

There was a clock on the wall beside the clerk's desk, and when Kilcoyne glanced at it so did Egan and Gold. Suddenly the time of decision was upon them all. Yes or no. Whatever was to happen would become, in a moment, irrevocable.

Kilcoyne raised the loudhailer to his mouth.

"Brown, there should be a clock in there somewhere. Take a look at it. In sixty seconds we're coming through that door. We have firepower on our side, Brown. We have shotguns. You won't stand a chance. There's no reason why you have to die. I'm asking you for the last time to put your gun down. You can make your point in court." When there seemed to be no response, Kilcoyne turned the loudhailer on again. "You have fifty seconds, Brown." He paused. "Forty seconds."

He glanced all around him. Craighead and his men had moved the battering-ram up to the door. The emergency service patrolmen in their armour had checked their weapons – there was a series of loud clicks – and they too now lumbered forward.

Then came Brown's voice through the door. "In forty seconds, unless I see my truck in the street outside, unless you agree to everything I want, Mr. Commissioner here is going to have a third eye."

It was as if Kilcoyne had not heard him. He was standing near the closed and locked door, his gaze shifting from the clock to his assault team and back again. "Ready?" he whispered.

Most of the men nodded, and those holding the ram began to swing it gently in its sling.

Keefe was looking at a clock too. On his side of the door it was on the judge's desk. It was almost equidistant between himself and Brown. His glance shifted from the clock down his leg. His ankle seemed as far away as the wall. He couldn't reach it. Time was moving too fast. There could be only a few seconds to go. He had no doubt that Kilcoyne and his men would come bursting through that door on schedule, or that Brown would immediately shoot him. The clock was moving too fast for everyone. At this short range Brown's bullets could not miss. His hand was moving downwards, but only by inches. He was trying to pretend to scratch his ankle. Brown was watching the clock, and did not immediately react. Keefe got his hand down out of sight. He got it around the gun's grip, and with a violent effort tried to yank it out. But its hammer snagged on the top of his sock.

"What you doing?" demanded Brown.

"Nothing, nothing," cried Keefe. His body had jerked upright in his chair, and he was as empty-handed as before.

As the battering-ram slammed into the door on the other side, Keefe went for the ankle holster again. He lunged for it. He was tugging at the gun and falling out of the chair at the same time, and Brown fired. The noise to Keefe was deafening, and then it was drowned out by the repeated smashes of the battering-ram against the door. He heard voices shouting, first Kilcoyne's:

"Again! Again!"

Then Rainey's: "Harder, harder!"

He had dived to the floor where he was trying to scrabble behind the filing cabinets and get his gun out simultaneously. Brown had run around in front of the desk, his head jerking this way and that, his concentration fixed now on Keefe, now on the door, his gun waving. The file drawer beside Keefe's head sprang open, hit by a bullet, or so he thought. He had not even heard the report: there was too much noise. The battering-ram was still smashing into the far side of the door, and people were screaming. The door was too sturdy. It did not budge. At last Keefe had his gun out and up. Clutched in two hands, he was firing it. Brown in front of the desk seemed to be firing shots at the door, and then at Keefe on the floor beside the filing cabinet. Keefe on his back was firing. He emptied his gun. He kept pulling the trigger even though now it gave off only clicks. Suddenly Brown went down. He lay on the rug and did not move, and Keefe got to his knees and then to his feet and looked at him. He tried to walk, but his knees melted and he nearly fell, and he had to grasp the desk for support.

The door came down. It fell flat and when it struck the rug it seemed to make Brown bounce.

Men ran across it into the room. There were a dozen or more of them, all with guns. The emergency service cops in their armor stood over Brown holding shotguns to his skull, but he did not move, and they did not fire. The other men surrounded Keefe. Someone had him by the shoulders and when he looked he saw it was Sergeant Rainey.

"Are you all right, Commissioner?"

"I just want to know one thing," demanded Kilcoyne. "How did you get yourself into this situation?"

"Are you sure you're all right, Commissioner?" said Rainey, who was practically embracing him. His voice sounded weak with relief.

But Keefe's eyes only flicked from one questioner to the other. When he tried to speak nothing came out.

The doctor and the stretcher-bearers were in the room. The doctor was working on Brown. There was blood leaking out of Brown onto the rug and the sight of it brought the contents of Keefe's stomach into his throat and he fought to keep from vomiting. He saw Brown placed carefully onto the stretcher. They wrapped him in blankets and carried him out the door.

The doctor approached Keefe. "How about you?"

"I'm all right."

"I can give you something."

"No."

The forensic unit was working quickly. Detectives had drawn a chalk outline around the spot where Brown had fallen. They stretched out tape measures to the wall. People were walking on the tapes and the forensic detectives were cursing them. A police artist began making a diagram of the room. A police photographer was working. He was shooting every possible angle.

Upon hearing the shots, the newsmen and TV crews who had been confined behind the barrier at the top of the staircase had overwhelmed the cops there. A second line posted by Kilcoyne at the outer door held them up briefly, but now they overwhelmed that one too and flooded into the judge's chambers. In a few seconds there were thirty of them inside, perhaps more. Cameramen filmed the PC, Gold, the angry Kilcoyne. They filmed Keefe and the detectives around him who were trying to take his statement. They began to push these detectives aside so as to film Keefe in close-up. Microphones were held to his face.

"Would you tell us what was going through your mind during the siege, Commissioner?"

"When did you become convinced that you would have to shoot your way out of here?"

More microphones appeared. Keefe looked numbly from one face to the other.

His gun was still in his hand. It hung beside his leg. "I didn't have any choice," he mumbled. "Don't you see? I didn't have any choice."

"I'll relieve you of your piece, Commissioner, if I may."

It was Lieutenant Roche from Ballistics. Keefe only stared at him.

"We'll have to match it against any slugs dug out of the gunman," Roche explained.

He reached down and took Keefe's gun from his hand.

Kilcoyne had rallied some uniformed cops and was helping them eject the newsmen from the room. One of the TV reporters held his ground. Lights were focused on him, and the mini-cam had him in close-up. He was in the process of signing off, and when the two cops pushing him realized this they grew immediately respectful, for they were of the generation that revered TV the way an earlier one had revered religion. Contrary to Kilcoyne's orders, they allowed the reporter to finish. Bathed in lights, facing his own camera, he said into his microphone:

"The cleaning woman is safe. Commissioner Keefe, who exchanged himself for her and who defied the gunman for over an hour, is safe. The gunman, badly wounded, has been taken to a hospital. Back to you, Jim, in the studio."

Lieutenant Roche, meanwhile, was searching for Brown's weapon, which would also have to be tested, but he couldn't find it. At first he imagined it was being trampled under so many feet. But now the room was emptying out. He said to Chief Gold: "There's a gun missing here, Chief. The perpetrator must still have his gun on him. Either that or –"

"It's under the desk," Gold said.

"How did it get under the desk?"

"I kicked it there before one of the reporters got it. How do you think it got under the desk?"

Gold stepped around the desk and stooped. When he stood up he had the gun. He was about to hand it to Roche when something about it caught his eye. He seemed to study it a long time.

"I'll take care of that now, Chief," said Roche, reaching for it.

But Gold dropped the gun into his side pocket.

"I don't understand, Chief."

"I'm keeping it."

"I don't know why you would want to do that, Chief."

"You want a receipt?" growled Gold.

"Well, at least let me take down the serial numbers."

Gold read him the numbers off the grip of the gun. "Satisfied?" he said. The gun went back in his pocket.

"Well," said Roche hesitantly, "this isn't the way it's usually done."

"This isn't your usual case," said Gold.

Roche made one last try. "Usually I take any weapons recovered at crime scenes straight to the lab and test-fire them."

"See me tomorrow or the next day," said Gold. He walked out, leaving Roche standing there.

Sergeant Rainey drove Keefe home. He kept up a line of cheerful chatter most of the way, but Keefe did not reply, and finally Rainey too fell silent. When he had stopped in front of Keefe's flat he said: "I'll walk you upstairs, Commissioner."

"I'm all right," Keefe told him, and he got out of the car and went into the building. Rainey watched him go.

Upstairs Keefe put his key in the lock, but before he could turn it Sharon pulled the door open from the other side. He stepped into his apartment, and for a moment only looked at her with what she would later describe as the most haunted eyes she had ever seen.

"I . . . I shot a guy," he said. She stepped forward and embraced him. With his chin on her shoulder and his face against hers he said the same thing again.

"I . . . I shot a guy."

Nineteen

THE PHONE RANG AFTER MIDNIGHT. THE POLICE Commissioner in bed in the dark came up out of befuddlement and groped for the source of the ringing.

"The mayor asks if you can come down to the hall."

It was one of the deputy mayors. There were a number of deputy mayors. Egan squinted at the clock on the bedside table, but was unable to read it. He brought the clock up to his face.

Beside him, his wife had stirred. "You can put the light on," she said.

As he did so, Egan's primary desire was to excuse himself to his wife, who got awakened by calls like this far too often. She not only put up with it, she never complained. He spoke into the receiver: "It's one o'clock in the morning."

"The mayor apologizes."

Egan thought: so it's started already. He had sensed it would start soon, though not this soon. They were not even going to permit him a good night's sleep first.

As the Police Commissioner began to dress, his wife put a robe on.

"What's it about?"

After studying her a moment, he said: "He didn't say."

"I'll look in on my little one," Edna Egan said, and went out.

He would need a ride to City Hall. Should he use the car on duty in front of his house? It would mean leaving Edna and the boys unguarded for thirty minutes or so. Surely nothing would happen in such a short period. The guards were probably not necessary at all. At this time of night the car could be back on post very quickly. But Edna might look out and notice it was gone. For all he knew its presence was important to her sense of security. She never said so. It was something they never talked about.

Stepping to the bedside phone, he dialed his own office: his night duty sergeant was to send a patrol car from the nearest precinct. He was also to order Egan's own driver to meet him at City Hall with his department car.

Edna Egan had come back into the bedroom. "He's probably dreaming about growing up to be a lion keeper at the zoo," she said.

"You should go back to sleep."

"I'll fix you a cup of tea before you go."

"I'm not sure I have time."

But he waited in the kitchen watching her pour boiling water in on top of the tea bag. Together they watched the tea steep. It was tea he didn't want, but she stood there watching him. He gave her a fond smile and drank about half.

"I'd better go." They stood at the front door. It was as if he were going on a long journey. He embraced her, and felt foolish about it. He was only going to City Hall.

"I'll wait up for you," she told him. It was what she always said.

"Please go back to bed," he said. He went outside into the warm moonlight.

The car he had called for had not yet come, so he walked down to the one on duty in front. Both cops, seeing him suddenly in the doorway, had already jumped out. The night was so quiet that he heard their doors slam. But the light remained on inside the car, and when he had approached he saw that they had been playing cards on the front seat.

"Evening, Commissioner," one cop said.

"Everything all right, sir?" the second cop asked.

Egan had never seen these two before. He asked their names, their ages. He asked what they hoped for from their police careers. They seemed pleased by his interest.

When the second car turned into the street, one of them preceded him through the parked bumpers and held the door open for him.

City Hall was a big building with a cupola in the middle of

a park. It dated from the early 1800s. There was a circular carriageway out front, blocked at both ends by wooden police barriers, and by cops on duty even at this hour, who lifted the barriers out of the way to let through the police car carrying Egan. He went up the steps. Just inside the doors there was a cop at the security desk who saluted him. He walked on down the long marble corridor. The corridor was dim. Only the night lights were burning. He walked past portraits of New York City mayors which lined the walls on both sides. Some of the portraits dated back more than 150 years. At the end of the corridor Egan pushed through the low iron gate that separated the mayor's offices from the rest of the building and went in.

The mayor was not there. Blumenstock, the deputy mayor who had called, stood in shirt sleeves in front of the mayor's desk. He was leaning backward with his rump on the desk. In the chair opposite him, in uniform, sat Dennis Kilcoyne. Kilcoyne looked freshly shaved.

"Sorry to bother you at this hour, Tim," Blumenstock apologized. He came forward, reached for Egan's hand and shook it.

The handshake seemed the most ominous signal yet.

"I've just been talking to Dennis, here," Blumenstock said, and he paused.

Egan said: "Are we waiting for the mayor?"

"The mayor won't be coming in." Blumenstock seemed to be choosing his words with care. "He asked me to handle this thing for the time being."

"I see."

Blumenstock folded his arms across his chest. "Not that his honor is snoozing in his bed," he said in a jocular manner. The tone, for this time of night, was completely wrong also.

"He's out in the city someplace, making his rounds," said Blumenstock jocularly. "On the job even in the wee hours." He threw his arms wide, as if to encompass the mayor's entire city.

Egan watched him, and waited.

"Yes, well," Blumenstock said, "the mayor wants to know

if he has anything to worry about as far as this Keefe business is concerned." He looked up expectantly.

Except for hello, Kilcoyne had not yet said a word. "Worry about?" said Egan. "Like what?"

"Well, for instance, do we have a good make on the perpetrator?"

Out of the mouth of such a man the police terms sounded ridiculous. Egan turned to his Chief of Operations. "Dennis?"

"We have a positive identification, yes," said Kilcoyne, and he handed across the yellow sheet on Joshua L. Brown, which he had been given earlier by Lieutenant Craighead.

Blumenstock placed it on the desk behind him. "I'll keep this, if I may."

Kilcoyne nodded.

"And how about the weapon in question?" said Blumenstock. "Are we satisfied that it was a legal weapon?"

"You mean Commissioner Keefe's gun?" asked Kilcoyne, surprised.

"Of course. We know that the perpetrator's gun was not legal. Or at least we assume it was not. But our deputy police commissioners are obliged to have a pistol permit, I believe. So did he have one?"

Blumenstock was looking to Kilcoyne for an answer. Kilcoyne, still apparently surprised, threw a sharp glance at Egan, who had begun studying his fingernails.

Kilcoyne said: "Those things are not my department. They're signed by the Police Commissioner."

"The permits themselves are printed up with my name already on them," said Egan. "I assume he has a pistol permit. In the case of deputy commissioners they are automatic."

"Automatic?" said Blumenstock. "I thought it was a .38 calibre revolver."

"No pun intended," said Egan. "The issuance of the permit is automatic, I meant to say. Or virtually so."

"But you authorised it?"

"Technically, I suppose I did."

A heavy silence descended on the room. "I'll check into it

first thing in the morning," Kilcoyne said.

"Just where is the mayor?" said Egan.

"Probably at the hospital," said Blumenstock.

To Egan this was a cryptic remark. Every time a cop got shot or a fireman inhaled too much smoke, mayors, this one or any other, were obliged by political tradition to rush to the bedside. However, no such hero had been hospitalized tonight as far as Egan knew. Of course the mayor might be visiting a suddenly stricken relative or high city official, but this seemed unlikely too. So who was he visiting? Egan looked into Blumenstock's smug smile and decided he did not need to know the answer. To ask the question would be a display of weakness.

Kilcoyne said: "Which hospital? Who's sick?"

"The mayor has had a lot of phone calls." Blumenstock's smile vanished and his face took on a grave expression. He pointed towards the mayor's telephone. "That thing kept ringing. The perpetrator may have been pretty well connected, which the mayor is checking out now."

"Was there anything else you wanted to know?" said Egan.

"No, that about does it."

"Is the mayor coming back here?"

"I think he'll go straight from the hospital back to the mansion."

Egan stood up. He was trying to maintain an outward calm, but despite himself his fingers went to his tie. "If there's nothing else –"

"No," said Blumenstock. "The mayor just wanted to know if there was anything he should be worried about."

"You said that before," said Kilcoyne. "I'd like to know what you are insinuating."

"Nothing," said the deputy mayor. He seemed surprised at Kilcoyne's tone. "I'm not insinuating a thing."

"The perpetrator took a hostage and threatened her life," said Kilcoyne. "He threatened her with what the law calls deadly physical force. One of our men got her out of there and was himself threatened by deadly physical force. In self-defence and in the line of duty he shot him. What could there possibly be to worry about?"

He and Blumenstock eyed each other. The deputy mayor was the first to look away. "I'm sure I don't know. The Boss just asked me to sound you fellows out."

"I'll be getting on home," Egan said.

"The mayor may be on the horn to you pretty early in the morning," Blumenstock said to their backs.

Egan and Kilcoyne came out on top of the steps in front of City Hall and stood for a time without speaking. Egan looked out over the trees at the Brooklyn Bridge. The floodlights were projected up the stone piers into the great Gothic arches. Even at this hour traffic on the bridge was heavy in both directions. The road bed gave out a loud hum from the cars moving across it.

"I'll check into it first thing in the morning, Commissioner," Kilcoyne said.

"Yes, that would be best," said Egan. He was still looking at the bridge. The moonlight played in the net of cables. It looked as if the bridge had got moonlight tangled in its hair.

"I'll call you as soon as I have anything."

"As soon as you have anything," said Egan.

Kilcoyne's department car was parked at the bottom of the steps. Egan's was behind it. The two men went down the steps together. "A common criminal," Kilcoyne muttered. "You saw his sheet. What does he mean, well connected? How could such a man be well connected?" To Egan, Kilcoyne sounded worried.

Egan was worried too. He was also determined that nothing would show. "We'll know more about it in the morning," he said.

When he got home he found his wife in the living room in her bathrobe. She had been knitting on the sofa. "You shouldn't have waited up for me," he told her.

"I didn't mind," she said. "Look." She held up a nearly completed baby's blanket.

"It's nice," he said. The blanket was blue with a white border. Suddenly he felt fearfully tired. "It's blue. Suppose the baby is a girl?"

Their oldest daughter was about to give birth. "It won't matter," Edna Egan said. She folded the blanket over the knitting needles and put it aside. "You look exhausted. Sit down and take your shoes off, while I make you a cup of tea. This time you'll drink it."

Egan sat down beside his wife and took her hand so she could not leave him. For a time neither spoke.

"What was it?" Edna Egan asked.

"I don't really know."

"Good news? Bad news?"

"I'll know tomorrow. I don't want any tea. It's going to be a short night. Let's go to bed." Hand in hand they went up the stairs to their bedroom.

Kilcoyne woke as always with first light; as he got older he seemed to require less and less sleep. Most mornings he would leave the house quickly, eager to get to headquarters and to work. Today he took longer. He had gone to bed uneasy, and was uneasy still. What was City Hall's position in all this? In his head he replayed step by step the events at the courthouse last night, and he did not see how his conduct could be faulted. He had acted quickly, ruthlessly, and most of all successfully. Nobody had got hurt except a single black criminal for whom, one assumed, no tears would be shed.

Perhaps this was to look at the matter with too much logic. A lot of people these days wanted to think of police work as being mostly polite, of force being used according to the rules of etiquette. They wanted to be protected unobtrusively, and totally without violence, which was simply not always possible. It had not been possible at the Bronx Courthouse, and Kilcoyne regretted the days when he was a young cop. Thirty years ago police response to a criminal situation was dictated by the situation itself rather than by the supposed wishes of the public or of politicians looking for votes.

Kilcoyne lived on a hill on Staten Island. From his bedroom window he could see part of New York harbor, part of the downtown skyline. Two blocks further up the hill was the house in which he had grown up. His father, nearing ninety, lived there still and was cared for by a daughter, Kilcoyne's oldest sister, who had never married. She cleaned Kilcoyne's own house for him too, and sometimes cooked his meals, for his children were grown and scattered and his wife had been dead for almost five years. The house was, of course, too big for him and he had been advised to sell it but had not. He was a traditionalist. It was where he lived.

And this morning he was uneasy.

Having reached no conclusions, he went out of the front door and locked it behind him, and his driver, a sergeant in uniform, came around and had the car door open for him before he reached the curb.

"Bridge or ferry, Chief?" the sergeant asked as the engine came on. He asked the same question every day, and unless in a terrific hurry, Kilcoyne always answered:

"Ferry."

He did not approve of the bridge. For most of his life Staten Island, one of the five boroughs of the city but disconnected from the others, had been almost entirely rural. Now the place was filling up with apartment buildings and condominiums – even factories – and of course people, and Kilcoyne barely recognized it any more. All because of the big new bridge.

As the ferry pushed out into the harbour the sun was squatting on the water and he got out of the car and went to stand at the rail. He pulled his gold braided cap down tight against the wind and looked across at the downtown skyline. It too had changed in recent years. Now it was dominated by the two square towers of the World Trade Center, a pair of 110-storey boxes set on end. Because of the way they were placed they looked asymmetrical though they were not. They reflected the light differently as well, and to Kilcoyne they were blocky and unaesthetic.

He was still wondering what could be City Hall's problem.

The ferry passed the Statue of Liberty and began to cross the tidal flow. Kilcoyne looked down on debris of all kinds. The ferry churned into it. The scum and garbage was floating out at the moment. In a few hours it would float back. Once each year a barge chartered by the New York

Police Department floated out with it bearing all the weapons cops had confiscated during the preceding twelve months, and these were dumped at sea and did not float back. But they were replaced soon enough by others.

The sun was still below the buildings as Kilcoyne's car moved through the streets of lower Manhattan. He got out and strode across Police Plaza and into headquarters. The interior of the building looked and felt empty. On his own corridor the noise of his shoes sounded too loud. Most of the offices he passed were empty.

At his desk he tried to forget City Hall. He made it a point to be the first commander in each morning, and the last to leave each night. He began to work on the memos and reports that awaited him. He liked to clear up all his paperwork before the phones started to ring, so he could approach the crises and surprises of the day – whatever they might be – with a clear desk and a clear mind.

But he had gone through the best part of the pile the previous night while waiting for the hostage situation to sort itself out and now, though he tried to study what was left, he could not keep his mind on it. So he went to the window and looked across the river and watched the sun rising above the roof tops of Brooklyn.

The deputy inspector who was his chief secretary came in with the morning newspapers at eight A.M. precisely; the men on Kilcoyne's staff were careful to come to work exactly on time.

"Coffee, Chief?"

Kilcoyne looked at him.

"Hell of a thing last night, wasn't it, Chief?"

Kilcoyne despised gossip. He had no intention of passing on juicy titbits to this subordinate or any other. "I want you to go around to Intelligence," he instructed him. "I want to know what they have on the perpetrator, this man Brown."

"Right, Chief. I'll send somebody over there."

"Go yourself."

Deputy inspectors were not used to serving as messenger boys, and this one fought to preserve his dignity: "I can send Captain Munger, Chief."

254

"You didn't hear me."

The deputy inspector, worried, was trying to puzzle it out. "Right, Chief. I'll bring your coffee, then go round to Intelligence."

"Forthwith," Kilcoyne said. But the deputy inspector looked so crestfallen Kilcoyne took pity on him. "They may not have anything," he explained. "You have enough rank to stand over them while they do a thorough search. Have somebody else bring the coffee."

When the deputy inspector had gone out, Kilcoyne spread out the newspapers. A sergeant came in with his coffee. "Send me Captain Munger," Kilcoyne said. Without looking up from the news reports he added, "Put it down there."

He scanned the newspapers one by one and was gratified. His decisions and tactics were neither questioned nor criticized. The mayor would have to take account of the newspapers. He could not be too far out in front of them on this thing. As for Keefe, the reporters seemed to imagine him an unalloyed hero, and this annoyed Kilcoyne.

When Captain Munger appeared Kilcoyne folded the newspapers and made a neat pile of them on the corner of his desk.

"Some shoot-out last night, right, Chief?"

Munger, too, hoped for details. Kilcoyne, after taking a drink of coffee, set the cup down on its saucer on his blotter. "Phone up the hospital and get me a medical report on the perpetrator."

"I already tried that, Chief," Captain Munger said. "He's still alive. Other than that they wouldn't tell me a thing. They said the Chief of Detectives has clamped a lid on."

Kilcoyne was not surprised. Gold was always quick to clamp lids on, after which all information had to come from him. Everyone had to beg him for it, even his superiors. This created the illusion that he was more powerful than perhaps was the case. One could know better, but the subliminal effect remained.

"Reach out for him," Kilcoyne ordered Munger. "He's probably in his car. Have him call in on a land line."

"Right, Chief."

Kilcoyne wanted to talk to Keefe too, and in his own office, and he gave orders for it. He was not bowing to protocol now. "He is to report to me as soon as he comes in."

Again Kilcoyne took his coffee to the window. He expected a phone call from Gold at any moment, though this would not happen, and did not really expect to hear from Keefe at all. Shoot-outs shook a man up. As a young cop he had been in one himself, and he doubted Keefe would come to work today – perhaps for several days. In shoot-outs a man came face to face with eternity and if he did not recognize this in the heat of the moment he certainly did afterwards. No one ever came away from shoot-outs unwounded, and the psychic wounds frequently went deeper than the lead ones. The loser could sometimes be made more comfortable, whereas the winner could not be helped at all, except by time.

If Keefe came to work, Kilcoyne reflected, he would have to face the hard questioning of the morning after. It would take as much nerve to come to work, in Kilcoyne's opinion, as to face that gunman last night.

So he was surprised when Keefe appeared in his office not ten minutes later. He and the deputy inspector came in simultaneously.

"Intelligence has nothing on the perpetrator, Chief. And I have Commissioner Keefe."

"Nothing?" Kilcoyne said.

"Not a thing."

Kilcoyne nodded. "Thank you. That will be all, Inspector. Good morning, Phil."

Keefe was young enough so that very little of his ordeal showed in his face. Nonetheless, he looked as if he had not slept. It was perhaps the expression in his eyes. His suit looked all right. There were the proper creases in his trousers. His shoes were shined. He had not nicked himself shaving. Nonetheless, his clothes seemed to hang off him, as if he had lost a great deal of weight in a few hours, and his voice when he spoke sounded odd.

"You wanted to see me, Chief?"

Kilcoyne gestured to the chair beside the desk and Keefe, after hesitating, took it. He sat there looking wary, though also subdued, gazing at Kilcoyne like a schoolboy waiting for the reprimand he knew was coming.

"You're in early," the older man began.

"I couldn't find out what had happened to – to that man. I called the hospital but no one would tell me. So I came in."

"Well, he's still alive, if that's what you mean."

"How bad is he?"

"I can't give you a medical report," said Kilcoyne somewhat sharply. The question reminded him that Gold should have called in by now. Why hadn't he? Where was he and what doing?

"I'd like to hear you tell me," said Kilcoyne, "whether or not you think you made a mistake last night."

"He was shooting at me," said Keefe defensively.

"That you shot him," said Kilcoyne, "was plainly justified. What I'd like to know is why you went into that room in the first place. I'd like you to tell me that."

Keefe did not immediately answer.

"You put your own life at risk, and you put us in the position of having to rescue you – meaning you put all of our lives at risk too." And all our careers at risk, Kilcoyne thought. Our careers may still be at risk.

Keefe's eyes had dropped.

Kilcoyne had had to deal with the mess. He had a right to speak harshly. "Do you understand how many other lives you risked?"

"What about the cleaning woman's life?" said Keefe.

"Getting the cleaning woman out of there would have been problem enough. Getting you out of there was ten times the problem."

Keefe said nothing.

"The whole thing might have been worked out without any violence whatsoever," Kilcoyne scolded him, "except for you."

"I went in there because I thought it was the only way to save the woman's life."

"You don't know what you thought," Kilcoyne told him.

"You didn't know then and you don't know now." From personal experience he added more kindly: "That's the way it is in situations of that kind."

Keefe seemed to remember his rank, or perhaps his dignity. He stood up. "Will there be anything else, Chief?"

"Normally we leave situations like that *∙ a sergeant or lieutenant." Kilcoyne had stood up too. "? ∙'s always a good reason for the way we do things in this ∖partment."

"Yes. I'm sure there is."

"You made a mistake in judgment, a grave one," Kilcoyne said, "and I would feel remiss in my duty if I were to refrain from telling you so."

Keefe was studying the floor.

"It's only your judgment I question," Kilcoyne said. "Nothing else."

Kilcoyne came out from behind his desk with his hand outstretched. "That much being said, I'd like to shake your hand."

Keefe looked surprised, but his eyes rose, and he gripped the hand held out to him.

"I never questioned your bravery," Kilcoyne said. "No one can question that. I've witnessed very few acts comparable in all my police career."

It won a tentative smile from the young man, and Kilcoyne showed him out.

When the door had closed, he turned to the window and again stared across the river at Brooklyn. Something was wrong and he did not know what. Never mind Keefe. He himself was the one who had had to make the tough decision. And that decision had been correct. Nonetheless, if no one backed him up today then retroactively it became wrong.

Where was Gold, and why did he not call in?

The PC was interested in the morning papers too. He read them in the back seat of his car as he was being driven to headquarters, and to his relief the notices were good. Once at his desk he sent word that he wished to see both Chief Gold and Deputy Commissioner Keefe. Like Kilcoyne, he expected to hear from Gold at once, and from Keefe not at all.

Instead the opposite occurred. About ten minutes later Keefe stood in front of the desk. He had come directly from Kilcoyne's office, but Egan didn't know this. He expected another scolding, and Egan didn't know this either.

"I've been trying to find out what sort of shape the – the perpetrator is in," Keefe said. "But no one can tell me."

Reaching forward, Egan buzzed his secretary. "Get me a medical report on the defendant from last night," he said into the speaker.

They looked at each other in silence.

"You're suffering," Egan told Keefe. "There's no reason why you should be."

"I don't know what I'm supposed to do about the press," Keefe said. "There have been a lot of requests this morning already."

"I know. I'm told we've had them here too."

Egan had decided he would handle the press himself at a news conference later in the day. He did not want Keefe present at the conference. Nor did he want him giving interviews on his own.

The light on Egan's phone began to blink, and he picked it up. The perpetrator was still alive, his secretary said. Otherwise the hospital would give out no information. Gold had clamped the lid on.

"Thank you," Egan said into the receiver, and hung up. "He's holding his own," he said to Keefe.

"I hope he's going to live."

Egan put his arm on Keefe's shoulder and led him to the door. "I want you to go home now," he told him. "Take the rest of the day off. Do any of the reporters know where you live? Take your phone off the hook. Maybe you should spend the day in the country."

Egan was sympathetic, but he wanted Keefe to understand that these were orders. "We'll handle the press from here," he said firmly. "You don't have to do it."

The important thing was that he be kept out of sight.

As soon as Keefe had gone out, Egan's first appointment

259

of the day, a black councilman from Brooklyn, was shown in. Egan greeted this man cordially. One of the Bedford-Stuyvesant station houses was to be closed at Egan's orders because the neighbourhood could be served more efficiently and cheaply by cops from the two neighbouring precincts.

Why did the black community have to bear the brunt of such economy measures? the councilman demanded. His constituents had the same rights as those rich white precincts on the Upper East Side.

For almost an hour Egan argued patiently. This was what he was good at. His graphs and charts were on the table in front of them. He proved conclusively that the new set-up would provide better police protection all around. However, the councilman was not buying, and as a result Egan's concentration began to go off. He wondered if he could depend on Keefe to stay out of sight all day. He wondered about Gold: where was he and why had he not called in? He wondered about the mayor, from whom he had not yet heard.

By mid-morning Anne Christianson had at last got in to see the elected District Attorney of Bronx County. It was the interview she had been waiting for. Standing before his desk, she was modestly dressed and coiffed, as always. Her manner and bearing were precisely correct. Her arguments, as she began to state them, were restrained and well-measured. She was almost prim.

At first the old man merely watched her. He was more conscious of the primness than of any sexual appeal. It made her seem just another young lawyer begging for a shot at better cases. This he was used to, and so was only half-listening. Part of the time his mind went off on other matters entirely, but it kept coming back to her. She was uncommonly pretty for a lawyer. Nice figure, too.

Anne's concentration, by contrast, was absolute. To her, much more than her future in this office seemed at stake. It was as if her whole life and career were now to be determined.

She did not mention the name of her supervisor, the

frump who had been holding her back, nor even allude to
the woman. Instead she made the old man concentrate on
Anne Christianson – not as a person but as a lawyer, which
was all that counted. She told him she was proud to be part
of his office, and she outlined her experience in the
complaint room, and in arraignment court so far. She spoke
of the one or two trials at which she had been allowed to
help out. In the meantime other less experienced and less
effective lawyers had moved up in grade. Unless her
performance to date was unsatisfactory, and she had
received no notices to this effect, then she thought he should
be aware that it was her turn now to be promoted.

The District Attorney interrupted her. He had seen her
name in the paper that very morning in connection with the
Keefe case, he said.

Anne had seen it too, a bare mention. The news reports
had focused not on her and on the low bail as she had
feared, but on the shoot-out.

"I'm asking for permission to keep the case," Anne said.

"It doesn't sound like much of a case to me," said the
District Attorney. "Justifiable shooting. Open and shut."

She mollified him. "I'm sure you're right. But for me it's a
start."

The District Attorney saw the investigation as short and
routine. The young woman saw it as sensitive, highly visible
and prolonged. Facts would be difficult to nail down. To
her, cops were men who shot first and asked questions later.
After that they routinely lied to protect each other. She did
not like them. To her, most police shootings were not
justified at all. At the very least her investigation would
prove both the independence of the District Attorney's
office and the sanctity of human life – no cop could gun
down a citizen without being subject to the closest possible
scrutiny.

It might be a case on which she could make a reputation.

The old man seemed to enjoy looking at her.

Anne risked a thin smile. "With your permission I'll keep
the case."

"Sure, if that's what you'd like. Keep the case." He had

Anne's personnel folder and he began to tap it unopened on his knee. All the while he stared at her. "It does seem to me you've been held back a bit too long," he commented finally.

Anne found his interest repugnant. She was satisfied he had never so much as glanced into her personnel folder, and possibly didn't remember her name. She was getting by on looks again, but after this case her looks would be irrelevant.

"I'll give instructions you're to be moved up," the District Attorney said.

"Thank you, sir," said Anne.

Once back at her own desk she put through a call to Chief of Detectives Gold. She was the one running this investigation now. He was not there. Next she phoned the hospital. No information on the victim could be released on the express orders of Chief Gold. We'll soon change that, she thought grimly.

She phoned Ballistics. No report was ready yet, according to a Lieutenant Roche. In fact, he had only been able to examine one of the two guns so far. The other was still in the possession of Chief Gold.

"Is that normal?" she asked. She knew it was not.

"Well," said Roche, "he's Chief of Detectives."

It was only what she had expected. She waited for Gold to call back.

Twenty

KEEFE DID NOT IMMEDIATELY GO HOME AS ORDERED, but instead went back to his office and waited to hear from Gold. The Chief of Detectives could tell him what the prognosis was on the man he had shot; Keefe also wanted to see what Gold's reaction to him this morning would be.

"Are you all right, Commissioner?" It was Sergeant Rainey in his doorway.

"Sure," said Keefe. "I'm a hero. Read the papers." He got

up and walked to the window. "Maybe I wanted to shoot him. Maybe I didn't care about the cleaning woman at all. Maybe I just wanted to know what it felt like to shoot somebody."

"Any cop who's ever shot a man has thoughts like that, Commissioner."

Keefe looked at him. He was no longer sure Brown had actually fired shots at him, though so far he had told this to no one, not even Sharon. He had tried to reconstruct the actual shoot-out most of the night. Perhaps it was his head that had knocked the file drawer open, not a bullet at all.

"Did I think it would make me a hero if I went in there and blasted him? Am I some kind of monster?" He gave a wry laugh. "It's not nice to have to confront such ideas, believe me."

"You don't want anyone to hear you talking that way," said Rainey cautiously. "The press would crucify you and –" He stopped.

"And what?"

"And some prosecutor might decide to indict you."

Keefe shrugged. The possibility of criminal prosecution had not yet occurred to him. "The worst of it is, there are never going to be any answers. I'm never going to know."

Rainey stood watching him, and Keefe was aware of and warmed by the older man's concern. "When you were in uniform on patrol, Ed, did you ever shoot anybody?"

"Yes, once." A grin had come on to Rainey's face, signalling that the anecdote was an amusing one, and that he was about to recount it.

"Who was it?"

"An innocent bystander."

Life was random, accidental, and therefore often comical. Rainey's anecdote would prove it. The idea cheered Keefe slightly.

It was a stick up run on an icy cold winter night. Rainey had fired a warning shot and the stick up man had kept on running.

"You never saw anybody run so fast. He was gone before I could pull the trigger twice."

Keefe was surprised at how funny this sounded. It made him laugh.

"Yeah," said Rainey, "there are hardened criminals who lead charmed lives. You could shoot at them all day and not hit them. And then there are the innocent bystanders. What can you do?" He sounded philosophical, good-humored. "I probably scared him, though."

Having missed the stick up man, his shot had hit a bag lady who, he said, was wearing the *New York Times* for an undershirt. "My shot went through about ten sections of the paper. It went through the sports section, through the financial section. Unfortunately it got her right in the heart."

Keefe laughed as if this were the funniest story ever told, and Rainey grinned.

"My partner said to me: 'You've done her a service. Now she won't have to sleep on any more of them gratings.'"

But it wasn't really funny, and Keefe fell silent. So did Rainey.

"My partner's grammar wasn't always too strong."

After another silence, Rainey said: "It shakes you up, Commissioner. That's the only shot I ever fired. Most cops never fire their guns in their whole careers. You'll get over it. It will take a few days."

After hesitating, Keefe said: "What happens – afterwards?"

"The case goes before the grand jury. They listen to a few witnesses, the assistant district attorney explains the law, the jury decides it was line of duty, and that's the end of it. Case dismissed. It takes about twenty minutes."

"That's all?"

"That's all."

Keefe wished Gold would call.

Rainey asked about the reporters downstairs. They were clamoring for an interview.

"The PC doesn't want me to be visible today."

Rainey's eyebrows went up. "Oh?"

"He'll give a press conference himself later. He suggested I not be there."

"You're the one the press wants to talk to."

264

"Well, the PC told me to go home and I think he's right."

"I see."

"He'll look after my interests."

"I think he'll probably look after his own."

"What makes you think that?"

"He could use that press conference to disassociate himself from you," said Rainey bluntly.

"Why should he?" Keefe considered the possibility and discarded it. The PC was too honorable, he decided. In any case, he did not want to be interviewed. Interviews were impossible to control. His ex-colleagues might decide he was bragging about shooting a man. It might be enough to tilt the media against him.

He tried Gold again, but there was still no reply. Before long the reporters would make their way up to this floor. Keefe did not want them to find him. He decided to leave. He could keep calling Gold from the street. From the garage, Detective Murphy drove him up the ramp and out into the sudden sunlight.

Left behind, Sergeant Rainey dialed Flora Bernstein's number at work. The previous night he had forgotten her completely, and had left her waiting for him for hours on a street corner. Now she would not talk to him. Every time she heard his voice on the telephone she hung up.

"Hello?"

"Flora –"

He had time to say no more before she had hung up again.

Rainey got up and left the office. He walked across Police Plaza, crossed Centre Street, and entered City Hall Park. He walked past the benches under the trees, coming out on Broadway where he stood on the sidewalk in the hot early morning sun and deliberated. The traffic went by in front of him. Finally he crossed Broadway and entered a florist shop.

The air was cold and full of heavy odors. There were glass refrigerators on all three of the walls, and he could feel the chill they gave off. It was like being in the morgue, except that here he could see into the lockers.

Rainey was a police sergeant. He was as unused to

flowers as he was unused to the situation in which he found himself.

"I want to send some flowers to a loved one," he began.

The proprietor's smile vanished; he appeared somber. "A loved one who has passed away?"

"Did I say passed away?" Rainey said.

The proprietor seemed caught between expressions. Congratulations or condolences? He tried one, then the other. "No, but –"

"I want to send flowers to my girl."

Noting Rainey's grey beard and strict business suit, the proprietor made a second mistake. He said: "Flowers for your daughter."

"Did I say daughter?"

The proprietor's remark – or the funereal odors of the shop – reminded Rainey of death. His own was not imminent, but it was more imminent than Flora's. Possibly she saw him as too old for her. How could he change her mind? He would have to change it. There was violence in Rainey. His voice became excessively low, his words excessively deliberate. "Do you want to make this sale?"

"Of course."

"Then try listening for a change."

Instead of smiles or sympathy the proprietor looked nervous.

A policeman was one who gave orders and other people obeyed. If they knew what was good for them, they did. "Girl friend," Rainey said. "You got that?"

After a moment the proprietor recovered. Stepping carefully among the potted plants, he moved to one of the glass lockers. "A small bouquet?" He indicated an arrangement behind glass. "This seems to be a very popular size."

To Rainey it was not substantial enough to impress Flora, and the proprietor seemed to have read him as a cheapskate. He might even have recognized him as a cop. There were other more important arrangements in that same locker and also in the ones next to it. "How about that one?" Rainey said. "Or that one? Or that one there?"

The proprietor began nodding as if confidently. "Well, of course, if price is no object –"

This remark too angered Rainey. "You think I can't afford it? There's nothing in your shop I can't afford." In one of the lockers was the biggest arrangement of all. "I'll take that one," Rainey said. "Wrap it and send it. How much?"

The proprietor studied the display for a moment and then Rainey's face. "You want me to leave the purple ribbon?"

"Put a white one."

"Okay," the proprietor said and he went behind the counter, and began writing out the bill.

"Put this card with it."

Rainey had known flowers were expensive. Nonetheless, when he stared down at the bill, the price shocked him. But his manhood had been challenged, and although reason argued that he should back down, he refused to do so. He handed over his credit card.

"When will it get there?" he said. "An hour? That's how much time you've got, an hour." He strode out of the shop.

Back at headquarters at his desk he imagined Flora reading his card. He had written: "Flowers for my flower."

He waited an hour, then dialled her number.

"Flora," he began, "did you get the flowers?"

"It took two men to carry that thing in here," she said. "What am I, a politician lying in state? Some Mafia guy who got shot? Were you deliberately trying to embarrass me, or what?" She hung up on him again.

Sharon had spent the morning walking in and out of Keefe's brownstone while cameras rolled. It wasn't really Keefe's brownstone, since he only rented the top floor, but she thought she could claim on her budget that it was, and thereby pay him a fee. It would be like giving him a present on his birthday.

There were two cameras and about twenty grips and technicians clustered on the sidewalk or sitting on the parked cars. Traffic in the street went by very slowly, while drivers and passengers gaped. Repeatedly she had approached the house along the sidewalk under the trees. DeForest had a list with all the various takes written down. She had approached from the right, then from the left. There was a doubleparked taxi standing by – she had approached out of the taxi. Once inside the house she had each time altered her appearance slightly, before coming out again. There was a prop man standing in there handing her things: sunglasses, a sweater, a raincoat, a mink – and even looking discreetly away as she pulled pants on under her skirt, then removed the skirt.

All these set-ups were completed before Keefe ever got there. DeForest was very quick. Between takes the director found time to try to charm her. When was she going to let him take her to dinner, he wanted to know.

When she saw Keefe's car come into the street she broke off the take and walked toward him – which apparently shocked DeForest.

"What the hell are you doing?" he cried out.

Keefe had come through the parked cars onto the sidewalk, and she stepped up and kissed him. Partly this was for DeForest. Mostly it was because of her concern for Keefe. "How did it go?" she said anxiously.

"The PC sent me home."

She was immediately alarmed.

"Don't worry," Keefe told her. "He's on my side."

"Sharon, we're waiting," DeForest called out. "We've got work to do here."

Sharon went over to him. "I can let you have about another half hour," she told him. "Then I have to break this off."

"What do you mean, break this off?" The director was fidgeting with the clipboard he carried.

"A half hour more," said Sharon. Keefe needed her and he needed her now. "That's all I can spare."

DeForest got testy. Finally Sharon compromised, agreeing to another hour late this afternoon at the courthouse, as planned. Additional footage could be done during her next trip to New York.

When she went up to the apartment thirty minutes later Keefe jumped up and put on what looked to her like a prepared smile.

"We can't stay here," he told her. "Sooner or later the press will be outside, and it's best if I don't talk to them."

She stepped to the closet and began once more to change her clothes. She put on slacks, a blouse and flat shoes; behind her Keefe was on the phone.

"Did he leave a message for me?" she heard him say. And then: "I see. Can you switch me to Chief Gold's office, please?"

Sharon waited for the call to end.

"Well, when do you expect him?"

When he had hung up they went out of the apartment and down the stairs. "I was trying to find out a few things," Keefe said. "The PC promised to at least leave a message." He sounded puzzled. "He must have forgotten."

They went window-shopping on Madison Avenue.

"My hero," said Sharon, giving his hand a squeeze.

"Me?" He grinned at her, "You got the wrong guy." But his grin soon faded. "I never thought I'd ever shoot anybody," he said. "I never thought that ever."

It was quite hot. They walked in the shade where they could. Cars and trucks went by in the street, and the sidewalks were crowded.

"He's still alive," Keefe told her. "He was when I left headquarters."

There were looking in a window marked: The Art of Nepal.

"Imagine," said Sharon, and she began to speak of artists working in that high cold land. She was watching Keefe carefully and saw that he was not really listening. Distracted, he was already moving on, and she followed.

They stood for some time at the window of a shop selling brightly-coloured ceramics from the south of France, and almost as long at a tiny jewelry shop whose speciality was antique watches.

They came to yet another art gallery and stood up close to the glass, shading their eyes with cupped hands.

They went into an Italian restaurant. Keefe ordered a bottle of Pinot Grigio and they sipped the wine while waiting to be served. He did not eat any bread or rolls while waiting, she noted, and afterwards left half his spaghetti on his plate.

"When I came into my office this morning, all the cops stood up and started applauding me."

She looked up at him sharply.

"They applauded me for having shot a guy, can you believe it?" Their expressos had been served and he was stirring it. "They just stood up at their desks grinning and clapping. Even the policewomen were doing it."

"They applauded you because you did something rare," Sharon told him. "Something they knew they were not brave enough to have done themselves."

"Any of them could have done it," Keefe insisted. He drained his cup. "I can't believe they would applaud me for shooting a guy."

When they came out onto the sidewalk the heat hit them, and they went into the Frick Collection where they sat for a time in the central atrium surrounded by ferns and trickling fountains. As they began to move from room to room Keefe seemed able to concentrate on the paintings and he made comments on several. The Holbein portrait of Sir Thomas More was everybody's favorite in the entire museum, he said.

"It's as perfect and as brilliant as if painted yesterday," agreed Sharon.

"It's either heavily restored, or a miracle," said Keefe.

"Now you're being cynical."

"Shooting people makes one cynical."

"Cops have a weird sense of values," he said as they came out of the museum. "And not just the cops who work for me. Cops in the garage congratulated me, even ones I passed in the hallway."

Sharon tried to get his mind off it. "Imagine," she said, "this man Frick actually lived in that house."

Keefe said: "If Police Commissioner was an elective office, the cops would make me run. If they could, they'd probably make me Commissioner by acclamation." He gave a laugh. "It's weird, isn't it?"

Sharon did not know what to do for him. These emotions were as new for her as for Keefe. They crossed Fifth Avenue and went into the park. They came to a pushcart

270

surrounded by children holding out money for Italian ices. Keefe stepped into the swarm and bought two. He looked like a giant among them. They strolled along under the trees digging out the sweet ice with flat wooden spoons.

At the lake Keefe hired a rowboat, and helped Sharon down into it. She pretended to arrange herself demurely in the stern like a maiden in a long dress sitting under a parasol and being courted during the Gay Nineties, but Keefe never noticed. Her suitor rowed away from the dock. Out on the lake he let the oars hang.

"Don't take it so hard," Sharon said in a sympathetic tone, then bit her lip. Everything she said sounded to her like a cliché. "You didn't do something shameful. According to the newspapers you're a hero."

He only shook his head negatively. Otherwise he did not respond.

She threw a handful of water at him. This won her a grin. He looked sheepish, vulnerable, and very young.

After leaving the park he phoned headquarters again. "Nobody's in," he said, when he had stepped out of the phonebooth.

An hour later they stood in front of the courthouse where DeForest and his crew were already in place, waiting. The director was brusque to Keefe, almost rude. Sharon glanced from one of them to the other. DeForest's antipathy to his supposed rival was almost amusing, especially as Keefe was so preoccupied. It all seemed to pass completely over his head.

Handing Sharon a briefcase, DeForest had her walk up and down the courthouse steps a dozen or more times. During each descent she could see Keefe over at the booths on the corner, telephoning.

He wandered back. "Did you get through this time?" she asked.

"No. The man is still alive. He was still alive an hour ago, according to the PC's secretary."

Sharon glanced in the direction of headquarters which was only a few hundred yards away. "You could walk over there. It would relieve your mind."

"The halls would be full of reporters."

The cameras and the big crew had drawn a crowd. People stared at Sharon and talked to each other behind their hands.

"You're being stared at," said Keefe

"It won't last."

"Don't underestimate yourself."

"It's kind of cute, though," Sharon remarked. She was amused by the attention.

"You might have to get used to it," suggested Keefe.

She was flattered, and responded on tip-toes with a quick kiss on the lips.

Later there was a lull while DeForest changed the position of his cameras, and Keefe came up to her with the afternoon *Post*. "Have you seen this?"

His picture was on the front page under a headline that read:

SEN. BUCKNER
VOWS TO PROBE
KEEFE SHOOTING

Underneath was a subhead in smaller type: *Use of Deadly Force Questioned.*

Sharon frowned. "What else does it say?"

"I haven't read it."

"Give it to me. I'll read it."

"Sharon," DeForest called out, "we're waiting for you."

She read the story all the way to the end. It started on the front page, then jumped to page three. A sidebar story went with it. She read that too. In the morning papers Keefe had been a hero. Now, only a few hours later, questions were being raised and the mood was changing, or changed. This could turn into a lynch mob, she thought. She didn't think it would, but it was possible.

She folded the paper and handed it back. "It's a sensationalist tabloid. I wouldn't pay a bit of attention to it."

"Is it bad?"

"It could be better."

"I assume they suggest that I never would have shot the guy if he had been white."

"Something like that."

She was watching his face, his mouth.

"Sharon," cried DeForest.

She was conscious of the cars going by in the street, of the cameras and crewmen waiting for her, of the passers by watching. "Coming," she called.

"Maybe it's true," said Keefe. "How do I know?"

"You're tired and not thinking clearly."

"They're waiting for you," he told her.

"Sharon!"

Leaving Keefe's side she started up the steps again. When she had reached the top she looked for him. There was a curbside trash basket at the corner, and he was just turning away from it empty handed. His unread newspaper lay at the top of the basket.

Twenty-One

CHIEF GOLD'S FIRST ACT AFTER CROSSING HIS LAWN and stepping into his department car that morning had been to reach under the dashboard and pull out a wire. The sounds of the police radio abruptly ceased. Gold's driver gaped at him.

"Something's wrong with the radio," Gold said. "When we get back to headquarters you'd better take care of it."

The PC, Kilcoyne and probably even the mayor would be trying to reach him, but he was out of contact, and would remain so until he had learned whatever it was he would learn.

His first stop had been the hospital where he imposed a complete news black-out and where the Administrator gave him an interim medical report. Brown was in bad shape. Then, in the corridor outside, Gold was practically assaulted by reporters and TV crews who had been staked out there for hours. He told them nothing.

According to the Administrator, Brown's son was in the

building and wanted to talk to him. The man was a Deputy Borough President of the Bronx, it turned out. This news made Gold wince. The son was about forty with a tan complexion – Gold was suspicious on sight of black men who were almost white – and a loud voice. Gold had been led downstairs to a private cafeteria to meet the son who had begun almost immediately to abuse him. Several interns at a nearby table were obviously listening.

"Keep your voice down," muttered Gold.

But the son started shouting. He threatened to hold a press conference at which he would denounce the police department in general and Gold in particular.

"Go ahead," said Gold tightly. "I can't stop you."

"Well, I will."

"Then do it."

Gold could hear running footsteps descending the stairs; he put down his coffee and dashed from the room. He barely got out in time. Behind him he heard the reporters begin to question the Deputy Borough President, and he waited in the hall to eavesdrop on the answers. They weren't answers at all, but angry charges. Police brutality. Violence against the black community. The usual horseshit.

There was a second press conference already in progress when Gold reached Senator Buckner's headquarters about thirty minutes later. This one too Gold overheard from the hall. The senator was more subtle, and for that reason probably more dangerous. His commission would "look into" the unhappy events of last night. It would "seek to determine" whether excessive force had been used, and a crime committed by Deputy Commissioner Keefe. It was police overreaction against black citizens that had provoked the formation of his commission in the first place, Buckner said.

Gold headed back to his office. Once there he took the pile of phone messages and stared down at them. This thing might ruin a number of careers, his own included. There was a public outcry coming, from which he must try to distance himself in some way. How?

His phone rang. When he picked it up he was informed

that Lieutenant Roche from Ballistics was outside and wished to see him. After hesitating, Gold ordered him shown in.

"Make it quick," he told the lieutenant as he came through the door. "I got a million things on my mind."

"Good morning, Chief. I was wondering if I could pick up a certain weapon from you."

Gold decided to stall. "So how many bullets did you dig out of the wall at the courthouse?"

"Not enough, Chief. There should be more."

Controlling Roche, Gold saw, might not be easy.

"That's why I need to examine the other gun, Chief. How many bullets are we looking for?"

"I can see your problem," said Gold and he began studying his messages, crumpling them up one by one and dropping them into his basket.

"We dug three out of the walls, Chief, all from Keefe's gun, and picked one up off the floor."

Gold looked at him. Finding themselves in the presence of the Chief of Detectives, most low-ranking cops were awed, and some almost trembled. Not Roche. "If I were you I'd send your guys back there," Gold said. "Make them keep looking."

"One of the slugs is totally deformed. That's probably from Keefe's gun too, but we're never going to be able to tell for sure."

Roche was a laboratory cop, Gold reflected. The headquarters brass would not impress him. He believed in instruments and in lab tests, which to him outranked rank. And he was right.

"So can I pick up the piece in question, Chief?"

"Would you believe it," lied Gold, "it's home in my house."

"Home in your house?"

"I forgot to bring it to work. I left in such a hurry this morning it slipped my mind."

There was a long silence. "What about the chain of evidence?" said Roche. "If this thing gets to court, the defence might call the chain of evidence into question." It was definitely a rebuke. A lieutenant was rebuking the Chief of Detectives. To Gold this was amazing, but he let it pass.

"Don't worry about it," he said. "It's in my safe at home."

"Well, could you perhaps tell me how many expended rounds there might be in the chamber?"

"No, I can't," Gold said. He had decided that he could ignore the messages from Kilcoyne – there were at least four of them. "I forgot to look," he lied. The ones from Keefe as well. The other important messages were from the mayor and from the PC.

"The assistant district attorney who has the case is bugging me for my report," Roche said.

"Fuck him," advised Gold.

"It's not a him, it's a her."

"Even better," said Gold.

"But Chief, I don't even know how many bullets I'm looking for."

"How many did you say you found so far?" said Gold with pretended indifference. He had heard Roche – and recognized the problem – the first time.

"Four, Chief. And there's at least one in the guy, right?"

"Four is not enough," said Gold. "Go back there and look again." The object was to keep Roche and his men busy, keep them from asking questions.

"We went over that place with a fine tooth comb," Roche said. Gold registered the cliché. Cops seemed to have memorized, and to use as often as possible, every cliché known to man. "All five bullets from Keefe's gun had been fired. How many from the other one? That's the question."

Gold said: "I once had a case, the victim was in the kitchen. The bullet went right through him. We looked everywhere for it. We scoured that kitchen for a week and couldn't find it. You know where we finally found it?"

"Where, Chief?"

"In a birthday cake in the refrigerator."

"It went through the door of the refrigerator."

"No, it didn't. There wasn't a mark on the door of the refrigerator."

"I don't understand, Chief."

"The first cop on the scene, he sees the birthday cake in

the middle of the kitchen table. It's starting to melt, so he picks it up and puts it in the refrigerator."

"He never should have moved that cake, Chief."

"He didn't want the cake to melt. The guy the cake was intended for is dead on the floor, and he's worried about the cake."

"Cops do funny things sometimes."

Gold made no comment. He was still staring down at his phone messages. He was brooding about his messages and he was brooding about Roche.

"So what's the point of your story, Chief?"

"The point is, I'd go back to that judge's chambers, and I'd look for the birthday cake."

"There was no birthday cake in there, Chief," said Roche mystified.

"The equivalent, you cluck."

"I don't understand, Chief," Roche persisted.

Cops could be brilliant on occasion, Gold reflected. Sometimes they were more intuitive than women. Other times you had to draw them pictures. When you lied to them even pictures weren't enough.

"There are filing cabinets in that office, aren't there? Those file drawers were open when you came into the room, weren't they? Did you look in those file drawers? Did you take out every paper in there?"

"No we didn't, Chief."

"If I were you, that's where I'd start," said Gold.

Roche looked puzzled. "All right, but it would be easier if I had the other gun and knew what I was looking for."

"I'll get it to you as soon as I can."

Brown's gun was in Gold's attaché case on his desk. After showing Roche out he sat down again, and with two outstretched thumbs released the catches on the case. Reaching inside, he withdrew the gun. It lay heavy in the palm of his hand and he looked at it. Roche was not going to find any expended bullets in those filing cabinets or anywhere else either, and that was the problem. The only gun that fired had been Keefe's, which fact was going to make a stink when it came out. Already Gold felt sorry for him.

He found a manila envelope, dropped Brown's gun into it and sealed the flap. He initialled the seal. That kept the chain of evidence intact. He put the envelope in the safe that occupied a corner of his office, closed the thick door on it, twirled the dial and then returned to his desk where he sat for a few minutes brooding. Finally he picked up his telephone and said into it: "Ask if the PC can see me now." He wondered how much he should tell him. It never paid to be the bearer of too much bad news.

About ten minutes later he was shown into the PC's office on the fourteenth floor. Chief Kilcoyne was already there. Gold, noting this, was not surprised. It was as if Kilcoyne and Egan could no longer be separated. Their interests had become identical. Both men looked worried, though little showed in their faces. They weren't as worried as all that, yet. The PC was probably the more worried of the two. He had a keen understanding of where political weight lay – always had had. Kilcoyne, in Gold's experience, never worried much about anything until it hit him in the face.

There was a sitting area off to one side of the PC's office: a sofa and two facing armchairs. The three men moved to this area. The PC sat down in a corner of the sofa and crossed his legs. Kilcoyne and Gold took the two chairs.

"Well, Al?" said the PC.

"I should start," Gold began, "by mentioning that there have been a number of press conferences already today, three in all. I attended two of them, one by Senator Buckner, and one by the wounded perpetrator's son, who is a Deputy Borough President of the Bronx by the way. The third was by the assistant DA in charge of the case. That one I missed but I've been briefed on it."

Gold saw Kilcoyne and the PC glance sharply at each other.

"Who his son might be doesn't change anything," Kilcoyne said.

"Please go on, Al," said the PC.

"Not a thing," said Kilcoyne.

"The assistant DA up there in the Bronx is young, and she's a female. According to her press conference she's

278

launching an investigation into the shooting. Naturally. It's what the law calls for. Senator Buckner is launching an investigation too. The son is just shooting his mouth off."

"What's he saying?" said Kilcoyne.

"He's just making wild charges."

"What kind of charges, Al?" the PC said.

Gold's original impression about Egan and Kilcoyne seemed to him confirmed. They were now running as an entry, and they were running scared.

"The usual stuff," Gold said. "That the shooting was racially motivated."

"It won't hold water," stated Kilcoyne.

The PC was pretending to be calm. Maybe he actually was. Gold had never been able to read Tim Egan very well.

"We don't have to listen to garbage like that," Kilcoyne added.

"He'll be believed in some quarters, Chief," Gold told him. "The black community will believe him. He was screaming about the hostage negotiating team. Where was it? Why was no effort made to talk his father into surrendering without the use of violence?"

"We did make such an effort," Kilcoyne said. "You were there, Al. It didn't work. We had no choice."

Gold looked at him. "You don't have to convince me, Chief."

"What else?" said the PC.

"The perpetrator was holding a hostage at gun-point," Kilcoyne interrupted. "He's got a list of priors as long as your arm and –"

"You put your finger on another one of our problems," Gold said. "It now appears that maybe he doesn't have any priors after all."

"What?"

"No prior record at all."

"You saw his sheet, Al," Kilcoyne protested. "I showed it to you last night."

"It may be that that was somebody else's sheet," Gold said. He glanced first at Egan, then at Kilcoyne. Both men looked stunned. "These things happen," Gold said. "Our record keepers are not infallible. In this case, it appears there may be two Joshua Browns. That sheet we had last night belongs to the other guy."

A heavy silence followed. Gold interrupted it saying: "After all, Brown is quite a common name."

"But Joshua, Al," said Kilcoyne.

"In Harlem Biblical names are common. All those people have them. Although names out of the Koran are gaining, I hear."

After another silence, Kilcoyne burst out: "It doesn't change the fact that he was holding a hostage at gun-point."

Gold decided he wished to smoke, and that as of today it was no longer necessary to ask permission. He got out a cigar, bit off the end and lit up.

"Who's responsible for the wrong sheet?" said Egan.

"That's not the question," said Gold. "The question is, who is the media going to hang it on?"

"The press will blame it on Keefe's inexperience," Egan suggested.

"He only used what the auto squad lieutenant gave him," said Gold. "Maybe they won't blame Keefe at all. Maybe they'll blame somebody else."

"Like who?" Kilcoyne said angrily.

Gold eyed him speculatively, and said nothing.

"What else, Al?" said the PC.

"This particular Joshua Brown, according to his son," Gold said, "was a sergeant in the United States Army until seven or eight years ago. He wasn't even in the country during the time the other Joshua Brown was running up that sheet we had last night. He had four kids. One, as I told you, is the Deputy Borough President of the Bronx. Another is a lieutenant colonel in the Air Force. Supposedly he's flying in tonight in his jet. The other two, from our point of view, don't count. One is a beer salesman in the South somewhere, and the other is a grade school teacher in Chicago."

He sucked in a mouth full of smoke, and blew it out again. There was not a sound in the room.

"He almost certainly did not belong to that car stealing

ring we broke up yesterday," Gold continued. "He just happened to be there and get caught in the raid. According to his son, he's been under terrific stress lately. His wife just died of cancer after about six months of agony, and he himself is a diabetic who since then often forgets to take his insulin shots."

Again Gold listened to the heavy silence.

"So you see how it is," he continued. "From our point of view we had every right to bust into the judge's chambers and shoot him. But the way the media is going to play it up we overreacted because he was black. He was an upright citizen all his life, and we turned him into a crazed aggressor and a victim in a single day by our incredible ineptitude. The Deputy Borough President and the lieutenant colonel are going to be listened to, believe me."

The PC said: "Deputy Commissioner Keefe led the raid on the junkyard and Deputy Commissioner Keefe fired the shots as well."

Gold nodded thoughtfully. "They might stop at Keefe," he said.

He did not think they would, and when he looked into the other two faces he saw that they did not either. Not if Brown died.

"What's the medical prognosis, Al?" said Egan.

"Not good, Commissioner."

"Fifty-fifty?" said Egan hopefully.

"He's terminal, Commissioner."

Egan winced. "They're going to say we executed him."

"They may, Commissioner," said Gold. He glanced over at Kilcoyne who had not spoken in some time. For Kilcoyne it must be an especially bitter dose.

"The press is all over me," Gold said. "So far I haven't told them anything."

"We've all had requests for interviews," Egan said.

Gold nodded. "Stall, Commissioner," he advised. "Play for time. If the guy should live, this whole thing might blow over."

"I think it best," Egan said, "to hold a press conference this afternoon."

The two men regarded each other. It was not going to blow over, Gold knew. "There're one or two other details in this case that won't look too good when they come to light," he added.

"What are you referring to?" snapped Kilcoyne, and Gold saw how edgy he had now become.

He had been about to mention the gun. Now he decided against it. "I got my own investigation going," he said. "I'll let you know as soon as I know." Knowledge was strength, as everyone knew. Knowledge also was time, which he himself needed – time to get well away from this thing before it exploded. Keefe, Kilcoyne and Egan were, he believed, lost, but he himself had a chance to get clear. All he needed was a little time, and he saw how the details he had been about to divulge would give it to him.

He said only, "At your press conference, Commissioner, they'll ask you if you approved the early morning raid on the junkyard. Hell, they'll ask if you approve of Keefe shooting a guy." Gold gave an airy wave of his hand. "The key question," he said addressing Egan, but watching for Kilcoyne's reaction out of the corner of his eye, "is going to be about the decision to bust in there. Why did you act so quickly? Why didn't you wait a little longer?"

"Because we were trying to keep Deputy Commissioner Keefe from getting killed," Kilcoyne burst out. "That's second-guessing. It's Monday morning quarterbacking. It's outrageous."

"Calm down," Gold said. "I'm just telling you what they're going to ask. These are questions the son was already asking up at the hospital. You'd better be ready for them."

Abruptly, Egan stood up. "I'll call the press conference for three o'clock," he said brusquely. "You'll both be on hand, I trust."

Egan, Gold knew, liked to conduct his press conferences with several high-ranking officers flanking him. Perhaps it was because of his relatively small physical stature: he seemed to need the weight of all that brass around him to give weight to whatever stand he was taking.

"I'll be there," said Kilcoyne grimly.

And Gold had no doubt that he would be. He would see it as his duty. He would stand up straight, and he would refuse the blindfold. To Kilcoyne the only manly way to face the firing squad was head on.

"You'll be there, Al?" said Egan.

"Sure."

But Gold had no intention of being there. To attend such a press conference would be to associate himself publicly with Egan, Kilcoyne and Keefe – with last night's debacle. So five minutes in advance he would have one of his captains telephone the PC to say that he had just been summoned by the mayor to City Hall.

"You can count on me, Commissioner," he said.

Twenty-Two

A HORDE OF NEWSMEN WAITED OUTSIDE KEEFE'S building.

"Back out into the avenue," he instructed Detective Murphy.

When the car was again pointed uptown, Murphy said: "Where to, Commissioner?"

Keefe was trying to decide.

"We could go to my hotel," Sharon suggested.

"What hotel?"

"The studio did reserve a room for me, you know. I wasn't expected to jump into just any bed I could find – yours, for instance."

He looked at her. It was nice to think she had come to his apartment rather than to the hotel.

A few minutes later Murphy deposited them in front of the Sherry Netherland. They rode upstairs and found that she had been accorded a suite. Together they explored it. Two of everything. There were flowers on the coffee table.

"Stick with me, baby," Sharon said, "and you'll be wearing

283

diamonds." They laughed, and in the center of the sitting room stood embracing. Then Keefe switched on the television for the evening newscasts. The screen lit up.

The "Keefe case" was the lead item. Senator Buckner commented that the ultimate police brutality was to take away a man's life without due process of law. His commission would investigate. Next on was the Deputy Borough President of the Bronx, who described his father as a devoted husband and father driven to desperate measures by racist police aggression. The son demanded justice.

Sharon, becoming more and more upset, said: "They're practically calling you a murderer."

"No they're not," said Keefe. Both these men were reacting as might have been expected, he said.

"The reporters are trying to appear impartial while making you out to be a criminal."

The reporters" reaction was programmed also, Keefe told her. Their role obliged them to take an adversarial stand against government – in this case against the police department.

"Not against the police department, against you."

Assistant District Attorney Anne Christianson spoke guardedly in the measured phrases dear to lawyers. A grand jury would investigate. If a crime had been committed, she would prosecute to the full extent of the law.

"They're not going to indict you," cried Sharon. "Are they?"

"No, of course not."

Part of the police news conference was shown. The PC sat hunched over microphones. He was flanked by Chief of Operations Kilcoyne and by Chief of Internal Affairs Sheridan filling the chair of Chief Gold. Keefe noted Gold's absence, but attached no significance to it. He did not know how long the PC had delayed the news conference while waiting for him, nor how angry he had been when at last he gave the order to start.

His own investigation, the PC said, was under way. If it should be determined that Commissioner Keefe had acted improperly then appropriate measures would be taken.

"He's abandoning you," cried Sharon. "He's throwing you to the wolves."

"No, he's not." Keefe, pacing, was too nervous to sit still. "He's trying to calm the whole thing down."

"You don't see it."

"I believe in the man, and I trust him." Did he? For the time being he had no choice.

Sharon ordered dinner from room service, including smoked salmon and champagne.

"Let the studio pay for it," she muttered, when she saw Keefe's eyebrows go up. She was still angry.

They dined in great luxury, though with no great pleasure. A waiter stood in attendance until, halfway through the meal, his presence got on Sharon's nerves and she sent him away.

Keefe was amused by her – by how worried she was about him, how fiercely she defended him.

She folded the tablecloth over the dishes, dropped the leaves and pushed the rolling table out into the hall.

"Now call your mother. If she's seen any of this, she'll be beside herself."

Later they walked to Keefe's apartment because they intended to sleep there if possible. But there were newsmen and vans still out front.

They stood on the corner hand in hand.

"We don't even have a toothbrush," said Keefe.

"I have one in my handbag."

Keefe looked at her in surprise.

"I like to brush my teeth on airplanes," she explained.

"Doesn't everyone?" said Keefe.

"Lots of people do," said Sharon defensively. "They get all icky. Stop grinning at me."

Keefe peered down the block at his building.

"You could go down there and talk to them."

Keefe only shook his head. "Not yet."

In an all-night drugstore he bought shaving gear, but when he started to buy a toothbrush Sharon said: "You could use mine."

They looked at each other. It was a moment of

unexpected intimacy. Shy smiles came on, and they touched each other's sleeves. Then Keefe paid for the shaving gear and they walked back to the hotel.

At eleven P.M. they watched the news broadcasts again. They were the same. This time Sharon made none of her previous comments. She did not have to.

When they had got into bed, naked because they had no night clothes, they clung to each other, or rather Keefe clung to her. The clinging became love-making, a speechless sweaty wrestling match. Keefe was capable of nothing tender or sensitive tonight, and when one bout ended he almost at once started another. He was inexhaustible, or perhaps only desperate.

All night he kept coming awake, seeking Sharon for comfort or else relief, he could not have said which, mouthing one part of her or another, manipulating her, clambering on top of her. Sometimes she woke and joined in the game, as if game were all it was. Other times she did not, or only half woke up, and lay there in an erotic dream while he employed her. When they dozed they lay with their limbs interlaced in every conceivable tangle, while their heartbeats slowed and the drying sweat, saliva and semen glued them together. Both of them even in sleep were dimly conscious of this sticky bond, which was perhaps the night's ultimate intimacy, and not to be disturbed by moving.

They called down for breakfast. Sharon hid naked in the bathroom. Keefe received the waiter wrapped in a sheet. They ate breakfast naked and giggling, making jokes about what the waiter must think, but once Keefe was dressed he phoned the PC at home, told him where he was and asked for instructions. He said he was considering releasing a statement of his own.

The PC said: "Let me handle it at this end a while longer."

They walked around to the flat. The reporters were already there and Keefe was tempted to talk to them. Instead he sent Sharon in past them to pack her bag and collect things for him as well, while he got his car out of the garage.

That day they drove up into New England through white

wooden towns, and looked into old wooden churches, some of which dated from Revolutionary days. They had lunch in one country inn and dinner in another where, after talking it over, they decided to spend the night. At least this time they had some baggage.

On Sunday morning they were awakened by the ringing of church bells, and lay listening to them. After breakfast they strolled through the village. It had a combination drugstore-post office that was closed, a grocery that was open, and a small public library, a white building no bigger than a one-car garage. A path through the woods attracted them and they walked in under soundless, timeless trees, and inhaled the odor of moist earth.

When they started back to New York they still had time, so they stopped here and there at antique shops. Finally they drove down through Connecticut to the Merritt Parkway, and across the Whitestone Bridge to the airport. This time when they reached the security checkpoint Sharon began to cry, and she clung to him: he could feel the hand that held her ticket pressed into his back.

"You're in trouble," she sobbed into his ear. "I don't want to leave you." He led her into a coffee shop and talked to her quietly. There was really nothing to worry about, he said. The PC would take care of him, or else he would take care of himself. In any case he had nothing to fear – he had done nothing wrong.

At last she went through security and when she was out of sight he went up onto the observation deck, something he had not done since childhood, and watched her plane taxi away and take off.

He walked downstairs and back through the departure hall where, from a wall phone, he spoke to his brother.

"You better do something, or you're going to wind up getting indicted."

"You're exaggerating," Keefe said into the phone. He looked around the departure hall: people with bags waiting in a semi-stupor for flights to be announced.

"Exaggerating?" Richard Keefe said. "They've lost sight of the felon and the felony. That must have been St. Thomas

Aquinas you shot, or Santa Claus or somebody. Have you been watching television? Have you been reading the newspapers?"

Keefe said nothing.

"Your silence is being read as guilt. You've got to tell what happened and why."

Keefe still said nothing.

"You were alone in the room with the guy. Nobody knows what happened in there but you and him, and he evidently is in a coma he might not pull out of. There were no other witnesses."

His brother's apartment overlooked Central Park. Keefe went there and they talked the rest of the afternoon away. The park was full of people strolling, of kids with kites and balloons, of softball players and frisbee scalers. He and his brother drank the many cups of strong coffee that his sister-in-law kept bringing, and they worked out the wording of the statement Richard Keefe thought he should make.

"You say you contacted the PC and he failed to respond? Put it in. And the Chief of Operations also failed to respond? Put it in."

Keefe said: "They both came eventually."

"They stuck you with it, you mean."

"But I need them in my corner. I can't accuse them like this."

"Why not? They're already accusing you."

"They're just trying to calm this thing down." It was possible. It was what he wanted to believe.

When the statement was finished it was his brother's advice that he give it out at once, but Keefe decided to hold it back until he could show it to the PC in the morning.

"Forget that guy," his brother told him at the door. "He's already dumped you. You can't trust him."

"I'll see how he seems tomorrow," said Keefe.

Twenty-Three

ON SATURDAY MORNING THE PC AND HIS WIFE HAD come downstairs early dressed in sweatsuits, intending to go jogging through the streets of Forest Hills. However, reporters had already congregated outside the front door. Egan had no intention of being photographed in a sweatsuit jogging. Not during a crisis of this magnitude.

Wearing sweatsuits instead of bathrobes, they lingered over breakfast, but when Egan looked again there were more reporters outside than ever, and the two cops on guard had got out of their car and were standing inside his front gate, arms folded across chests. Egan went back upstairs and changed into a business suit, while his wife began to vacuum the rooms downstairs.

He had not wanted to talk to any newsmen that day at all, but now decided to go out front and, for Edna's sake, try to get rid of them. However, his appearance in the doorway was enough to send them like a school of sharks into the equivalent of a feeding frenzy. For the most part their questions were the same ones he had refused to answer previously. If they thought he was going to answer them now they were mistaken, and so this first interview of his day served no purpose on either side. He went back into his house and tried to calm himself by drinking another cup of coffee standing up in the kitchen. Outside his front door the press remained on post.

His phone began to ring. The mayor wished to see him. Gold wished to see him also. Neither the mayor nor his Chief of Detectives chose to tell him in advance what to expect, and he did not ask, hiding his emotions, and therefore his cards.

"Can it wait, Al?" was all he said to Gold, who told him it could not.

The press vehicles trailed him all the way to headquarters – at least now Edna was free to move about without being harrassed. He took the private elevator from the garage up to his office. Presumably the newsmen were waiting for him in the pressroom downstairs. Presumably it was their hope that at some time during the day he would make a statement. But his conversation with Gold, which now took place, only reinforced his decision that there was not going to be one.

The Chief of Detectives broke the seal on the manila envelope he was carrying and spilled its contents – a revolver – out onto Egan's desk blotter. Guns were nothing new to Egan.

"That's the gun," Gold told him, "with which the perpetrator not only threatened Commissioner Keefe's life but supposedly fired shots at him."

Egan, looking it over, winced.

"As you can see, Commissioner, it's a starter's pistol. The barrel is plugged."

Egan recovered quickly. Already his face showed nothing. "You're sure," he said carefully. "There can be no mistake?"

"That's the gun, Commissioner."

Egan put it down on his blotter and ran both hands over the top of his thinning hair. He walked to the window and looked out, then walked back to the desk.

Finally he said: "So in effect Commissioner Keefe shot an unarmed man."

"He didn't know he was unarmed, Commissioner."

"The press is going to say he did know, or at least that he should have known."

"Maybe the grand jury, too," Gold said.

There was a long silence. Egan picked up the gun and put it down again.

"You have to look at it pretty carefully to tell what it is," Gold said.

"What's the latest medical report?"

"Unchanged."

"If he pulls through," Egan temporized, "this whole thing might blow over."

"It's a possibility, Commissioner," said Gold.

"So maybe we should keep it under our hats and see what happens." This was one possible decision, and he toyed with it.

"If you say so, Commissioner." Reaching across the desk Gold lifted the gun and dropped it back into the envelope. "When it's pointing at you," he said agreeably, "it's awfully hard to tell it's not a real gun."

"He was probably terrified," said Egan. But he was only stalling for time.

"No more terrified than I would have been," Gold said. "Or you would have been." It was a half-hearted defence of Keefe, but Egan did not bother with it.

"How many people know about this? Chief Kilcoyne? Commissioner Keefe?"

"None of the above, Commissioner. If you give the word, we can keep it quiet a few more days."

Egan, having made up his mind nodded. "Let's do that." Probably this decision was exactly the one Gold had hoped for. The person withholding information – and evidence – from press and public had become Egan himself. Gold was now in the clear, but Egan was caught. He had no choice.

Gold had turned away and was halfway to the door. "One other thing, Commissioner."

More bad news was coming. Egan looked up sharply.

"If the guy dies, the autopsy report will become public. It will show that he was hit by only one bullet." Gold added: "In the back."

This time Egan had his emotions under tight control. He only nodded. There was no change of expression. "Thanks for coming in, Al," he said.

An hour later he was driven up to the mayoral residence. His car went in through the gates, past the sentry booth and up the long winding driveway lined with trees. The mansion was a relic from the gracious living of an earlier New York, a great white wooden Victorian house replete with towers and turrets. Its grounds, bounded by the East River on one side and by apartment buildings on all the others, were the size of a park.

Egan was put in a reception room and told to wait, a bad sign. Finally the mayor came bustling out of an office. He was dressed not for a confrontation with his Police Commissioner but for a summer Saturday – blue jeans and a tee-shirt. It was his right. This was his house, and besides he was mayor. The tee-shirt bore the slogan: *I Love New York*, the word "love" being represented by a heart.

"Come on outside," the mayor said. "Let's go for a walk."

As Egan followed him across the veranda and down the steps he saw that the back of the tee-shirt was decorated with a large red apple.

They strolled through the grounds under the trees. The mayor's bald head, Egan noted, was sunburned and peeling.

"So what do I have to look forward to?" the mayor said.

There was bad news in all directions, bad news as far as the eye could see, but Egan meant to withhold it for the time being. "If the man lives," he said carefully, "I think we can contain this thing."

The mayor shook his head with annoyance. "I've spent my career going to the funerals of people who 'tried to contain this thing', as you so hopefully put it." He shot Egan a calculating glance. "If there's any news out there that the city doesn't know about yet, you don't have a chance. Even if there isn't anything more, you don't have much of a chance."

They walked several paces in silence.

The mayor said: "So what are your contingency plans?"

Egan decided to give him a smile: "Contingency plans? I haven't started thinking of contingencies yet."

"So start." The path they had taken brought them ever closer to the wrought-iron fence that surrounded the grounds. On the sidewalk outside some pedestrians had gathered. Having spied the mayor in the garden, they had begun waving and calling out to him.

Suddenly he broke away from Egan's side and loped over there. He was grinning broadly. Egan watched him shaking hands with people. He had both hands extended out through the fence over the sidewalk. He was touching flesh and apparently making wise cracks, for some of the people laughed.

The mayor came back and they resumed strolling side by

side. "So tell me about all the swell contingency plans you just thought up while I was over there charming my public."

Egan tried for another confident smile. They were getting harder to do. "You don't give me much time."

"You got to find answers to the questions people are asking," the mayor told him. "For instance, a deputy commissioner is an administrator, right? So why was this Keefe armed? Who signed his pistol permit?"

"Deputy commissioners are usually armed," Egan said.

"Why, for Chrissake?"

Egan looked at him.

"It's only what the public is asking," the mayor said. "And goddamn it, they have a right to know."

"Everybody in the department is armed," responded Egan with some heat. "I'm armed and I'm an administrator. Why shouldn't deputy commissioners be armed?"

"Not good enough. You're a cop twenty some years, he's a newspaper reporter. Who signed his permit?"

"It's automatic for a deputy commissioner. My name was on the permit, but I –"

"Yeah," the mayor interrupted. "Your name. How many questions is that you haven't answered right so far? Here's another one. Who's responsible for the press being given the wrong rap sheet? And last and most important question of all, what don't I yet know about this thing?"

Egan could not read the man's mood very well. He seemed both congenial and demanding – even slightly angry – all at the same time. Probably, Egan told himself, I ought to inform him about the starter's pistol, and about Keefe's bullet striking the man in the back. But the words would not come.

Again they strolled along in silence.

"So whose head is gonna roll?" demanded the mayor. He did not pause for an answer. "The public doesn't even know it yet, but that's what they want. Which heads are you going to give them?"

"I hadn't thought about it in those terms exactly."

"So start thinking about it."

"Keefe?"

293

"That's a good start. Who else?"

After a few more paces, Egan said: "If I demanded Keefe's resignation it might seem like we're trying to convict him without a trial. It might rebound against us."

The mayor's eyebrows went up, and he began nodding his bald head. "You may have something there."

"It's not an easy situation," said Egan.

"You can say that again."

Having reached the end of the path, they turned and started back toward the mansion. Nothing more was said by either man until they had reached it.

"You might start by disciplining some of those sergeants and lieutenants on the scene," the mayor suggested. "And higher guys than that, if you got them. That might quiet things down a little. It would make it look like you're doing something, at least. Instead of just standing there with your finger up your ass." He had paused halfway up his front steps, thereby towering over Egan who stood on the pavement, peering up at him. "That might do for a start," the mayor said. "Give the sons of bitches a look at some heads rolling. They'll love it."

Suddenly he glanced out towards the fence. There seemed to be a new group of sightseers there now, and a big grin came on his face, and he waved both arms over his head in their direction. They began applauding. Finally the mayor's attention returned to Egan. The grin was gone, and he said: "They like to see blood. You give it to them, and they're happy. Let me know what you decide."

He turned and went into the mansion.

I give them the heads of a few sergeants, Egan thought, and if that doesn't work he gives them mine.

He walked along the driveway, got into his car and told his driver to take him home.

The next morning was Sunday. When Egan stepped out onto the front stoop in his bathrobe to bring in the newspapers, his yard was still clear. The police car was on post; no one else was in sight. But by the time he and Edna and the two little boys were ready to leave for mass, less than two hours later, there were a dozen or more newsmen there jostling for position.

"They're going to ruin my hedges and plantings," his wife muttered to him in the doorway.

Pushing forward with their microphones and cameras they began trampling Edna's flowers, and one of them, having lost his balance, fell face down in a mixed bed of petunias and impatiens.

As he waded toward the curb, a fixed smile was glued to Egan's face. He was trying to smile while warding men off. He kept saying: "I don't know anything more than I knew last night, fellas. Why don't you just let us go to church? That's all we want, fellas. To go to church."

The two cops from the guard car had hurried forward to help. They were willing to restore order, wrestle people to the ground, crack heads; but when no such instructions came from the PC they did not know what to do.

Finally the Egans reached the sidewalk. Egan's own department car was doubleparked in front, but he had no intention of being forced to get into it. St. Brendan's was only two blocks down the street. He had a right to walk there if he wanted to, not ride. He was furious, though still smiling. He had an arm around the shoulders of each of his sons. All three were moving along the sidewalk as fast as he could make them. Edna Egan, face down, was half a pace behind him. The cameramen, some of whom receded backwards in front of him, were still filming.

At the church Egan led his family into a pew and sat down. He sat quietly for a moment as if the siege were over, though he knew it was not.

The pew was close to the altar and the newsmen had remained outside – or so Egan imagined when he glanced around.

The mass began. Presently all four Egans marched up to the altar rail to receive communion, walking back to their pew a few seconds later with clasped hands and downcast eyes.

A few minutes after that, leaning over, Egan whispered in his wife's ear. He grabbed one boy, she the other. With each adult dragging along a surprised child, the family hustled quickly out the side door. Egan's car was parked there according to instructions he had given his driver earlier.

"Quickly," Egan ordered the driver, when they had all jumped in. "Let's go."

The car took off with a squeal of rubber that bounced the little boys into the backrest to either side of their mother. They were giggling with excitement. Seated up front beside the driver, Egan had turned and was peering through the back window.

"We've lost them, I think," he reported, and his satisfaction was so great he almost smiled.

The car sped through the streets of Forest Hills and dived down into the Queen's-Midtown Tunnel. Like a dolphin, it crossed the river, coming up for air on Second Avenue where presently Egan stopped it in front of a delicatessen. His wife got out and disappeared into the store. When she returned ten minutes later she was carrying bags containing what would be their lunch.

The car turned crosstown. It crossed between rows of buildings that at first were short. In the center of the island they became very tall; then they shortened again. As the Hudson came into sight at the end of the street the buildings stopped altogether and the car drove uptown along the waterfront toward the place where the Circle Line excursion boats were berthed. There the Egans all got out and the PC joined the queue at the ticket window. The boys were excited about their coming boatride and were jumping about. In a moment Egan came away with four tickets. His car was still parked nearby. He stopped to speak to the driver, who was instructed to return for them at a specified hour. Standing with his family, Egan watched the car pull away. He was feeling much better, for at last he had shaken off the reporters – shaken the tail, so to speak – and once aboard the boat he would be out of contact with the city and with the press for several hours.

The Egans went aboard. Egan had the impression that the hawsers had already been cast off when suddenly came the sound of screeching brakes. Two cars had pulled up. Out of them spilled newsmen. One of their number was already racing to the window to buy tickets, and the others were running toward the boat, toward their quarry, himself.

His first reaction was shock. Not until afterwards did he become angry. He was shocked because only now, as he realized the effort these newsmen had put into finding him, did he understand what a very big story the media considered this to be. They must have sent scouts out in every direction. One of them was in that phone booth over there – Egan could see him through the glass – no doubt informing his colleagues that the Police Commissioner had been found. Since the boat was about to sail, the other reporters, which meant most of them, would be left behind: a small blessing. He would have to deal only with the two car-loads already on board. He considered grabbing his family and getting off, but there wasn't time, and the boys would be in tears. The boat was backing out into the current. Having turned, it aimed itself downriver and began to surge forward.

Other reporters had waited outside Kilcoyne's house that morning. He too had walked to church, and they had trailed him there. He too smiled a lot. He called some of them by name and wished them a good day, but he ignored their questions. He strode five blocks through the streets of Staten Island to attend mass, a very tall, somewhat heavy white-haired man wearing today a brown suit, brown tie and brown wingtip shoes, striding along surrounded by a swarm of reporters.

After mass, Kilcoyne stood outside the doors chatting with other parishoners and with the priest. Then he walked home, still ignoring their questions. When at midday he walked over to lunch with his father and his sister they were still outside his house and they followed him. He strode the two blocks briskly, swinging his arms, looking straight ahead. Their questioning by this time had become ugly. They were virtually accusing him of incompetence or malfeasance or both. Many times he was asked if he intended to resign. He paid no attention to them, making no statement of any kind.

Still more reporters, first one then several, began to congregate in front of Gold's house in the Long Island suburbs. He watched them covertly from an upstairs window. When a good crowd had collected, he stepped out onto his lawn and gave them what they had come for. He had been wearing a sportshirt, but changed to a business suit first. He spoke with his thick arms folded across his chest. He spoke of "the deplorable events," of the other night, a good phrase. Did he mean the hostage taking was deplorable, or was he criticising the police response? They could take it either way. Perfect.

Under questioning he admitted that the police response had perhaps not been "suitable". This statement too was vague. It was always better, was it not, to solve disputes without firing shots, he said; but he himself had arrived very late, and had not been on the scene in time to influence events one way or the other. Talking about it now was not going to change anything. Yes, police procedures in matters of this kind could possibly be refined. Police procedures could always be refined. That's what each new police commissioner tried to do as he took office.

Was he himself a candidate for Police Commissioner, a reporter asked.

He said he was Chief of Detectives, and that was all. Tim Egan, he added piously, was one of the finest police commissioners in recent years, and Dennis Kilcoyne was a man of such honor and rectitude that it was a privilege to serve under him.

Yes, Keefe had commanded the raid on the stolen car ring, not himself, he admitted reluctantly. At no time had Keefe conferred with him, much less asked his advice. Since Keefe was acting with the blessing of the Police Commissioner, Gold had been obliged to step aside and let him run it.

After the reporters had decamped Gold went back inside his house and poured himself a stiff drink. It was not yet noon. He realized that his hands were moist. His wife was out of the house, a good thing. She was a woman who couldn't keep her mouth shut. If the reporters had got to her she would probably have said something stupid. He felt himself begin to tremble. He believed he had just saved his career. From now on press attention would have to focus on the other three men only. The mayor might start firing people. But he couldn't fire everybody, and Gold was in the clear. In fact he might seem to one and all the viable alternative to Egan – the savior, the man of the hour. It was entirely possible. He had a good chance.

When he had downed his drink he felt better. If his statements just now were accepted by the media, then his next move was to send Joshua Brown's starter's pistol to Ballistics. It all depended on tonight's newscasts, on tomorrow's morning papers. If they were good, the pistol went to Ballistics, which was the same as sending it to the *New York Times*. Cops talked too much. A titbit this juicy would reach the reporters before the day was out. His own hand in the leak would be invisible to all. That gun was going to destabilize the situation for good; he was sure of it.

The Egans were still on the water. Edna Egan sat under an awning with a book, while the Police Commissioner, a little boy dangling from each hand, circled the deck pointing out landmarks. Newsmen followed him. Cameramen went down on one knee. Egan gave the cameras his best tight smile.

"Are we going to be on television, Daddy?"

"I'll be probably the youngest kid ever on television."

"How old were you, Daddy, the first time you were on TV?"

"When I was a little boy there wasn't any television."

The youngster didn't believe it. Neither did his brother.

"Daddy's kidding you," the older boy advised him.

"Television hadn't been invented then," Egan said. He muttered so the newsmen would hear: "And the world was probably better off for it."

The boat went down the Hudson. He watched pass all the empty piers where the ocean liners used to tie up. Some days there had been whole rows of them, and the boy Tim Egan would stand looking up at the prows, and dream of places more exotic than the streets of New York through which he walked to school, in which he was confined.

There was no point saying any of this to his sons.

The towers of the financial district passed. They sailed under the Brooklyn Bridge, and as Egan pointed out police headquarters to his sons he heard the cameras turning.

"Commissioner, would you mind pointing out headquarters a second time?" a cameraman requested.

He must have missed the shot. Good, thought Egan.

The boys were constantly gazing straight up at the bridges, or else out at the river tugs and barges. At a certain point hunger drove them back to their mother who began to pass around sandwiches. Egan opened soda for the boys, iced tea for Edna and himself, and the family ate lunch while cameramen and reporters clustered near, photographing them, trying to eavesdrop.

People were eating all around them. We didn't need to bring our own lunches, Egan thought, they sell food on board. He felt he should have known this, and was annoyed with himself.

He went to stand by the rail. The boat entered the East River, and he watched the high brick apartment complexes of the Lower East Side, and then the massive hospitals that seemed to hang out over the river, Bellevue, the N.Y.U. Medical Center, New York Hospital. To the other side of the boat was first Brooklyn, then Queens, vast sprawling cities in their own right, low cities that extended toward the horizon. The outer boroughs were not New York to Egan. They did not look the same as Manhattan, and they were not the same. Manhattan was compact, crammed full. It was limited and without limit at the same time.

When his sons rejoined him, he pointed out the town houses of the very rich along Sutton Place. Then came more bridges. The river changed its name. It was the Harlem now, with Yankee Stadium on one shore and another housing project on the other side where the old Polo Grounds used to be.

"The New York Giants played there," Egan said, and he found himself telling his boys about that once famous stadium, though there was no way they could ever understand about the old Polo Grounds, or about the former New York Giants, or about so many half-forgotten memories that were this city to their father. He knew the city as intimately as his own house. As a young cop he had dreamed of being Police Commissioner, and he had managed his career skilfully enough to be appointed. His head now was filled with plans for his department, and he was more worried about what would become of these plans than of what would become of him personally. His new training programme, for instance: there were cops in the precincts who hadn't been back to the Police Academy in ten years. They knew nothing about new theories in crisis intervention, or even changes in the law. Egan wanted to set up courses to be attended on a staggered basis by every cop in the department. They would last two weeks at first, and he would extend them to a month each year as soon as it was practical to do so.

But he could not put in such a program without co-operation. The department was too big, too unwieldy. Commanders, who were only foot cops with insignia on their shoulders, had no more belief in training than the average patrolman. They would not want to give up their men for such extended periods. Egan would have to meet with them in small groups, explain his ideas, make them want to co-operate. The program would have to be financed by City Hall, meaning that Egan would have to convince the mayor too.

He had dozens of ideas of this kind, all of them suddenly not viable. This was no time to ask the mayor for money, or to ask his subordinates to embrace one of his programs either. The Mayor would wait to see how the Keefe case came out. So would Egan's subordinates. They would wait to see if he survived it.

The boat passed between the Riverdale section of the Bronx and the Baker Field sports complex of Columbia University, including a boat basin. They passed under the Henry Hudson Bridge high above, then through the former railroad bridge which stood frozen open forever. At last they were in the Hudson again. Much of the northern end of Manhattan island was a park, and from the deck Egan could see how his city must have looked to the Dutch sailors who first found it, and he mentioned this to his sons. They sailed down the great river past the stately buildings that lined Riverside Drive, most of them decorated with stonework and majestic in appearance.

During the last part of the ride Egan sat beside his wife and let the boys wander off. He was thinking about that morning's news stories. They were bad. Questions were being asked that would be difficult for Egan to answer and perhaps impossible for Keefe.

Why had Keefe, a civilian administrator, been permitted to mastermind a police raid despite a total absence of prior experience or training? Who was responsible?

As for spotting Hot Harry's truck on the road in the first place, what was he doing driving a department car not only outside of the city limits but even across into a neighboring state? Was he using a department car as personal transportation to his weekend house? Did this constitute a theft of service? And was not theft of services a crime?

When the boat had docked, Egan went down the gangway holding his two sons by the hands, and all the reporters who had missed the boat earlier seemed to be waiting for him on the pier.

"Do you have anything to say about Chief Gold's statement?" they asked him.

Another shock. What had Gold said? Egan gave a wave and the same fixed smile as before, and without answering moved to his car.

When they got home the Egans watched the early newscasts, and the boys giggled to see themselves on TV. Egan himself waited only to hear Gold's statement, whatever it was. He kept switching channels, hoping to pick up more of it. Gold's message was all too clear. He was the last of the high-ranking commanders to reach the courthouse, and the decision taken was not his decision. When asked if he disagreed with that decision, either then or now, Gold was careful not to answer.

I should have ordered him not to speak to the press, Egan told himself. He was furious at Gold, but at the same time felt a grudging admiration for him. With this one stroke he had managed, it seemed to Egan, to extract himself from the swamp in which all the rest of them were still sinking.

The next morning Keefe came into his office with a prepared statement. He wanted to give it out to the press, he said.

Egan read the statement. Then he read it again. Having been abandoned on the scene, Keefe had had no choice but to act as he had.

Abandoned? Egan at his desk looked up at him. Abandoned by whom? That's what the world would ask. "Yes," he said, "well." He put the statement down. "I really don't think it would be wise to release this just yet." When Keefe's mouth seemed to set itself stubbornly, Egan added: "It doesn't put you in a good enough light."

It took him twenty minutes to convince Keefe to hold the statement at least one more day.

"Let me handle it a while longer," he told him. "Give me time to work behind the scenes." This was Keefe's best chance, Egan told himself, and his own as well.

When Keefe still looked unconvinced, Egan said: "Trust me," and with his hand on the young man's shoulder he showed him out.

How much longer could he keep Keefe in check? Egan thought he could convince him to hold back his statement a few more days. Faith and trust existed at hot temperatures, and he realized this. They tended to consume themselves. They were as perishable as certain foods. But at the very least Keefe would warn him first, wouldn't he? Wouldn't he?

After that Gold came in and announced that the perpetrator's starter's pistol had been sent over to Ballistics for tests.

"Did I authorize that?"

"No, sir."

"Then on whose authority –"

"The DA's office ordered me to do it," said Gold defensively. "I had no choice."

Discipline him, Egan ordered himself. Punish him.

For a moment Gold looked worried, then confident again. The two men eyed each other across Egan's desk. There was nothing Egan could do about the gun now without being accused of attempting a cover-up; and he could not afford to be seen to punish Gold. Of the two of them he was in the more vulnerable position, and Gold knew it.

"So you can expect that information to leak out any time," Gold advised him, adding, as if to rub it in: "I don't know what the media might make of it, when they find out."

Egan knew, or could guess. He was reasonably certain Gold knew too. The Chief of Detectives was not stupid.

As soon as Gold had gone out Egan buzzed his chief secretary, a deputy inspector in uniform, and demanded a list of all officers who had responded to the Bronx courthouse four nights before. It was handed to him about an hour later. As he took it he instructed the deputy inspector to hold all his calls. He began to study it. The list was by rank. His own name came first of course. Then came Keefe, Kilcoyne and Gold. Which could he sacrifice at no risk to himself? The answer, at this stage, was none of them. It took no great genius to realize that only their names protected his own. Gold was especially safe. The public outcry was focused for the moment against Keefe and Kilcoyne.

But other names, some of them commanders who had arrived too late to be any use, were not protected at all. Sooner or later there would have to be a blood bath. But the mayor had seemed to be urging haste, whereas Egan still saw, or thought he saw, the need to move cautiously. When he acted he had to stop this thing dead in its tracks, not add impetus to it.

He was looking at about twenty names. Included were Lieutenant Craighead of the Auto Squad, Sergeant Carmichael of the Stakeout Squad, and Sergeant Rainey of Keefe's office. Egan began to put checkmarks beside some of the names, then to erase them and to check others. His decisions kept changing. His eyes and pencil kept going up and down the list.

He put it aside and began to study a report he had ordered on the Stakeout Squad. The report put him in a worse mood than before. The Squad had been established by his predecessor presumably to terrorize prospective stick up men. A squad of sharpshooters. A squad that had been put in place to kill people, and for some months had been doing so. But its existence had never been publicized – who knew why? This made it a secret squad. A squad of secret killers. Cops who terrorized nobody because nobody knew they were there. They prevented nothing, they merely killed stick up men in the act. They hid in the backs of stores and when a stick up man came in they executed him. They executed one after the other, twenty-one dead bodies in the last year and a half, nineteen of them being guess which color.

Egan decided to abolish the Stakeout Squad at once, before anyone found out about it. He wanted all those sharpshooters – killers, he almost called them – back in uniform, back on patrol. He wanted it done fast before word got out that the squad had ever existed, but he also wanted it done silently – which was impossible. Whenever men were flopped back into uniform they screamed. These men would scream. In the very act of abolishing the Stakeout Squad, Egan would have succeeded in calling public attention to it. He could see the headlines in advance, and they were hideous. He could visualise the street demonstrations in Harlem and Bedford-Stuyvesant – demonstrations that could turn into riots if some panicky cop used his gun.

Senator Buckner phoned. He thought they should meet in some place where they would not be seen, the better to talk of "events".

Again Egan had a decision to make but he was too upset to make it calmly. "Call me back tomorrow," he snapped. "I'll see if I can work it in."

Buckner began trying with heavy-handed charm to talk him into a meeting that very afternoon. He sounded like a man trying to talk a girl's clothes off. Exasperated, Egan finally burst out: "Did it ever occur to you I might be busy? We've been very busy here the last day or two. I don't know if you've noticed?" He hung up on him.

A moment later the prosecutor assigned to the case, a young blond named Anne something, was shown in by the deputy inspector outside Egan's door. Although surprised that such an important case had drawn a female and that she was so young, he did not show this but came around the desk all smiles and shook her hand. As young as she was, and as inexperienced as she must be, she was in a position to cause Egan trouble, and in fact had already tried to. He had enough trouble and did not need to add her. He drew her attention to the portrait of Teddy Roosevelt, painted at the end of the last century, that hung on his wall.

"One of my predecessors as Police Commissioner," he said. He patted the desk. "This is his desk too." She had tried to get him to come up to the Bronx to her office for this interview. He had instructed his deputy inspector to refuse. He had not spoken to her himself. Now he led her to the sofa at one side of his office and sat down beside her, knees drawn in, almost facing her, but not too close. He was careful not to threaten her personal space.

"Tell me how I can help you," he said.

She arranged her tape recorder on the leather cushion and turned it on. He saw that she was intimidated, which was good. He wanted to get rid of her promptly.

No, he could not remember at what time he had reached Judge Baum's chambers, he said. "Surely someone noted it down. I was at a banquet with the mayor and the cardinal, you see."

He saw her digest this: he moved in the highest circles. She was taking up his time.

"Well," she said hastily, "when did the banquet begin? How long do you think you were there before you left?"

He wanted no part of her investigation, and had no intention of testifying before the grand jury if he could help it.

"Let me see. The cardinal was at the microphone. I remember that much, because his chair was the one beside me, and it was empty." He gave her a nod as if this detail was important.

She asked him to describe the scene when he arrived at the courthouse, but he said he couldn't. "I was listening to a briefing from Chief Kilcoyne and others."

She fell silent. He looked down and watched the tape spool turn, recording for the moment nothing.

"Did you know that Deputy Commissioner Keefe was armed?"

Another subject Egan intended to avoid. "The door was closed and locked. None of us had any way of knowing what was on the other side, don't you see?"

Her brows had come together, probably in frustration, but she continued down her list of questions.

"Who devised the plan for breaking into the judge's chambers?"

"When I got there it seemed to be the consensus. I don't know where the various components of the plan came from. You'll have to ask someone else about that."

He glanced at his watch, and made certain she saw him do it. About ten minutes later she finally gave up – she packed up her tape recorder and left. He was smiling with apparent warmth as he showed her out, and he remained smiling after the door had closed, savouring his small triumph. Then he went back behind his desk. His smile disappeared and he began to study his list again, and the Stakeout Squad report, and Keefe's proposed statement, grave matters all. He sat trying to decide what to do.

Twenty-Four

THEY WERE TEN WHO SAT DOWN TO DINNER. ON THE table was a casserole of indeterminate nature, and a bowl of clotted rice, a big wooden bowl almost overflowing with salad, and several two litre jugs of red wine. This was at the apartment of Anne's best friend, formerly her college roommate. Anne's own date was a former classmate from law school – everyone at the table was still influenced, if not dominated, by relationships formed in school, and by ideas formed in school. Some of the couples had brought babies who whimpered from time to time in the next room.

Dinner was accompanied by animated conversation about baseball among the young men, and about pregnancies among the young women. Only Anne was silent, for her focus was elsewhere and details about her case churned through her head.

"What?"

One of the husbands had asked her a question.

She looked around in something of a panic while people stared at her. The question, repeated, was about Deputy Commisioner Keefe.

"Anne's famous," her college roommate explained. "Her name is in the papers every day."

This was flattering, but it also made her impatient. She did not want to talk about herself, nor about Keefe either. She wanted to be left alone while she sorted through the possibilities, decided what to do next.

"So is the guy guilty or not?" one of the women said.

"You know as much about it as I do."

"They'll bury this case," said her roommate's husband, "you watch."

"The cops and the DA are in bed together," said another of the men.

"I'm the DA," said Anne hotly.

"You'll do what you're told, I imagine."

"I'll do what the law calls for."

"She interviewed the Police Commisioner," said the young lawyer who was her date. He worked for a major Wall Street law firm.

"And?"

"He stonewalled her."

Anne was furious, and when he had taken her home she dismissed him at the downstairs door.

The next morning she phoned Senator Buckner at Brutality Commission headquarters. To her surprise he invited her to lunch, and gave her an address in midtown.

She rode the subway down from the Bronx, arriving too early. He wasn't there yet. It wasn't a restaurant at all, but a small and probably very exclusive club. She had never been in such a place before. There were only about eight tables, and she sat at one and watched nervously. When Buckner finally arrived she didn't know whether to stand or remain seated. This man was a senator. She had seen him on television many times. She began to be afraid that when he found out why she wanted to see him he might consider her presumptuous.

Buckner sat down, summoned the waiter, and pressured her into ordering a drink she didn't want. He behaved as if this luncheon was the most natural thing in the world. He addressed the waiter by name, called for menus, described the best dishes, and practically told her what to order.

"You're a very beautiful girl, you know that?"

Anne frowned. She wasn't here to flirt with him.

"Yes, sir," said Buckner, taking a gulp from his drink. "I like the way you handle yourself in court."

Flattery of this nature was far more pleasing. Momentarily disarmed, Anne smiled.

"When I saw your picture in the paper, I said to myself, I've got to meet that girl." He flashed her a large grin.

Young as she was, Anne was extremely sensitive to men who came on to her. Since she didn't want to offend Buckner, she blinked her eyes at him, and said with attempted lightness: "And here I thought you were only interested in my case." But she had become more nervous than ever, and her voice cracked slightly. She had wanted her remark to sound charming. Instead it came out as a rebuff.

In his turn, Buckner frowned. He was a big man in an expensive suit. He wore a gold wristwatch, and there was a red handkerchief in his breast pocket. "So why did you phone me?" he said.

Anne dropped her eyes. "I – I wanted to ask you for advice."

She had lost all control over this luncheon and all confidence in herself. Perceiving this at once, Buckner began to interview her. His manner was brusque, his questions increasingly specific. Anne answered all of them. Everything she had refused to tell the press, had intended not even to tell the District Attorney, she told Buckner. The waiter came and put plates of steaming food in front of both of them.

Finally Buckner picked up his fork. "Let's eat." He did not speak again – did not even look at her again – until the waiter came to take the plates away. His attitude completely unnerved her.

Coffee was served.

"You didn't get me here to ask for advice," Buckner said. "You want something. What do you want?"

It was Buckner's job to investigate alleged police brutality, Anne began hesitantly, was it not? And what was the ultimate in police brutality? It was the taking away of a man's life without due process of law, was it not? And not by some patrolman in a police car either, but by a deputy commissioner. As she spoke her voice had gradually become firmer.

Buckner eyed her. "Nobody's dead yet."

"True." Anne bit her lip.

"So what do you want from me?"

Anne took a deep breath. "Support."

"Support?"

"My Boss, the District Attorney of Bronx County, seems disposed not to indict."

"How do you know that?"

"He as much as told me."

Buckner studied a spot halfway up the opposite wall. "But you want to indict?"

"Do I think Commissioner Keefe should be indicted?" said Anne carefully. "If the evidence points that way, yes. Absolutely. You're a lawyer, what do you think?"

Buckner, watching her, said nothing.

"That's what the system is for," Anne said earnestly. "That's the way it's supposed to work."

"You want to nail a deputy commissioner," said Buckner.

"It's a high-visibility case," Anne admitted.

"Nail a deputy commissioner, and your career takes off."

"I don't care about my career."

Buckner gave a harsh and unfriendly laugh. "That's a hot one, honey."

"I want to see justice done," said Anne stubbornly. "I don't want to see someone protected just because he's got high rank."

"That may not happen."

"That's what usually happens. They're already trying to cover it up."

"The safest thing for you is whatever the DA wants."

"I know that." She hesitated. "If I felt I had some support, your support, I'd –" she stopped.

"You'd indict the guy anyway."

Anne said nothing. She met his eyes, but when his stare lasted too long she looked away.

"You want me to speak to the District Attorney for you, so that if something goes wrong you don't lose your job."

They looked at each other.

"I want you to tell him –" Anne took another deep breath – "to let the case go through normally."

"Normally? You mean to let you run it, not him. Yes, sure. I'll give you my support." Then he said: "I'll make a deal with you, honey. You keep me informed every step of the way, and I'll do what you want."

"You will?" Anne was elated. Buckner's hand lay on the tablecloth. She picked it up and shook it. "That's wonderful. Thanks a lot."

"I want to know everything that happens, got that? Everything."

"It's a deal."

Buckner pushed back from the table. "Now, if you'll excuse me, I have work to do."

As he vanished out the door, Anne had barely risen from her chair. Suddenly abandoned, she glanced about the room in some embarrassment, then made her way out of the building. She was excited. She had had the nerve to approach Senator Buckner, and had got his support. She was no longer alone in this thing. Buckner would back her up, and by her reading he had more power than anyone. She walked along Fifth Avenue with a big grin on her face, from time to time looking into the windows of the swanky shops, but not seeing much. She was safe now. She could take this case as far forward as it should go, and the District Attorney would have to let her do it. On the corner of Fiftieth Street she came to a hot dog stand. Crowds swirled around it and her. She was famished, she realised. She had hardly eaten a thing. She bought a hot dog and walked along eating and grinning. When it was devoured, she licked the mustard off her fingers, crossed to the Lexington Avenue subway, and rode back up to the courthouse.

Buckner, meanwhile, strode through the streets back to his office. Many people glanced at him in recognition, and some stopped him. He gave each his brilliant smile and shook a number of hands. He had no intention of contacting the District Attorney on this woman's behalf because it would seem, if word got out, that he had meddled with the cogs of justice itself. Cops were fair game for everybody, but at the line where the cops dropped off and you came up against lawyers, the system suddenly became sacrosanct. It could not even be breathed on except at great peril. Still, he felt pretty good. He had secured himself regular access to privileged information about an important case, and all it had cost him was the price of a meal.

At headquarters little police business was done. Egan chaired the usual meetings. He put Gold at the head of about five study groups, loading the work on him, letting the other men see his displeasure. Gold only nodded politely. The commanders one and all watched, and they waited. Each night Egan went home and switched on the television news. He was like a competitor in one of those sports whose outcome was determined by a panel of judges: figure skating or gymnastics, perhaps. He could no longer influence his score, and all eyes were now fixed on whatever cards his judges were about to hold up. Egan's judges were the newsmen. In any political crisis they had more collective power than any mayor, certainly more than any police

312

commissioner. They illuminated the road they wished the politicians to take, and once they had done this most politicians most times thought it wisest to take it. Politicians were always quick to go whichever way the noise went.

The ballistics reports leaked out within two days. Citing unnamed sources, anchormen on all three channels described Joshua Brown's weapon and the location of Deputy Commisioner Keefe's shot.

Egan's phone rang. It was on a low table next to the sofa, and he picked it up. It was the mayor.

"Is it true?"

"I'm looking into it now," said Egan.

He let an hour go by, then phoned the mayor back. "It's true," he reported.

"What are you going to do about it?"

"Let me put a programme together and bring it to you for your consideration in the morning." The mayor began a ten-minute lecture that was not pleasant to listen to.

The next morning Egan found that Keefe, without any further consultation, had released his own statement to the press. A copy must have reached City Hall as well, or else a reporter there had shown one to the mayor, for the red phone on Egan's desk rang.

"I'm still waiting for you to do something, for Chrissake."

"I'm making an announcement later in the day," said Egan.

"You can't wait until later in the day. You've got to get out in front of these sons of bitches. You can't always be behind. That's why you're in this mess. You're always a step behind." He hung up.

Egan got out the list he had studied for days, and called for Kilcoyne. The Chief of Operations was shown in, and stood there as tall, as heavy, as immutable as an ox, and Egan began issuing orders. He went down the list with an axe. The two-star Bronx borough commander was out, and so was the –

Kilcoyne interrupted him. "May I ask why?"

"Don't fight me on this, Dennis."

"He wasn't even there."

"And the division commander as well," Egan said. "He's out too. His name is –"

"I know what his name is," snapped Kilcoyne. "He wasn't there either."

"Did it ever occur to you that both of them should have been there?" said Egan angrily.

Kilcoyne pursed his lips and said nothing. Egan continued down the list until, figuratively speaking, there were seven heads in Kilcoyne's lap. Among them was Lieutenant Craighead's.

"I've already removed him," muttered Kilcoyne. "At least he bears some responsibility for this mess. What do you want me to do with him?"

"Put him back on patrol. Send him out to Jamaica or the North Bronx. Send him far enough away so that if some reporter wants to talk to him, it will cost him a very long cab ride."

"The North Bronx then. He's already there." Kilcoyne remained tight-lipped. "Is that all?"

"I want the Stakeout Squad abolished." Egan opened the folder on his desk. "Why wasn't I told about that squad? The sergeant in command – Carmichael his name is – I want him sent to Jamaica or the North Bronx too. Put him in a different precinct from Craighead."

Kilcoyne did not care about Craighead and Carmichael, only the older men of high rank. He studied his notes. "The borough commander, the division commander – they're good men. Might I ask you to reconsider?"

"I want it done today."

"It can't all be done today," responded Kilcoyne hotly. "Not by me it can't."

"Why not?"

"Because they're men who have devoted their lives to this department. They deserve better treatment than that. Besides which, they're friends of mine. If you think I'm going to send them an order of dismissal through the department mails you've got another think coming. They deserve to be called into my office individually, and then I have to talk to them. You've got to give me time to try to soften the blow."

The two men stared at each other. Finally Egan said: "Do the top three commanders today. I'll be satisfied with that. The rest you can do later."

Kilcoyne stood up. "Will there be anything else?" When Egan shook his head the Chief of Operations turned on his heel and left.

Kilcoyne did call in and talk to all three commanders that afternoon – Egan's deputy inspector was able to verify this for him – and when it was evening Egan himself went home, turned on his television set and attempted to watch all three newscasts at once. There was nothing on them about the three dismissed commanders, and Egan began to wait for the next set of newscasts at eleven. The mayor, whom he had talked to earlier, was probably doing the same. Egan's wife tried to calm him. She brought him a scotch and soda, and when he didn't drink it she got him a cup of tea. About ten-thirty he sent his guard car to the nearest all-night news stand to buy the next day's papers, and as soon as he had them in hand he spread them out on his coffee table. The police crisis so dominated all three papers that he did not know which to start reading first. It had been like this every day, and he scanned the headlines, looking for one about the dismissed commanders that would tend to show his own firm hand at the controls. It wasn't there.

STAKE-OUT SQUAD DISBANDER

MURDER INCORPORATED AGAINST BLACKS

KEEFE CLAIMS POLICE COMMANDERS FAILED TO RESPOND

SUSPECTS TORTURED, SEN. BUCKNER CHARGES

Egan took off his reading glasses and rubbed his eyes.

There was no story about the three sacked commanders. The press had not been told about it or had chosen to ignore it.

He was waiting for the mayor to call. If he was going to do it, why did he not get it over with?

Finally the eleven o'clock newscasts came on. By then Egan was in pyjamas and starting to relax. The mayor would not call now; it was too late. There was nothing further to fear, Egan thought, but suddenly he looked up and his Chief of Operations, bathed in floodlights, was reading from a sheet of notepaper. Egan watched with

315

increasing consternation. All the day's earlier stories, bad as they were, had just been relegated to the category of stale news. The recent news was much more sensational. It was so unexpected as to be stunning. The lead story on all three channels – Egan switched rapidly back and forth to make sure – was the resignation of New York's highest ranking uniformed officer, Chief of Operations Dennis Kilcoyne.

Speaking to newsmen from the front stoop of his house in Staten Island, Kilcoyne wore full uniform. There were four stars on each shoulder and gold braid on his hat, and the TV floods gave more than enough light to read by. This afternoon, he said, he had been obliged by political forces outside the department to summon to his office certain high-ranking police officers, men who had devoted their lives to the department. He had been obliged both to relieve them of their commands and to compel them to retire if they wished to avoid being disgraced.

At least he is not blaming me by name, Egan thought.

It was impossible in good conscience, Kilcoyne read, to stand still and say nothing while such injustice was perpetrated. The men forced to resign were innocent of any wrong-doing. The events in question had been his responsibility, and his only. The decisions taken had been his decisions, and his only. "If blame is to be apportioned among devoted police commanders," he read – his statement was not entirely without eloquence – "then I must accept my share. I have served the city and its police department faithfully for thirty-three years. I will serve it again tonight by embracing the only honourable course open to me."

Kilcoyne folded his notes and looked directly into the cameras. "I am resigning from the department effective immediately," he said. "I will make no further statements of any kind."

And knowing Dennis, Egan thought, he won't.

For a moment longer Kilcoyne remained on his doorstep bathed in light, bombarded by questions he did not answer. Instead he turned around, stepped inside his house and closed the door.

I'll have to appoint Gold to replace him, Egan thought. I

have no other choice – because Gold seems to be in the clear on this thing. To promote Gold to Chief of Operations should help me. Maybe it will.

He was staring down at the newspapers spread on his coffee table. The editors are going to have to redo tomorrow's front pages, he thought.

Edna was already in bed, perhaps even asleep. He saw no need to wake her. But neither could he crawl calmly in beside her. Sleep was not going to come right away, perhaps not for hours. He went into the kitchen and prepared himself a cup of hot milk, hoping it would calm him down. He kept glancing at the telephone on the kitchen wall. If it rang it would be the mayor, and he did not know what he could tell him. He had been caught by surprise again – to a politician the one indisputable sign of weakness.

Although he had finished his hot milk, Egan continued to sit in the kitchen, drumming his fingertips on the table.

I can trust Gold, he tried to convince himself. Gold will be a big help to me. Dennis's resignation might even put an end to the crisis. Dennis tonight has done me a service. It's the best thing that could have happened.

But it wasn't, and Egan knew it.

Twenty-Five

SERGEANT RAINEY SAT AT HIS DESK DAY AFTER DAY and his phone did not ring and no projects were assigned him. At other desks sat other cops and policewomen. There was no loud talk or laughter, no jokes, no explosions of pleasure or frustration. Everyone's phone had stopped ringing. Rainey watched Keefe come to work in the mornings and go into his office and stay there, most often with the door closed. The only calls he received, according to Captain Fallon, were from family and friends.

Much of Rainey's time was spent trying to think how to

repair the damage with Flora. It still seemed to him that the right gift would do it. His older daughter was Flora's age. He might have asked her for suggestions. But this particular daughter adored her father, Rainey believed. She admired his strength, decisiveness. So he could not ask her.

With nothing to do in the office he went out into the street and walked along in search of ideas; and near the subway station across from City Hall he came upon a street vendor who had set out costume jewellery on a trestle table on the sidewalk. The guy had no permit, Rainey could see at once, but instead of taking police action he looked over the merchandise and brooded. The illegal vendor became excited, thinking a sale was coming. Rainey's daughters certainly liked big jewellery of this kind. Finally Rainey made his decision, and when the vendor came forward, all smiles, he flashed him his shield. He had no intention of paying inflated prices. At first the vendor misunderstood. He panicked, and started to fold his table and dump his stuff into the satchel at his feet. He was hurrying and apologising at the same time, but Rainey stopped him.

He picked up a bracelet, then a brooch. "How much you want for this? And this?"

Prices were never hard with such people. There were many different items on the table. Rainey selected one of each. He was a man for whom gifts needed to take up space. "How much for this? And this?" He swept two dozen items to one side.

Seeing that he was not going to be arrested and might even make a sale, the vendor was calming down. But when he had named a price, Rainey said: "You ought to be in jail." A pause. "Unless, of course, you're kidding me."

They bargained. As the vendor pocketed Rainey's money he looked almost grateful.

"You got wrapping paper?" Rainey said. The vendor did not, nor did he have a gift card.

So Rainey still needed a card and some nice gift wrapping. In addition, the costume jewellery didn't quite satisfy him. It didn't express well enough himself and Flora. He had a friend named Sol who had a small jewelry store

318

between two porno movie houses on Forty-Second Street. Rainey took the subway up there. Sol said he was glad to see him, and sold him a heart-shaped locket in fourteen carat gold. There was a tiny red heart on the outside and room for two tiny photos inside: just the thing. Sol wrapped both packages and handed over a gift card as well.

Rainey went back to headquarters, studied the blank card and tried to think what to write. This time he decided to skip the poetry. He wrote: "From a secret admirer," and stuffed the card into the wrapping. Then he sat at his desk and worried about how to effect delivery.

He was interrupted by Captain Fallon. "He wants to see you." Fallon jerked his thumb in the direction of Keefe's office.

Rainey got up and went in. Keefe was at his desk in shirt sleeves, and he looked tense. Standing up, he handed Rainey a three-page statement and asked him to read it.

As soon as he saw what it was Rainey began to read carefully, lifting each page with his thumb and flopping it back. He realised he was about to be asked for advice.

This was on the Tuesday following the shooting. The statement was the one Keefe and his brother had concocted two nights before. He had shown it to the PC the previous day.

"What do you think?" he asked.

Rainey thumbed through the pages again. The anxiety in Keefe's tone was slight, but Rainey had detected it.

"What's the status of this thing?" he asked.

"It's on hold."

"On hold?"

"The PC asked me not to give it out to the press just yet."

"I see."

"I was wondering," Keefe said hesitantly, "what your ideas might be?" He really did want to know his opinion, and Rainey was flattered.

From time to time in the past Rainey had allowed himself to serve as mentor toward rookie cops. At the end of a week they looked up at him as if he were their father. This was the way Keefe looked at him now, he believed.

There were many ifs in a man's life. Early in his career he himself had made some wrong steps that had not been his fault. If intelligence and character were all that counted, he would be on Keefe's side of the desk now. Circumstances had stopped him.

He did not resent Keefe, and lately had come to admire him. Partly this was because Keefe seemed to like and respect him. Keefe's image of him matched his own image of himself. And although Keefe had started out with advantages, it was clear to Rainey that he had made the most of them. Furthermore, his deportment the other night had won Rainey over completely. In any cop's scale of virtues bravery came first, and Keefe had displayed bravery that to Rainey was stupefying.

Once again Rainey thumbed the pages of the statement. "Why did the PC object to your giving this out right away?"

"He asked for time to work on my behalf behind the scenes."

Rainey was not sure of the exact nature of Keefe's relationship with the PC. "Do you believe him?"

"I'm so shell-shocked by now I don't know what to believe."

Rainey had worked for many commanders in his long police career. None before Keefe had ever given him the respect he believed he merited, or hung on his every word as Keefe did now. "Let's talk about the pros and cons on both sides. If you give the statement out, what happens? If you don't, what happens?"

He took the chair beside the desk, and Keefe got out a yellow pad and drew a line down the centre. The office door was closed. The phone did not ring. No one disturbed them.

If he gave this statement out as written, Rainey told him, he might lose the support of the PC and other members of the hierarchy. Could he risk that? How valuable was the PC's support? Unfortunately no clear answer was possible.

Rainey suggested toning the statement down, especially where it related to Keefe's attempts to bring the PC and other superior officers to the courthouse to take command. It was best also, Rainey said, to eliminate Chief Gold's foreknowledge of the junkyard raid.

320

"He has claimed he knew virtually nothing about it," Rainey said. "We both know he's lying. But if you accuse him of a lie in your statement, he will be obliged to defend himself, and the only way he can do that is by attacking you."

He watched Keefe pencil corrections into the margins of his statement.

"But do I give this statement out today," said Keefe with a wry smile, "or hold it as the PC has requested?"

Rainey studied the edited statement. His own name was in there, and had been from the beginning. He wished it wasn't. He was identified as the driver of the car that had tailed Hot Harry Hamish into Connecticut. Like Gold, he would have preferred to disassociate himself from the case completely, but he could not say so because Keefe's admiration for him seemed to have grown even greater during the last ten minutes. Rainey did not want to risk diminishing it.

"I do not trust the PC as much as you seem to," Rainey said. "I don't trust headquarters" brass in general. But you apparently do trust him, and you've made him a promise." He paused. "In your place I would give the statement out immediately."

Keefe nodded. He looked grateful. "Well," he said, but then he stopped. After a moment he said: "Thank you for your opinion."

Rainey went out. Back at his own desk he thought about Keefe for a while, then he thought about Flora. He was reasonably certain Keefe would not release his statement right away or even tomorrow. As for Flora, he decided he would take his gift-wrapped packages out to her house and present them personally.

He rode the subway out to Coney Island in the middle of the evening rush hour. The train he boarded was filthy and covered with graffiti, and when he had forced his way through bodies into a car he found that the fans did not work. The train lay stopped for some time in the tunnel under the river. Rainey was standing up in the crush unable to move. By the time the train finally came into the Coney Island station he was soaked with sweat.

It was still light out. The streets were full of traffic and blaring horns. The surf was pounding only a few blocks away, but he could not hear it. When he reached Flora's house he could not decide what tactic to follow. While deliberating, he took up position in a doorway across the street and began watching the house. Maybe she would come out, or approach along the sidewalk. That would make it easier.

He waited an hour or more in the doorway and nothing happened. Maybe he should just go across the street and ring the bell. Suppose Flora answered? Suppose she was friendly? Suppose she was unfriendly? If she was unfriendly, he might not even have the chance to hand over his gifts before she slammed the door on him. Or suppose her mother answered? Suppose she was friendly? Suppose she was unfriendly?

Though it began to get dark, Rainey remained on post. The sweat from the subway had dried on his body. Twilight had turned into night. The lamp posts had come on. The lights were on in the houses. His bladder was so full he was practically dancing from one foot to the other.

Finally he crossed the street, pushed open Flora's gate, and stepped up to the front door, where he pressed his ear against the panel. He thought he could hear movement in there. There was an alley along one side of the house. He walked down it toward the tiny back yard. When he came to a window bright with light, he climbed on top of a garbage can and peeked in.

Flora and her mother were seated at the kitchen table eating dinner.

Rainey peed in the bushes, then went back to the front door. Finally he punched the bell. But when he heard footsteps approaching, he thrust his packages down against the door, turned on his heel and ran. Over his shoulder he saw the door open, for light flooded out, and someone bent to pick up the packages. Before that person – either Flora or her mother – could straighten up and begin to glance up and down the block, Rainey had rounded the corner and was out of sight.

322

When he came into his sister's apartment about an hour later he asked if there had been any calls for him, but the answer was no.

"Have you had dinner?" his sister said.

"Sure," answered Rainey, who had eaten a doughnut and drunk a bowl of soup in a coffee shop after he had come up out of the subway. He went into his small room and closed the door and turned on his small television set. He had nothing to say to his sister, any more than to his wife. The television set was a portable and the image was poor. He lay on his bed watching and thought about F. Hyman Effrat's acting class the following day. If Flora was wearing the locket or some of the jewellery he would have his answer before he even spoke to her, and it would take the pressure off.

The grand jury investigation into the shooting had begun. The prosecutor, Anne Christianson, was working from the same list the Police Commissioner had called for. In fact she had a copy before he did, and she employed it before he did. For her it was a list of witnesses to be heard. She would interview all of them to find out what they knew and from these witnesses would construct her case. When ready she would throw a selection of them into the grand jury to testify. Out of the grand jury might come – or might not come – one or more indictments.

She had studied the list like a menu in a Chinese restaurant. The names at the top – Egan, Keefe, Kilcoyne, Gold, one or two others – were the best dishes. They would be the succulent ones: any prosecutor would find them so. She would talk to them last. The hors d'oeuvres were all the other men on the list, and she prepared and sent out Notices of Appearance to all their commands.

After that she had subpoenas drawn up that would compel the top four men to report to her office and to testify, for she assumed in advance that they would otherwise not appear, or would obfuscate facts to protect themselves and each other. She had no notion of how isolated from each other and how vulnerable all four had now become.

But when she had the subpoenas in hand she had found herself afraid to send them out. Instead she had made an appointment to interview the Police Commissioner – she would take him first – in his office at police headquarters. This interview, from her point of view, had turned out a disaster. All future interviews, she resolved, would take place on her turf, by her rules.

One of those who had received a Notice of Appearance was Sergeant Rainey. For the trip up to the courthouse Keefe had loaned him his department car, saying it would save time – time for what? In the office there was absolutely nothing happening.

Upon reaching the courthouse Rainey left Detective Murphy at the wheel saying: "I shouldn't be long." He assumed he would ride up in the elevator, make his statement to the prosecutor, and come back down again. In a week or so he might return to testify to the grand jury. Today it should take about twenty minutes.

When Rainey got off the elevator on the fourth floor and saw the mob ahead of him he was shocked. There were already more than two dozen cops waiting. The men were milling about in the hall because the reception area of the prosecutor's office was already jammed. Her office door, he saw over heads, was closed. There was no one at the reception desk, no one keeping order, no one to provide information.

Rainey no longer believed he'd get back to the car in twenty minutes. Still, protocol would surely be observed. The interviews would be conducted by rank. He would have to wait for Lieutenant Craighead and any other lieutenants to be interviewed first. Then would come the sergeants: himself, Carmichael and a few others. Say an extra hour. His own interview would be brief and did not worry him. Rainey still saw this case as cut and dried. Later the grand jury would hear four or five witnesses, himself included, would rule the shooting line of duty, and would dismiss the case. That would shut the newspapers up and in a month it would be forgotten.

The office door opened and a young uniformed cop came out. The door was shut behind him immediately by someone inside. As the cop pushed his way out toward the corridor he looked sheepish.

Rainey stopped him. "What's happening?"

The cop peered a moment at the shield on Rainey's lapel. "Beats me, Sarge."

"Is it just a Q and A, or what?"

"Yeah. She's taking it down on tape."

The door opened again and a young woman appeared. She was nearly six feet tall with a long nose and kinky hair.

"There's a blonde in there too," the young cop said.

He must mean the one from arraignment court, Rainey thought. Anne something.

The young woman in the doorway, Rainey would learn, was named Josephine Croker. "Keep the noise down," she said. She had to shout to be heard. "Nobody leaves." She had a list in her hand and read off a name from it.

"Here," sang out a voice. It belonged to one of the detectives from the Auto Squad, and he began to push his way toward Miss Croker. Rainey pushed forward too and said to her: "There are superior officers here. They should come first."

Young Miss Croker eyed him coldly. She couldn't have been more than twenty-five years old. "You'll be called in good time, Sergeant," she said. When she had followed the detective into the office she closed the door in Rainey's face.

Every twenty minutes or so after that a cop would come out of the office, followed five minutes later by Josephine Croker who would call out another name. At length Rainey began to feel uneasy. Protocol was not being observed, and, once interviewed, only a few of the men were being allowed to leave.

He went downstairs and sent the car back to head-quarters.

Each time Josephine Croker appeared in the doorway more and more cops protested loudly or badgered her for information. There were two FBI agents in their Brooks Brothers suits present. They thought they deserved special treatment, and they kept jumping to their feet.

"We're from the FBI. We got cases we're working on."

Josephine Croker ignored them, and the cops in the room hooted them down.

There was a one-hour break for lunch. Josephine Croker announced it. "One hour exactly," she said.

Rainey went across the street to a Jewish delicatessen that was already full of cops, and ordered a pastrami on rye.

"What you want to drink?" the proprietor asked him. "You want a nice cold beer?"

All around him cops were swilling beer. The delicatessen reeked of beer like a bar room, and Rainey felt the familiar pangs of desire. "Give a me Pepsi Cola," he said.

He ate his lunch at the plate glass window, and peered out at the neighbourhood which had once been prosperous and heavily Jewish. Now it was a slum, except for the courthouse opposite, and most of the Jews were gone. This delicatessen owner was probably too old to find some place new.

Rainey passed most of the afternoon in the corridor. The air was better. The men had raided neighbouring offices for chairs. They made a lot of noise, and from time to time other young assistant district attorneys came out into the corridor to tell them to pipe down. But Anne Christianson herself never came out of the office once, and Rainey did not see her all that day.

The anteroom remained crowded. At six o'clock the office door opened and the final cop to be interviewed came out. Behind him Josephine Croker stood with her back to the door and read off a number of names. These men were dismissed. The rest were to report back tomorrow morning at nine A.M.

In the elevator going down a number of the men who had actually seen the mysterious Anne Christianson were making ribald remarks about her. She was a lesbian or a suppressed nympho. They discussed what she needed and how they would supply it. Rainey made no comment.

From a callbox on the corner he phoned in and was surprised when Commissioner Keefe came on the line. "Are you coming back to headquarters?"

Rainey planned to grab something to eat and then go to F. Hyman Effrat's studio. "Is there something you would like me to do, Commissioner?"

"I was working on the statement again," said Keefe hesitantly.

Why doesn't he just give it out, Rainey asked himself.

"I guess it can wait," Keefe said.

They've taken all the steel out of the guy, Rainey thought. He hung up and started toward the subway. He forgot Keefe and thought about Flora. After the class he might take her to a restaurant, then back to his friend Hennessey's apartment which he had borrowed again. If she were wearing the locket or some of the jewelry it would be a good sign. He was glad he had displayed patience and left the jewelry on the doorstep last night. Patience was one of the advantages that came with age. Tonight he would get this relationship back on track, and as he ran down the steps into the subway he began to picture her smooth body and he was smiling.

Thirty-five minutes later and several miles away he ran up another set of steps onto the street again. By then it was beginning to get dark, and he walked along under the trees past the brownstones and he was whistling.

Anne Christianson at that moment was entering the office of the elected District Attorney of Bronx County.

He had called her twice during the day. On each occasion she had been certain it was to tell her she was off this suddenly important case in favour of a more experienced lawyer. Perhaps Buckner had not yet called him. The first time, she had pretended to be too busy to take the phone. The second time, late this afternoon, she had not dared.

It was his secretary. "He wants to see you."

"Just give me a couple of minutes."

As she made the same long walk across the Persian rug toward the old man's desk, he seemed to be measuring her figure once again, weighing her flesh.

"Sit down," he invited, and she took the chair beside his desk. She wore a severe charcoal grey suit whose skirt was a

327

bit longer than the year's fashion called for, and she crossed her legs.

"Well, now," the DA began. His tone was both excessively hearty and somewhat diffident. "How's your case coming on?"

He not only wasn't angry or impatient, he even sounded a bit afraid of her. Buckner must have called him after all, Anne decided. He did not dare intervene now. There were convulsions occurring at the top of the police department, and he did not need them to spread up here.

"The case," said Anne, "is coming very well." She smiled at him, volunteered nothing more, and waited.

"You're interviewing a lot of people."

"I'm obliged to interview every officer who responded to the scene, don't you agree?"

"Of course." He hesitated. "How many would you say you've interviewed so far?"

"About half."

The old man said suddenly: "Those cops are lined up out into the hall."

"According to the newspapers this has developed into an important case. I'm trying to get to the bottom of it as fast as I can."

The DA tried a smile. "But I'm wondering if you couldn't schedule them a bit better." His tone became more brisk. "There are cops waiting all day to be interviewed. Some people might say that's wasteful of police man-hours."

Anne said: "In the interests of speed and efficiency, I thought it warranted."

He looked at her.

"There will be fewer tomorrow," Anne promised, and the District Attorney nodded.

"You can't throw thirty or forty witnesses into the grand jury anyway," he said with an unexpectedly false smile. "Or can you?"

Anne realised that he wanted to know what her investigation had turned up so far but was unwilling to ask for information outright.

"I think I should call as many witnesses as are necessary to establish the facts," she said, and watched him. "Don't you?"

328

"Five or six witnesses?" he persisted. "Does that sound about right?"

"I really can't say as yet." How much would he push? She had been held back a long time, and for the moment the power was on her side.

"Well, let's count them up, shall we?" said the District Attorney, still falsely amiable. "Someone from Ballistics will have to testify, right?"

Anne nodded, and watched him.

"And the Medical Examiner, and Deputy Commissioner Keefe, of course. Have you interviewed him yet?"

Anne was saving Keefe for last, and so shook her head.

"The Chief of Operations too, I would think. That makes how many?"

Anne let him add it up for himself.

"And what? Four or five of the cops and detectives who were there. That ought to do it, wouldn't you say?"

Anne studied the back of her fingernails.

"And the cleaning woman," the District Attorney said almost triumphantly. "I forgot about her."

"Up to now, unfortunately, I haven't been able to find her."

"She's important," said the DA. "You should throw some detectives after her."

"I already have. They're not even sure they know her name. They certainly haven't found her."

"Do you need more help on this thing?"

Anne judged that this question was supposed to alarm her, and it did, up to a point. Then her confidence returned. He doesn't even mention Buckner's name, she decided. Her manner changed, became much less outwardly cocky, almost demure. "If I get in any difficulty, I know I can call on you for help." She even smiled at him.

"So what are your findings so far?"

"I don't have any findings. I've only done preliminary interviews."

"You talked to fifteen or twenty cops today."

"But none of the important ones yet," said Anne stubbornly.

He studied her and did not look friendly.

I'm not going to tell him, Anne thought. She was no longer the inexperienced young woman who had been awed almost to silence by the PC. With Buckner behind her, she was not a bit afraid of the District Attorney. The PC had been in no position to hurt her whereas this man was her boss.

"As for those cops waiting on line to be interviewed," the DA said suddenly, coldly, "the citizens want them on the street protecting them, not waiting around in corridors."

By not meeting his eyes, Anne managed at least to deflect this rebuke, and perhaps reject it altogether. "If they show the same incompetence on the street that they showed in the judge's chambers the other night, the public is probably better protected if I keep them out of circulation."

Abruptly the District Attorney stood up. His manner became falsely jovial once more, and he put his hand on Anne's shoulder as he walked her to the door. "You know you don't mean that," he said. "Keep up the good work and be sure to let me know when you're ready to go to the grand jury."

Anne had a two-room apartment in Manhattan on the West Side; her father sent her money to cover the rent. She studied the transcripts at home for two hours before supper, and after supper she studied them until midnight.

Twenty-Six

FLORA ARRIVED LATE, SO THAT RAINEY DID NOT GET A chance to talk to her. She was not wearing any of the jewelry. About an hour into the class, F. Hyman went into his office to take a phone call, and as the students crowded toward the coffee urn, Rainey came up behind Flora and whispered into her ear: "We have to talk."

She turned on him. "Not now."

"Later is fine," said Rainey hastily, adding: "What if I take you home?"

Flora's eyes narrowed.

"Or some place else," said Rainey, thinking of Hennessey's apartment.

"I'm going home with Jason."

Jason was one of the fags, and Rainey glanced around for him. He stood at the coffee urn filling two cups and wearing his extra tight pants. Perhaps Flora meant that Jason lived near her. Maybe the two families were related.

Rainey said to Flora: "We'll talk about it later."

Flora turned on him. "Look, you're an awfully nice guy, but – I'm seeing Jason now."

"What?" said Rainey. He glanced over at Jason holding two mugs of coffee.

"I won't be able to see you any more."

The verb *to see*, a euphemism. It said everything and nothing. "What do you mean you're seeing Jason?"

"Just what I said."

"He's a homo."

"Homo? What's a homo?"

Rainey realised his mistake. Homos were no longer called homos. They were now called gays, and everybody protected their so-called rights. The world had entered into a conspiracy to consider them normal. The world changed and the language changed and to use outdated language no doubt made him seem outdated too.

"He's a homosexual."

"Oh no he's not."

"You don't see it."

"Believe me," said Flora fiercely, "I can attest personally to his virility."

"Oh."

"I'm seeing Jason, and I'm not seeing you any more."

"But –" Flora was looking over at Jason and she gave him an almost imperceptible nod of her head. The nod said: I'm taking care of it. She said to Rainey: "We were going to tell you the other night –"

He did not understand her use of the word "we."

"We were waiting on that street corner to tell you, but you didn't show up."

"But Flora –" Rainey realised he was begging, but could not stop. "Just tell me why."

"I had a long talk with my mother."

"Your mother?"

"She was concerned that you were too old for me, and also about – about the other thing."

"What other thing?"

"She was very dismayed to hear you were not Jewish. She would prefer I was seeing someone of my own faith."

"What's religion got to do with it?"

"She would prefer it."

Rainey's head swivelled around and he stared at Jason. "He's Jewish?"

"It's very important to her."

The students, carrying their coffee cups, began to return to their places. The sight of Jason, who waited a short distance away, infuriated Rainey.

He said to Flora. "What about the jewelry I left you last night? It was pretty nice stuff, didn't you think?"

"Was that you?"

"Yes. Did you like it?"

Flora frowned. "You must think I'm some kind of kewpie doll."

She reached out and took a coffee mug from Jason.

Rainey turned on him. "We're talking here."

"It's time to go back to our seats," said Jason mildly.

"So I won't be seeing you any more," said Flora.

Rainey batted the remaining mug out of Jason's hand. The coffee sloshed onto the young man's shirt, and maybe his neck, for he squealed and jumped back. The mug itself went bouncing into the corner. "You stupid son of a bitch," Jason said.

"You want to make something of it?" Rainey began breathing through his nose. He was forty-six years old with a grey beard and clenched fists wearing a business suit. Jason, though twenty years younger, took a step backwards. He knew Rainey was a cop. Also that he would be armed.

"We'll see about this," Rainey snarled and stormed out of the studio.

The next morning at the Bronx County Courthouse Rainey again waited for his turn to be interviewed. The mob was smaller today, though not much, and more resigned to the delay, though not much. Cops who had been interviewed were at least being allowed to leave, and some arrangement had apparently been made for the two FBI agents, who were not present.

Waiting, Rainey swallowed and reswallowed last night's experience.

It was nearly noon when he was at last admitted to the inner office. The prosecutor preparing the case, he noted, was indeed the blonde from arraignment court. She directed him to take the chair beside the desk. The other female prosecutor, the six-footer with the long nose, nodded at him briefly from her chair in the corner.

The tape recorder was turned on.

"To save time," Anne Christianson said, "please tell us in your own words exactly what happened at the courthouse."

Rainey did this. It took him about twenty minutes. He put in all the details he could think of, but it was hard for him; his mind kept going off on Flora. By the time he came to the end of his account he had worked himself into a rage so that he said to the young woman behind the desk: "I'm a sergeant. So why did you make me wait two days? Who do you think you are?"

"I'll ask the questions here, Sergeant," said Anne calmly.

It was exactly the reply he expected. She wants to show us our powerlessness in the face of the law, he thought. She's insecure and possibly stupid as well and so makes two dozen cops wait most of two days, and some of them no doubt longer.

He said coldly: "I have to get back to headquarters. What else do you want to know?"

"You'll go back to headquarters when I release you, Sergeant."

"Is that so?" said Rainey, and they had a staring contest, which he lost. It was indeed so, and he knew it.

"Please calm down, Sergeant," she said. "Let's go back over a few points, shall we?"

The tall one came to the desk and the two women whispered together. Rainey's impotence was total, and his rage increased.

The tall one went back to her corner. The blonde said: "Deputy Commissioner Keefe was in direct command of the raid on the junkyard allegedly operated by one Harry Hamish, is that correct?"

"No, that's not correct."

"Although he had no police experience to speak of, it was his raid."

"It was the Auto Squad's raid. Lieutenant Craighead was in command."

"I see," the blonde said, and Rainey knew he was about to be called a liar. "Let me read to you from the transcript of the interview with one of your colleagues." She got the transcript out and turned pages until she found what she was looking for. "Question: Who was in command? Answer: It was the Deputy Commissioner's raid from start to finish. Question: But on an operational level, the commander was you, is that correct? Answer: I obeyed orders."

"Lieutenant Craighead," said Rainey. "I don't know what he's trying to pull."

"If you keep interrupting, it will take longer," said the blonde calmly. "Answer: I went to the Chief of Detectives. He said the man was a deputy commissioner. He couldn't help me. He said I'd better do what I was told."

Rainey had turned in his chair and was staring out the window.

"What do you have to say to that?" the blonde said.

"I already told you what I have to say to that."

"Let's go to the night of the shooting. I'm told that Commissioner Keefe simply marched into the courthouse and took command even though he could hardly be called qualified."

Rainey spun around in his chair and faced her. "He didn't take command. It devolved on him. There was nobody else with any rank. He had us making calls all over the place. We couldn't get anyone else to come in."

"Let me read to you from another part of the transcript."

Rainey saw that it was the same transcript as before. "Lieutenant Craighead again," he muttered.

The blonde said: "Question: When the hostage was first taken, who was in command on the scene? Answer: I was. Five minutes later the Deputy Commissioner shows up and takes over."

Rainey stared at the blonde, and she stared back at him just as hard. "I don't know what you're up to here," he said.

"I'm trying to put together a picture of what happened in that room, Sergeant."

"I just gave you the picture."

"Unfortunately your picture differs from the one described by the other witnesses."

"You better call them in and talk to them again."

"I don't need advice from you, Sergeant."

Her coolness infuriated him. "Have you ever put a case into the grand jury before?" he asked.

"That's neither here nor there."

"You haven't, have you? Well, this isn't the way it's done. You don't keep two dozen men waiting outside, and interview cops and detectives while making superior officers wait."

"Let's go on, shall we?"

"It's about time you started treating cops with respect."

"Respect? Don't you talk to me about respect. I took the trouble to go downstairs to Judge Baum's chambers. I paced off the dimensions of his anteroom. What do you think it measures?"

"Go ahead and tell me. You're dying to."

"Fifteen feet by twelve, even though the evidence is that more than forty men, and possibly as many as sixty, were jammed in there at one time. That's my picture of this thing. It's a picture entitled pandemonium."

"What do you know about the kind of incidents cops get involved in? You've probably never been out of arraignment court. How many cops have you encountered so far?"

"You're right, Sergeant," the blonde said. "Most of the cops I encounter are the ones who get up in arraignment

335

court and perjure themselves in order to support bad arrests. This incident we're discussing here has not increased my appreciation of cops. We're talking about mass panic that ended in a shooting. Sixty men in one room and a hostage on the other side of the door. You want to know what my reaction is, Sergeant? It's not surprise, it's disgust."

The tall one in the corner was doodling on her yellow legal pad.

"Tell me about the sharpshooters in the window across the courtyard, Sergeant. As I understand it, it was Commissioner Keefe who placed them there."

"It was not. In fact he ordered them to get out of the window."

She sighed. "Let me read to you from the transcript." There was a pause as she searched in a folder. It was, Rainey saw, a different transcript from the last one.

"Question: You had your sharpshooters in a window across the courtyard, is that correct? Answer: I went over there with the Commissioner. He looked over the line of sight. He approved it."

"Carmichael," Rainey said. "Absolutely not true."

"Now we come to the moment when Commissioner Keefe takes it into his head that he will go into that room and possibly exchange himself for the hostage."

"He didn't 'take it into his head'. The gunman asked for him by name. Everybody heard it."

"Everybody? So far I have found nobody who heard it."

"I was there."

"All right," the blonde said, "we will again consult a previous transcript." She read from it aloud. "Question: Did the gunman in the next room call specifically for Commissioner Keefe? Answer: He was asking for Judge Baum. We were offering him a make-believe judge. I volunteered to go in there wearing robes. So did one of the other guys, I think. Question: But Commissioner Keefe decided he would go instead? Answer: Yeah. He said he had to go. And he did."

"Whose testimony is that?" Rainey demanded.

The blonde ignored the interruption. "Let me go on.

336

Question: You say you strapped an ankle holster on Commissioner Keefe's ankle? Answer: Yes, I did."

"Carmichael again," interrupted Rainey.

"Question: He instructed you to do this? Answer: Of course. Question: And he went into the room wearing your holster and gun? Answer: You crazy? My gun stays with me. My holster. His gun." Suddenly she stopped reading and looked up at Rainey. "Were you one of the others who volunteered to go in there as a make-believe judge, Sergeant? Were you hoping to go in there and shoot the fellow between the eyes?"

"I volunteered, yes. It seemed like somebody had to do it, and I was the most experienced cop there."

"Seemed, Sergeant? You mean the state of panic in that anteroom was so great that nobody was using any restraint? Is that what you're trying to say?" She turned and looked over at the tall one, her accomplice, who was smirking.

"The gunman was asking specifically for Commissioner Keefe."

"Question: And you never heard the gunman ask specifically for Commissioner Keefe? Are you willing to so testify under oath? Answer: That's the way it happened." She looked up expectantly.

"Did you talk to the cleaning woman yet?" said Rainey. "She should remember that he asked for Keefe by name."

Instead of answering, the blonde closed her case folder, put both palms on top of it, and said to Rainey: "Why don't you go outside and think it over, Sergeant? Try to remember what you actually saw, what you actually heard. We'll talk again."

Rainey tried once more for his freedom. "I have to go back to headquarters."

"I can't permit that. Please wait outside and this afternoon or tomorrow we will talk again." She turned casually to the tall one. "Let's break for lunch, shall we?"

Rainey got up and stalked from the office.

The delicatessen was again filled with cops, a few already eating, most waiting on the same unruly line as himself. The store still smelled like a saloon. He inhaled its moist beery

337

aroma and remembered the vivid bars of his past. They paraded one by one through his mind. He used the memory of bars to blot out the humiliation he had just experienced. As he kept breathing in the fumes, his nostrils began to tingle – the start of the usual physical reaction. That the blonde was getting ready to indict Commissioner Keefe, Rainey did not now doubt. She was unsupervised. One day next week it would just happen, and everyone would look up surprised. What could he himself do about it? What should he do about it? Keefe had become the point of stability in Rainey's life. If he lost Keefe, they would send him back to patrol. Back in uniform in a radio car in the street. He wasn't going back on patrol no matter what. Oh no? What would he do if assigned? If they sent him, what choice would he have?

He had reached the counter where he watched the old grocer make him a pastrami on rye. Well, he could speak to Sergeant Carmichael and Lieutenant Craighead, refresh their memories, perhaps get them to change their testimony.

"You want ice cold beer?" said the old grocer. "I got Budweiser, I got Michelob, I got –"

The blonde had shaken him badly, and the beery air shook him even more. I deserve a beer, he told himself. The afternoon session might be even worse. One beer can't hurt, he told himself. "Give me a bottle of Bud," he said. When he held the cold wet bottle in his hand he felt a tremor go all the way through him, and a voice to his rear said:

"Back on the sauce, I see, eh, Rainey?"

Rainey recognised the voice without turning around. "Fuck you, Carmichael."

Carmichael only laughed. "You were a terror in your day, Rainey. How long you been back on the sauce?"

Rainey lifted the bottle and began to drink. He swallowed about half before he paused for breath. To the the grocer he said: "Give me another."

Draining the first bottle, he handed it back, took the second and went to stand again at the window looking out. He ate his sandwich. Carmichael stood at a shelf along the wall. Beside his plate he had a six-pack of beer. He kept wrenching the cans out of the plastic holder, working his way through them. Cops, Rainey thought, drink a lot of beer.

Having finished his lunch he went outside and leaned against a fender. When Carmichael came out Rainey joined him and they crossed the street.

"I'm worried that she may be planning to indict somebody," Rainey began.

"Probably." They stood on the centre line waiting for cars to pass.

"Maybe me. Maybe you."

"Your boss, more likely."

They reached the opposite sidewalk. A swarm of people, mostly cops in uniform, converged on the courthouse door. "We ought to get together on our testimony," Rainey said. "For instance, the gunman did call for Commissioner Keefe by name, don't you remember?"

"What are you talking about? He called for the judge."

"And he had nothing to do with placing your guys in the window."

"He okayed it."

"He gave you express orders not to fire across that courtyard."

"What would you know about it?"

"I was there," said Rainey.

"You want to hear something, Rainey? I never liked you much."

"Your testimony might be crucial."

"What do you want me to do, perjure myself? I told it the way I remember it."

About an hour later Rainey managed to separate out Lieutenant Craighead, making much the same plea. Craighead's testimony and his own differed, he said, and –

"What you're trying to do is the crime of subornation of perjury, Rainey. I ought to lock you up." Craighead's career was in ruins. "I'm up in the Bronx in uniform," he muttered, "and it's your guy's fault. I don't owe him nothing and you less."

In mid-afternoon came a surprise interruption: Chief

Gold appeared suddenly in the crowded reception room. He seemed startled to see so many cops waiting their turn, though only for a moment. He had a cigar between his teeth and he pushed forward on a straight line toward the inner office door.

"Is she in there?" he growled, but did not wait for an answer, and the door closed behind him.

There were three people in the office. All three stared at Gold who studied only Anne. His sudden appearance made her immediately nervous.

"You," Gold said to the cop in the chair, "Out."

His eyes had never left her, and he ignored her assistant entirely. As soon as he heard the door slam behind the cop, he dropped his subpoena on her desk saying: "I got this letter from you, honey. So here I am. Let's get this over with."

She was not prepared for him. He sat down in the cop's chair, crossed his legs and re-lit the dead, foul-smelling cigar in his mouth. As she fumbled to start her tape recorder she realised that in addition to cigar smoke he reeked also of some terrible perfume.

"I made a statement on the television the other day," Gold said. He blew smoke at her. "I don't know if you saw it."

"No, I didn't."

"By the time I got to the courthouse everything had been decided."

"What was it like there?"

"I took no part in any of it."

"Yes, but –"

"You're wasting both our time."

Though Anne continued to try to press for details, he would not give any: he wasn't there until the end, had taken no part. His fingers began drumming on his knee. From her point of view, this interview was even worse than the one with the PC, and her nervousness increased. "Would you say correct procedure was followed?"

"I was in my car."

"Why did it take you so long to get there?"

"There was a lot of traffic."

He stood up, ending the interview, and when she tried to prevent this he snapped: "You're on the wrong track, honey, I got nothing you want to hear." He walked towards the door.

"I may ask you to appear before the grand jury." But she was talking to his back.

"Honey, that wouldn't be wise." Gold's hand was on the doorknob. "I had nothing to do with it." He turned to face her. "You put me on the stand, you'll only fuck up your case."

Puffing on his cigar, he went out through the door which he did not bother to close behind him. She saw him pushing through the crowd of men, outside.

Rainey was the last man left in the waiting room, and when the blonde called him this time she said: "Now that I know who you are, perhaps we can come to an understanding."

On her desk was his personnel folder.

"If you fail to co-operate in this investigation," she said, "then given your past record, you might find yourself in serious trouble."

"I'm not afraid of you," Rainey said, but he was.

"So I'll ask you again. Do you remember anything differently?"

"No." But he could not take his eyes off his folder on her desk.

"Your loyalty to your superior is touching. But the grand jury takes testimony under oath."

"You can't threaten me."

"If the grand jury finds your testimony in conflict with that of the other witnesses –"

Rainey had fallen silent.

"Let's shift to a different topic," the blonde said after a moment.

"Did you find the cleaning woman?" demanded Rainey.

"I'll ask the questions here, Sergeant."

"Find the cleaning woman. See what she says."

"Tell me about driving Commissioner Keefe across the state line in a department car. Was that something you did often?"

Rainey was as shocked by this sudden question as by the idea of being indicted for perjury. "That question sounds to me peripheral to your investigation."

"I can compel you to answer it."

"Not without a lawyer present to represent me," he said and got up and left the room.

"You'll be hearing from me, Sergeant," she called after him.

In the anteroom Rainey and Chief of Operations Kilcoyne met head on. They were equally upset, moving equally fast in opposite directions, and they nearly knocked each other down.

"Excuse me, Chief," said Rainey. Kilcoyne went into the office and slammed the door.

She had imagined that her subpoenas would cow these men but the reverse seemed to be happening. Chief Kilcoyne was not overbearing like Gold; he was outraged.

"Are you the one who sent me this?" he said, and threw his subpoena down on her desk.

She looked up at an immensely tall man with white hair and with gold braid all over his uniform.

"Over thirty years I've been in this department," he sputtered, "and no assistant district attorney has ever felt obliged to subpoena me yet."

The young woman's face was burning. "I'm sorry you feel that way."

"If you don't know how to use the telephone, get somebody to teach you. Get somebody else to teach you how we do things around here. Otherwise you won't last long."

From this beginning the interview progressed nowhere. The tape recorder was on the desk with its microphone on its little stand pointing up at Kilcoyne at a forty-five-degree angle. From time to time he would glance at it distastefully as he answered her questions. Like Gold he refused to discuss how Keefe had found himself alone inside Judge Baum's chambers face to face with a crazed gunman. He had no knowledge whatever of what had taken place inside the room until the moment came when his men broke down the door. He would offer no testimony whatever, neither for nor against Deputy Commissioner Keefe.

Though thrown off-balance by Kilcoyne's imposing person and by his responses so far, the young prosecutor clung doggedly to the position she was trying to establish.

"Was it Keefe's duty to act as he acted?"

"A course of action such as Commissioner Keefe took has never been taken before in the history of the department to my knowledge."

Kilcoyne's hostility was so intense that she felt herself on the verge of starting to tremble. "In other words, he usurped authority that belonged to someone else."

"He shouldn't have been there."

"Will you so testify before the grand jury?"

"If summoned to testify I will answer every question truthfully to the best of my ability. Now, if you'll excuse me, I have work to do."

He was gone. She could not have held him, and in fact had been afraid to try.

It was that night that Kilcoyne read his statement of resignation from the doorstep of his house in Staten Island. As she watched this on the late news Anne related it to her subpoena. Good, she thought, the rats are on the run, and I'm doing it, me. In this she was at least partly correct. During the previous few weeks Kilcoyne had been watching his stature erode, and with it his dignity. They had eroded first slowly, then in recent days with increasing speed. The mayor was not supporting him, and Tim Egan was trying to save himself by blaming others. He would blame Kilcoyne next. For Kilcoyne now to be subpoenaed to appear before a twenty-five-year-old female assistant district attorney as if he were some Mafia hoodlum who could be made to appear in no other way was to him the ultimate affront. There would be worse coming if he chose to wait for them. He did not so choose. Instead, at a time and place determined not by the mayor, nor by Tim Egan either, but by himself, he had resigned from the department.

Anne Christianson, watching on television, was gleeful.

To her Kilcoyne was as responsible for Brown's shooting as Keefe was. They were both guilty and ought to be charged with the same crime. Unfortunately Kilcoyne stood one step removed and could not be charged; but at least she had driven him from the department, her first victory in this case though not, she was confident, her last.

On the other side of the city Rainey too watched Kilcoyne resing on TV.

That night he had gone out and walked the streets. He was desperately worried and desperately wanted a drink. He had not had a drink of hard liquor in over four years. Finally he compromised with himself. He would go into that bar there – not because he craved alcohol but because he craved sweetness. He had no intention of ordering whiskey or even beer. He would sip a Bristol Cream, and probably only one. He had an absolute craving for sweetness, he told himself. If he stuck with sweet sherry it was not as if he had started to drink again.

The bar had an Irish name and a green neon harp in the window, and inside it was dark and pleasantly cool and the odours he inhaled were familiar to him and warm and pleasant. The glass felt good in his hand. Along the bar the other drinkers came and went but Rainey stayed, sipping, talking, sometimes glancing up at the television screen on the wall.

It shocked him to see Kilcoyne resigning. The top of the police department was about to implode like a lightbulb. It was getting really bad. When Rainey looked down his glass was empty, so he ordered another. Drink did not seem to be a problem with him anymore. He had begun to feel good, and he remembered the two beers for lunch yesterday which certainly hadn't hurt him.

Tomorrow he would tell Keefe how important it was that the cleaning woman be found. He should send detectives out to find her. He was a deputy commissioner and could order it. No point mentioning Carmichael and Craighead and the testimony they were ready to give. No point worrying him. Keefe was the one in trouble, not himself. He

344

was not worried about himself. There was no fear in him, only the nobility that came with concern for another.

When he asked for his bill it was midnight and he was surprised to see that he owed so much.

"You drank seven of those things," the barman told him.

"I didn't think it was that many," said Rainey.

"I never saw anybody drink so much of that sweet stuff at one sitting. Jesus, it makes me want to puke just to think about it."

Rainey looked at him. "Let me have one more," he said.

Which certainly shut that barman up, he saw with satisfaction. He drank it in two swallows, paid and went out into the night.

Twenty-Seven

KEEFE TOO TOSSED THE SUBPOENA DOWN ON HER DESK. The young prosecutor, expecting to be abused by this man too, got up and moved to her window, looking out and down the hill in the direction of Yankee Stadium. Let him shout at her back.

But Keefe was intent on seeming friendly, and he complimented her on the plants that grew on her windowsill. "How do you keep them looking so healthy?"

She read his uncertainty, his desire to please.

"We're not here to discuss plants, are we?" she said, returning to her desk.

Keefe was studying her diplomas, which were from Ivy League universities. "So how did a nice girl like you wind up here?" He tried a warm smile to which she did not respond.

"Do you have a lawyer, Mr Keefe?"

He had talked to Rainey and another veteran cop who worked for him, and had concluded that he did not need a lawyer for a preliminary interview like this one. He still believed his problems were political, not legal. There were ways to keep this woman's questioning within bounds, and he could always get up and walk out.

"I like to think I don't need a lawyer."

"We can postpone this until you get one."

"I've been talking to my brother. He's a lawyer." Keefe waited.

"He should be here."

"No, let's see how it goes."

Josephine Croker came into the office, took the chair against the wall. Anne gestured Keefe into the chair opposite her desk, and activated her tape recorder. "Let the record show that Deputy Commissioner Keefe has been advised of his right to legal counsel, but has waived it."

She and Keefe studied each other in silence. Then: "Tell me about your gun, Mr Keefe."

It was not the subject Keefe had been prepared for.

"Were you advised by your superiors to carry a gun?"

"No, I was not."

"Were you trained in its use?"

"Of course I was trained in its use."

"Who told you to take the training?"

"I went through what every cop goes through. Anybody untrained walks around this city with a gun is an idiot. Also a menace."

"Ballistics tells me that you fired five shots and hit the defendant once."

"Lots of cops in combat situations don't hit anybody at all."

"I see."

"How many shots did Brown's gun fire?" When she did not answer, Keefe said: "I've been hearing rumours."

"That it was a starter's pistol?"

"Yes. Was it?"

"Would that make a difference to you?"

"I don't know. I guess so."

"You mean you would no longer be able to brag about how brave you are, and about the shootout you won."

Keefe looked shocked.

"This gun, do you have it with you now?"

Keefe withdrew it and ejected the bullets into his hand. Having stood the five bullets up on the edge of Anne's desk, he pushed the gun across towards her.

She looked at it distastefully.

"Ballistics gave it back to me after the tests."

"I would think," she said, "that after shooting someone you wouldn't be so anxious to carry it anymore."

"You can't just leave it somewhere. Somebody could steal it. Or pick it up and shoot somebody else." Keefe gave a wry laugh. "One thing I found out: I don't own the gun, it owns me." After a moment he added: "I assume it's the same with every cop in the city. They're more careful of their guns than their wallets."

"Please put it away."

Keefe reinserted the bullets and jammed the gun back into his belt.

She pursued him. "All right, you're armed and trained. Now you begin to wonder what it would be like to shoot somebody."

Perhaps he had. It was a possibility he had brooded about a good deal lately.

"This daydream in which you shoot somebody becomes more and more real to you, is that correct?"

"Are you crazy or something?"

"You keep wondering what it would be like to shoot somebody. Finally you get your chance and you do it."

"What is this?"

"A man lies near death, and you shot him."

"In self-defence in the performance of my duty."

"My understanding is that your duty had nothing to do with carrying a gun or using it."

"Maybe I do need a lawyer."

Anne turned off the tape recorder. "We can stop right now, while you retain counsel."

After hesitating, Keefe said: "What else do you want to know? I want to get this over with."

Anne restarted the tape. "On what authority did you take command of the raid on the junkyard? And then of the hostage situation?"

"I didn't take command of the junkyard thing. I suggested that Lieutenant Craighead put the case together."

"You did not go through the Chief of Detectives?"

"What's that got to do with it?"

"Do you deny that you took command of the hostage situation outside Judge Baum's chambers in this building?"

"I never intended to take command."

"But you did take command?"

"It was an emergency situation. Somebody had to do something. Instead of grilling me you ought to be talking to that cleaning woman. My sergeant tells me you can't find her. Have you talked to her yet?"

"I have detectives looking for her. They'll find her."

"I hope so."

Keefe tried another smile, to which she did not respond. She said: "Are you willing to testify before the grand jury?"

There was a formula that went with this question. Keefe had been briefed on it. "Do I testify under a grant of immunity?"

"There will be no immunity."

This was as expected.

"I'll be glad to testify without immunity assuming you can assure me that I am not a target of this investigation."

Josephine Croker coughed.

Such a state of tension had been achieved in that small office that it sounded as loud as a door slamming. Anne and Keefe were staring at each other.

"I cannot give you that assurance."

"Jesus," said Keefe. He stood up. "Jesus," he said again, turned on his heel and strode out through the door.

Keefe returned to headquarters and phoned the Police Commissioner, but the PC was tied up.

"When can he see me?"

There was another long pause before the deputy inspector came back on: "Possibly tomorrow or the next day."

Keefe rushed up the stairs to the fourteenth floor and burst in on him.

Egan, who was in shirtsleeves, looked surprised.

"I've just come from the Bronx Courthouse. I was interviewed by the woman who has the case."

"Yes, she was here too," said Egan soothingly, pointing toward his sofa. "Sat right here. Very pretty girl, wouldn't you say?"

"She's planning to indict me."

"You're imagining things, I'm sure," said Egan even more soothingly. "Come over here and tell me about it." He led the way to his sofa, but Keefe did not sit down.

"You've got to help me."

"Of course, of course," said Egan.

"You've got to talk to her for me. Or talk to the DA, or something. Once she indicts me it will be too late."

Egan patted the place beside him on the sofa. "I'm sure you're exaggerating."

"No I'm not."

"Of course I'll help you," Egan continued. "I'll help you in any way I can." But Keefe read his face, or thought he did. The situation to Egan was too tender. It was too big a risk. Even to try to help Keefe would be unwise.

He's not going to do anything for me, Keefe muttered to himself as he strode back to his own office. Who could he count on? His only ally seemed to be Sergeant Rainey, and he sent for him.

"Suppose she indicts me? Then what?"

"Indicts you for what?" said Rainey. "I don't see where you committed any crime."

"She's the one who will present the case to the grand jury."

Rainey nodded. "Yes, but my understanding of the procedure there is that it all gets reviewed by the DA first."

"He'll believe whatever she tells him," said Keefe, "and the grand jury will believe whatever she wants it to believe. All she has to do is pick her witnesses carefully and ask only the questions she wants answered. A grand jury hearing is not a trial. There's no cross examination to bring out my side of the story."

"That's true. But –"

"All it takes is a couple of witnesses testifying that I acted irresponsibly, and the grand jury will vote to indict me."

"If you're that worried," Rainey suggested, "you could phone up the DA. Ask what's happening."

"The way the papers keep blasting me day after day I've become a non-person. I doubt he'd talk to me. He might think it improper if I even called him."

Rainey said nothing.

"Craighead, Carmichael and the others. How will they testify?"

"Maybe I can find out," said Rainey.

"Could you?"

"Try to relax," Rainey advised. "Grand jury hearings go on over a period of days. There's still time for them to find the cleaning woman. And the last witness to be heard will probably be you. So you'll have a chance to testify yourself as to what happened."

"I just told her I wouldn't testify."

Rainey said: "Oh."

"Not if I'm the target."

"I'll try to talk to Craighead, Carmichael, and the others," Rainey said. "And I'll see if I can't get a line on that cleaning woman too."

Rainey took half a step forward, as if he meant to clasp Keefe on the shoulder. The simple physical touching might have helped both of them. But there were barriers of rank between them.

"I'll let you know," Rainey said, and left the office.

Keefe dialled his brother's number. From now on, Richard Keefe advised him, he should speak to no one except through his lawyer. This lawyer would be the firm's star litigator, Joseph Kilsheimer. "I can't represent you myself for obvious reasons. I'll have Joe call this assistant DA and see if he can find out what's going on."

Keefe waited an hour before his brother called back.

"She wasn't very forthcoming, but she did tell Joe that the grand jury hearing would extend over several days. She promises to talk to him to see if you want to testify or not."

Keefe said: "Thank him for me."

"You're in good hands. Joe Kilsheimer is one of the best

there is. From now on, you let Joe Kilsheimer worry about it."

As Keefe hung up, there was a knock at his door and Captain Fallon stuck his head in.

"We've got a problem, Commissioner." Fallon hesitated, then said: "The new headquarters telephone directory has just been published." He paused dramatically. "The Chief of Personnel sent us only two copies."

Keefe looked at him.

"We need at least six, Commissioner. I called down to ask for four more, and they won't give them to me."

Keefe's life was about to be destroyed, and this man was worried about in-house phone directories.

"I thought if you intervened personally with Chief Flynn, Commissioner, we might get the extra four copies we need."

"Get Chief Flynn on the phone for me," Keefe said. It was something to get his mind off himself, and it was a favour he could do Fallon.

"Thank you, Commissioner."

There was no reason why Flynn should not send over the four extra directories at once. He had always been eager to please in the past. When Flynn came on, Keefe explained his needs.

"I'm sorry, Commissioner, your quota is two directories."

"But we need six, or so I'm told by my staff."

"Two."

"I think they've always had six."

"Two is all I can spare."

Keefe began to get annoyed. "I'll be right there to pick up four extra ones." And he got up and hurried down the hall.

Flynn was a three star chief and his staff of clerks and computer experts was a large one. His outer office was full of uniformed officers at desks, and there was a captain at his door who attempted to hold Keefe up.

"You can't go in there, Commissioner."

Keefe went in past him. He managed to smile and, at least at first, to keep his voice friendly. "Jerry, you've just got to give me those four extra directories."

Flynn was an officer with a long habit of obsequiousness.

Seeing Keefe only a few feet away, he seemed almost to cringe, and his evasive eyes began to dart this way and that. "The quota for your office is two, Commissioner," he said.

"Look, we need more. What's the big deal? It's just a phone directory."

But Flynn, as the interview continued, got stronger, and although Keefe kept bringing forth arguments, Flynn insisted he could have two directories, and two only.

Keefe got angry. Flynn did not. Keefe's voice rose, Flynn's did not.

"We'll see about this," Keefe cried, and stormed out of the office. But he had already come to the realisation that his power within the department was gone, his rank notwithstanding. Flynn did not have to take orders from Keefe any more. No one did.

"How did you make out, sir?" said Fallon.

"You'll have them soon," said Keefe. He went past him, closed the door, and sat behind his desk. He became more and more angry. Having determined to test this thing immediately, he picked up the red phone to call the PC. But instead of dialling he put the receiver back down and went to stand at his window.

After a while he called Sharon at work in California. She came on sounding out of breath, and also slightly impatient. "What is it? They're shooting. I have to get back."

"I just felt like talking to you."

Her voice grew warmer. "That's very nice. I feel like talking to you too. But I can't right now. Is everything all right?"

He assured her it was, promised to call her that night, and hung up.

Keefe continued to go to work each day, but took to going out for long walks at mid-morning, and again in the middle of the afternoon. He liked strolling through Chinatown and into Little Italy. He liked to smell the Chinese food cooking and then, a few streets further on, the odor of coffee from the espresso bars.

He talked to Sharon every night and during each call he

worked hard to keep the conversation sounding breezy.

Sergeant Rainey had been unable to find the cleaning woman. She was a temporary who had worked for an agency that had a contract with the city, he said. He had gone to her last known address.

"Supposedly she went to live with some friend. I went there as well. No one has seen her since the day after the shooting."

Rainey had the names of the two detectives assigned by Assistant DA Christianson to find her. He wanted Keefe to call up the inspector who was their commanding officer.

Keefe frowned.

"She might have gone back to the South," Rainey said. "I have two possible addresses for her, one in Alabama, the other in Georgia. You could ask the two detectives if they've checked them out."

"Sure," Keefe said.

"The inspector's name is Henning. I'll be at my desk if you want me, Commissioner."

It took Keefe most of the afternoon to get up the nerve to call Henning. Like all inspectors Henning was anxious for promotion to one-star rank. Normally such men were eager to respond to any request from a deputy commissioner.

"The two detectives are to report directly to me," Keefe said.

A week ago a command this forceful would have been more than sufficient. Henning said: "I don't think I can do that, Commissioner. I'm not even sure it's proper."

"I want them here forthwith."

"I won't be able to reach them until tomorrow, Commissioner," said Henning curtly.

"Tomorrow then. First thing in the morning." He slammed the receiver down.

But in the morning a message from Henning was waiting when he reached his office. Both detectives had reported sick and would not be able to report to Commissioner Keefe as ordered.

A Lieutenant Coffey from the licence division called. Keefe's pistol licence, he said, had been found to be invalid.

He was requested to turn in his gun while a new licence was prepared.

"What?" cried Keefe. "Who's behind that?"

Lieutenant Coffey began to stammer. Apparently no one had informed him that this particular deputy commissioner had been stripped of the power to hurt anybody.

"Tell whoever put you up to this to write me a letter." Again Keefe slammed down the receiver.

An hour later came a call from Chief Sheridan of Internal Affairs. There had been a complaint about Sergeant Rainey from two patrol officers who, some weeks before, had found him after hours illegally parked in Keefe's official car on a midtown side-street. Also in the car had been an unidentified female.

"When was this?" said Keefe levelly. He was trying to keep his emotions under control. "Which officers signed the complaint?"

Sheridan, as he read out this information, was amused. "You know how it is. They've been reading about this car of yours in the press and they saw Rainey's name. They got scared. They began to worry about being drawn into this mess. So they came forward." He gave a laugh in which Keefe read cynicism, not warmth. "I assume the transportation of this tootsie was not authorised by you. You look into it at your end, and we'll look into it at ours."

In the meantime an order had been cut transferring Sergeant Rainey back into uniform. He was assigned to patrol in the Forty-First Precinct in the Bronx. Keefe rushed about trying to get the order countermanded but there was no First Deputy Commissioner, no Chief of Operations, and the PC claimed to be too busy to see him. He could not even find out where the order had come from.

He told Rainey he would straighten this out in a matter of days, and Rainey nodded stoically while cleaning out his desk.

Ten minutes later Rainey was gone. Within the police department Keefe for the first time was truly alone.

Twenty-Eight

EGAN STOOD BESIDE THE BIER AND GREETED THOSE WHO came. He had taken up his position about five in the afternoon and had remained there unmoving except for the need from time to time to shift his weight from foot to foot. He wore a dark suit and a gentle smile, and spoke in a soft voice. He shook hands with everyone, and remembered nearly all the names.

"Thank you for coming." he said over and over again. "I know Jill appreciates it."

Jill was John Gaffney's widow. She was bearing up well, sitting in a straight chair across the room surrounded by female relatives. Most of the many dignitaries who came, after standing a moment at the bier, would go over to her briefly, then go out. It was Egan's presence that had brought them. It had forced them to come and pay their respects. He knew this. He was determined to send John out in style. After so many years it was the least he owed him.

For the first two hours John's oldest son had stood beside him, but the flowers kept arriving, so many that at length the great masses of them had obliged the man and the boy to move back several paces. Flowers in Egan's mind represented funerals only. When you grew up in New York City in an Irish Catholic working-class family you encountered them nowhere else. It was the too pungent odours that drove the boy away from the bier after a time. Egan, who hated flowers, assumed that was what it was. By the time this wake was over Gaffney's son perhaps would hate flowers too. He himself found them overpowering, the hardest part of the job he had assigned himself.

About ten P.M. the mayor came. There was a commotion near the door and he came in accompanied by several other men. He made straight for the bier where he stood with his

head down for the required minute, perhaps contemplating John Gaffney's death, perhaps his own. Perhaps
his mind was on the next election. Egan had no idea what
mayors thought about at wakes. They attended, after all, so
many. The entourage stood a pace or two behind the mayor,
also heads down, with their hands clasped at their crotch.

At last the mayor's head came up and he glanced over at
Egan, as if noticing him for the first time. His hand came
out, and Egan shook it.

"When did he pass away?" he asked in a sombre voice.

"Early this morning."

The mayor nodded. "It's a blessing."

"Yes."

The entourage had faded backwards. None of the three
men, Egan noted out of the corner of his eye, bothered to
approach Jill Gaffney. That was not their function. He
wondered if it was the same three men who accompanied
the mayor to every wake, and he wondered what their
function was.

"Good crowd?" inquired the mayor in the same voice. He
showed no sign of beating a quick retreat, which meant that
he hadn't come here solely to gaze at the mortal remains of
John Gaffney.

"The cardinal was here," Egan said, and for a moment
considered naming the other dignitaries who had come: two
congressmen, a senator, the fire commissioner, some
judges, assorted councilmen. He chose not to do it. Most
had signed the book, shaken hands with Egan, and gone out
again, a few of them without even approaching Jill Gaffney.
That was all right. The book with all those signatures was
going to be important to her when this was over. To the
mayor, Egan said: "The cardinal said the rosary."

The mayor's bald head nodded. The two men stood
together and gazed down on John Gaffney.

"You don't see uniforms like that anymore," the mayor
commented. "Those choker collars went out in, I don't
know, the sixties."

Gaffney was wearing his patrolman's uniform from long
ago with the simple patrolman's shield on his chest.

"He wanted to be buried in that uniform," Egan said. "It was one of his last requests."

"Last requests are a pain in the ass usually," the mayor said.

Egan looked down on his friend.

"He looks pretty good," the mayor said.

The dead man wore a grey wig parted, Egan knew, on the wrong side of his head. It was more grey than John's hair had been too. Furthermore, John had lost sixty or seventy pounds by the time he died. But the mayor wouldn't know that. The mayor had not known John Gaffney well. The saddest thing to look at was how skinny John's hands had become, clasped now on his breast with rosary beads entwined in thin fingers.

The mayor had turned away from the bier and was surveying the room. "Which one is the widow?" he asked.

"I'll take you over there, if you like," Egan said.

"In a minute," said the mayor. He paused. "I understand that deputy commissioner of yours is still carrying around a gun."

"Keefe?" said Egan, surprised.

"I don't even like to say his name."

Chief Gold had just come in, Egan saw. Probably timed it so as to be here at the same time as the mayor. At the moment he was bending over Jill Gaffney, holding her hand and talking to her.

"So get it away from him," the mayor said.

Egan said nothing.

"I had one of my people make a move in that direction," the mayor said, "but it didn't take."

"He's got a legal right," said Egan, adding quickly, "of course the news he's still carrying it is news to me."

"Get it away from him."

"I don't know how I'm going to do that."

"Find a way."

There were candelabra behind the bier, five flickering candles on each one. The reflections bounced off the side of the mayor's bald head. But the candles created heat as well as light. Egan realised he had begun to sweat.

"I'll look into it," he said.

"Don't look into it. Do it."

Across the crowded room Gold was still talking to Jill Gaffney. To change the subject, Egan said to the mayor: "As Chief of Operations, what would you think of Gold?"

The mayor nodded. "A good choice. Provided he's clean."

"He seems to be clean."

"Wait a few days to be sure."

Why doesn't he leave? Egan thought. There were others waiting to approach the bier, but none would come up for as long as the mayor remained there.

"I don't know if you heard," the mayor said, "Gaffney's not the only one who died today."

"Oh?" said Egan.

"Joshua L. Brown."

"I hadn't heard," said Egan.

"It's unusual, don't you think? Two deaths in the family, so to speak, the same day."

Egan could think of nothing to say in response to this remark.

The mayor said: "I got to go up there now."

"What?" said Egan. "He's a felon."

"Not in Harlem, he's not."

"I see."

"He passed away about an hour ago."

It was John Gaffney who had passed away. Brown didn't pass away, Egan thought. He was shot and killed during the commission of a crime. But no one's going to have the nerve to say it.

"Anyway," the mayor said, "in death there are no felons."

Egan gazed for a moment at his friend in the casket, still sleeping peacefully.

"So when is the grand jury going to decide?" said the mayor.

"I don't know."

"Another day or two at the most, wouldn't you say?"

Egan was having trouble continuing this conversation. "I'm sure you're right," he said.

"If I were you, I'd give Harlem my full attention right

away," the mayor advised. "I'd get on up there tonight. Make sure everything's quiet – and stays that way."

"Do you want to meet the widow?" said Egan.

"Let's go meet the little lady," said the mayor.

Egan, leaving his post, led the mayor across the room. At their approach the group around Jill Gaffney parted. There were several women, all of whom stepped back, plus Al Gold and, Egan now noticed, Deputy Commissioner Keefe who must have just come in. The mayor shook Jill's hand, and put on his most doleful voice and manner.

"So sorry for your trouble," he said.

It was a line out of the old Irish wakes of Egan's boyhood. The mayor was not Irish. Jill, to her credit, gave him a sad smile and thanked him for coming.

Turning away from Jill, the mayor shook hands with Gold and even paused to murmur a pleasantry. He had no handshake for Keefe whom he eyed briefly before giving an even briefer shake of his head and striding past him. The entourage fell in behind, following the mayor out the door. To Egan the room suddenly seemed half-empty.

"What did I do to him?" inquired Keefe at his elbow.

"I think I'll pay my respects to the deceased," said Al Gold, and he joined the queue waiting to approach the bier.

"Brown just died," Egan said to Keefe.

"I know. I heard it on the radio a while ago."

"How do you feel?" asked Egan in a kindly voice.

"I don't feel much of anything. I thought I would. I hoped for days that he'd pull through."

"There was never much chance of that, apparently," said Egan.

"I never thought I'd kill anybody ever," Keefe said. "These last few days have been so hard. I've been reading such awful things about myself in the papers and I guess I just don't have any sympathy left for Joshua Brown. Maybe I'll feel different in the morning. I don't know."

Egan realised he had business to conduct here, and so began to conduct it. "What happened to that gun you had?"

"Ballistics gave it back to me."

"You didn't get rid of it?"

"At first I wanted to. Then I started to get a lot of death threats. I don't know how serious any of them were."

"Death threats?" Egan had not known about this.

"Phone calls. Some letters. Somebody called up CBS and said I would be killed that very night." Keefe gave a hollow laugh. "That was two nights ago, and I'm still here."

To Egan this was serious. "What did you do with these threats?"

"I sent the letters over to the intelligence division. Supposedly they're investigating them now."

Egan nodded. This was correct procedure.

"The newspapers want me disarmed by force or by the courts. Somebody called from the licence division. He wanted me disarmed too, and I got angry and said to myself: I'm not going to let them push me around."

"So you still have the gun," said Egan.

"It's been as if I had no legal right to carry it, or, under circumstances like the other night, to use it."

Egan said nothing. The silence that built up became uncomfortable for both of them. Keefe was waiting for some expression of support from Egan, who was unwilling to give it.

Finally Keefe said: "I gather the mayor is not my friend."

"Oh no," Egan said. "The mayor's on your side."

"Sure."

"There are drinks and refreshments in the next room."

"I would have appreciated his support."

"Help yourself to the refreshments if you'd care to."

"I would have appreciated the support of somebody."

But Egan, who was in no mood for rebukes from Keefe, had already turned away from him. He had spied Gold who, having been to the bier, was on his way back through the crowd. "Al," he called sharply, moving toward him. And then: "May I speak to you for a moment, please?"

He began giving orders. In the morning Gold was to assign someone to institute proceedings that would strip Keefe of his pistol licence and gun. When Gold glanced at him, Egan said defensively: "Just do it. And I don't want it known that it comes from me. Is that clear?"

Over Gold's shoulder Egan could see the banks of flowers that surrounded the casket. He could see the rosy-cheeked profile of his best friend whom he was about to bury.

"Brown died," he told Gold.

"I know."

His second order from the mayor was that he should take personal charge of Harlem beginning tonight, but this he would not do. His place was here with John and with John's family. He would go just so far for the mayor and no further.

"You are to take personal charge of Harlem beginning tonight," he told Gold, "and ending when the deceased is safely in the ground."

He saw Gold's face light up. Gold knew what this meant. For the next three or four days he would be acting Chief of Operations, and the promotion would be confirmed in due time.

"I'll take care of it," said Gold.

"Good."

Jill came over to him. "Who was that young man just now?"

It took Egan a moment to realise whom she meant. "Deputy Commissioner Keefe. You met him once, I think. Just before John got sick.

"He seems very nice."

"Yes," said Egan.

"He's the one who's in trouble."

"Yes." Because of him, Egan thought, we're all in trouble.

"It was nice of him to come, don't you think? He didn't have to."

"Yes." There was perhaps no room for niceness in the police department, or in the city government as a whole, Egan concluded, and the sooner a man learned that the better for everybody.

Josephine Croker stuck her head into the office. "The DA would like you to come down."

"I wanted to talk to him anyway," said Anne. Locking the case folder in her desk, she walked down the corridor and

361

went in past the secretary into the DA's office.

This time as she crossed his Persian rug she remarked on it and flashed him a too bright smile. "I like your rug. You're a collector of rugs, it seems."

The elected District Attorney of Bronx County gave her a puzzled look.

"I've been reading up on you." She nodded several times. "Very interesting."

The DA studied her. Every time he saw her she surprised him. She wore a blue print dress – silk, perhaps – with a white collar. She had smooth cheeks and a blonde girl's high complexion.

"So how many rugs do you collect?"

He had called her in for several reasons, one being to scold her about the subpoenas. He had meant to do it gently, given her youth and inexperience.

"On a DA's salary, I don't get to collect too many", he said, and smiled back at her, the better to conceal his thoughts. There she stood in front of his desk, this big bosomed girl who held in her hands this suddenly incredibly sensitive case. How did I let this happen, he asked himself.

Finally he said: "I've been hearing about those subpoenas you sent out."

But she ignored the implied reprimand. "I came in to ask your advice," she said, smiling as if he had praised her. "What should I do about this potential theft of services charge against Deputy Commissioner Keefe?"

She never behaved as the DA expected. As he studied her, the word "nubile" came to mind. Yet she seemed both to him and to others he had talked to as unapproachable as a statue.

He chose to say: "Tell me about the rest of the case. Is it ready for the grand jury?"

"I've interviewed everyone who is available. I have probably eight potential witnesses."

The DA nodded. Eight sounded about right, and he was encouraged to think that she was handling the case with all due care and restraint.

362

"You didn't answer my question," she said.

"About the theft of services?" the DA said, startled. "I don't think any jury would send Commissioner Keefe to jail for driving a police car into Connecticut, do you?"

This was no longer the uncertain girl he had talked to a few days ago. He did not know she had been to see Senator Buckner. He had no idea why she felt so confident. He thought she was merely reading the signs – it was a big case, and it was hers. He hoped she wasn't reading some of them wrong.

"Then you think I should just let that part of it go?"

"The rest of the case is serious enough. Let's not compound our problems."

She was nodding. "I thought you'd see it that way. That's the way I see it too."

The DA felt uncomfortable in this young woman's presence but blamed it on the nature of the case rather than on her personality. He said: "So how is the grand jury going to rule?"

"I beg your pardon?"

It was as if he had just taken some liberty with her person, put his hand on her breast or something, yet he had a perfect right to ask this question, or any other. He said impatiently: "Are we dealing with a justifiable homicide or not?"

"That's for the grand jury to decide."

"True." But the prosecutor – any prosecutor – could usually control a grand jury's decision. Prosecutors always denied this in public but it was simple fact.

He tried again. "Legally speaking, it certainly seems justifiable to me."

"The grand jury will tell us whether it was or not."

This case is a hot potato, he told himself. Watch out. In his head he was already backing off. The climate was all wrong. The newspapers had whipped themselves into a frenzy. Senator Buckner, to whom he had never spoken, was out there somewhere as well. To charge a district attorney – himself for instance – with trying to manipulate a grand jury so as to cover up a police shooting would be

363

the biggest triumph Buckner could imagine.

It would be madness for the DA to get too close to this case.

"By the way, five of my witnesses have already testified," she advised him.

"What?" he said. "What?"

"I put them in yesterday. The grand jury has already heard them."

"Why wasn't I told?"

"I'm telling you now."

"I want to see the minutes."

"Certainly. I'll send them down."

It meant that it was too late for him to do anything, control this in any way, even if he dared. He was the elected District Attorney of Bronx County but the case was beyond his control. The only good thing was that, however the case came out, he had been re-elected less than a year ago. His term still had more than three years to run.

"Keep me informed," he told Anne Christianson.

It was not until he heard her footsteps receding down the hall that he realised he had not even managed to reprimand her for the subpoenas.

John Gaffney was buried from St Patrick's Cathedral at ten o'clock in the morning on the third day. The Egans sat in the front row pew along with Jill Gaffney and her children. The cathedral was not full. Funeral masses were long and John had been only a first deputy commissioner – and in an administration now rocking with scandal.

The mayor had not come. He was represented by one of the deputy mayors. Many of the elected officials who had signed in at the wake were not there, nor was the cardinal – one of the auxiliary bishops spoke the homily. So John had at least rated a bishop – not too bad under the circumstances.

The auxiliary bishop identified John as a good policeman, which he was, a lifelong public servant who had given his energies and aspirations, his ideas and at times even his physical strength to the city of his birth and its people, who had stood as a symbol for justice in a world that frequently mocked justice.

Egan in his pew was much moved, and Jill beside him was sobbing silently into her handkerchief. Because it was all true. It was true of John, and it was true of every honest cop, including, perhaps, Egan himself. Being a cop was a holy calling or it was nothing at all. Egan had believed that from the first day, and believed it still. It was true about protecting people who perhaps did not even realise they needed protection, and who almost never thanked you afterwards. And the only thing that was not true was the notion that John had devoted every waking moment to such idealism. He had not. Nor had Egan. Not had anyone. It wasn't possible. What the auxiliary bishop had neglected to say was that only a small portion of a man's energy and time – of a man's basic idealism – could be directed toward helping others. The rest of it had to be spent wastefully, uselessly on self-protection or self-aggrandisement. A good man's life – and Egan hoped he was a good man, as good a man as John had been – in some ways resembled one of those charities that gave away only a small percentage of the donations received, the rest having been consumed by the expenses involved in keeping the charity in existence. In the career of a cop like Egan – or even one like John, whom Egan thought a better man than he himself would ever be – only about ten per cent of a man's effort went outwards at all, perhaps less. The rest was devoted to trying to survive in whatever job he held at the moment. Egan in his pew, as the auxiliary bishop droned on, regretted this. Nonetheless he justified it to himself. It must be the same in every business, he thought, but at least in ours the small percentage directed outwards does help people. We're not just trying to foist useless products off on gullible buyers. We are better than other people. In general we're despised by our fellow citizens everywhere in the world, even though, for the most part, we are better men than they are. And some of us, John for instance, lived truly honorable lives.

Presently the mass ended, and a police bugler blew taps.

The individual notes echoed and reverberated in the great cavernous church, and Jill Gaffney choked back a sob that must have been audible to everyone. Six cops carried John's flag-draped casket out of the church and down the steps and thrust it into the hearse.

Egan, as he was about to step into the limousine that already contained Jill Gaffney, Edna and the two Gaffney chidren, was stopped by a small group of newsmen. He was locked inside his own thoughts at the time, and the questions they put to him at first failed to penetrate.

"The indictment of Deputy Commissioner Keefe has just been handed down, Mr Egan. What are your reactions?"

"Any comments on the Keefe indictment, Commissioner?"

There was a microphone in front of Egan's mouth and a camera lens was pointed at him over shoulders.

Reporters with notebooks leaned close.

"Any reactions, Commissioner?"

"No comment," said Egan, and he climbed into the limousine and slammed the door. The windows were tinted, fortunately. They could not photograph him through the glass.

"What was that?" inquired Edna Egan.

"Nothing," he said.

As the car pulled away Egan turned and peered out the oval-shaped rear window. The reporters now had surrounded Keefe; Egan had not even realised the young man had attended the funeral. Keefe's face looked ashen.

He didn't know in advance either, Egan thought.

At the graveside there was a second shorter service. Under its flag John's casket lay athwart boards atop the hole. All of the dignitaries had dropped away by now including even the auxiliary bishop. The service was read by Monsignor Kelly, the police chaplain.

There were no clouds. The summer day was brilliant, but very windy. Egan's whispy hair was being blown about, and the wind got under Jill's veil and blew it up over her hat.

Monsignor Kelly closed his missal. After kissing his stole, he rolled it up and put it in his pocket.

Egan's own department car had followed the cortège.

366

Now his driver came up to him and said: "The mayor wants you to call him." Egan looked around at the mourners climbing into the limousines.

"It just come over," the driver said.

"*Came* over," corrected Egan. "We're going back to Commissioner Gaffney's house," he told the driver. "You can follow us, and wait for me outside."

About twenty family members and close friends crowded into the small house not far from Egan's in Queens. What amounted to a very late lunch was served. The cold cuts, salads and sandwiches stood around on a sideboard covered by Saranwrap. Edna Egan had arranged for this earlier, and now she and Jill Gaffney plucked the wrapping off and began heaping the food on to paper plates. The plastic cutlery was already wrapped in paper napkins and there were clear plastic glasses for the wine and hard liquor. People ate off their laps. The first gin bottle was emptied, then the second, and there was a good deal of laughter as people recounted anecdotes out of John's past. Everyone laughed fondly at familiar stories.

Egan waited until he was good and ready before phoning the mayor – who at that point refused to take his call, and he was switched to one of the deputy mayors. It was all a game, Egan reflected. He waited on hold until the deputy mayor came on. The mayor's message was that a demonstration was planned for Harlem that evening. A thousand people were going to march in support of the late Joshua L. Brown. Maybe it would be five thousand, or fifty thousand. Egan was to take personal charge.

The deputy mayor waited, perhaps for Egan to acquiese. He made no comment at all. He merely hung up, and returned to John Gaffney's living room. About an hour later he phoned Chief Gold and informed him about the proposed demonstration. Gold was to take charge. There was always the possibility that the demonstration could turn into a riot. Gold was to take all reasonable precautions. He hung up.

By late afternoon John Gaffney's house had begun to empty. Finally only the Egans and Jill Gaffney were left.

Edna Egan cooked supper, but Jill did not eat much of it. Afterwards they sat together watching television. About ten o'clock Jill began to weep silently, and Edna, sitting beside her on the sofa, put her arm around her. Presently Edna put her to bed, gave her some pills and sat beside her until satisfied she was asleep.

When Edna returned to the living room Egan was on his feet watching a news programme – it was about the indictment of Deputy Commissioner Keefe. Edna stood beside him. No words were spoken, but she must have realised how upset he was, for her arm came around his waist and she lay her head on his shoulder.

After that came live shots of the demonstration in Harlem. It seemed peaceful enough. The mob was walking across 125th Street. There were few cops visible. Then the cameras showed the two parallel streets, 124th and 126th, which was where Gold had put his men. They wore helmets and carried nightsticks and they were lined up nearly shoulder to shoulder – but invisible to the demonstrators. A block further away still were the communication trucks, the Mounted Squadron standing beside their horses, and Gold's command post. Good, Egan thought, he's done everything he can.

He went over and turned off the TV.

"She's sleeping," said Edna.

"I guess we can go now."

They went out into the warm summer night. They got into Egan's department car and were driven the few blocks home.

The phone rang, and it was Gold. The demonstration in Harlem appeared to be over. The crowds had dispersed peacefully.

"How many people were there, would you say?" Egan asked.

"Hard to say, Commissioner. Between five and ten thousand, I would guess."

"Any arrests?"

"About five youths assaulted a police officer. We grabbed them and hustled them down a side street right away. The chances are that most of the demonstrators never knew it had happened."

Then it's over, Egan thought. The indictment is over, the demonstration is over, and I'm still here. "Nicely done," he said to Gold. "Tomorrow you'll be named the new Chief of Operations."

There was a momentary silence. However, Gold did not appear surprised. "Thank you, Commissioner," he said.

"I've already cleared it with the mayor," said Egan. He hadn't, but he was afraid that the mayor, to express his displeasure with Egan, might bypass him, appointing Gold directly. He had no desire to lose any more face than he had lost already.

"I'll try to do my best for you and for the department," Gold added, before ringing off.

Later that night Egan, only half-conscious, heard a telephone ringing and sirens blaring simultaneously. Stupefied with sleep he sat up and grabbed the phone, and the voice in his ear cried excitedly: "Commissioner, we have information that a bomb has been planted in your house. It's set to go off any minute. Get your family out of there at once."

Already there were cops downstairs banging on all the doors, and he could hear their shouts as well.

Egan threw on the lights. "Get out of the house at once," he shouted to Edna beside him. "I'll get the boys."

He saw her run toward the closet for slippers and a bathrobe, and he shouted: "You don't have time for that. Out. Run."

He himself was sprinting down the hall and into the boys' room. He scooped up one in each arm and ran for the stairs. The boys, not knowing what was happening, were wriggling and kicking though they were still half-asleep. Egan got them out the front door and out to the sidewalk under the trees. Edna was already there. There were three police cars in the street with their lights flashing, and more on their way obviously, for Egan could hear the approaching sirens. There were cops banging on the front doors of each of the adjacent houses as well, and within several minutes about

369

twenty people stood on the sidewalk in their night clothes. All the front doors were agape, and neighbours were running up to Egan demanding to know what was going on.

He pretended to be calm. "I think it's a threat of some kind," he said. "I'm sure it's completely unfounded."

He was trying to reassure them, and at the same time reassure himself. He was not a bit sure it was unfounded.

About twenty minutes later the bomb squad truck pulled up, and in its wake came the van that carried the dogs that were trained to sniff out explosives. The bomb squad men were wearing armour plate so that Egan thought: whatever the information is that they're acting on, they believe it.

The bomb squad lieutenant who had circled the house carrying a protective shield and a flashlight reported to him: "No sign of any forced entry, Commissioner. That's good. Maybe it's just a false alarm. My men are going through the house now room by room."

Edna's nightgown was by no means transparent, but she stood beside him looking embarrassed nonetheless. She was barefoot, and in the Lieutenant's presence was trying to cover herself with her hands. There were cops all around, and the little boys, who were very excited, were trying to talk to them.

"I'll get you something," said Egan to his wife, and he started back toward the house.

"Tim, for God's sake," said Edna. "I don't need anything. Don't go in there."

Egan went in anyway. When he came back he was carrying bathrobes and pairs of slippers.

He began trying to urge the boys to get into the police cars and try to go back to sleep, but they wouldn't do it. Edna had begun following them, watching over them. Most of the neighbours had clustered around Egan. Of course they knew who he was, and they were begging for information and muttering about bomb threats, interrupted sleep, reduced property values. He tried to soothe them. The houses across the street had not been evacuated. The lights were on and people were hanging out of the windows. Egan walked away and stood under a tree, and closed up inside

370

himself to review his entire career. He remembered all the promotion exams he had passed, and how fulfilled he had thought himself when, as a very young captain, he had been brought to headquarters. He had been part of a so-called think team, and had been promoted to inspector. It was then that his police ideas had begun to flower. He had written papers which had achieved some notice, and some of his ideas were actually implemented by the then commissioner. He had never even been promoted to deputy chief as a New York cop. Instead he had accepted the job of Chief of Police in Atlanta, which was going through a corruption scandal at the time, and from Atlanta he had been hired by Cleveland, a much bigger city. It was in Cleveland that his youngest son had been born. But the incumbent mayor there was defeated for re-election, and Egan had resigned as police chief. He had had no choice really. Every mayor in every city always wanted his own police commissioner, always called him his most important appointment – and usually got total obedience from the man in question, because the chief law enforcement officer in every city was the mayor, whatever the voters thought. The mayor could remove the chief or commissioner on a moment's notice, giving no reason at all, and the chief or PC, if removed, would have a hard time proving that it been done for political reasons only, and not for cause – cause being some crime or other, probably corruption. Becoming Police Commissioner of the City of New York had been Egan's ambition from his first day in uniform as a patrolman, and he had achieved his goal, and the result here and now was to stand out on the sidewalk in the middle of the night in his pyjamas with his wife and youngest two children waiting to find out if some madman had planted a bomb in his house. Edna won't complain, he thought, and the boys think it's fun.

About an hour passed. Finally the bomb squad lieutenant again reported to Egan. "We've ransacked the place, Commissioner. There's no bomb in there that we can find. I think it's safe to go back to sleep."

"Thank you," Egan said.

371

"I don't know what the information was," the lieutenant said. "I'll look into it tomorrow and send you a 49 on the subject."

"Yes," Egan said. "That would be good. Tell your men how much we appreciate it. Good night."

He led his family back into their house. Edna put the boys back to bed. When she returned to their bedroom Egan was sitting up against the headboard with the light on.

"Are you all right?" she asked her husband.

"Sure. No problem."

She got into bed on her side. Egan turned off the bedside lamp and slid down under the sheet, which was all that covered them on this warm night.

"Good night, darling," Edna said.

He reached over and stroked her face.

Presently he could tell from her breathing that she was asleep. She is a remarkable woman, he thought. I don't deserve her. His mind felt totally alert, which meant that sleep would not come for him for a long time, if at all.

Egan waited a week to make sure that the city was indeed quiet, that the Joshua L. Brown crisis was indeed over. Then he took up a memo pad with the following words printed across the top of it: *From the Desk of Police Commissioner Timothy Egan*. No one was calling for a new police commissioner and the mayor was again cordial to him when they talked on the phone. Sitting at Teddy Roosevelt's old desk on the fourteenth floor of headquarters Egan wrote out one line, and signed his name, and asked the deputy inspector outside his door to carry the envelope to City Hall. He was to give it to the mayor personally, if possible.

The memo he had just sent forward read: "I am resigning as Police Commissioner of the City of New York effective immediately."

And that's how a career ends, he thought. One line. He did not even clean out his desk. Into his attaché case went a few personal items only, including Edna's picture and another taken the previous Christmas of his entire family, and he went down into the basement garage and got into his car.

"Take me home, please," he instructed his driver.

Edna and the boys were ready. He backed his personal car, which was already packed, out of the garage and drove out of the city, heading south-west. They stopped for the night in Virginia, and the next day Egan showed the boys Washington's house, and after that Jefferson's. From time to time he thought about the future. Perhaps someone would offer him a job. If not he would have to find one. His police pension would carry them until then. They drove west, for the boys wanted especially to see where the Indians had massacred Custer, and Egan had promised to show it to them. It was while passing through southern Illinois that Egan managed to buy a copy of the *New York Times,* and to learn that Alvin G. Gold had just been appointed the new Police Commissioner of the City of New York.

Egan at the wheel continued driving west.

Twenty-Nine

CONFRONTED BY REPORTERS OUTSIDE THE CATHEDRAL after the funeral, Keefe was at first too shocked and upset to say anything. He pushed through to his car which was waiting doubleparked at the corner. He jumped in and slammed the door.

"Drive," he said. The reporters had followed him out into the street.

Detective Rodriguez put the car in gear. "Where to, Commissioner?"

"Anywhere. Just go."

The car moved down Fifth Avenue. It moved slowly in traffic and at first the cameramen ran alongside filming in. It moved past the windows of luxury stores, past airline ticket offices plastered with posters of exotic places. He could jump out, buy a ticket and fly away. He could run. Chase a pipe dream instead of a nightmare. But life was long and human beings by nature were sprinters. What happened when he could run no more?

They crossed Forty-Second Street and for a time were stalled in traffic in front of the two-block-long public library. He could not run from himself, nor from the indictment. The sidewalks were crowded with pedestrians, who had their own problems, and didn't care about his. He might live another forty years, perhaps more. He could hide, but not for long. He had to get past this thing, which meant he would have to face it. By now he was filled with equal parts of rage and frustration. Other emotions would be along later, and he knew this, but for the moment rage and frustration were enough. He stared straight ahead, his jaws clenching and unclenching regularly, almost imperceptibly.

The car continued to move downtown in heavy traffic, and he saw that Rodriguez, unasked, was merely heading back to headquarters. The horse knows the way, Keefe thought.

"Turn around," he said. "Take me home."

"Right you are, Commissioner."

The car stopped in front of his building. He went up the stairs to his flat, but kept Rodriguez waiting below, for he was unwilling to give up the perks of his office, much less the office itself, any sooner than he had to. His first phone call was to Joe Kilsheimer, supposedly his lawyer.

"I think I've just been –" it was harder to say than he had imagined – "indicted." He had a dozen questions, but Kilsheimer cut him off. He would check into it and call back.

Keefe paced his small flat, waiting. He turned the radio on. There were two all-news stations. He listened first to one, then the other. The announcers went on and on about his indictment. It was as if no news event of such magnitude had ever occurred before.

Finally his phone rang. "Well," said Kilsheimer, "it's true. I just confirmed it with the District Attorney's office."

Keefe had never had any doubt that it was true. "How could it happen without us knowing about it?"

"You got me there."

"You promised to keep on top of this. You were supposed to decide whether or not I wanted to come in and testify. Supposedly there was not even any urgency."

"Well, we were wrong."

Keefe thought: it's no good crying on this guy's shoulder. "What's the worst that can happen to me?"

"You can get convicted. But it's not going to happen."

"What's the maximum sentence?"

"That's no way to think. The jury's going to laugh this case out of court. They're going to give you a medal."

Juries were not empowered to confer medals, only verdicts. "What's the maximum sentence?" Keefe demanded again.

"Eight and a half to twenty-five. But we'll work something out long before then."

Twenty-five years was a number that took getting used to. To Keefe it was a number so enormous it could not even be comprehended. It was like trying to imagine being buried twenty-five feet deep.

"What happens next? What do we do next?"

"I come up there, and we march into the nearest precinct, and we surrender."

The editorial "we". Kilsheimer did not surrender. Keefe did.

"I don't need you to surrender," Keefe said. "I know where the nearest station house is, and I can surrender by myself."

This caused Kilsheimer to pause. Then he said cheerfully: "Where are you? Are you home? Stay put. I'll be right there."

"No," Keefe said, "you misunderstood me. The time when I needed you was before this. I don't need you now." He rang off.

His mind was stuck on the number twenty-five. He might come out aged sixty, more or less, having missed all the years in between.

He phoned his brother, who came on the line. "You just fired Kilsheimer," he said.

"Yes."

"Not one of the brightest things you've done."

"I haven't done much lately that was bright, so it seems." Keefe paused. There was a silence between the two men. "I have to go in and surrender," Keefe said. For a moment he thought he might burst into tears. "I don't – I don't want to go alone. Will you come with me?"

"Of course," his brother said. "I'll be right there."

Keefe hung up, and as he did so the tears came in a flood. Then he washed his face and tried to think how to begin fighting back.

He surrendered at the Nineteenth Precinct station house on East Sixty-Seventh Street at two o'clock that afternoon, having walked there from his apartment because, when he went downstairs to his car, he found that it was gone. Rodriguez had been withdrawn, probably by radio.

His brother met him at the station house. The paperwork was done in the second-floor detective squad room. A detective at a typewriter filled out the forms, and Keefe was obliged to hand over his gun and shield. The detective was extremely apologetic. "I don't like to have to do this, Commissioner."

The detective led him to the fingerprint stand where his fingers were inked and rolled. "This is a waste of time, isn't it?" Keefe said. "I was fingerprinted when I came into the department. You already have my prints on file."

"Well, Commissioner, this is the way they tell us to do it."

He was taken downstairs to the muster desk and booked. A number of cops, obviously sympathetic, stood watching.

"I think they screwed you, Commissioner."

"I seen what you done on TV," another cop said. "You don't deserve this."

Keefe was both touched and embarrassed. "I'm not a commissioner any more," he mumbled.

Two detectives were assigned to escort him to arraignment court. One had his handcuffs out.

"Is that really necessary?" Keefe said.

The detective looked sheepish. "We're supposed to," he said. "I'm sorry."

"Screw procedure," the other detective said to his partner. "Put 'em away."

"Thank you," Keefe said. Outside they waded through the mob of newsmen without speaking. This was a scene Keefe had watched many times on TV and also, since joining the department, in real life: the prisoner, handcuffed, being led to the car with his coat over his face. But Keefe was not handcuffed, and he did not try to hide his face. Instead he walked as proudly as he could to the unmarked car.

There was a similar gauntlet to run when the car pulled up outside the arraignment court. One of the detectives went to get a docket number, then they had to wait in the courtroom for about a half an hour until the case was called. Assistant District Attorney Christianson asked that Keefe be held on $250,000 bail.

"What?" cried Richard Keefe angrily. "Are you crazy?"

The judge on his dais rapped his gavel for order.

"The defendant until an hour ago was a deputy police commissioner of this city, your honour," Richard Keefe said. "He surrendered voluntarily and has no intention of fleeing. I ask that he be released without bail."

"Your honour," said Anne Christianson, "the defendant has lived for a number of years outside the country, has many friends abroad, and conceivably even concealed bank accounts. There is a very real danger he will flee the jurisdiction of the court. In view of the seriousness of the charges against him, I think $250,000 is only fair." She never once looked in Keefe's direction.

"I haven't even heard a plea yet," the judge said, looking down on them.

"Defendant pleads not guilty," said Richard Keefe.

"Defendant will surrender his passport to the court."

"Yes, your honour," said Richard Keefe.

"Released on his own recognisance pending trial," said the judge. He rapped his gavel. "Next case."

Keefe and his brother went out of the courtroom.

"Whew," Richard Keefe said, "that was a close one."

As the reporters crowded around both of them, they began to walk faster and faster. In the street they hailed a cab, and got into it.

"You'll have dinner with us," Richard Keefe said.

Their mother and father were there too. Dinner was

interrupted by a long telephone conversation with Sharon, who was soon in tears. She had called to comfort him; instead he was obliged to comfort her, and it was debilitating work. From the dining room he could hear his father muttering: "It's an outrage" over and over again. When he got back to the table his food was cold, his mother's eyes were damp, his brother and sister-in-law had given up any pretext of cheerfulness, and he had to work hard lest the dinner table mood become totally funereal. This would be his job from now on, he saw: to cheer up every relative and friend who called or crossed his path, and he found himself daunted in advance.

He went home. There were no newsmen outside his building. They had their story for today, his arrest and arraignment. They would not bother him again until tomorrow. However, once he was upstairs the phone began to ring incessantly. He assumed it had been ringing most of the day. He answered it the first few times: people who wished to commiserate. Some were friends, others only acquaintances, who had perhaps called not to offer solace but to satisfy purient curiosity. One call was from a total stranger who cursed him and threatened his life.

He got an answering machine out of his closet and attached it to the telephone.

He needed a lawyer, and soon settled on a young man named Harold Bloom, an ex-assistant district attorney who, after successfully prosecuting a number of important cases, had recently left public service to open his own law office. Bloom, Keefe reasoned, knew first-hand how a District Attorney's office worked. He had few clients as yet, and therefore could give Keefe's case all the time it required. Furthermore, he would see the defence of ex-Deputy Commissioner Keefe as a case on which he might acquire enormous publicity, and therefore new business. It was a case on which he could base his career as a criminal lawyer.

Nonetheless, his fee made Keefe wince. Bloom was extremely apologetic, but he had rented an expensive suite of offices in the financial district – necessary, if he was to attract clients – and his expenses were high. He was even more apologetic as he asked for half his fee up front.

Keefe sold his few stocks, and his car, cashed in his Keogh plan, paying a significant penalty to do so, borrowed money from his father and wrote out Bloom's cheque.

In strategy conferences Bloom was full of ideas. First of all, he would file a motion asking the indictment be set aside. Good, Keefe responded, Bloom should do it as soon as possible, and if that failed he should move for the earliest possible trial.

Negative, Bloom told him. Time was Keefe's ally here. Passions had been raised. It was necessary to allow them to die down. In a few months the press and public would begin to see this case more rationally.

Keefe could see that this was reasonable, but to him time was not his ally but his enemy. He sat down and counted his money at least once a day, because he had so little left, and none coming in. Each day had to be paid for in other ways too. With nothing to occupy his time, his brain fixed itself on his predicament. He could not stop thinking about it. He was sleeping badly. He woke before dawn and lay in the dark and brooded.

"And stay away from the press," Bloom warned him.

The reporters and camera crews had returned, waiting in droves on his doorstep. The big scoop now would be an interview with him. What were his thoughts, hopes, emotions, plans? He looked down from his window at the doubleparked vans and trucks, the milling reporters, and felt himself a prisoner. He paced his small flat and listened to the ringing telephone that his answering machine promptly cut off each time.

He took to going out very early or else very late. Several times, having left his flat before breakfast, he remained away all day, despite having no plans at all, because if he went back he would be stuck in there until dark. But if he stayed out, what was he to do with himself? He took to going to museums. He saw a good many movies, once paying his way into three in one day. He sat under the trees in Central Park, watching the children as they roller-skated, or tried to fly kites. He ate in cheap diners to save money.

As soon as he got home he would play back his messages to see who called.

By the week's end the reporters had mostly been withdrawn. It was too expensive, obviously, to keep them on his doorstep. Besides, the editors had decided on a new strategy, and Keefe's answering machine began to fill up with messages from reporters, some extremely well known, some friends of his.

He reported all this to Sharon. They spoke every night. Keefe pretended that his existence was actually quite amusing. Sharon pretended to believe him, but suggested he escape to California: "I have plenty of room for two." Because she couldn't come to New York, couldn't get time off from the show before a month or six weeks at least.

But Keefe, who could not leave the jurisdiction of the court, answered bitterly: "You never should have gone out there in the first place."

"You're not being fair."

"You're the one who wasn't fair."

"I can come for the weekend."

"What good would that do?"

Three days passed before they spoke again.

One call on Keefe's machine was from May Fondren. He thought about it a while, then called her back. For no particular reason, or perhaps for reasons too deeply rooted in his psyche for him to explain, he was anxious to talk to this woman he had once been close to, to feel even over the telephone whatever warmth she might offer him.

She came on the phone sounding effusive, almost giggly, obviously pleased with herself and with him because he had cared enough to return her call. "I felt so bad when I heard," she said. "I wanted to put my arms around you."

"Well," he said. He was quite touched.

"I wanted to send you flowers, as if you were in the hospital. But you're not in the hospital, are you? You're perfectly healthy."

He laughed. "In most ways, yes."

"I mean, what do you send to someone who's just been indicted? Do you send chocolates?"

"You send the name of a good lawyer, May."

It was pleasant to talk to her, and he was glad she was not mad at him any more.

"I didn't know what to send. I never previously had a boyfriend who managed to get himself indicted."

Perhaps it was the use of the word boyfriend that put him on his guard. It was the wrong word.

"So what are your plans?"

"I'm still trying to work them out," he said.

"Who's your lawyer? Do you feel sure you'll be acquitted?"

She was a reporter, and this was an interview. She had been assigned to it because she could perhaps get through to him by playing on the relationship that used to exist between them, whereas other reporters couldn't.

"What about you, May?" he interrupted. "What stories do they have you working on?"

"Nothing very interesting, I must say. Would you get a job? You'll have to, won't you? I mean, the trial is several months off, isn't it?"

"Let's not talk about me, May," he said gently. "Let's talk about you."

He heard her receive and accept the rebuke. "Oh," she said.

"Do you think you'll be sent overseas again soon?"

There was an awkward silence. May was embarrassed too. "I'm sorry you're in trouble, Phil," she said. "I really am sorry."

"I know you are, May. I appreciate your concern." A moment later he rang off.

Seymour Becker called, or rather his secretary left a message on the machine. Keefe thought this over for some time too. Am I that important a story, he asked himself, so that even the Executive Editor feels obliged to have a try? But he dialled the paper's number.

"How are you?" Becker demanded when he came on. "What kind of shape are you in? Is there anything we can do for you here?" His tone was brusque. He sounded like a man holding a telephone in one hand and doing something else with the other – signing letters, perhaps.

Keefe decided to say: "I need a job, Seymour."

The paper employed about five thousand people. Some were visible to the public, sure, but not all. Becker might be able to find room for Keefe, if he wanted to. The paper also owned a number of smaller papers in small cities.

"I'm not asking to be assigned to Paris as bureau chief," Keefe said.

"I know you're not," said Becker gently, and for a moment he sounded like a man with a heart. He had once had all the heart in the world, Keefe knew. But that was a long time ago.

"I'd go to Atlanta. I'd go to Indianapolis. I'd go anywhere."

"Why don't we meet and talk it over?" Becker said briskly, and he named a time and place: lunch at the Princeton Club two days later. For Phil Keefe he would clear his calendar.

Arriving first, Keefe was shown into the dining room and led to a table which, he saw with alarm, had been set for three. Becker arrived a few minutes later, and he greeted Keefe with false joviality. "I've brought along a friend of yours," he said, grinning broadly.

The friend was May Fondren.

"Hello, Phil."

Keefe had risen to shake hands with Becker, and after hesitating briefly he came around the table to kiss May on the cheek. Then all three sat down, and there was a moment of silence. A waiter came over and took an order for drinks: beer for Keefe, Perrier with a twist of lime for Becker, a glass of white wine for May. While they waited Keefe stared at his hands and wondered what to do, what to say.

"I don't know what you expect of me," he began.

"You're among friends," said Becker. "Say whatever you please."

"I thought we were meeting as friends."

"And so we are."

"I can't afford any publicity at all," Keefe said. "You understand that."

"Be that as it may," said Becker.

May said nothing, but she seemed to eye Keefe cautiously.

"I thought we were going to talk about a job," said Keefe.

May looked surprised. Becker attempted to give an easy laugh. "We'll get to that. So how are you feeling? What are your plans?"

"Anything I might say in the course of this meeting," said Keefe carefully, and he raised his eyes to meet Becker's, "is personal between us and off the record." This was a condition which newspapermen agreed to and honored all the time. If Becker agreed to it now he would honour it. Keefe believed he would. In any case, in May he had a witness.

Becker took off his thick glasses and polished them with his handkerchief. Then he managed another laugh. "You are the most suspicious guy."

"Is it agreed?" said Keefe.

"I'm not used to having people impose conditions on me," snapped Becker.

Keefe stood up. "In that case, I have to go."

"What about the job you're hoping for?"

There would be no job if he left. There might or might not be one if he stayed. That is, he lacked the conviction simply to stalk out. For twenty seconds, perhaps longer, he stood between his chair and the table, trying to decide what to do.

He did not want to embarrass the Executive Editor either. As far as any future in journalism went, he would be worse off than ever. In the headlines of Becker's paper, he might be worse off than ever as well.

The twenty seconds had passed and he still had no answers. He simply sensed that to remain at this table would diminish him forever, not so much in Becker's eyes as in his own.

"I'm sorry," he said again, "I have to go now." And he went out the door.

Later that afternoon there was a message on his machine from May. Her voice sounded plaintive.

"He made me go to that lunch," she had cried into the machine. "I didn't want to. He made me." She had then hung up.

Keefe played the message back several times before he turned off the machine.

Thirty

BLOOM'S MOTION TO SET ASIDE THE INDICTMENT HAD been rejected.

"Barring new evidence," Bloom said, "it did not figure to work."

"No," said Keefe. Although he had known it was a long shot, he was bitterly disappointed.

They were sitting in an Eastside restaurant eating lunch. Around them sat businessmen presumably discussing deals, and at a few other tables sat obviously rich women lunching with each other.

"So how about it?" said Bloom. "How about some new evidence? What is there?"

"The cleaning woman, if we could find her."

"Is there any hope of that?"

Keefe did not know where to look, and Rainey was no longer available to help him.

"I'll file some more motions," said Bloom encouragingly. "We can delay this trial almost forever."

But Keefe did not want it delayed. "Do you know what it's like, living like this?"

"No, I don't," Bloom said. "Though I can imagine."

Keefe looked at him.

Bloom gave a warm grin. "Imagining is the best I can do," he said. "You'll have to be satisfied with imagining."

On the sidewalk outside the restaurant, Keefe said: "I'd like to go to California."

Bloom shook his head. "You're not allowed to leave the jurisdiction of the court."

"Can you request permission for me?"

"On what grounds?"

"I can't get a job here."

Bloom shook his head again. "Not good enough."

"I've had some death threats on the telephone. You could say that I fear for my life."

"Do you?"

The death threats had stopped about the same time as the requests for interviews. He was old news now and would remain so until the trial. "No," said Keefe, "but I fear for my sanity if I don't get to California."

"I'll give it a try," said Bloom.

A week later he phoned triumphantly. "Permission granted," he said.

Sharon met him as he came off the plane. She had thought a long time about what to wear, and had decided finally on a sleeveless white dress that showed off her brown arms, and white open-toed shoes, and she carried a white handbag. But Keefe's reaction to her was so restrained she worried that she had decided wrong. Perhaps he thought she looked dressed for a wedding.

Keefe wore a medium-weight business suit, for it was fall now in New York, and he carried a topcoat over his arm. He looked into her smiling face and imagined that he was bringing her only problems, and he hoped she wouldn't come to regret her invitation. He had just spent five and a half hours in tourist class in a full airplane with his knees almost under his chin. For her it was nine P.M. For him it was midnight. He was tired. He felt he hardly knew her.

They stood at the baggage carousel.

She was shocked by his appearance. He had lost at least ten pounds, most of it in the face. "You look wonderful," she told him. I should have realised, she told herself, how badly he must have been eating and sleeping. "Your face has changed," she said. "Now you look, well, distinguished."

They stood smiling at each other."

"You're the one who looks wonderful."

Bags began to appear on the belt. Keefe watched them carefully, because for reasons he could not understand it was easier than talking. One of his suitcases came by, and he lifted it off. He waited, and the other came. Both were big, and he hefted them.

"Going to stay a while, are you?" Sharon said. She had meant the question to sound droll, but it didn't, and she frowned. The length of his stay was a subject about which he was perhaps supersenstive. "I mean, I hope you are." She put her arm through his. "A good long while."

People always wanted to know how long house guests were staying, Keefe thought, did they not? So how long?

A series of possible replies passed through his head.

I'm here until the trial.

I'm here as long as you'll have me.

Perhaps he should say: We'll try it and see how it works. That was the kind of thing lovers seemed to be saying to each other these days, many of them even as they married. This to Keefe was amazing. It was like telling someone – like telling Sharon – that you loved her just so much and no more. It was like acknowledging that her feelings for you were just as thin. If it could be quantified it could not be love. Love to Keefe was without dimensions. It was an extreme emotion and could not exist otherwise.

"I don't know how long. I thought we could figure that out together."

Sharon thought this a lovely answer. She was very pleased with him. "When's the trial?"

They had walked out of the terminal and were crossing the street into the parking lot.

"Several months, I think."

"We'll have all that time together," Sharon said. "That's wonderful."

He glanced at her, unwilling to take this remark at face value. Had he detected a hesitation in her voice, a suggestion of doubt? His psyche had become so fragile that he was likely to see slights where none was intended, and he warned himself about this even as he lifted his suitcases into the back of Sharon's car. For God's sake be careful, he thought.

It was a red Italian sports car and he was sitting very low. He was a passenger, neither more nor less, which had been his role for weeks and would remain so until the trial concluded, if not beyond.

"Now I'm going to take you to a lovely restaurant for

dinner," Sharon said brightly. He looked so thin. She had decided that the first thing to do was feed him. Having pulled up at the exit booth she handed across a five-dollar bill. Keefe had got his wallet out; he had been holding bills out to her, but she pretended not to notice. He didn't have any money anymore and she had plenty. She hoped he wasn't going to get all manly and virile and sticky on the subject of money. She took her change, and the barrier in front of the car lifted, but before driving off she leaned over and kissed him on the cheek. "We'll have a lovely dinner, and then we'll go home."

"Well, I like the going home part." Keefe would have preferred to go there directly. He did not want to share her with the patrons of a restaurant. The width of a table could be an immeasurable distance. Besides which, he had eaten dinner on the plane, bad food, but he had eaten it. He was not hungry for dinner, and given the mood he was in he wondered if he was even hungry for her. He was disoriented. He had imagined that by coming here he could leave his problems behind, some of them at least. Already he had begun to see that this wasn't true. They were not only still with him, but, like a backpack he had sought to get out from under, they now seemed to sit crookedly on his shoulders, making them heavier.

It was a restaurant with starched linen and heavy silver on all the tables. It was an expensive place but one Sharon liked and therefore frequented, and she was known there. Still, she never expected the maître d'hôtel to bow them to their table with such ceremony. She was embarrassed. Keefe might think she was trying to impress him with how successful she was, so she turned and gave him an elaborate wink over her shoulder, meaning: You're in Hollywood now, this doesn't mean anything. But she couldn't tell if he understood the gesture or not, and for a while worried about it.

"Tell me what you've been doing with yourself," he said to her, and his voice sounded cooler than she would have hoped. He was studying his menu and she could not see his face. Lately they had telephoned each other less and less frequently.

"It's so marvellous that you're here," she told him,

reaching across the tablecloth to take his hand. Soon he seemed a good deal more cheerful. She felt more confident too, and it became possible to imagine that although the stature of both had changed recently, their feelings for each other had perhaps not.

A candle burned between them inside a red globe. This was part of the illusion to which Keefe had temporarily succumbed. Life could be rosy after all, and things would work out. They held hands across the tablecloth as the restaurant gradually emptied out. Finally the bill was presented, and Keefe reached for it.

But Sharon took it. "Tonight I'm treating you, right?"

"No. I'll pay."

But she held on to the bill. "We're in my town now. You can pay in your town."

And that, Keefe thought, is how we're going to handle the delicate question of money between us. She would want to eat in restaurants a lot. She worked all day and would not want to stay home at night. But he could not afford many restaurants.

She drove them to the apartment she had taken in Studio City near the Burbank studio, which was where her soap opera was produced. Her key turned in the lock, she preceded him inside, the lights coming on ahead of them as they advanced.

Keefe looked around him in confusion. Obviously she was proud of her apartment and wanted him to admire it. But the furniture was all strange to him, as were the pictures on the walls, the rugs on the floor. These were her possessions and he had never seen any of them before. It was the first he realised how long she had had a life of her own that he was not part of. Everything about the place put him off, even the fact that she knew where the light switches were and he didn't. If he was ignorant about something as intimate as her apartment, how much else of her intimate life was he ignorant about? It caused an immediate lesion of confidence, one he had not been prepared for.

"Would you like something before we go to bed?" She had noticed the uncertainty in his manner. She wanted to relax him, to make him feel as completely at home in her house as possible. "A cup of tea, maybe?"

It was three o'clock in the morning New York time. He was exhausted, and afraid.

"I don't think so, no." A spotlight shone on a big abstract painting over the sofa. He stood between his two heavy suitcases looking at it.

"The bedroom is this way," she said. She switched off the lamps and led him down a short hall.

"You can have that closet there."

He looked into it, then threw one suitcase onto the bed and opened it. A few weeks ago, he realised, there would have been no unpacking of suitcases. They would have fallen on each other in the doorway, and in the morning awakened to a room strewn with clothing. Which was perhaps the normal, natural way to do it. Only this situation as it existed now was not normal, not natural – at least not for him. He undid catches, lifted things out, began hanging garments in the closet. Sharon stood smiling, watching him. When the first suitcase was finished he emptied the other.

"You are the most meticulous guy. Are you finished now? Are you ready?" She came up and put her arms around him.

They fell sideways, kissing, down on to the bed, which was queen-size, with a satin coverlet. This was what she felt Keefe needed. It was her solution to the tension between them, and to her relief it worked. Or so she thought.

Keefe had never seen her bed before either. The other beds they had shared, in his New York flat or hers, had been normal double beds. A queen-size bed to him was new, and so strange that he wondered who else had shared it with her prior to his arrival. Who else was perhaps waiting for him to vacate it so that he could return? Such questions became so insistent that he almost asked her. He stopped himself just in time.

Only when they were under the covers clinging to each other in the dark was he able to chase such thoughts away; but he needed more than to be hugged and held close. In some obscure way he needed her to know exactly what his needs might be, the way a mother would know, without

389

being told. He had been alone so long, and he didn't want to be alone any longer. She might have liked being told this but he was afraid to do so. There wasn't enough intimacy between them, or so he believed, even as they began the most intimate ritual that man and woman ever perform together. If he showed weakness he might lose her.

Sharon, meanwhile, was offering him not comfort but eroticism. She was being sexually playful, and this was a deliberate decision. In her experience it was what men loved. Certainly Keefe always had. She was doing her best for him. With her touches, her kisses, her coyly crossed legs she was teasing him. She was giggling and squirming. He couldn't hold her down. She would not let him get to the place he wanted to be.

The place he wanted to be was, in a manner of speaking, home. The teasing eventually stopped. It became not a game any more, and for Keefe there was a gratifying sexual release at the end of it – for her too, he hoped – but not the other kind of release which was the one he craved. He was not home yet, and perhaps would never be.

She lay quietly in his arms and admitted the truth to herself. I've got an invalid on my hands. And then: I hope I'm woman enough to handle this.

Keefe lay awake telling himself: You want too much. You want what she can't give you. Be careful or you'll ruin it, both for her and for yourself.

She took him to work with her the next day, introducing him to the other actors and to some of the technicians. She did not introduce him as her husband, since he was not, nor as her live-in boyfriend either. There were rules for this. Close friends would soon get the idea. Others did not need to know.

She was dressed like any young female business executive. She wore a severe grey skirt, belted in at the waist and fitting snugly about her hips. Above that she wore a silk blouse and a blue blazer. She wore medium high-heeled shoes. Together with the other actors she walked through those scenes that would be shot later in the day and her open blazer flowed this way and that. Her secretary stood close

390

by, and during moments when she was not needed on the set the two of them conferred. Sharon opened and read a number of letters and memos. She gave directions which the secretary, an older woman than herself, took down on a steno pad.

Watching Sharon work, Keefe was struck by her competence. Few young women had moved as far as fast in their careers as Sharon had. He stood off to one side as the scenes were blocked out. He was, relatively speaking, at ease. The others had all been cordial when introduced to him. No one had seemed to recognise his name. No one had stared.

She came over. "I have to go to my office now and make some phone calls. Will you be all right here for a while?"

"Sure."

It occurred to her that he had little choice, for he had no car. This was Los Angeles where there was almost no public transport of any kind. She considered offering him her car but decided against it. Better to behave normally in every way.

Keefe was thinking about a car too. He would have to get one. How he was to pay for it he did not know.

"After that, we'll go to lunch," Sharon said brightly.

Keefe sat down in a chair, opened the *Los Angeles Times*, and began to study the want ads. From time to time he looked up and watched the other actors moving through additional scenes. An hour passed and Sharon did not return. He read the used car ads. He could not buy just any old wreck. He could not risk causing Sharon embarrassment. This was a town, he had always been told, in which people judged you by the car you drove. You are your car.

Finally, smiling, she reappeared. "Let's go to lunch."

As they went out the door into the parking lot, DeForest was on the way in. Sharon introduced Keefe to the director. "Phil is staying with me for the next few weeks," she explained.

"I think we met in New York," DeForest said.

Keefe knew very well they had met in New York, but his mind was stuck on Sharon's introduction.

Phil is staying with me for the next few weeks.

Why had she said that? It was against the rules. His mind reverted to her queen-size bed. A single young woman – Sharon for instance – had no need for a queen-size bed to sleep in alone.

Phil is staying with me for the next few weeks.

A message to DeForest, then. What else could it be? And if she needed to give him such a message, what did this mean?

"See you later," Sharon told DeForest, and she led Keefe toward her car. He got into it. It was not very big. It was very expensive. He was thinking about DeForest. He wanted to say to her: You were warning him off back there; why was that? But his attention was divided. He was also thinking about her car. He would have to get a car like it if he was to regain – or to hold – any stature in her eyes.

When he tried to pay for lunch, Sharon stopped him. Here we go again, she thought. "All I have to do is sign it," she lied. "The studio pays."

"I don't believe you."

"It's true." In any case, she had already signed it.

Keefe was unsure what was true any more.

Soon they were back on the set. This time the other actors did stare at him. Or else they talked behind their hands and stared at everything else.

DeForest, Keefe thought. He's told everybody they have a felon in their midst, and they're staring because they want to see what one looks like.

He stared right back at them. He tried to stare them down. When this didn't work he stared at his shoes. The afternoon seemed endless.

Finally it was over and Sharon came for him. "We can go now."

He had watched the filming of the entire episode, and could not have told anyone what he had seen. In the car driving home Sharon said to him brightly: "Tomorrow's Saturday. What do you want to do?"

Everything she said, however innocent, threw him further off-balance. He wanted to say: I want to spend the entire day in bed with you. It was what he might have said some months ago, batting his eyes at her and giving a grin. It would have made both of them laugh, then reach out to touch each other.

But it was not a remark he could bring off now.

The freeway was very wide, and absolutely jammed with cars. Sharon at the wheel said: "One thing I'd like to do tomorrow, I'd like to go look at a house I might buy."

She felt Keefe glance over at her. She was determined to behave absolutely normally. It was the only therapy she imagined might help him.

"The real estate agent called this morning. She had several houses she'd like to show me."

If she was buying a house, then she meant to settle down here, and this too he had not known. Each discovery seemed proof to him that their former intimacy no longer existed.

And they did spend most of the next day looking at houses. The real estate agent, an elderly woman, was heavily made-up and expensively dressed. She drove a Mercedes. The houses were all in the Hollywood Hills section. They drove back and forth along Mulholland Drive plunging down side streets into canyons to look at houses. They were all small, and the property on which they sat was small. They were hardly more than bungalows set on slabs on the sides of mountains, but their prices to Keefe were astronomical.

One house particularly caught Sharon's eye. It was inhabited by an aging actor and his fourth wife, a girl of about twenty. On the back porch was a hot tub, and the actor and his wife were both in it, both apparently naked. They called out that the agent should not worry about them, just show the house. The downstairs was all one room – kitchen, dining room, and living room together – and the walls were decorated mostly with posters from the actor's movies. Upstairs there was a single vast bedroom with a bathroom alcove containing a vast sunken tub.

Keefe drew the real estate agent aside. "What's the asking price?"

When the woman told him, it made him want to whistle. Could Sharon afford this?

He realised he had no idea how much money she made now.

Sharon was studying the house, not Keefe: "I think I ought to have a house, don't you?" she said finally. "If I'm going to live here. Everybody here has houses."

Keefe said nothing.

"I'm hoping you'll want to live here too."

Again Keefe did not respond.

"I mean, I can always sell it again if I want to leave."

Houses to Keefe were permanent. If you were transient, you took an apartment. Sharon had felt this way too in the past, he believed; but she was changing – had changed – in ways beyond his imagining.

"Well, we'll think about it," she told the real estate agent. Keefe was grateful for the "we", and annoyed by it at the same time.

"You have to like it too," Sharon told him.

"Can you afford such a house?" They were back in her Italian car driving home.

"Sure." Sharon gave a laugh. "I think I can, anyway." Her new contract called for what to her seemed a stupendous sum, so much she was afraid to volunteer what it was. It might sound like she was bragging. It might upset him, even estrange him. It might diminish him in his own eyes. If he asked she would tell him. Otherwise not.

Keefe wondered why he hesitated to speak the only question on his mind. How much did she earn? But suppose she refused to tell him? He would have no choice but to leave her, go some place else; and he had no place else to go.

Thirty-One

On Monday morning in the kitchen Sharon put her breakfast cup in the sink: "Do you want to come to the studio with me?"

She was fully dressed, whereas Keefe was still in bathrobe and slippers. All relationships were precarious but this one had become as brittle as an icicle, and she had no idea what to do about it.

"No."

"You can't just sit around the apartment all day." This rebuke came out stronger than she intended. "I mean, you can, you're welcome to. But it won't be very nice for you."

"I'll rent a car and look for a job." DeForest had been, and perhaps still was, her boyfriend; he was sure of it. DeForest would move back in as soon as he moved out.

At the mention of a job, Sharon brightened, and she hesitated only briefly over his need for a car. "You don't have to rent a car. Use mine."

"You need yours."

"Just drive me to the studio. You can have my car the rest of the day."

"How do you get to lunch?"

"I'll go with somebody."

Yes, Keefe thought, and I know who. "I'll rent a car."

Sharon laughed at him. "You are so silly. Can't I lend you my car if I want to?" She came over and put her arms around the neck of his bathrobe. Dressed for work she looked very nice. She knew it and he knew it.

He held her tight, a weakness he could not at that moment resist.

"Throw some clothes on and drive me to the studio."

He did so, and kept the car all day, but found himself unable to go job-hunting. Instead he only drove aimlessly around, a metaphor for his life at this point: no destination. The trial was three months off, or six, perhaps longer. No date had been set. California, it seemed was no better than New York. He could not live off his father there. He could not live off Sharon here. Even to borrow Sharon's car was costly in self-respect.

He had to support himself, sure. But how? Who did he ask for a job, and how much did he reveal? Job-hunting was a job like any other, and too much for him today.

After that he would drive Sharon to work each morning, and then just drive. He liked to put the convertible top down and drive out past Santa Monica and get out and watch the surfers. His face began to be tanned like theirs, and even a little windburned. If Sharon noticed she did not say so. Nor did she nag him about the job he still didn't have. If she noticed the extra mileage on her car, she never mentioned that either.

The surfers were wearing wetsuits this late in the year. The waves were steep with suds blowing off them and the water looked cold. The boys all seemed to be big, long-haired blondes. Even the girls were usually big and blonde. The wetsuits came in all colours, and flattened bosoms down, and it was hard to tell the sex of anyone from any distance at all. It was not a sport Keefe had ever tried, but there was a fascination to watching it, a lack of reality.

Lunch was usually a hamburger and a beer at a lunch counter off the beach. Sometimes the surfers would come in, having leaned their boards against the wall outside, and he would listen to their mindless conversations.

Sometimes he walked on the beach. The sand was golden brown and hard-packed. He could walk a long way. One day one of the girls came up out of the plunging surf toward him, her board under her arm, her hair hanging like ropes down her back. Beads of water ran off her face and tight yellow wetsuit, and when she shook her head she flung water around like a dog.

"The ocean's great," she said to him. "You should try it."

He stood with her. "You look like you can hardly breathe in that thing."

She unzipped the wetsuit down to her naval.

"It's like wearing a very tight bra," she said, and laughed. Her face was very tanned, and the skin down her middle quite white. The wet suit had puffed up considerably across her chest and no longer covered much.

She said: "Are you the guy with the little red sportscar?"

"Well," said Keefe.

"So where would you like to take me in it?"

She was pretty, and one of the few dark-haired girl surfers he had seen. "Where would you like to go?"

"Anywhere."

How much did her invitation imply? Perhaps nothing. Yet he read a quality in her eyes, or thought he did. She was very appealing.

"Okay. Get in."

He was excited. He was in the mood for a new person, a new girl, a new life.

"I'll go anywhere at all," the girl said, "just so long as there's a beach and good surf." She laughed again.

She left the car full of sand and Keefe full of guilt. Before picking up Sharon he was obliged to stop at a car wash and get out and vacuum the floor, the seats. Getting rid of the guilt would take considerably longer, and he decided not to go back to that beach.

He bought a map showing the locations of the homes of the stars, and began to hunt them down. It took up hours, and then days. He would drive up to an address indicated on the map, turn the ignition off and muse, or perhaps brood. He wasn't interested in the current stars who were fighting their battles for survival in the same world he inhabited himself; he was interested in the old ones, the older the better. He was aware of what big, big stars those big stars had been. Perhaps he was trying to come to terms intellectually with a world of which he had never been a part. More likely he merely sought escape – the same kind of escape that the supposed glamour of the old stars, and of course their films, had once offered – escape from real life, escape from the haunted present.

He drifted in the direction of Forest Lawn, where he left

the car in the parking lot and strolled among the tombstones. There was a map for this tour too. He had still not looked for work. Some of the tombs of the stars were as grandiose as their former houses. In death they were still stars.

Finally, most afternoons, he shopped for dinner. By the time he drove the red car into the studio parking lot its small Italian trunk held a bag of groceries. He was never late, though sometimes she was. He might wait an hour in the slot with Sharon's name on it before she came out, but he never complained, merely gave her a kiss on the cheek and turned the key in the ignition.

"Any luck today?" Sharon always asked hopefully.

"Nothing yet." She always frowned, or bit on her lower lip, and after that stared out the windshield and did not look at him for a while. He always waited for her to nag, but she never did, and on his good days he was grateful. On his bad days he only resented her the more.

He had begun to resent her for a lot of things. As soon as they got home he would prepare dinner. In New York they had split this chore, but now that she was in effect keeping him, the preparation of dinner to him had become an obligation. He had a limited repertoire. She had a limited repertoire too, but it was different from his, and in New York their dinner for two had rarely been boring.

"I think it should be my turn once in a while," Sharon told him gently.

"You're working, I'm not."

"You'll get something soon."

To him this sounded like an accusation.

She stood with him at the stove, her arm around his waist.

"I was talking to them at the studio publicity department today." She hesitated. "I don't know if you'd be interested, but they're looking for somebody."

"How much did you tell them about me?"

"Nothing. Just that you were a New York newspaperman who had recently moved out here."

"That's all? I don't believe you."

"I told them you were writing a book, and were looking for something to tide you over."

"I'm not a PR man." Keefe threw the spatula down on the stove. "Is that what you think of me? You think I want to be somebody's flack?"

"Well, you have to do something."

"I pay for the groceries, don't I? I keep your stupid little car gassed up, don't I?"

"That wasn't what I meant."

"Stop bawling, for Chrissake."

Instantly contrite, Keefe put his arms around her. "I'm sorry. I didn't mean to shout at you, Sharon. It's just that –"

But she was stiff in his arms, and in a moment shrugged him off, wiped her eyes, and went into the other room where she remained until the plates were on the table.

They ate dinner in silence. The next day Keefe dug into his dwindling resources and bought her a pair of gold earrings, and they were friends and lovers again for a while.

The evenings were often long. They went out to an occasional movie. Otherwise they stayed home. They invited no one in. After dinner most nights she sat watching TV, and he went into the bedroom to read. She was studying the actors, she said. The shows were all stupid, he informed her in reply. She was trying to learn from watching others, she said.

It annoyed him. He sat against the headboard but it was difficult to concentrate because of the noise coming through the closed door. Ultimately he always came out, and usually he reinstituted the same argument, or another.

"Nobody acts on TV. There are no rehearsals and there are no second takes."

"No, I think you're wrong," she said mildly.

"Television is people speaking lines in close-ups. The lines are all dumb and the actors don't know a thing about acting."

Her small apartment felt to him like just another prison. He was aware that he had never met her friends. She must have some. She hadn't just sat in this apartment every night before he came. Probably she had had lots of dates with men. With good-looking, empty-headed actors, as well as with that director. That's what the queen-size bed was all about.

"I better start paying you rent," he told her.

She was sitting on the sofa, eyes glued to the screen, but this remark seemed to make her stiffen.

Without looking up she said: "What for?"

"That's what people do. They pay rent on where they live."

She looked at him.

"Well, I have to pay the rent whether you're here or not." She had turned back to the screen, but he doubted she saw it.

"Let's get this settled." .

"I don't want you to pay me rent."

"Then I'll go back to New York."

"You take up one closet, and one side of the bed. I wouldn't know how much to charge you."

"Say half."

"We'll talk about it tomorrow. I really want to watch this show."

He walked over and turned off the set.

"I don't know what to do," Sharon said. "I've tried everything. I just don't know what to do."

Keefe did not know what these words meant, and in fact scarcely heard them.

"From now on I pay half the rent."

"All right," Sharon said in a small voice. She got up, walked to the set and switched it back on. She stood three feet away from it, staring at it.

If he had a job, it would be normal for him to pay half the rent. If he paid rent they would be equals again, or nearly so.

"Who do I make the cheque out to?"

"I don't know."

"To the rental agent, or to you?"

"Whichever," said Sharon. "I really want to watch this show."

When the weekend came they drove down to the border and crossed into Mexico. It was absolutely forbidden for Keefe to do this. Legally speaking it amounted to fleeing the jurisdiction of the court. If caught he would be returned to

New York in custody and most likely be remanded to jail to await trial.

It was a hot sunny day, but it must have rained heavily here less than an hour ago. He drove into the border town and there were enormous potholes even in the main street. They were filled with water, and the street itself seemed to be steaming. He saw the poverty right away.

And odours: diesel fuel, unfamiliar cooking, uncollected garbage, a sewerage system that had been improperly designed and irregularly maintained. Keefe was back in the Third World, which was where he had made his reputation. There was a sense of recognition. He suddenly felt confident again.

There were many shops, and some specialised in Mexican handicrafts. The prices seemed ridiculously low. He bought Sharon a hand-embroidered linen tablecloth, a pair of shoes and finally a silver bracelet inset with two large flat obsidian stones incised with Aztec designs. To his satisfaction she became giggly with pleasure. Later they went to a bullfight. It was incredibly hot and dusty inside the arena, but scary and exciting as well. They selected a local restaurant for dinner and ordered a selection of dishes studded with hot peppers and other spices that set the mouth aflame. They ate hot corn tortillas and drank cold Mexican beer.

All day Keefe had used his Spanish. It was a pleasure as always to communicate with people in a language not his own, and it greatly impressed Sharon, or at least so she pretended.

"I knew you spoke French. I didn't know you spoke Spanish."

At the beginning of his career he had made a tremendous effort to learn the languages of the countries to which he was assigned. To him a foreign correspondent without languages – and there were many – was one-dimensional. He had paid for the lessons himself, and had kept on with them for months.

"English, French, Spanish. What else do you speak?"

"I used to know a good deal of Italian."

"Four languages," Sharon enthused. "Wow."

She was perhaps overdoing it a bit. Nonetheless, he was very pleased.

When they came out of the restaurant it was nearly night. Keefe was comfortable here and did not want to go back, so they drove further south along the Baja Peninsula as the last of a lurid sunset disappeared from the Pacific sky. They drove on in the dark with the top closed now but the hot wind still blowing in the windows. They found a good-sized town, and then a hotel room with a modern shower stall in which they showered together, washing off the day's sweat and dust.

In the morning they ate a Mexican breakfast at a café: hot tortillas and huevos rancheros and bitter Mexican coffee.

They started out to explore the streets and alleys of the town but when they came to the church they went in. It was Sunday morning and a mass was in progress. The church, which was rococo in design, was old and decaying and smelled musty. Everything was gilded, but the gilt was mostly peeling. There were many bleeding saints, and the lighting was principally by candles.

They drove further south through more dusty villages, and in one of them came upon a street market. Indian women with long black braids sat on mats in front of pyramids of fruits and vegetables. Lunchtime found them at a restaurant under some trees behind the beach. They sat outdoors on camp chairs and ate lobsters cooked over an open fire, and the inevitable tortillas, and drank more cold Mexican beer.

But the weekend ended, and they went home.

The next day Keefe began to look for work. His first call was to the Executive Editor of the *Los Angeles Times*, a man named Gardner whom he used to meet occasionally when they covered the same stories in Europe.

They met at three P.M. that same day. Gardner came around his desk to shake hands. When they had made small talk for a few minutes, Gardner remarked: "You're in a bit of trouble back in New York, I gather. Are you working?"

"I'd like to work for you if there's an opening." It was

402

easier to say than Keefe might have expected, and he was grateful for the chance to say it so soon. He would have to go back to New York for the trial, he explained, if indeed there was a trial. His indictment was a political thing. He would certainly be acquitted. He was asking for a job as a reporter or correspondent. He meant to make California his home from now on. Of course he would not be averse to a foreign assignment, should one arise.

It was a long and not entirely comfortable speech.

"Let me call my City Editor in here," Gardner said. He got up from behind his desk, and was gone a few minutes. When he came back he was trailed not only by the City Editor, whom he introduced to Keefe, but also by a reporter carrying a steno pad who took a chair against the wall, opened the pad and prepared to take notes.

"So why don't you tell us about this case you're involved in?" Gardner said cordially.

The shocked Keefe looked from one face to the other.

"I didn't come in here to be interviewed for tomorrow morning's newspaper," he said quickly. Realising how harsh this sounded, he said: "I mean –"

It was the Seymour Becker experience all over again. Why should I be surprised, Keefe asked himself. All men have one liver, two kidneys, one spleen. They have two eyes, two ears and one brain. Their bodies work identically and their minds, given similar training, work identically. All editors respond to exactly the same stimulus, in almost exactly the same way. The stimulus here was himself. No editor could be expected to react to him any differently from any other.

And unfortunately no editor could be expected to present Keefe to the world as a curiosity in tomorrow morning's newspaper and then hire him as a professionally anonymous reporter for that same paper on the day following.

He stood up: "If a job opens up that you would like to offer me," he said, "I'd be pleased to come in again. I'll leave my address and phone number with your secretary on the way out. Thanks so much for your time and courtesy."

Courtesy? He attempted to stride out of the office, to escape with as much dignity as he could.

Having made a start he was able to continue. He made more calls. An FM radio station was looking for a news director. He was interviewed by a man named Wohlgemuth, and was hired at once. Wohlgemuth did not seem to recognise his name. Los Angeles, after all, was a long way from New York. Keefe told him he had recently moved out to the coast and the radio business was the one he wanted to get into.

"Your future here is great," said Wohlgemuth.

Pertinent information had been withheld on both sides. Keefe had failed to mention his impending trial; whereas Wohlgemuth's station was about to be sold and his employees dismissed.

"In a few years" time," said Wohlgemuth, "you'll be general manager and a rich man."

On the strength of Wohlgemuth's commitment Keefe arranged to lease a car the following day. It would only be a Chevrolet, but would disgrace neither himself nor Sharon, and he would not have to worry about getting rid of it when he went back for trial.

"Guess what?" he said to Sharon in the studio parking lot. She had just come out of the building.

"You got a job," she said.

Keefe was mystified. "How did you know?"

"I can see it on your face." She began to laugh. "Congratulations."

He saw that there were tears in her eyes.

When they reached the apartment Sharon went straight to the refrigerator and pulled out a bottle of champagne. "I knew you'd get a job," she said. "I've been saving this. Let's celebrate."

The celebration lasted all through dinner and even, once they had gone to bed, far into the night.

The station was on top of a bare brown hill behind Hollywood. The hill was almost high enough to be called a mountain, and the station on its peak thrust its great spiky finger at the sky. The road climbed up there in a series of sharp switchbacks, and from Keefe's office window he could see other bare brown mountains, and a collection of canyons and arroyos, but no houses. Inside the building the station's programming, which was mostly rock music, blared from speakers in every room. It took getting used to.

It was Keefe's job to prepare the newscasts every hour on the hour from eight in the morning to six in the evening – a long day. Mostly this amounted to no more than tearing paragraphs off the UPI teleprinter and stapling them together in the order in which they were to be presented. It took him about five minutes per hour. He did not read the news broadcasts on the air himself. The disc jockeys did that.

Sharon's principal reaction was relief: the worst was over.

They began to go out in the evenings to restaurants, to the movies, and on one occasion to a concert. Once she arranged dinner in a restaurant with another couple – the first of her friends that she thought Keefe was ready to meet. The other couple was amusing, dinner turned out to be quite pleasant, and when it was over Sharon allowed Keefe to pay their share of the bill. However, the sum involved that night represented for Keefe a week's pay, and once they got home she tried to reimburse him for their entire share. She pressed money into his hands.

He refused it.

"Well, take my half of our share at least."

He still refused.

About once a week from his office Keefe telephoned Bloom, and also Sergeant Rainey. No, he had not located the cleaning woman yet, Rainey said. He had put feelers out. The trouble was he no longer had an office in which to make and receive calls, nor did he have much time. He had put in for time-off, but he was new in the precinct and so far had been refused.

Bloom always seemed confident. There were more legal motions he could try, he reported. He was running through them one after another, and he expected to come up with a winner any day: not to worry. In the meantime, a trial date had been set. Keefe reached for his desk calendar, and drew an "X" across what would perhaps turn out to be the darkest day of his life.

He still slept badly, and on nights when he had talked to Bloom and Rainey he hardly slept at all. In his dreams he would see himself standing as the jury gave its verdict, which was always guilty. Sometimes he would come awake with a start with the word *Guilty!* pealing in his ears like a bell. He would turn to Sharon sleeping peacefully beside him and want to shake her awake, make her understand the awful thing that had happened to him, was still happening to him. Instead he would lie there and when the daylight began to come up outside the window he would get out of bed and go make the coffee.

He learned of the sale of his radio station from the *Los Angeles Times*, which was delivered outside Sharon's door every morning. He brought it inside and dropped it on the kitchen table where it fell open to the correct headlines as if by magic. *Immediate lay-offs threatened. Newest employees to go first.*

He set Sharon's coffee down on the bedside table beside her head. He also dropped the paper, folded, on top of the covers. Although she opened the paper and read several stories, she never noticed the one about the sale.

He went to the station at the regular hour and waited for Wohlgemuth to appear. Instead a letter came. A smiling secretary came in and handed it to him. Obviously she did not know what it was. She had a handful of them that she was distributing.

It was a form letter signed by the incoming general manager. It was addressed: Dear Staff Member.

Keefe would receive one week's severance pay, which would come in the mail. He was to leave the premises immediately.

At the bottom of the page Wohlgemuth had scrawled: "Dear Phil, sorry about this."

Wohlgemuth did not appear. Every ten minutes Keefe went down to his office. Finally he found Wohlgemuth's secretary on the phone to him.

"He wanted to know if all those who had been let go were out of the building," she said when she had hung up.

Keefe said nothing.

"I told him yes," the woman said, eyeing him.

So he packed his things, took them out to his Chevrolet, and drove down the mountain. He drove straight to Sharon's studio. He had some idea of taking her to lunch, before sharing with her this new calamity.

However, the guard at the door said she had already gone out. "A number of them went out together."

"Mr DeForest with her?"

"Sure was."

That night at the dinner table Sharon said: "You're awfully silent."

He kept his feelings inside him until they were getting ready for bed, a masterpiece of self-control, he believed. He was amazed at his ability to do it. "I drove by the studio this noon," he began, and he folded his trousers and hung them in the closet. "I was going to ask you to lunch."

"We broke early today," Sharon said. She was sitting on the bed taking off her shoes. "I must have already gone out. I'm sorry I missed you."

"Did you go alone?"

She glanced up sharply. "What's the matter?"

"Did you go alone?"

She took the time to stand up, take her dress off over her head, and shake out her hair. "Yes, alone," she said. "I couldn't find anybody to go with today." She walked to her closet and hung up the dress. "I guess because it was so early."

She was unable to meet his eyes. She's not a very good liar, he thought. Not brazen enough, probably. He said: "No you didn't."

"Didn't what?"

"Go alone."

Her face got dark. She got very angry very fast. "Have you been spying on me?"

"And another question I've been wanting to ask you for a long time –"

"How long have you been spying on me? What gives you the right?"

"I want to know what you had in mind when you bought this queen-size bed. And who else has been in it."

"I don't have to tell you that."

"I'm leaving."

He began to get dressed again, and then to pack. In silence she watched him. "I bought it so that when you came out here we could sleep in it together," she said.

"I'll bet."

"Why shouldn't I have a queen-size bed if I feel like it?"

"Who else has slept in it besides me?"

"What's the matter? What happened today? What went wrong?"

"Nothing went wrong." His suitcases were on the bed and he was throwing things into them.

Her anger had appeared quickly, and as quickly vanished. She came toward him and embraced him from behind. She bound his arms to his sides and laid her face on his back. She said: "Let's get married."

"Married?" He turned on her. "I might have to go to jail."

"I don't care. Let's get married."

"So you can drive up to the penitentiary every weekend to visit me? There are wives who do that. They have special buses for them. Most of them are Mafia wives, or else the wives of black stick-up men. I don't think you'd feel quite at home on the bus. Or do you just want to show the world how loyal you are? You have a thing about loyalty, is that it?"

"What's the matter? What's happened?"

"And I hate it when you cry like that."

"Tell me what's happened."

"I lost my job."

The phone rang. They stood staring at each other, while the phone rang and rang, and neither spoke. The phone was on the bedside table and closer to Keefe than to Sharon. Finally he snatched it up.

It was Dolan, one of the night duty sergeants in his former office.

"I hate to be the one to tell you this, Commissioner, but something's happened to Sergeant Rainey."

408

"What?" said Keefe. "What?"

Sharon, listening to Keefe's end of the conversation, saw tears in his eyes, and when he had hung up he began to shake as if with chills.

"It's not your fault," said Sharon, holding him. "Whatever it is, it's not your fault."

Thirty-Two

THE FORTY-FIRST PRECINCT IN THE BRONX, SERGEANT Rainey's precinct, was known to cops, and to a lesser extent to the city, as Fort Apache. The station house was the fort, and all around it were the savages. The savages lived like savages and were as dangerous, cops said. Rainey had worked Harlem, but this was worse. The typical tenement was four storeys high, twenty-five feet wide. They stood ten to a block – those that still functioned. A good many had been torched and gutted by fire, either before the inhabitants moved out or after – no other precinct could match the Four-One in incidence of arson. There were many rubble-strewn lots where buildings had been demolished. They looked like gaps in teeth. Most served the community as garbage dumps. Atop such lots were deposited wrecked appliances, rusted-out pieces of cars, sodden rugs, broken-down furniture, and sometimes items to quicken the interest of any cop, such as corpses.

Not all the torched buildings were subsequently torn down. Some were only condemned but left standing, which meant that in some of them people continued to live, usually without heat and sometimes without water.

Some years the Four-One led the city in murders – it was the one precinct where death by knife was as frequent as death by gun. Death by drug overdose was common too. Alleys and stairwells served as shooting galleries for junkies and hopheads. Their suppliers stood in groups on street corners, but did business in vestibules whose splintered doorjams no longer held locks, or in the backs of candy stores, or in doubleparked Cadillacs adorned with two thousand dollars' worth of exterior chrome accessories. Meanwhile, burglars in sneakers prowled the staircases and rooftops in search of a score; they swung their loot out of windows on to fire escapes, and then down.

The population of the precinct was about 200,000, nearly all of them Blacks or Hispanics, and they were policed by about 250 cops who worked out of a station house that was little better than a tenement itself. Both sides lived in what amounted to a war zone. The cops wore bulletproof vests, sometimes carried two guns each, and worried about staying alive. Many of them had been there too long and were as burned-out as the buildings around them.

There were nine sector cars, except on nights when one or more were in the shop for repairs, which was often. The cars were old too, were driven around the clock by heavy-footed cops, and so broke down regularly – which, however, was not usually a problem for Rainey. If the car assigned to him stopped running he merely commandeered another, because he was the sergeant. In theory a patrol sergeant's job was only to supervise; it was the cops in the sector cars who answered the emergency calls, and in most other precincts the sergeant merely drove up and down streets for eight hours, checking that the cops standing fixers were on their posts and awake, that the cars were in their sectors and answering their calls. He initialled their memo books each time he stopped and he sometimes responded to a request for assistance from a sector team that had run into something puzzling. Otherwise there was little enough for him to do.

But the Four-One was not such a precinct. The calls were so numerous that Rainey's vehicle operated most times as an extra sector car. There wasn't time to supervise anyone. He was back on patrol, exactly what he had never wanted, back to dealing with poverty, with violence, with victims and perpetrators who seemed to be trying to outdo each other in their numb acceptance of whatever life did to them.

Earlier in his career Rainey had sometimes been able to achieve a corresponding degree of numbness himself, but not now. It was age, probably, or perhaps despair.

During his second week the precinct received an infusion of rookies straight from the Police Academy. They came to work early and stood around the station house trying to learn how to twirl their sticks. They wanted to look like veteran cops. Their sticks dangled from the thongs and when they attempted to twirl them their thighs and shins took a beating. Their legs after a day or two were black and blue. They were all in their early twenties, fresh-faced and eager. They were there to clean up the world, and they hoped for the chance to become a hero. Achieving these two goals would make them real cops, they believed. Rainey listened to such nonsense and said nothing. Their two goals were stupid and impossible. The day they would become real cops was the day they admitted that the world could not be cleaned up, that there was no such thing as a hero.

Each night Rainey selected one of them as his driver, and took him out on patrol. It was a boy named Mannion who was with him when the maternity call came over the radio.

Mannion was twenty-two. Skinny kid. Long stalk of a neck. Six feet two, but he couldn't have weighed more than 135 pounds. It was impossible for Rainey to believe that he himself had ever been as young as this young man.

"Report of a maternity," Central said, and gave the address. "Which car responding? K."

"Let's take that call, Sarge," Mannion begged, as they moved down the dark street.

"That location is in Sector Boy," said Rainey.

"We're only two blocks away."

Mannion's enthusiasm made Rainey sullen. He said: "Let Sector Boy handle it."

But Sector Boy did not respond.

"Is there a car available? K," Central demanded.

Evidently there was not, for no answer came back.

"It would have been my first time delivering a baby," said Mannion wistfully.

The kid probably thought of birth as a religious

411

experience. His wistfulness further irritated Rainey. Doctors in white would be looking over his shoulder and coaching him while he did everything right. He imagined the process antiseptic, wondrous, the miracle of a new life.

"Is the sergeant's car available? K," came Central's bored voice.

Rainey plucked the microphone off the dash. "Four-One sergeant's car, Central. We"ll take that call. K."

"Great," cried Mannion, stomping down on the pedal. Rainey was pitched backward into the headrest.

They doubleparked beside two derelict cars. Both were burnt to scorched and rusting shells. From the look of them, they had occupied the same kerb space for weeks, if not months. In the Four-One the Department of Sanitation was under no pressure to tow such hulks away.

Rainey and Mannion went up four flights of stairs. Even from below they could hear the screams of the mother-to-be. Doors were open on the hallways, and staring faces watched them go by. Black faces. Puerto Rican faces. Faces without expression.

The strangled screams were coming very close together. At the top floor apartment they knocked. There was no response. Rainey shouldered into the door, and it flew open.

The light was on and so was an enormous TV set. On a sprung sofa lay a man snoring. He was either drunk or stoned, for his face was beaded with sweat. They went down the hallway, for the screams were coming from the back of the apartment. The hallway was dark. Rainey's shoulder hurt. His flashlight found the switches along the wall and he tried each one, but no lights came on. Mannion, who was trailing, shone his flashlight into rooms, illuminating broken pieces of furniture, and walls that seemed to him to quiver.

"Sarge, the walls are moving in there."

For a moment two beams played on the same wall. "Cockroaches," said Rainey. "You're lucky you're not walking on them. It makes a noise like the building is on fire."

At the end of the hall was the bathroom. The mother-to-be was in the tub.

"See if the lights work," said Rainey. He played his flashlight all around. The bathtub stood on four claws. The girl lay in the tub with her legs hanging over the sides, a ghetto version of operating room stirrups. She was about sixteen and screaming for her mother. Rainey pointed his beam into the tub. The baby's head was half out. Beneath it the tub was streaked with rust. Blood and slime leaked toward the drain.

"The lights don't work," said Mannion at the sink. There was a choke in his voice and Rainey spun around, afraid the boy was going to be sick.

"If you're going to puke, do it in there." His flashlight beam moved from Mannion's face to the toilet.

But a glance into the toilet made Mannion gag again, and very nearly Rainey. It had no seat, and the bowl was filled close to the top with used paper mixed with faeces.

"There's no water, either," Mannion said.

"Go downstairs and wait for the ambulance."

"I'm all right Sarge."

"You can go down if you want."

"I'm fine, Sarge."

"All right," said Rainey. "Do you want to do it, or shall I do it?"

"I'll do it, Sarge."

The boy stood over the tub staring at what was happening between the girl's legs.

"What are you waiting for?" shouted Rainey. "Haven't you ever peeked between a girl's legs before? Haven't you ever seen a cunt before?"

"Sure, Sarge, but –"

Rainey held both flashlights. "Well, this is what it's for," said Rainey. He was outraged. "I hate to start your sex education so young. It's not for fun and games, like you always thought. It's for this."

One flashlight pointed at Mannion's chest, the other between the girl's legs. "Bend down over the tub, you stupid prick." He was shouting at him. "Ease the head out. Didn't they teach you anything at the Academy?"

Then a little later, a little more gently: "That's right. You're doing fine. Watch out for the afterbirth. If it gets on

413

your uniform, it's ruined. The cleaners can't get it out. I don't know why."

The girl looked unconscious. The baby, still attached to the cord, lay between her legs on the floor of the tub. It was a girl and it was squalling.

"Sarge, we don't have anything to cut the cord."

"Forget the cord. Let the doctors cut it." He was still angry. "That's what they get paid for. You're not a doctor. You cut the cord in a place like this and the infection will probably kill both of them."

Supposedly an ambulance was on the way. Rainey, who had been listening for the siren, still did not hear it. "Look in one of the other rooms," he said. "See if you can find something to wrap the baby in until the ambulance gets here. Find something for the girl too."

At the sink he tried the taps himself. He played his flashlight on the girl and on her bloody, slimy baby. How can people live without water? he asked himself. The baby's cry had dropped to a whimper. I can do nothing more to help either of you, Rainey thought. He had assisted at still another ghetto tragedy – a tragedy for the mother, and for the baby as well.

Mannion came back with a thin blanket which Rainey tore down the middle. He wrapped the baby in one half, and with the other covered the mother.

The rookie had found a dish towel too, Rainey saw. He had his flashlight tucked under his arm and was trying to wipe his hands.

From the street came the noise of the approaching siren. Rainey went out onto the landing. When he heard the heavy footsteps climbing the stairs he called out: "Up here."

The paramedics came into the bathroom and set up a light on a stand. Mannion watched them. Rainey saw that he was elated and smiling.

"Did you fill out the aided card yet?" Rainey demanded.

"Not yet, Sarge, but –"

"Fill it out."

Rainey went out into the front room and shook the sleeping man. The man sat bolt upright, then fell back on the sofa again. He lay there blinking.

"Congratulations," Rainey said. "You've just become a father. What's your name?"

The man went on blinking.

"What's your name?"

The man seemed unable to answer.

"All right," Rainey snarled, "what's her name?" Turning to Mannion he said: "Make him give you a name. Write it down on the aided card. See that you fill out that aided card properly. It's the most important job you'll do here tonight, because if you don't get it right and some Boss finds out, you'll get in trouble."

He went down to the street and stood on the sidewalk. The traffic moved under the El tracks, dodging the stanchions, dodging also his own double parked radiocar. He stood under the light of a lamp post, the only one for blocks, he noted, that had not been stoned to death by vandals.

Mannion came down. He looked very pleased. "I got the aided card all filled out, Sarge."

"Next time you want to deliver a baby, go by yourself."

They went out between bumpers to the car.

"My hands are all sticky, Sarge. Can we go back to the station house for a minute?"

"You're a cop on patrol in the Four-One. That means you can wash your hands on your own time. The city doesn't care about your sticky hands, or about your cleaning bills either."

Rainey got into the car and slammed the door. "Turn right at the corner." The new street was very dark. Most of the streetlights were out here too.

"Will she be all right?" said Mannion.

"How the hell should I know if she'll be all right?"

Rainey eyeballed the vestibules and the alleys they passed.

"I guess you've delivered a lot of babies, Sarge."

"Twenty-three years I've been in this job. You got any other stupid questions?"

A little later, breaking the silence inside the car, Rainey said: "You did a pretty good job with that baby."

Behind the wheel the boy beamed. "Thanks, Sarge."

Cops dealt only with abnormal people in abnormal situations, Rainey thought. But cops themselves were not abnormal at all. Not starting out they weren't. They were like Mannion. And afterwards?

Each morning Rainey would shave the unfamiliar face in his mirror. His beard was gone, and his three-piece suits were zipped up inside the plastic bag in his closet. At work each night he took to asking for Mannion as his driver. The boy was his lineal descendant, and he realised this. Mannion and a few other cops scattered throughout the department were all he would leave behind him that he could be proud of.

But the desk lieutenant, as soon as he saw the pattern, began to assign Mannion elsewhere.

"You don't have no privileges around here, Rainey," the desk lieutenant said. His name was Ritkowski. He was Rainey's age, only one rank higher and he was often in command at night. He sat behind his desk in the big muster room and glared at Rainey.

"It's not a question of privilege," said Rainey carefully. "I need someone who can drive down these dark streets without sideswiping the parked cars."

"Just watch yourself, Rainey. You're here on sufferance."

"Sufferance? Where'd you get that word from? Do you even know what it means? Tell me what it means."

"I don't have to give no explanations to you, Rainey. Just remember who you're talking to."

"The year you made lieutenant it must have been a very easy exam."

"You're about this far, Rainey – about this far – from a complaint for insubordination and disrespect to a superior officer. Now get out of my sight."

It was later that same night that Mannion, having just made his first arrest, approached Ritkowski's desk for advice on how to process his prisoner. The prisoner stood beside him, a hulking black man so drunk he could barely remain upright.

"What's this, what's this?" Ritkowski demanded, looking up. "Why isn't this prisoner handcuffed?"

The scene had attracted the attention of every cop in the muster room: the clerical man, the mop man, the cop at the switchboard, one or two others. Ritkowski was impressing them all with his authority. He had not yet noticed Rainey, who had just come in from patrol and who moved closer.

Mannion tried to explain that the prisoner was too drunk. Handcuffed, he couldn't walk at all, and he was too big for Mannion to carry over his shoulder. But Mannion realised that he might be in trouble. He began to squirm.

Still seated behind his desk, Ritkowksi started on a lecture about crime in the streets, about the level of violence in the Four-One. His voice kept rising. "They're animals out there," he shouted. "You bring this baboon in here without handcuffs and he might assault a police officer. Because of this gorilla the entire station house might go up in flames."

At first Rainey was amused. What did Ritkowski know about crime? He was a desk lieutenant. He would avoid the street for every day of his police career if he could. But the kid did not know this, Rainey saw, and he listened to the lecture attentively, and as he did so he seemed to become more and more worried about his "arrest".

Finally Ritkowski, having run out of air, demanded: "So what's the charge on this hump?"

"It's, er, well, Lieutenant –"

"Speak up. I don't have all night."

"Drunk and disorderly," Mannion admitted.

"*What?*" Ritkowski said incredulously. "Do you know where you are? This is the Four-One, for Chrissake. We arrest these germs for torching buildings, for carving each other up. I got homicides. I got stick-ups. I got rape. There's whole blocks burning down out there, and you got the balls to bring me a drunk and disorderly."

Mannion began trying to defend himself. The drunk had been wandering into stores along Prospect Avenue, knocking over stacks of merchandise, falling into display cases. The outraged merchants had virtually forced him to arrest the drunk, and –

The desk lieutenant interrupted with another tirade. "You

rookies are like virgins with hot pants. Can't wait to lose your cherry."

Rainey stepped forward. "I'll help the kid process the prisoner, Lieutenant."

"You stay out of this, Rainey," the lieutenant shouted. He turned back to Mannion.

"What's the matter?" he shouted at him. "You couldn't wait to make a real arrest? You bring me the arrest of the year and –"

The drunk meanwhile had for some time been concentrating on his fly. He was trying to unzip it. He was totally intent on his overfilled bladder, and at last he managed to bring forth his hose, and a smile came onto his face, and his eyes closed, and he sent a stream arching out into the kneehole of the lieutenant's desk. Rainey saw this happening and said nothing. The rookie cop, standing at attention, saw it late and his eyes opened up like plates.

"Excuse me, Lieutenant," he said, but the desk officer shouted him down.

"Don't you interrupt me when I'm talking to you. You know what you can do with this bullshit arrest –"

Suddenly Ritkowski jumped to his feet. "What's this?" he demanded. "What's this?" He stared with bewilderment at his drenched pants. He watched amber liquid running down into his shoes.

Mannion looked terrified. The drunk was shaking himself dry. This too took all his concentration. His eyes were still glazed, but the smile on his face was of beatific proportions.

From various corners of the muster room came bursts of smothered laughter, but when Ritkowski glared at each man in turn there was silence. Mannion, meanwhile, stood in front of the desk as if frozen.

Ritkowski began hollering for the mop man – on each tour there was one cop assigned to housekeeping duties – and then at Mannion. "I want that prisoner locked up," he shouted to the rookie cop. "Take him upstairs and process him. Throw the book at him. Take him across town and arraign him." Ritkowski was aware of the incipient hilarity in the room. The room rocked with it, though there was no sound. He glared at Mannion, but saw no hilarity there. He could sense it everywhere else, however, guffaws that could not be restrained much longer, faces that had gone red with the effort. His rage fixed on Rainey. "What's so funny, Rainey?"

But Rainey had not even smiled. "I don't see anything funny at all," he said. "This is serious. This is far more serious than you seem to realise, Lieutenant."

"What? What are you telling me?"

"I hate to say this, Lieutenant, but we're not just dealing with a man whose shoes are full of piss. Your life may be in danger."

"What?"

The prisoner, eyes closed, weaved unsteadily as if asleep on his feet. Rainey pointed to him. "How do we know that man doesn't have herpes, Lieutenant? How do we know he doesn't have AIDS?"

"Herpes? AIDS?"

"People think those diseases come from sexual contact only," Rainey said. "It's not true. Piss is a thousand times more virulent than sperm. I don't know how you're going to explain it to your wife."

Ritkowski stared at him.

"Do you have any lesions between your toes, Lieutenant? A little athlete's foot, maybe? That's how it gets into the blood stream. I hate to say this, but you may be doomed. The rest of us may be attending an inspector's funeral before long."

Ritkowski's hands were balled into fists.

"It's definitely a line-of-duty death," said Rainey. "You don't have to worry about that. Your name will be enshrined on the department's roll of honour, just as if you had got shot intervening a stick-up."

Ritkowski stared fixedly at Rainey.

"I'd get those shoes and socks off immediately, if I were you. The shoes are gone. You'll have to get rid of them. The socks too of course. And probably the uniform trousers."

The mop man had come forward with a bucket of

ammonia. He started to mop under the desk. "Never mind the puddle," Rainey told him. "That puddle will be absorbed into the floor. Save the ammonia for the lieutenant's feet." He turned again to Ritkowski. "With prompt treatment it may not be too late. If you soak your feet in ammonia for about twenty minutes, Lieutenant, it might save your life."

The desk lieutenant's jaws worked, but no sound came out. Suddenly he spun around and stormed off into the captain's office, which was empty at that hour, and slammed the door.

Rainey turned to the mop man. "He's going to want that bucket of ammonia. You better take it into him. If he refuses, you better just dump it into his shoes."

The other cops in the muster room could restrain themselves no longer. They laughed uproariously, hysterically, and even Rainey smiled, though not Mannion, who said: "What do I do now, Sarge?"

"Take your prisoner upstairs," Rainey told the rookie cop. "Lock him in the cage and let him sleep it off."

"And when he wakes up?"

"When he wakes up, you might consider cutting him loose. Don't let the lieutenant see you do it."

The captain's door opened, and the mop man came out followed by a stream of shouted obscenities.

"I guess I had best be getting back on patrol," Rainey commented and he went out into the night.

After missing several meetings, Rainey on a swing night put on one of his three-piece business suits and returned to F. Hyman Effrat's acting class. Everyone seemed glad to see him. The young people crowded around the distinguished-looking older man and remarked about his missing beard. Some of the girls stroked his smooth cheek, though not Flora, who only watched warily from a distance. Jason the fag stood beside her and would not meet his eyes. When asked, Rainey chose not to reveal that he was now back in uniform, back on patrol, but blamed his recent absences on a troublesome virus.

"Life's most embarrassing moment," F. Hyman said when

420

everyone had taken chairs facing the chalkline that represented the stage. "Everybody's got one. Tonight we're going to act them out one by one in pantomime, followed by a class critique."

For more than an hour Rainey sat and watched his fellow students perform. His attention was far from total. He kept stealing glances at Flora who, however, stole none back. Her hair was longer and she had combed it out. It almost reached her shoulders.

Rainey pondered his problem. What had gone wrong? How could he break through her resistance, make her see both his stature as a man, and the depth of his feeling for her?

His favourite line from *Othello* was never far out of his head: "She loved me for the dangers I had passed, and I loved her that she did pity them." Make Flora see the "dangers", then. It had worked once and would again.

The others, meanwhile, strutted and postured in front of his front-row seat. Jason's charade involved laundry blowing off a clothesline in the wind. Every item on the line wrapped itself around him, apparently. The laundry was mostly ladies' undergarments; the wind flung a bra into his face. It blindfolded him. Fellow students laughed. Rainey was not even watching. Instead he watched Flora, who was laughing hard. She applauded Jason all the way back to his seat.

Rainey was already on his feet. It was not his turn but he took it. He stepped past the beaming Jason and ended the fag's applause by holding a hand up for silence.

"Up to now you've been watching trivia," he said truculently. "What I am about to show you is either high comedy or low tragedy. Or perhaps both."

He had their total attention. "My playlet is in several scenes. In the first there are three characters: two cops in a radio car and the radio itself, which announces a violent crime in progress."

He turned his back on his audience to compose his thoughts, his face, his hands. The unfamiliar three-piece suit seemed to fit him awkwardly, and he gave a jerk to his shoulders.

Then he turned around and began to mime.

A bitterly cold night, cold even inside the police car. Both cops are half-frozen. One steers. The other swills repeatedly from a bottle.

A bottle for a blindfold, Rainey thought, not a goddam bra off a clothesline. He mimed the emergency radio call – both cops harken to it. He mimed the short wild ride through the streets. He mimed first the one cop whirling the steering wheel, then the drunken one who, having got the cork into his bottle, works his gun out of its holster. The audience was as silent as Rainey, and he was aware of this. It was always the case, he told himself. People may not like us, but when a cop recounts his experiences mouths drop open and the attention is total.

But eye contact with Flora had been lost. Her face was down. Didn't she realize that this performance was for her alone?

The police car skids to a halt. As the drunken cop attempts to jump out of the car he trips, and the gun goes off in his hand.

The shot is silent. The hand of Rainey the actor jumped upwards from the recoil. The drunken cop stares down at the gun aghast. It is live, has performed this act all by itself.

Flora, look at me, Rainey almost shouted.

The attention of both cops is divided. The suspect is running away, but they ignore him. The drunken cop's bullet has found an unexpected target, an innocent bystander, and they bend over and begin to give assistance.

Please, Flora, Rainey cried silently.

The two cops lift the victim into the back seat and race to the hospital. The driver stares grimly over the whirling wheel. The other cop, no longer drunk pitches his flask out into the frozen night. He stares into the backseat at his victim. He pleads with his partner to believe him. He wasn't drunk, he only slipped on the ice.

Rainey on stage had moved forward as far as the chalkline. Sometimes Flora looked at him. Mostly her gaze was fixed on her lap. He stood directly in front of her chair. The subject here was nakedness. He stood naked in her presence as he had stood naked in the presence of no one ever before.

The two cops deposit the victim on the emergency room table. The sheet is drawn up over the face. Superior officers arrive. The formerly drunken cop gives his story, but is not believed. The live heads are all shaking negatively.

The final scene: a courtroom. The formerly drunken cop is sworn in, tells his story. He slipped on the ice. The second cop is sworn in, backs him up. Outside the grand jury room both wait. Presently a third man comes out, stares for a moment into their anxious faces, then shakes both their hands. It is over.

All this Rainey pantomimed, and no one coughed or shifted position or looked away – with the exception of Flora of course – and now the applause started. It was real applause. Rainey had even Flora's full attention, though she wasn't applauding, and so felt a great bodily catharsis. He felt he had won – he had purged the past and so won the present.

At the chalkline he stood head down feeling the wash of applause, and, when he looked up, F. Hyman was grinning broadly and applauding as he advanced.

But Flora's face was the only one that interested Rainey. It bore an expression that could best be called quizzical.

Everyone else also crowded forward. "You should take that act into a real theatre," F. Hyman said. "That's a true story, right?

"I made it up," said Rainey.

"The guy driving the car was you, right?"

Rainey said nothing.

"No," said Flora, "he was the other guy, the one that did the shooting."

Rainey looked at her.

"Am I right?" said Flora.

Rainey decided not to answer.

"I just want to know one thing," said Flora. "Why aren't you in jail?"

"Flora –" said Rainey.

About twenty minutes later came what F. Hyman always

called intermission – as if his studio were a theatre, as if what went on there was a play. Rainey called it recess, like at school, and he came up behind Flora and in a low voice spoke into her ear: "Why don't we go out and get a hamburger later, Flora?"

She said: "I thought I told you I was with Jason."

"There's something I want to say to you."

"It's all been said. Go get the hamburger by yourself."

She was not making it easy for him. But then girls – the desirable ones – seldom did. Or so he remembered from his adolescence. "What I just did up there on stage," he said carefully, "that was for you."

"It was for you yourself," she said bluntly. "You wanted to get it off your chest."

"I meant it to mean something to you."

"Look, I don't want a hamburger, and I don't want to go out with you."

"Afterwards, we could maybe go to a nightclub, or a disco. You have to eat. And you know you like discos."

"You don't make it easy for yourself, do you? When this class ends, Jason and I are going back to his apartment, and when we get there we're going to go to bed and screw."

"You shouldn't talk that way, Flora." Rainey hesitated, then said, "if you're tied up tonight, maybe we could see each other tomorrow?"

"How can I make myself any clearer?" said Flora. "Let me try. With Jason I don't have to wait an hour for him to get it up again. Is that clear enough?"

When the class resumed and it was Flora's turn on stage. She did a pantomime of a girl in bed with her boyfriend who is disturbed by the ringing of the front door bell. Both lovers get up and go to the door. On the doorstep is a gift-wrapped package from another admirer, and the girl and her boyfriend both step out onto the stoop looking for whoever put it there. At last they spot the admirer some distance off running away, and they point at him, both of them laughing derisively.

Rainey got up from his chair, walked across the floor to the door and left the studio.

424

Thirty-Three

TWO MEN FROM INTERNAL AFFAIRS CAME. ONE WAS a Detective Flood. Rainey did not catch the other's name. They stood just inside the station house door and flashed their shields in cupped palms. Rainey had been called in from patrol to meet them. They did not offer to shake hands.

The precinct commander's office was empty at this hour. "Come into my office," said Rainey.

He sat down behind the captain's desk and put his feet up. "What can I do for you?"

"Maybe you didn't hear me too good," said Detective Flood. "Internal Affairs. IAD."

"I'm terrified, said Rainey. "You going to tell me what you want?"

Before they could reply the door was flung back to reveal Lieutenant Ritkowksi. "Who do you think you are, Rainey? This office is the captain's office."

"We need about five minutes of privacy here, Lieutenant."

"You're not allowed in here. Out."

Although the two detectives had begun to move toward the door, Rainey remained as he was. "Lieutenant," he said, his voice full of concern, "you don't look at all well to me."

"Never mind my health, Rainey."

"Can you trust your own doctor, that's what I ask. Sometimes they cut open a cancer patient and sew him right up again, and then tell him they got it all."

"You can't scare me, Rainey."

"Something terrible happened to our lieutenant the other night," Rainey explained to the two detectives. They had stopped halfway to the door. "We thought we had lost him for sure."

The desk lieutenant began to sputter.

"Why don't you tell these two gentlemen the story, Lieutenant? I'm sure they'd like to hear it."

"You'll get yours, Rainey," Ritkowski shouted. "You'll work midnight tours all winter, if I have anything to say about it." He slammed the door, making the whole room shake.

The two detectives looked at each other mystified.

"Now, gentlemen," Rainey said blandly, "where were we?"

"There's been a complaint against you," said Detective Flood after a moment. He was carrying a manilla envelope, from which he withdrew some papers. "Unauthorised use of a department vehicle." He gave the date, the time of day, the location and the names of the two police officers who were the complainants. His tone was both threatening and accusatory.

"Is that the only charge?" said Rainey.

"You want more, you got more," said Flood. "Not present in assigned area. Improperly allowing a civilian to ride in a department vehicle, namely an unidentified female."

"An unidentified female?"

"This is a general order 15 inquiry," Flood said. "Don't get smartass with us, pal."

"General order 15," said Rainey. "Imagine that."

"You want me to put down failure to co-operate with an official inquiry? It's immaterial to me. Just another charge, that's all."

"Another charge," said Rainey. "How many does that make?"

The second detective had not yet said a word. Both men stared hard at Rainey.

"You're right," Rainey said. "This is serious. What do you want to know?"

"The identity of the unidentified female."

The second detective said: "And what the unidentified female was doing in a department car."

"Are you gentlemen sure you have the right unidentified female?"

"Failure to co-operate," said the second detective. "Put it down, Paul."

Flood said: "Let me explain to you about a general order 15 inquiry."

"An unidentified female in a department vehicle?" said Rainey. "Do I look like a man who would do such a terrible thing? Would either of you gentlemen do such a thing? You would? I don't believe it."

He stood up and began ushering the two IAD men out into the muster room.

"You deny each and every one of these allegations?" said Detective Flood stolidly.

"The incident doesn't ring a bell with me. I was hoping it might ring a bell, so as to help you two gentlemen out. Because you look like real nice guys. But it just doesn't ring one."

"They'll nail your ass," said the second detective.

"That's what I'm afraid of," said Rainey. "They might take away my cushy detail. They might go so far as to assign me to patrol duty in the Four-One."

The two detectives went out the station house door. Rainey followed behind them. His radio car was parked out front. He stood with his hand on the roof and watched them drive away. Not until their tail-lights went around the corner did the smile disappear from his face. He knew this was not the end of it. Normally the offence of which he was accused was worth at worst the loss of fifteen days" pay, but unfortunately it and he were part of the Keefe case. He doubted the department advocate or the press would be satisfied with fifteen days. They were going to put him on trial in the department trial room. They would move to dismiss him for cause, with loss of pension. They wouldn't admit it was because he – that car – was part of the Keefe case. They would blame it on his past record: this officer does not deserve to remain a member of the department.

He was still staring down the street, though the IAD car was out of sight now. He got into the blue and white vehicle assigned to him and went back on patrol.

An hour later he was standing in a dim hallway, his gun in his holster, trying to take a machete away from the berserk Puerto Rican who was swinging it.

427

His partner was another of the rookies, not Mannion. This one's name was Billy DeVito. He was short, with black curly hair. He laughed a lot, and had an endless supply of jokes. He too looked up to Sergeant Rainey as a role model.

It was by then about eleven P.M. Central had sent them to an address on Hoe Street – man with a knife. They loosened their guns in their holsters as they climbed the stairs. Both had flashlights and DeVito had a nightstick. Sergeants did not carry nightsticks.

The third floor hallway was narrow. On one side was the wall, on the other the railing protecting the stairwell. It was in this cramped hallway that they found the man with the knife. It was a machete. He was slashing the air with it and muttering curses in Spanish. From the landing they could have shot him in perfect safety. To disarm him they would have to get much closer and could approach him only one at a time.

DeVito had whipped his gun out faster than Rainey could believe. He was faster than Wild Bill Hickock or Wyatt Earp. In addition to learning to swing his stick, the rookie must have been practising his quick draw too.

"Drop that knife," DeVito shouted. He was crouched in the combat position. "Drop it or I'll blow your head off."

There were many rites of passage for a rookie cop, Rainey realised: first arrest, first shooting –

"No," he shouted at DeVito, and he grabbed the gun hand and pushed it toward the floor. He also jumped in front of him, leaving the boy staring incredulously at him.

The only light came from a dim bulb that hung down on a cord. The Puerto Rican stood almost immediately under it. His next swipe or the one after was likely to lop the bulb off or sever the cord, confronting Rainey with total darkness and an even worse set of problems.

"You must be crazier than he is," Rainey shouted at DeVito over his shoulder. "Shoot him and you'll get indicted. Cops aren't allowed to shoot any more. Didn't you see what happened to Commissioner Keefe?"

Slicing open the air, the Puerto Rican lunged at them. But the lunge was not full-fledged. He jerked just as fast to a stop and resumed posturing.

"Look out, Sarge," DeVito had cried, jumping backwards.

Rainey, however, had stood his ground. Every cop in the city, himself included, was afraid to fire his piece, Rainey thought. Perhaps this was what the politicians wanted. Certainly it was what the liberal press wanted. "Give me your nightstick," he muttered. "I'll show you how we deal with babies like this."

The duel was joined: club against sword. As he advanced into the arc of the machete, Rainey was still muttering, releasing not words but weeks of accumulated venom. He stepped toward the Puerto Rican not in the attitude of a fencer but with the nightstick hanging beside his leg. This was contrary to all he had been taught, and potentially suicidal.

Doors were open on the hall. Rainey was aware of it. Eyes showed, noses. No one came to his assistance, nor did he expect anyone to.

The madman was swinging the machete about like a scimitar. Once again he lunged, this time taking a roundhouse slice in the direction of Rainey's tie. Rainey heard the sharp swoosh. He felt the blade go by under his chin. Then he moved.

For an instant the advantage lay with Rainey. The machete was past him, and the Puerto Rican's weight had followed it. He was off-balance. Rainey might have thrust the nightstick into the man's midsection, or brought it down on his head – his choice was somewhat large. But either blow might fail to immobilise him, and the machete might cut his arm off coming back, or the roof of his skull.

No, the club's proper target was neither midsection nor head but rather the hand that gripped the machete, and Rainey swung the nightstick at it as hard as he could. Smash the knuckles, he thought. Make the assailant drop the blade, and crack him on the cruller after. What could be more satisfying?

The theory was perfect. However, Rainey's blow missed its target almost completely. It caught the machete halfway out along the blade and slid off, and now it was Rainey who was off-balance and defenceless.

"I cut your balls off, man," the Puerto Rican shouted, and

the machete swept across Rainey's middle like a scythe. He thought it had missed him, for he felt nothing. At the end of the stroke the machete seemed to hang there a second in the air. The light was so bad that the man himself was in silhouette, but the upraised blade caught reflections like a mirror and Rainey clubbed at it with all his might. He missed the knife but caught the arm in mid-bicep, and then he brought a second blow down across the forearm.

The Puerto Rican wailed at the first blow and again at the second, and the machete struck the floor and bounced. It made a shivering metallic sound almost like cymbals. Rainey kicked at it. He swept it off the landing with the side of his foot and sent it clattering down the staircase. The Puerto Rican was dancing frantically about, his right arm limp, his left hand clutching it in support.

The doors on the hall opened wider – all danger apparently was over. Rainey glimpsed whole faces now, and it was a sight that enraged him. These were the people he had just risked his life for, had risked his life for repeatedly during most of twenty-three years, and all of them had always hid behind doors, had let him take the risk alone, had not only never offered assistance at the time, had never even thanked him afterwards. Quite the opposite: more often than not they had come into the station house the next day to lodge civilian complaints against him. He hated them all. "A dollar a look," he shouted at them. He had his gun out. He aimed it at the several doorways. Every door slammed instantly.

DeVito was grappling with him, pinning Rainey's gun arm to his side. "Easy, Sarge. Easy, Sarge."

Jamming his gun back, Rainey ordered DeVito to go down the stairs and recover the machete. He was breathing hard. "We bring this hump in without it, they'll claim we assaulted an unarmed civilian."

DeVito's head disappeared down the stairwell, which gave Rainey a moment to examine himself. He was having trouble catching his breath. His left trouser leg was sliced open at testicle level. He spread the cloth with his fingers and under it there was blood. His thigh was sliced open. The machete had missed his manhood by an inch. He swallowed hard to think of it. He would need stitches. Blood was running down his leg. His eyes focused on the man who had done this to him, the would-be cop killer.

"Pull a knife on a cop, will you?" said Rainey.

"My arm," the Puerto Rican moaned, "my arm."

The emotions that dominated Rainey were rage, residual terror and, perhaps most of all, desperation.

"You break my arm," moaned the Puerto Rican.

"Only one of them so far," cried Rainey, grabbing the man by the other. His hands encircled the thin bony wrist, the fleshless elbow, and he ran him forward to the banister crying: "Let's try for two, shall we?" From over his head he brought the prisoner's arm down on top of the railing. It was the equivalent of a man snapping a stick across his knee, though the noise it made was louder.

The Puerto Rican screamed.

DeVito was on his way up the staircase carrying the evidence, and he brandished it. "Got it, Sarge," he said. His face then lost all its colour. "Jesus Christ, Sarge," he said, "Jesus Christ."

They brought the prisoner back to the station house. He was weeping with pain and they booked him for attempted murder of a police officer. DeVito took the arrest, his first, while Rainey went to the hospital to have his wound dressed. The other rookies crowded around DeVito and congratulated him and were envious. "Me and the Sarge, we had to subdue him," DeVito said soberly. Perhaps no further questions would be raised.

Rainey by then was in the emergency room at Bronx Lebanon. His wound was dressed and some stitches taken. He went back to the station house and changed to civilian clothes and signed out. In the last few days he had taken to wearing one of his business suits to and from work, and an hour later he stood with one foot on the rail in a bar on the Upper Westside, near F. Hyman Effrat's acting class. In front of him was a double Manhattan with two cherries. He sucked on each cherry for a long time. He liked Manhattans for their sweetness, and because they erased each night's tour from his brain. He liked talking to barmen. He certainly could not talk to the rookies who drove the sergeant's car.

"The other night I assisted at the birth of a baby," he said, and took a sip of his drink.

"A baby," the barman said. "I never seen that."

He had thin hair and a red nose. Otherwise he was like Mannion. To him the whole idea was romantic.

"Yeah," said Rainey into his glass. Good barmen were the ones who listened but asked no questions.

Rainey withheld some of the gorier details, but on the whole he described the birth accurately. "So who was that lout asleep or stoned on the sofa?" he asked rhetorically.

"You got me there, pal," the barman said.

"Was it her boy friend? Maybe it was her father."

"Niggers don't think like you and me," the barman said.

"You'd be surprised," said Rainey, and he stared into his Manhattan. "You want people to be humane," he said. "How can people be humane amid so much inhumanity?"

"You got me there, pal."

Rainey drained his glass. "Give me another one of these."

He watched the barman mix it, shaking the shaker close to his ear.

"This will kill you," Rainey said. "This is rich."

He told the story of the drunk pissing into Lieutenant Ritkowski's shoes. He began to laugh, remembering. Peering into his glass he was unaware that the barman had moved off and was speaking to someone else. "You should have been there," Rainey concluded, and he began to giggle, "it was really funny."

When he looked up he noted the location of the barman, and realised he had been talking aloud for a long time to himself. He put money down, and left that bar.

A little later he was in another one talking to another barman, who insisted that a bullet had more penetrating power than an arrow, which was absurd. "Do you think a bullet would go through that wall there?" demanded Rainey.

"Of course," said the barman.

"That's how much you know," said Rainey. "An arrow would, though."

"It would not."

"I'll prove it to you," said Rainey.

He left the bar and took a cab to the apartment of Hennessey, his former radio car partner, who liked to hunt deer with a bow and arrow in the Adirondacks every fall. Rainey still had his key, and he let himself in and took Hennessey's hunting bow and a quiver of arrows down off the wall. He got back into the same cab and was driven back to the same bar.

When he came through the door carrying the bow and quiver, the barman's eyes opened very wide. Those patrons who stood at the bar moved several paces back to give Rainey room.

"What's behind that wall?" demanded Rainey, pointing at the rows of bottles behind the bar. They stood on shelves, and above them was a clock. He was already fitting the notched arrow to the string of his bow.

"The crapper," said the barman. He reacted much too slowly.

"Do you still say an arrow wouldn't go through that wall?" said Rainey.

"Yes, I mean, no," the barman said hurriedly, though not fast enough.

By then Rainey was more sober than he had been. He realised vaguely that he was making a fool of himself and that what he was doing was dangerous. Although he had control of his eyes and his hands, he was nonetheless still in the grip of a vast carelessness. Screw it, he said to himself, and drew the feathers back to his ear and let fly.

The first arrow glanced off the side of a bottle and cleared half the shelf. Almost instantly Rainey fitted another and let fly again. The first bottles hadn't even stopped falling yet.

The second arrow went through the face of the clock and through the wall as well, just as Rainey had promised, for only about eight inches of the rear of the arrow protruded.

"See that?" said Rainey. "Did you see that?"

"He shot out my clock," said the barman. He stood awash in liquor and broken glass. "Guy comes in here and shoots out my clock."

He looked from the clock to Rainey and back again. He

looked down at the wreckage at his feet.

"What did I tell you?" said Rainey triumphantly.

To the barman the event was so incomprehensible that he could speak of nothing but his clock. "Look at my clock," he said. The arrow had nailed the clock to the wall. "How am I supposed to get that thing out of there?"

"I got an idea for you," said Rainey, and he nodded sagaciously. "You could leave it there for a motif and you could change the name of your bar."

"Change the name of my bar?"

"You could call it 'The Wigwam.' Of course that harp in the window would have to go."

"I'm calling the cops," the barman said. "That's who I'm calling." He lifted a receiver from behind the bar.

Rainey turned to the other patrons, all of whom took an immediate half step backwards. "He gets some buffalo robes and hangs them on the walls, right?" said Rainey. "He plants a few tomahawks in the bar, and he calls the place 'The Wigwam'. How's that for an idea?"

"Great idea," said the man nearest him, who was edging toward the door.

"Got any more beauties like that one?" said a second man.

Behind the bar the barman had dialled 911, and now the police operator came on. "There's a guy in my bar with a bow and arrow," the barman shouted into the phone. "This is an emergency. He just shot out my clock."

Laughing silently, Rainey turned and fled into the night.

He walked down one dark sidestreet after another. He was trying to attract a mugger. He dared one to accost him now – just dared him. He wouldn't fire shots at him, he'd fill him full of arrows. A little later he came to the Waldorf Astoria and realised he had been heading toward it all along. He decided to check in. He had chosen the Waldorf because to him it was the symbol of luxury in the city. As he stood in the lobby in his three-piece suit with the quiver of arrows on his back and the bow in his hand and glanced around, he remembered that he had occupied this same exact space in this whirling city and universe twice before, both times when as a young cop he had been part of the detail guarding the President who was in town for something or other and probably boozing it up in a suite upstairs. On those two occasions Rainey had gazed all about him with awe and admiration, but this was not his mood now.

"Any luggage?" inquired the clerk.

"Only this," Rainey said, indicating his bow and quiver.

The clerk pushed a key across and rang for a bellboy. "Are you taking part in a competition of some kind?"

"Yes," Rainey told him. "The object of the competition is to stay alive as long as you can."

"Check-out hour is noon."

"Oh, I expect to check out well before that," said Rainey.

His room was on the thirty-ninth floor, and he stood at the window looking down on the city that had nurtured him, the city he had loved since childhood and which, once he had become a cop, he had tried so hard to understand. He had never wanted to move out onto Long Island. Moving him out to Long Island had been like partially uprooting a tree. All the roots were stretched thin, and the tree could not get the nourishment it both needed and craved.

There were two beds with a telephone table between them. He had deposited the bow and quiver on one of the bedspreads and now he sat down on the other to use the telephone. His first call was to room service. He ordered up two double Manhattans. "Make sure there are two cherries in each one," he said into the receiver.

He went back and stood at the window again. It was a clear night and he was facing south. His view included most of Brooklyn. There were lights as far and as wide as he could see. He could discern the three bridges linking Manhattan with Brooklyn, and the Verrazano Bridge leaping from Brooklyn across to Staten Island. From so far away they looked like toys. But they were not; they were absolutely vital to the life of the city. Without bridges the city will die, he told himself. Without bridges a man will die too – the man even quicker than the city. Maybe it is principally bridges that separate men from animals, he told himself.

Maybe it has nothing to do with the ability to laugh or the awareness of death. Men build bridges, animals don't.

Maybe it was just a question of bridges.

He would do nothing until the drinks came.

For a while he watched the tail-lights winking on and off as cars moved down Park Avenue. They could not move far, however, because a few blocks ahead the avenue was completely blocked by the Pan Am building, fifty-five storeys high and shaped like a tombstone. Cars had to go around it. The tombstone's name in giant letters, its logo, surrounded its top storeys and still blazed with light even at this hour. The man who built that building had had the right idea, Rainey mused. Not for him a marble tombstone in the corner of some suburban cemetery. No, sir. He built his tombstone fifty-five storeys high with a heliport on the roof and planted it in the city in the way of everybody. Probably decided he would make the city remember him whether anybody wanted to or not.

There came a knock on the door. The waiter came in with the two double Manhattans on a tray. Rainey signed the bill and plucked a tip out of his wallet. He had meant to give the waiter a dollar, but in his hand was a twenty. He shrugged, and gave it to him anyway.

When the door had closed he carried one of the glasses over to the window and sipped it for a while, still looking out at the city, remembering incidents of which he had been a part which had taken place in one or another of the streets and towers that he could see. No one knew a city as intimately as a cop did. No one saw a city the way a cop did. No one, he supposed, felt he owned his city as much as a cop did.

He went over and sat down on one of the beds and picked up the telephone. He had a number of calls to make – four calls, it would turn out – and he began to make them.

The first was to his daughter Lisa, who was the favourite of all his children. He was sucking on a cherry as she came on the line.

"Daddy," she said sleepily, "it's you."

"I guess I woke you up."

"What time is it?"

Rainey saw that it was nearly four A.M. "It's late," he conceded, "but –"

"That's all right, Daddy, I'm always there if you need to talk."

Daddy. The most noble word in the language. "I like it when you call me daddy," Rainey said.

"Well," said Lisa, "you haven't always been the perfect father, I guess, but you've been a lovely daddy.

Rainey did not know what to say next. He did not really know why he had called her. Was it just to hear the sound of her voice?

"What's troubling you, Daddy?"

"I had a little problem tonight," Rainey said. "As a matter of fact I had to go to the hospital."

Lisa was immediately alarmed. "What happened?"

She was twenty-three and had just moved into her first apartment, which she was sharing, thankfully, with another girl, not with some long-haired hippie with no interest in her except to bang her. She was in her first semester as a grade school teacher.

"This Puerto Rican cane-cutter was swinging a machete around. I had to take it away from him."

There was a short silence. "So why did you have to go to the hospital?" his daughter asked cautiously.

"He cut me in the leg a little."

"A little?"

"It bled a little. They took some stitches. You know how queasy I am. I didn't look."

"He slashed you?"

"I gave him something to remember me by."

"Daddy, you didn't?"

"No, of course not." He took a long sip from his Manhattan. In six weeks" time Lisa was getting married. He was expected to take her to the church and give her away, and that would be that. The term "to give away" was entirely accurate. In six weeks' time he would lose her forever. She would still call him "daddy", and she wouldn't even complain if he called her up in the middle of the night, provided it

437

didn't happen too often. But she would belong to someone else, not him.

"I thought you were through with patrol forever," Lisa said.

"So did I," said Rainey. Then he added: "They needed me, though. They asked for me personally. I volunteered. They've got me training these recruits up in the Bronx." He smoothed the bedspread with his hand.

"Is it temporary?" the girl inquired. "Do you go back to headquarters again?"

"Of course."

She knows I'm lying, he thought, or at least senses it. She always understood me better than anyone. Better even than her mother.

"So when are you coming home, Daddy?"

"I don't think your mother would be too glad to see me."

"I think you're wrong."

This sounded hopeful. "What has she been saying?"

"She'd be glad to see you, Daddy. I know she would and you know she would. I never understood why you moved out in the first place."

Rainey's gun was digging into his midsection. He drew it out and laid it down beside his drink on the bedside table.

"You didn't answer my question, Daddy. When are you coming home?"

Why does a father feel closer to one of his children than to any of the others? Rainey wondered. Why would he worry in advance over something he was about to do because he knew how much it would hurt that one particular child? The special closeness between himself and Lisa – when had it begun?

He said into the telephone: "Do you remember the night of your birthday party when you were about four or five, Lisa? When I put you to bed, your arms came up around my neck and you said, 'You spoiled me today, Daddy; thank you for having spoiled me.'"

Lisa laughed. "I don't know if I remember it, or if you've told the story so often that I only think I remember it."

438

"You taught yourself to read in kindergarten," said Rainey proudly. "You kept staring at books and working out what the words meant."

"I really wanted to learn to read." She was enjoying the conversation, he thought. These reminiscences pleased her.

"And then one day in the street," Rainey reminded her, "we were walking along hand in hand and we passed a bar and you looked at the window and you spelled out the letters there, B, A, R, and you said to me, 'It spells bar, Daddy, that's what it spells'."

Lisa gave a low, throaty, pleased laugh. But when it ended she said: "When are you coming home, Daddy?"

It was not a question he was prepared to answer, though for several minutes he tried, after which the conversation seemed to run down. When he had hung up on his daughter he carried his drink to the window again and looked out on the lights and shadows of his night-time city. Then, having drained this first glass, he returned to the telephone and dialled his home number.

His wife came on the line sounding extremely worried. Calls at this hour were usually serious. But as soon as she recognized his voice she became merely disgruntled. "Do you realize what time it is?"

"I was just talking to Lisa." He was on the defensive already.

"You're drinking."

"No, I'm not."

"I can hear you."

"I'm sucking on a cherry."

"Out of a cocktail glass, most likely."

"Listen, Nora –"

"I won't speak to you while you're drunk. The only time you call me is when you're drunk. What did I ever do to you?"

So there was no possible bridge left there. "All right," he said, "I'm sorry I woke you. Go back to sleep. Goodnight." He hung up. Picking up the second Manhattan, he returned to the window.

His third call would be to Keefe in California. He was

thinking of it as the next to last he would have to make. One more to go after this one.

Sitting down on the bed, he dialled Keefe's number. By now it was so late that, despite the three-hour time difference, he woke Keefe up too. Where had the time gone? Well, he didn't have time to worry about that now. Check-out time was the time he had to worry about. Check-out time was near.

Despite the lateness Keefe did not complain.

Nor did he demand immediately to know how Rainey was progressing in his supposed search for the cleaning woman, presumably the only subject of consuming interest to him. Rainey noted this and appreciated it.

Instead he was immediately solicitous about Rainey. How was he? Was he fully settled into his precinct yet? How was he getting on in his job?

To Rainey a tremendous feeling of warmth came across the 2,500 miles that separated them. He still had Keefe. Keefe still liked and admired him. There was a bridge there still standing – part of one, anyway. The telephone line across which they spoke was a bridge, and the warmth was a bridge.

But almost immediately Rainey was ashamed. Keefe was counting on him to find that cleaning woman in time for his trial. The trial must be close now, and Rainey hadn't done it, hadn't had enough time, or enough energy, or perhaps only enough hope. He would never find her now. The reason he had called was to confess this one failure among so many others, and to beg Keefe's forgiveness, and he began to do it.

Keefe interrupted him. "I know you gave it your best," he said. "I appreciate the tremendous effort you must have made."

"Thank you, Commissioner, but –" He wanted to try to explain it. He had made preliminary inquiries, sure. He had called on men in the department he had known for years and had asked for help, but no one had been willing to help him. Most of them, it seemed to him, had glanced furtively around and had cut the interview short as if embarrassed by his presence, as if they had put their careers at risk just to talk to him, as if a friendship or at least an acquaintanceship going back many years could not even be acknowledged. In some cases he had tried to call in old debts, but had been refused.

But he found that he wanted Keefe to continue to think of him as well-liked and influential within the department, and so he said only: "I just haven't been able to find her." He lifted his glass from the bedside table where it stood beside his gun, and took a long swallow of his Manhattan. "I don't know where to look for her next, Commissioner."

Again Keefe cut his confession short. "That's Fort Apache where you are," he said. "Is it as bad as they say?"

Rainey was grateful for the question, for it meant that his confession need not be continued.

"Some days it's even worse," he said. Then he added hurriedly: "But I'm enjoying it a lot." He put enthusiasm into his voice. His tongue felt a bit thick, and so he enunciated carefully. "I'm putting my experience to good use there. They have me training a bunch of rookies. I'm really enjoying myself."

"I'm awfully glad about that," said Keefe, and to Rainey it sounded as if he meant it. "I've been a little worried about you."

"Worried about me?" But the idea delighted Rainey. "Why would you worry about me?"

"No reason," Keefe said.

This conversation was revealing too much about their feelings for each other, or else too little, and both were somewhat embarrassed.

"It's just that, well, I was afraid you might be unhappy up there, and it would be my fault."

"Don't you worry about a thing, Commissioner. I'm having the time of my life in fact. I wouldn't want to go back to headquarters if they asked me."

But what about the plans Rainey had made, the dreams he had allowed himself? Never going out on patrol again was the least of them. With Keefe as his rabbi it might have been possible in a year or so to resign from the uniformed force and get a civilian job with the department. This would have given him more authority and especially more prestige than a sergeant's stripes. He might have gone on working in headquarters at this higher level. Or he might have switched to some other city department. There were several with police functions where his background and experience might have been seen as valuable. He had imagined himself living down his past. Before long his past would be forgotten.

But no man could live down his past, Rainey realised. A man's past was always there, like a tangle of barbed wire, and he stood in it, and when he moved all the barbed wire moved with him. The man at the other end of this phone line would find all this out in time. Keefe and I are alike in that respect, Rainey thought. Both of us now have pasts that we'll never live down.

"I wish –" Rainey began. What he wanted to say was: I wish we'd never seen Hot Harry's truck that day. The words had nearly burst forth of their own accord. He had stopped them just in time. You wouldn't be in the mess you're in, he wanted to say, and I wouldn't be in the mess I'm in. But it was no use articulating what might have been. Keefe would think less of him, and what good could it do?

"Has headquarters been bothering you at all?" Keefe asked.

"I don't know what you mean, Commissioner," Rainey said, though he knew very well what he meant.

"Just before I left, Chief Sheridan came to me with a problem he had. I wonder if he spoke to you about it."

"Two guys did come to see me," Rainey admitted. "Tonight as a matter of fact. Something about your car."

"Now I remember," said Keefe, "That's what it was about. My car. I hope they didn't cause you any trouble."

"Two guys from Internal Affairs. I guess I satisfied them all right. They went away. I don't expect to hear from them again."

"I'm glad to hear that," said Keefe. Once more he sounded relieved.

"Nothing for you to worry about, Commissioner."

"Then there was nothing in it?"

442

It was true that he would hear no more from the detectives. He could expect to hear from the department advocate, though. He would be brought to trial in the police department trial room before the deputy commissioner for trials, who would serve as judge and jury, and who would interrogate him under oath about the charges of which he was accused. Contrary to Fifth Amendment guarantees, the department could force him to testify against himself. The Supreme Court had so ruled on the grounds that no man had any absolute right to be a police officer. The department could take any steps it liked regarding its own.

So Rainey in front of the deputy commissioner for trials could lie under oath, and perhaps face a criminal trial for perjury; or he could refuse to answer the deputy commissioner's questions; or he could tell the truth. No matter which of the three options he chose he would be convicted, for the verdict in police disciplinary trials was virtually preordained. Given his past record the sentence almost certainly would be dismissal. They would take away his gun and shield. His pension, too. They would take away twenty-three years of his life, scattering the pieces so completely that he would never be able to put them together again.

"It's not something I'm losing any sleep over, Commissioner," he said into the phone. "And you shouldn't either."

"I'm glad you called," Keefe said. "Don't worry about the cleaning woman. I know you did your best."

If I could testify on his behalf and be believed, Rainey thought, we wouldn't need the cleaning woman. Rainey himself had heard the gunman ask for Keefe and could so testify from the stand. This would clear up the central, essential point, that Keefe had been forced to exchange himself for the hostage. He had had no choice.

But Rainey, given his past record as a cop, would not be believed. He doubted Keefe's lawyer would dare put him on the stand. The prosecutor would cross-examine him not about the night in question but about each and every incident out of his own past. Life had not been easy for him, and there was too much there of which he was not proud. The prosecutor would rub his face in it, destroying his credibility and so any possibility that he might help Keefe.

And so you shot and killed a bag lady, Sergeant. Were you drunk?

And despite your dubious past, Sergeant, the defendant kept you on his staff at headquarters, is that correct?

Would you say, Sergeant, that you owe him a debt?

And a little perjury from the witness stand today, Sergeant, would you say that was small payment, considering the size of your debt to him?

"I wish I could have done better, Commissioner."

"We'll see each other when I come back to New York."

No, Keefe's lawyer would not dare call him to testify, and he would have failed twice, once in not finding the cleaning woman and now a second time in failing to provide credible testimony in court.

"My trial comes up soon. We'll have dinner."

"It will be good to see you again, Commissioner."

"Thanks for calling," said Keefe, and he broke the connection.

Rainey lifted the glass to his mouth. He reclined on the bed with his ankles crossed and his shoes pointing up, and the headboard bit into the back of his three-piece suit. His gun still lay on the bedside table, and he thought about his conversation with Keefe. What had he hoped for? That Keefe would say to him: Good news, Ed, I've been reinstated as Deputy Commissioner, and I've asked for you, and you've been reassigned back to headquarters. Was that the miracle he had hoped for? Rainey allowed himself to imagine it. Starting over. Not only Keefe and himself, but Egan, Kilcoyne and Gold all returned to their original places. John Gaffney not dead.

Rainey gave a shake of his head. Any reconstruction of the past was like trying to put the pieces of bodies back together again after certain car crashes he had cleaned up after.

He uncrossed his legs and patted the bedspread. He reached for his glass and drained it. Then he lifted the phone and made his final call.

As it happened, he woke up Flora's mother.

"Is Flora there? Please put her on. This is an emergency."

He waited so long he imagined Flora wasn't coming. By now he was no longer reclining against the headboard. His feet were on the floor beside the bed, and he reached for his off-duty gun and stuck its two-inch barrel into his mouth. That was the way cops generally did it. People sometimes tried to claim that this proved latent homosexuality, or some such drivel. It proved instead that cops knew about recoil and were afraid of it. Put the gun in your mouth and do the job cleanly. Otherwise your hand might jump, and you might only blind yourself, or turn yourself into a vegetable. It had happened often enough.

Rainey was amazed at how bad a gun tasted, and he took it out and looked down at it. There was a purity to it. A cop's best friend. It would never let a cop down.

In Coney Island the phone must have been lying on a table, for he heard the clatter as Flora picked it up.

"Hello?" She sounded breathless. "Who is it? What's the emergency?"

He spoke her name and stopped.

"Oh," she said. "It's you." Then, after the briefest of pauses: "This better be good. Do you realise what time it is? What's the emergency?"

Rainey licked his lips. "Listen to me, Flora. I just found out I'm dying."

It gave Flora pause. She was young and had hardened herself to him, but she was not totally heartless. She said carefully: "I certainly am awfully sorry to hear that."

"Flora, I –" Again he paused.

She was treading carefully. "How did you find out? What is it exactly? Are you calling from the hospital?"

"I might die today," Rainey said. "Or I might live a while longer. It depends."

Immediately Flora sounded suspicious. "It depends on what?"

"I love you, Flora."

"We've been all over that." There was exasperation in her tone. "What, if anything, are you dying of?"

"Call it," Rainey said, "– call it unrequited love."

"You're not dying at all, and I'm going back to bed."

"How long I live depends on you."

"What's that supposed to mean?"

Rainey was again trying to build a bridge he could walk out on, but according to the rhyme from his childhood that now popped into his head this was not possible: London Bridge is falling down. There was a tune that went with it, he remembered. Bridges didn't get built, they only collapsed. All fall down.

All of them. So many attempted bridges so far tonight. London Bridge every one. All fall down. So many London Bridges in his life for years and years.

"All fall down," he said into the phone.

"What? You're making me very angry, you know that?"

"Let's go to Tahiti together, Flora. Would you like to go to Tahiti with me?" But where did Tahiti come from, he asked himself. Why Tahiti?

"No, I don't want to go to Tahiti."

"We could go together. I could get the tickets tomorrow. By the day after we could be lying on a beach in Tahiti."

"The only place I want to go is to 168th Street to see Jason."

"Flora, please –"

"I'm going back to bed."

"Flora –" he called quickly.

The desperation in his voice must have stopped her, for she did not hang up. He could hear her breathing into the phone. And suddenly he began to recite the lines from the death scene in *Othello* into the phone, and then when his own first long speech was ended and he paused, to his delight and amazement Flora came in with the lines of Desdemona.

"Will you come to bed, my lord?"

"Have you prayed tonight, Desdemona?"

And you, Rainey asked himself, have you prayed tonight? He hadn't, unless this phone call was a prayer – this one and the others that had preceded it.

Meantime, the scene continued by telephone, like a bridge Rainey had made that would keep him alive a little longer.

"Kill me tomorrow," said Flora. "Let me live tonight . . . but half an hour! But while I say one prayer!"

"Flora," Rainey interrupted, "it's not Desdemona who will die tonight, it's Othello."

"What?" she said, a note of alarm in her voice. Then she snorted. "I don't believe you."

"I have my off-duty gun here. When you hear the noise you will understand it's all over."

"I'm hanging up," she said, but she didn't.

So he had her full attention. Possibly he had never before so captivated an audience. "It is too late," Rainey intoned, continuing Othello's death scene a moment longer.

"Now wait a minute, Ed –" Flora said hurriedly, "you just wait a minute."

"Will you go with me to Tahiti, Flora? I have my gun pointed at my temple." This was not true. The gun still lay in the flat of his hand and he studied it.

"I won't go with you to Tahiti, and you're just trying to scare me."

Rainey put his finger inside the trigger guard, gripped the handle tight and stuck the muzzle into his right ear. They're not going to be able to rent this room for a while, he thought. Sergeants usually died in fleatraps, where you heard moans from next door and the rhythmic creaking of bed springs. But this was the most luxurious hotel in the city. The walls here were thick. He did not expect anyone to hear the shot and come running.

"Here goes," he said, and pulled the trigger.

The bullet exploded out of the gun, and his brain exploded out of his skull, and in a brief moist shower rained down upon the bed.

The telephone receiver swung down and banged against the leg of the bedside table.

"Ed? Ed?" said the earpiece. "Are you still there? Eddie?"

The receiver swung in silence. "Say something, Eddie," the earpiece said, into a room now empty of any living presence. The receiver swung gently back and forth on its cord.

There was a long pause, and then the same voice said: "I don't believe you shot yourself. Not for a single second. You're just trying to get a reaction out of me. Well, you're

447

not going to get one." In the frame house near Coney Island she slammed the receiver down, and this noise too made its muted reverberation in the hotel room.

Thirty-Four

BY THE TIME FLORA WENT TO WORK SHE WAS ANNOYED at herself for having been upset earlier. No one killed themselves over love affairs any more, and certainly not over a broken love affair with her. She was sick of Rainey's histrionics and sick of him, and would tell him so the next time she saw him. That would be at acting class next week, she supposed. She wondered if she would have trouble with him there. Several times during the day she worried about it.

Rainey's body was not found until a maid came in to clean just before noon. It was the first suicide for the maid, but not for the Waldorf Astoria, whose executives were used to them – although usually they had to deal not with cops who had access to guns, but with overwrought businessmen who bounced off set-backs. In any case there was a procedure. The room became crowded with hotel staff men and then with police forensic personnel. Procedure prevailed. The corpse was hurried out of the service entrance, the media was not informed, and hotel personnel were cautioned to keep the whole thing quiet.

The incident did not therefore reach the papers – since Rainey was only a sergeant it might not have been considered newsworthy in any case – meaning that Flora never found out about it. Rainey simply disappeared from her life. From time to time during the weeks and months that followed she wondered what had happened to him, but before long she forgot him completely.

His death caused a big stir only within the police department itself – all police suicides did – and every cop during the time that Rainey remained above ground looked at his own revolver at least once and asked himself what had driven Rainey to it, and wondered if he would be capable of committing such a desperate act himself.

The wake was held at a funeral home in Stony Point, Long Island, about fifty miles from New York. It was a wooden Victorian house done over into candlelit chapels, one of them for Sergeant Edward Rainey. Not many mourners came, and no dignitaries or officials. There were flowers from the Sergeants' Benevolent Association which also sent a representative, and from Rainey's children, and from Keefe – not even enough to make an embankment around the coffin in its corner. The casket was closed. A framed photograph of Sergeant Rainey in uniform stood on the lid.

Rainey's wife was there and Keefe met her; and her children, and other members of the family, all dry-eyed, except for one daughter. There were a number of cops. Several were from Keefe's and Rainey's former office, none of them in uniform or in their official capacity; the highest rank present was sergeant. Most of these men came over to Keefe.

"They ought to make us leave our guns in our lockers after work," one muttered. "Having guns around night and day makes it too easy."

Keefe made no reply.

The next day was the funeral. It was not an inspector's funeral. Those were for murdered cops, not self-destructive ones. At inspectors' funerals thousands of cops in white gloves saluted in the street. The Police Emerald Society Band provided bagpipes and muffled drums. Entire pews were filled with police brass, and the coffin in the aisle was always flag-draped, making of the slain cop even more of a symbol in death than he had been in life.

Rainey's funeral was a simple mass of the Resurrection. The crowd in the church was sparse. There were fewer cops than the night before – most were probably on duty in the distant city. No flag covered the coffin, and the photo was gone, back to its place on the mantlepiece, or perhaps already in a drawer.

At the appointed time, as requested by the family, former Deputy Commissioner Philip Keefe rose to give the eulogy. Although he had sat on a bench across the street in a park for an hour trying to work out what he would say, to speak this eulogy at all was hard for him. It was painful to realise that he was probably the highest-ranking dignitary with whom the Rainey family had ever had close personal contact. They were attempting to send Rainey off in as much style as possible. Keefe did not feel he should be there. He was not a dignitary at all, but a man under indictment about to go on trial.

These thoughts and others moved through his head even as he praised Rainey's leadership qualities – qualities the world at large never saw, and would never believe in now, measuring Rainey merely by the rank he had attained, which was only sergeant, and by the death he had died, which was by his own hand.

"He was the only man in my office who understood that change within the police department was essential," Keefe said, "and who saw the directions which ought to be taken, and who led me to see these directions. I believed in his leadership, and I followed where he led, and one night I followed him even into a stick-up, and I suppose not many men would follow another man there." He told the story of the stick-up, "how quickly Ed sized up the situation", striving for a lightness of tone, attempting to make the mourners see this bright competent man in action near the end of his life.

But no one smiled at the tale, and certainly no one laughed. Keefe had no idea what the mourners were thinking, or how their vision of Rainey differed from his own. "He deserved to be much more than a sergeant," Keefe said. "I don't know what went wrong." He looked over at the family, especially at the weeping daughter. "Maybe the next generation will be better." He started to say something else about guns, but lost his train of thought and broke off. "I cared about Ed Rainey," he said. "I depended on him, I needed him.

"Ed Rainey was more than a friend. In a police department sense, he was my father."

He broke off again, hesitated for a moment, could think

of nothing to add, and so went back to his pew, and as the mass continued he sat there, feeling a mixture of gloom and grief and thinking: I wasn't able to describe the Ed Rainey I remember, I wasn't able to put into words what he meant to me.

Presently they were all outside on the sidewalk in front of the church. The casket had been slid into the hearse, and Rainey's son came up to Keefe and handed him an envelope. "We found this among my father's effects. It's got your name on it. Perhaps it means something to you."

On the train back to the city, Keefe opened the envelope. In it were Rainey's notes on his search for the cleaning woman: scribbled names, phone numbers, notations.

Keefe held in his hand a number of starting points, but no destinations. Still, it was something. Rainey had been in no shape to conduct a proper search – his suicide proved that much – but Keefe was fighting for his life. Where Rainey had failed, he told himself, he would succeed.

From the station he went to see Bloom, whose office was high up in a financial district tower. From the window could be seen most of lower New York Bay. There was no more time for self-pity or any other emotion. I'm going to get out of this thing, Keefe assured himself. He would get out of it with Bloom's help, and Rainey's help, but most of the work he would have to do himself.

"I'm going to find that cleaning woman," he told Bloom.

"She's the key to your acquittal," the lawyer agreed.

"I'm confident I can find her," Keefe said. "Assume we have her, what else?"

"Who could you get to come in and testify in your behalf?"

"You mean character witnesses?"

Bloom shrugged. "If that's what you want to call them."

"Kilcoyne maybe," Keefe said. "And maybe Egan, the former Police Commissioner. I don't know."

"How about Al Gold?"

"I doubt it."

"He's the one we need. He's PC."

"Right. And now that he's PC he's probably afraid to raise his head. All those guys are afraid to raise their heads, and the higher up they get the more afraid they become."

Keefe had never articulated this notion before, and had perhaps never even thought it.

"Kilcoyne," Bloom mused. "Egan." He was tapping his pencil on his thigh. "It would be great if you could get them. Do you think you can?"

"Egan always liked me, I think." Liked him? Or only thought he could use him? Keefe had discovered cynicism only since leaving the police department. It had shocked him. He was afraid it meant he was now a cynic himself, never again to be fully open to idealism or love or even friendship. When this was over, assuming he survived it, he was going to have to decide on new tenets on which to base the remaining years.

"Kilcoyne told me he was proud of me," he said. "He will want to stand up in court and say what he thinks. Furthermore, he's out of it now. Egan has nothing to lose either. But I don't know what Egan will do."

"All right, I'll call them," said Bloom.

"No, I'll go see them myself. After I find the cleaning woman."

He began to redo the investigation that had already been done twice, once by Anne Christianson's detectives, once by Rainey. He started as they had with the agency that had employed the cleaning woman, whose name was Lavinia Spencer.

The clerk who took his call seemed to be chewing gum as she listened to him, and she was still chewing as she gave her answer: "We don't give out no information over the phone."

He asked to be put through to her supervisor, who was more patient. But he too was not permitted to give out information over the phone.

"Why don't I come down there and we can talk about it?" Keefe said, and hung up before the man could refuse him, and went out and got on the subway.

The supervisor, who kept him waiting half an hour, was an enormously fat man with a soft, sweaty handshake. A dossier marked with Lavinia Spencer's name on the tab lay on his desk.

"I got a thousand things to do," he said.

"I am terrifically sorry to bother you, busy as you must be."

The supervisor read from the folder as Keefe made notes. Then: "I never do this for anyone. Don't say you got it from me. That way is out."

"There's just one more thing –"

The supervisor began to look angry.

"On a big job like the Bronx County Courthouse you must send these women out in pairs, or groups."

"This is against regulations."

"If I could talk to one of the women who worked with her, I might be able to come up with some additional information."

The two men gazed at each other. Finally the supervisor opened the dossier again. "She was on Theda Childress's crew."

"You've been most kind," said Keefe, and he meant it.

There was no mention of Theda Childress in Sergeant Rainey's notes, and Keefe began to hope that he had stumbled on a lead no one else had thought of. Deciding to search for Theda Childress first, he boarded the subway to the address given, which was in Harlem. However, the apartment indicated was empty, and a neighbour told him that Mrs Childress had moved out weeks ago, leaving no forwarding address.

He wrote her a letter care of the agency he had just visited, but four days later it came back marked: "Not at this address." He sent a letter to the Harlem address, with the same result.

Meanwhile he had begun to check out the references used by Lavinia Spencer. One had been a housewife in the suburbs and the other a New York hotel.

Keefe went to see the housewife. She was cordial. She remembered Lavinia Spencer well, and said she had done good work. No, she had left no address or phone number.

When he phoned the hotel at which she had worked no one could remember her name. Addresses and phone numbers of employees were not given out in any case.

He went to the hotel and talked his way into the office of the general manager. They chatted for a few minutes, and the man made an effort to find some trace of a former employee named Lavinia Spencer, but he failed.

If she had worked in one hotel she had perhaps worked in others, was still working in others, and Keefe went back to his flat and began telephoning hotels on the East Side. He called these hotels off and on for the next three days, without finding any trace of Lavinia Spencer.

The trial was now two weeks away. He went up to the Bronx County Courthouse three evenings in a row and walked the empty corridors listening for the hum of vacuum cleaners, the banging of pails. He found and interviewed nine cleaning women on two separate shifts. None knew Lavinia Spencer, nor Theda Childress.

He phoned the two detectives who had worked on the case for Anne Christianson. He talked first to one, then the other on successive days. Both refused to give him information of any kind. They did admit that they had not found the cleaning woman, and had long ago ceased looking for her.

"Let me throw out some addresses," Keefe said hurriedly. The second detective was about to hang up on him. He read the addresses off Sergeant Rainey's notes, one in Macon, Georgia, the other in Birmingham, Alabama. "Just tell me if you checked out those addresses," he begged.

There was a long silence at the other end of the phone.

"Yes, we checked out both those addresses. I already told that to the sergeant who was working for you."

"Did you check them personally?"

The hand went over the receiver again and there was another delay. Then the voice came back on. "We asked the local police to check them out for us."

"And the results were?"

"The results were negative, Commissioner. Look, I can't help you." The detective hung up.

One day Keefe searched for Theda Childress, the next for Lavinia Spencer. The two became confused in his mind. Sometimes he didn't know which of them it was most urgent to find. He sat making phone calls until the blood became choked off in his elbows and he could no longer hold the telephone to his ear. Time was closing down on him. Haste and worry made him erratic. He rode subways into benighted corners of Queens and Brooklyn chasing down possibilities that evaporated before his eyes. Sometimes he found Rainey had been there before him, sometimes not.

He went back to the hotel on Madison Avenue, he rode the train out to see the suburban housewife, retracing his steps because he was unable to go forward. The housewife was again extremely cordial. She sat him down at her kitchen table and gave him a warmed-up cup of coffee left over from breakfast. She had discovered who he was in the interim, and wanted to hear all about his case. She did not seem alarmed to sit alone in the presence of the killer, who was himself. She was perhaps only lonely or bored. Unfortunately she could remember nothing further except a conversation one time about Birmingham, which was where Lavinia had grown up. Had Keefe tried Birmingham yet?

"Not yet," he admitted. If the Birmingham police had tried and failed, what chance was there for him? Macon, Georgia, was another possibility, of course, but the police there had failed too. If the woman had gone back to the South she could be anywhere, and Keefe had no money or time to waste on wild goose chases.

Birmingham seemed the best bet to her, the housewife said.

Maybe she was right. He had exhausted all leads in the New York area. He had exhausted himself as well. He took the subway downtown to the telephone building and bought phone books for Birmingham and Macon, then he went home and started dialling. There were fifty-five Spencers listed in Birmingham. He called them all. He got nibbles. Sudden, heart-stopping nibbles.

"Lavinia Spencer?" the voice said with recognition.

It made Keefe's whole body go tense, and he waited.

"Not Lavinia Spencer," the voice said. "You must mean Ramona Spencer."

But he didn't mean Ramona Spencer at all, and he went on to the next name, the next telephone number. Finally he came to the end of the Birmingham listings. No Lavinia Spencer. Nothing. There were twenty-one Spencers listed in Macon, Georgia. He started in.

"Lavinia?" the voice said. A woman. She sounded like a black woman. "Lavinia ain't here."

"Let me make sure I have the right Lavinia," Keefe said, made almost breathless by this response. It was only the third Macon call he had made. He began to describe Lavinia Spencer. "A light-brown woman. With a high-pitched voice. Heavy-set." He realized this was all he knew about Lavinia Spencer personally. He recited her date and place of birth. "She's been working up in the New York area for a number of years."

"You got the right Lavinia. But like I said, she ain't here."

"When will she be home?"

"She don't live in Macon. I ain't seen her for years."

Such a sense of hopelessness invaded Keefe that he doubted he would be able to call anyone else after he hung up now. "But you do know her?"

"Sure I knows her. She kin. Last I heard she was over to Birmingham, working for some lady there."

"Birmingham? You wouldn't know where exactly?"

The woman did not know where. The family had received a postcard from Lavinia about a month ago. So at least the information on her whereabouts was fresh. Fairly fresh. It was just not exact, and Birmingham was a big place, with about 300,000 people. Keefe could feel the sweat running down his face, running down the middle of his back. He kept trying to worm additional information out of the woman at the other end of the phone, but failed. She knew nothing more.

Keefe went to LaGuardia Airport, handed over his credit card, and bought a ticket to Birmingham via Atlanta on Delta. He phoned Bloom from the departure lounge.

"Christ," Bloom said, "you're not allowed to leave the state, and the trial's Monday. You haven't even talked to those other guys yet, Kilcoyne and Egan, or Police Commissioner Gold."

Keefe did not need to be told.

"Would their testimony be enough?"

"There's no way of knowing in advance what's enough. A trial is a trial. You don't know what's going to happen. You never know how the jury's going to see it. But it's certainly better to make certain of what you have than to take a trip to Birmingham and wind up with nothing at all."

"I've got to try it," said Keefe.

Counting the stop-over, it took him four hours to reach Birmingham. He took a taxi directly to City Hall, where he went upstairs and asked to see the Chief of Police. Chiefs of police were men who made access to themselves as difficult as possible at all times. Keefe had chosen the direct approach rather than a telephone call because a man in a waiting room was harder to get rid of than a voice on a line.

At length Keefe was admitted into the great man's presence. He turned out to be an ex-New York police captain. He knew not only Keefe's name but all the details of the case, and he began by apologising for his men who had kept Keefe waiting.

"You probably came down here hoping you could find that cleaning woman," he said.

"How hard did your guys look for her?"

"They gave us some addresses, and we checked them out." The Chief shrugged. "The people my men talked to said they hadn't seen her in years."

"Can you give me the addresses you tried?"

"Of course," the Chief said, and he sent for them.

For a time the two men sat in silence. "What are you thinking?" said the Chief.

"I have an informant who told me Lavinia works for a lady here." Informant? The police terminology had come to Keefe's lips because in this office he was back inside the police world. Such terminology was perhaps what this man would respond to.

"How reliable an informant?"

"I don't know. But it's my last and only hope. The trial begins Monday."

The Police Chief nodded. "I'm on your side. I'll help you if I can."

"If she's working for a 'lady' it would be a rich lady," said Keefe. "Maybe you could point me towards the richest section of the city."

"You'll ring doorbells?"

"I'll ring doorbells."

A clerk came in with the list of those addresses that had already been checked out, and the Chief handed it over. "I'll lend you a driver and a car," he said.

Keefe had not expected kindness of this magnitude, and so much gratitude rose up into his throat that for a moment he did not dare attempt to speak.

"I'll ask one favour of you," the Chief said. "I'd like to get back there."

"Back to New York?"

"That's right. As PC. As a deputy commissioner even. Everybody here knows it. If you find the woman you're looking for, if you get out of this thing, I'd like it to be known that I helped you."

"Sure," said Keefe.

"Otherwise –"

Keefe tried a smile. "Otherwise I won't mention your name," he said.

The Chief unfolded a map of the city and began marking areas with a red pencil. "You don't have time to do all of them," he said. His pencil came down hard. "Start here. Cherokee Drive. Lots of posh houses in there. It's as good a place as any to start."

He called in a sergeant in uniform and gave instructions, then waved off Keefe's attempts to thank him. The sergeant went downstairs to drive the car around in front. The Chief accompanied Keefe to the elevator. "I think what they've done to you so far is an outrage," he said. "It's a goddamn miscarriage of justice. That black sergeant driving you, he's working a four to twelve, so you can keep him until midnight if you want."

Cherokee Drive. The houses were indeed large and expensive. They were also widely spaced with patches of forest between them, and it was sometimes a long walk from the road up to the front door.

"I'm looking for a maid named Lavinia Spencer," Keefe said each time. He said it over and over again. The black sergeant in uniform stood each time at his side – Keefe was afraid, especially after it got dark, that householders would not open to him otherwise. But he did not find Lavinia Spencer. He did not stop for dinner either, which the sergeant took with good humour.

"It'll take a few pounds off me," he said, showing a mouthful of large white teeth. "Easier than jogging. The Chief don't think cops have a right to get fat."

"I guess we'd better stop," said Keefe at last. In many of the houses now no lights showed at all. The sergeant drove him to a hotel, and he checked in. The hotel bar was the only thing open. He bought himself a beer and bowl of pretzels. There was nothing else in the hotel to eat. He went to bed.

The next morning the search resumed. The black sergeant was as cheerful as the night before, but this time had brought with him a picnic lunch. "Got enough in there for you too, Commissioner," he said cheerfully. They were back in the same neighbourhood. The sergeant pulled the police car into a driveway, and they both got out. "You gonna find her today," the sergeant said. "I feel it in my bones."

They walked up to the door, and Keefe rang the bell. They waited.

The door was opened by Lavinia Spencer.

She was wearing a dark brown uniform, darker than her skin, with white cuffs and a white collar and a kind of white doily on top of her head. She said: "Miz Floyd ain't home."

Keefe was so surprised that he was, for the moment, speechless. "It's her," he said to the sergeant beside him.

The sergeant grinned. "Well, well, well," he said. "Ain't we lucky?"

Lavinia, perplexed, looked from one of them to the other. She did not recognise Keefe. He gave her his name, but she did not immediately make the connection. "Is I suppose to know you?" she said.

"We've met before."

"Where was that?"

"At the Bronx County Courthouse on a certain night –"

But her face lit up and she interrupted him. "– You the Commissioner that man was calling for. That man that had me. You the man got me away from him." She took half a step toward Keefe as if intending to kiss him, or shake his hand, but she stopped herself abruptly, and began blinking back tears. "It sure give me pleasure to meet you." Her head was nodding up and down. "I be in your debt forever."

The sergeant, still grinning, turned and was looking back across the lawn toward the road. It was between Keefe and this woman now.

"I've come all this way to find you, Mrs Spencer."

"Most folks calls me Lavinia."

"I've been looking for you for weeks."

"Everybody hereabouts know Lavinia," she said.

At this point Keefe fell silent, uncertain how to continue. It seemed to him that whatever he said next would only frighten this woman. She was looking past him at the police car in the driveway and was perhaps half-frightened already. She certainly did not understand how law enforcement functioned, and would not agree to testify. The very notion would terrify her, he believed, and she would refuse.

"At first I looked for you in New York," Keefe said.

"New York a dangerous place," said Lavinia seriously. "The man that had me, he prove it to me once and for all. I didn't hang on for no more evidence. The next morning I was on that bus, and I come home. And from now I's gonna stay home."

Keefe, not knowing how else to phrase it, said: "Lavinia, I'm in terrible trouble. I need your help." He began to speak rather too fast, afraid to look at her steadily, catching only glimpses of her face from time to time as he explained exactly the nature of the trouble he was in, and the help he was asking her to give. Her brows seemed to knit together as he spoke, but there was no other reaction he could discern. "It will only take you a day or two," he concluded hopefully, meeting her eyes for the first time, "and I'll pay your expenses and any wages you might lose. I can make it worth your while."

Before his eyes she seemed to take on immense dignity. But she also had begun shaking her head, so that all his hopes collapsed.

"You got it all wrong," she said.

"Yes," said Keefe, "well –"

"You can pay my airplane ticket," Lavinia said. "I ain't got no money for that. And you can fix it with Miz Floyd. You didn't take no money to help me, and I ain't taking no money to help you. When you want me up there?"

Thirty-Five

BLOOM'S REACTION WHEN KEEFE BURST EXUBERANTLY into his office was not what he had expected.

"What's the matter?" Keefe asked him. "I thought you'd be thrilled."

"So she agreed to testify," Bloom said. "That's very nice. Assuming she comes." He was a tall, dishevelled young man. His desk was dishevelled too. "But what exactly is she going to testify to? Did you ask her what she would say?"

"She'll describe exactly what happened. I think she will. What more do you want?"

"She'll describe what happened according to her. What she thought she saw, what she thought she heard. For all you know, it may be completely different from what you thought you saw, and heard."

Sobered, Keefe stared at his lawyer.

"Trials are live theatre," Bloom told him. "Witnesses have to be carefully prepared. We don't like to use the word rehearsed. They have to have their lines – the lines you want them to speak – almost memorised, but even then you can't be sure what they'll say on the stand. Some get stage fright and can hardly talk at all. Some start to sweat and forget everything. They can't remember their own names."

Keefe looked at him.

"Maybe I better call her."

Keefe thought about it. "Maybe you better not." He found he was afraid she might change her mind.

"Trials are tricky," Bloom said. "You can never tell in advance what's going to happen. You can't be sure what witnesses are going to say, and you can't be sure what a jury is going to believe."

Keefe said nothing.

"Hey," Bloom said. "Don't look so glum. You did a great job. You found her. She'll probably be on that plane."

His office, despite its gorgeous view, was nearly empty of furniture, and outside the door, Keefe knew, Bloom had only the one girl working for him. All his money, so far, probably went on rent.

"All right," Bloom said decisively. "I won't call her. We'll meet the plane and I'll get a chance to talk to her before I put her on the stand. It'll work out, I'm sure it will."

He came around the desk and clapped Keefe on the shoulder. "Not to worry. I'm an expert at this. That's why you hired me, right?"

Keefe tried to smile. Bloom had won big cases as a prosecutor. He was an excellent lawyer, Keefe had been told and believed. In any case, his life was in Bloom's hands.

"So what about these other witnesses you promised to bring in here?" Bloom said. "I'm talking about Kilcoyne, Gold and Egan."

"I'll go see them."

"Let's talk about it for a minute. Who do you go to see first? What do you say? What kind of testimony are we looking for from them?"

"The truth," Keefe blurted out. "That's what we're looking for. I'm going to see Kilcoyne first. I'm going to see him right now."

"Why him first?"

"I don't know. He feels like my best bet."

"What are you going to say to him?"

"I don't know."

"All right, and after him, who do you see next?"

Keefe said nothing.

"Think it out," Bloom said. "Plan it."

"I can't. I'm going out to Kilcoyne's house now. After that, I'll see."

Keefe walked through the financial district toward the ferry slip. The tall narrow streets opened out. It was a cold winter day, the sun was going down and the wind hit him suddenly. He paid his fare and walked on to the ferry. He went up to the top deck and stood below the bridge in the wind and watched Staten Island come towards him. There was no one else out on deck. When the ferry docked he took a taxi to Kilcoyne's house and rang the bell. He had not telephoned first.

He's the most likely one to testify for me, Keefe told himself as he waited. Telephoning wouldn't have helped. What could he have said on the phone? Of course Kilcoyne might not be home. The cold seemed to be increasing. He stamped his feet on the rope doormat.

The door opened. Keefe was immediately aware of how big Kilcoyne was. He wore corduroy trousers and a baggy woollen sweater. His white hair was dishevelled and he was wiping his hands on a rag. Even his shoes were old and scuffed. It was difficult to recognise the former police commander in the impeccable blue uniform. Kilcoyne looked older. The stiff military bearing was gone too. His face seemed to have sagged in unaccustomed places.

"Come in," Kilcoyne said, "you're letting in the cold air." He stepped back.

Keefe followed him into the small hallway.

"I was working downstairs in my shop," Kilcoyne said.

He was a man not used to receiving visitors, apparently. He did not seem to know what to do with Keefe now that he was in the house. Finally he said: "Let me take your coat." A living room had opened up to one side of the hallway. "Why don't you sit down in the parlour?" Kilcoyne said. "Just let me go downstairs and turn off my machines."

Left alone, Keefe looked over the 'parlour'. During his boyhood every Irish Catholic home in New York had had its 'parlour'. It was a word you never heard any more. This one seemed left over from those days. There were Venetian blinds left over from those days also, and the low sunlight shining through the slats showed that the windows behind them had not been washed in years. There were faded slipcovers on the upholstered furniture.

Keefe realised that he was standing in the house of a man who had lived alone for a long time.

Kilcoyne came up the cellar steps and into the parlour.

"Well, Dennis, what have you been doing with yourself lately?" began Keefe.

"Mostly some carpentry," said Kilcoyne. "I was making a rocking chair just now. For my daughter-in-law."

Keefe was uncomfortable.

"She likes rocking chairs," said Kilcoyne, who seemed equally ill at ease. "They live in California."

"I was out in California for a while."

'Is that so?"

"My trial begins Monday."

"Yes, I know."

"I was wondering if – if you would be willing to testify on my behalf?"

Kilcoyne nodded as if he had known all along that this was the purpose of the visit. Then he looked away.

"I don't see where I can be much help to you, Phil."

Keefe's gloves were in his hands. He had not sat down and neither had Kilcoyne.

"Just to lend me a bit of your prestige –"

"Not much of that left, I'm afraid."

"Oh yes," said Keefe. "You have enormous prestige in this city."

"If I came to court, the reporters would be all over me."

Keefe said nothing.

"Detestable people," said Kilcoyne. "Even though once you were one of them, I'm sure you agree with me now. After what they did to you."

Keefe said: "You called me into your office the morning after the... the incident. You told me you were proud of me."

"I also said you shouldn't have been there. That by your presence you escalated the level of violence."

Keefe tried to smile. "You wouldn't be obliged to mention that part of it. Maybe you could just say the first part of it, and stop."

But Kilcoyne did not smile back, with the result that Keefe's own smile faded.

"Who else has agreed to testify for you?"

"I thought I'd ask Gold next, and then the PC."

"By the PC I suppose you mean Tim Egan. He's a private citizen now, just like the rest of us."

Keefe waited.

"Any testimony I could give might hurt you more than help you."

"If you feel that way, then I would appreciate it if you refused to testify." After another long silence, Keefe said: "And do you feel that way?"

When Kilcoyne did not immediately reply, Keefe added: "Perhaps you blame me for – for causing you to resign from the department."

"I resigned from the department of my own free will because I chose to do so. You didn't cause me to do anything."

"Yes," said Keefe. "I could understand if your personal feelings –"

"My personal feelings do not enter into it." Kilcoyne selected a calmer tone. "My personal feelings have never been allowed to colour any testimony I gave in court."

This produced the longest pause yet. "I didn't know woodworking was your hobby," Keefe said.

"Oh, I've been making most of the wooden furniture for members of my family for years." Kilcoyne smiled unexpectedly. "Especially since my wife died."

Perhaps it was the mention of his wife that caused him to frown.

"Let me think about it," the former Chief of Operations said. "What's your lawyer's name? I'll call your lawyer with my decision." He led the way back to the front door. Bitterly disappointed, Keefe followed.

At the front door he said: "Dennis, can I ask you a favour? Could you let us know as quickly as possible?"

Kilcoyne patted him on the shoulder, and Keefe stepped out into the cold. "I'll call your lawyer," Kilcoyne said, and the door closed.

On the ferry recrossing New York harbor, Keefe sat on a bench below deck sipping coffee out of a styrofoam cup. The deck plates throbbed beneath his feet, and for a time he only listened to the hum of the engines. He looked out the window. It was dark now on the water. Across the river the city would be all lit up, the world's most gorgeous Christmas tree. It would be approaching ever closer like a celebration, like the biggest non-stop party in the world. But Keefe did not want to see it. If he could not count on Kilcoyne, who could he count on?

When Keefe had gone Kilcoyne went back down to his basement workshop, fixed his goggles in place and switched on his machine. He was turning the upright spokes for the back of the rocking chair. His daughter-in-law would be very pleased with it. Three spokes were done. This was the fourth and last and he held the wood to the machine to shape it. The floor where he stood was half an inch deep in sawdust, and he shuffled his shoes so as to plant them more firmly. As he worked, the tone of the machine increased in pitch. The raw odor of wood was pleasing to Kilcoyne, as was the way the wood felt in his fingers. He told himself now to forget Keefe. He was happy in his workshop. He could stay down here forever and if he did he would miss nothing of consequence. It was not his fault that Keefe was in trouble, and he owed him nothing. He had warned him against the raid on the junkyard, foreseeing any number of possible catastrophes though not, of course, the one that actually occurred. Keefe had spurned his advice then and had no right to call upon him for help now. To go back into that arena even to testify at the trial would be a mistake.

Although he did not see it precisely in those terms, his workshop had become his sanctuary, and he was loath to leave it for any reason at all. From time to time, even while shaping wood on a machine, he did think of the future. He thought of it again now. He was only fifty-six. In a year and a half there would be another mayoral election, and perhaps a new mayor. A new mayor would want a new police commissioner, his own man, someone new but with prestige from the past, and if nothing was heard publicly from Kilcoyne between now and then he might come to seem the ideal choice.

He had nothing whatever to gain by trying to help Keefe.

His machine whined, the dust dropped toward the floor. His expert fingers shaped the spoke he was working on. There was a phone down in the workshop. The department had put it in. From time to time he looked at it. It never rang any more. Presently he turned the machine off, picked up the receiver and dialed a number.

When he got off the ferry Keefe took a taxi to police headquarters. There were two cops on security duty in the lobby. Both recognized him. They called him Commissioner, and wished him luck. He asked if by chance the PC was in the building. They said he was.

"Can I go up?"

"Of course," both men said at once, and he went past them to the elevators. The car rose up. It was empty except for Keefe. He walked down the fourteenth-floor corridor. The building felt totally empty to him, though of course it was not.

The sergeant on duty outside the PC's door, recognizing him, looked surprised.

Keefe said: "Will you ask the PC if he can see me for about five minutes?"

The sergeant got up and went into Gold's office. Keefe considered walking in right behind him, but discarded the idea.

The sergeant came out. "He says go right on in, Commissioner."

Gold had come around his desk with his hand outstretched. "Good to see you, Commissioner," he said.

Keefe thought it important to strike a cheerful note, if he could. "You're the Commissioner now, Al."

Gold gestured towards his telephone. "I was just talking on there with a friend of yours."

Keefe looked mystified.

"Dennis Kilcoyne," Gold said. "You've just been to see him, I guess. He told me you might come here next."

Kilcoyne had phoned Gold, had warned him. Keefe needed time to orient himself to that, and to this room, and to Gold as PC. The room was the same as before. Teddy Roosevelt's portrait still hung on the wall. Teddy Roosevelt's desk still served the incumbent Police Commissioner. But to Keefe this office belonged neither to Roosevelt nor to Gold but to Tim Egan, who would never be there again.

Keefe said: "Then you know why I'm here."

"Yes, and I wish I had better news for you."

Keefe pretended ignorance. "I don't understand."

"I'd testify for you in a minute if I thought it would help. But I arrived at the courthouse when the thing was just about over." This was the stand Gold had maintained throughout. It had served him well till now. Why should he budge from it?

Keefe had one thought and one only: Don't give him a chance to say no outright. Keep him talking.

"You're working late, Al." He flashed a bright and probably inappropriate smile. "And on a Saturday too."

"This is an unending job," Gold commented. "I don't know why I ever agreed to take it. It's killing me."

"What were you working on right now?" asked Keefe. "What was it I interrupted?"

A pile of folders stood on Gold's desk. He lifted the pile in two hands and let it drop back again. "Personnel problems, traffic problems, major case squad problems. You name it."

"It would mean a lot to my defence," Keefe said.

"If I thought you were right, Commissioner," Gold said, "I'd testify for you in a minute. But I don't see where I could add anything."

"Just to testify that you knew about the raid on the stolen car ring in advance – that would help me. It would prove I wasn't some power-mad maniac going off half-cocked on my own."

"Even there, Commissioner, my advice was not sought. I really didn't know anything about that raid."

"Sure you did," said Keefe in surprise.

"Did I?" said Gold.

"You were sitting in the room when Kilcoyne tried to talk me out of it."

"I may have been. I don't really remember."

"And you told me that Lieutenant Craighead was keeping you advised."

"See," said Gold. "I've got a rotten memory. I'd have to try to dredge all this stuff up out of my memory, and I don't even know how successful I'd be."

"I can see why you might not want to get involved," Keefe said. He had begun to badger Gold but could not help himself. "I hate to bother you, Al, but –"

Gold had come around the desk again, and was walking Keefe to the door. "If I were in your place," he advised, "I'd go see Tim Egan. If you get him in your corner, and Dennis Kilcoyne, it should be clear sailing. I'd help you if I could, but I didn't get to the courthouse until it was pretty much over. There's nothing much I can tell the court that can be of any use to you."

"Even an expression of support," Keefe said, "even that would help."

"I've got to think about my department," Gold said. "I've got to think about that scumbag Senator Buckner and his hearings coming up. I've got a lot on my mind. I'll give your request a lot of thought, though. Maybe I'll be able to remember some detail that might help you. Let me have your lawyer's phone number. If I think of anything, I'll call him."

They had nearly reached the door of Gold's office, where Keefe stopped and got out a pen. He was about to write down Bloom's number on an envelope, but Gold stopped him.

"Leave the number with the sergeant outside, Phil. Good to have seen you again. Thanks for stopping by."

The door closed behind Keefe. He was in the outer office and the sergeant looked up at him from behind the desk. To his shame, knowing it was hopeless, Keefe swallowed his pride and wrote out Bloom's number. It seemed essential to conceal his emotions from the sergeant, so he handed him the number, fixed on him an impossibly broad grin, then went out of the office and down in the elevator.

It was dark outside, and cold, and the cars went by with their exhaust pipes steaming. He went into a diner, its windows so coated with condensation that he could not see out, and ordered a coffee. He sat in front of it for about twenty minutes. He should go to see Egan now, but he did not know if he could make himself do it. It seemed to him certain that Egan's answers would be the same as the ones he had already heard. The trial began in less than forty-eight hours.

He went down into the subway where he waited about fifteen minutes on the platform listening to the wind in the tunnel. When he came up into the street in Queens there were no taxis. He started for Egan's house on foot. He trudged head down, from time to time beating his gloves together, his breath vaporising in the cold night.

The door was opened by Edna Egan who said: "Oh, it's you. I don't know if Tim – you look cold. Please come in. I'll get him."

She led him into the living room, took his coat and left him there. At the window he peered out at the street. Something was missing and after a moment he realized what it was: the guard car was gone from out front.

Egan came into the room behind him. He was wearing brown slacks and a tan cardigan sweater over an open-neck shirt.

His manner seemed neither more nor less cordial than in the past. Keefe, who was looking for some clue to his feelings toward him, realized that there would be none.

"You've been away," Keefe began.

"We took the boys on a trip through the West. But we've been back a good long time now."

Keefe found he did not know what to call him. He had never called him Tim. To continue to call him Commissioner seemed to Keefe subservient.

"How's your new job?" Keefe asked him. Egan had been named vice-president for security at one of the city's major department stores.

Egan smiled. "The hours are better and the phone doesn't ring in the middle of the night."

Keefe decided to call him Mr. Egan. "You're looking very relaxed, Mr. Egan."

"What can I do for you, Phil?"

"My trial begins Monday."

"So it does."

"I was wondering if you would consider testifying on my behalf."

Egan hesitated so long that Keefe expected outright refusal. Instead the former Police Commissioner said: "I don't know what I could say, Phil."

"There are a number of things which, if you said them, might help my case a good deal."

Egan nodded, but did not ask for specifics. Keefe thought: now he'll tell me he'll think about it, and he'll ask me for the name of my lawyer.

Egan said: "How many of the other men have you talked to?"

This seemed a bit more hopeful. At least no one – meaning Kilcoyne or Gold – had warned him off. "I've been to see Chief Kilcoyne, and Al Gold."

"And have they agreed to come in?"

"I think they will," Keefe said. "I'm hoping they'll come in." It wasn't an outright lie. No matter what happens, he told himself, I'm not going to lie. "My lawyer thinks it would help a lot if, for instance, you testified that I led the raid on the stolen car ring at your request."

"My request? I'm not sure I recall it quite that way."

"With your permission, then."

Keefe waited for Egan to acknowledge this, but he did not do so.

"What else was your lawyer thinking about?"

There was a whole list of possible topics, and Keefe brought them forth. Egan could testify to Keefe's good character, and describe him as a responsible man – he was not a cowboy. He could testify to Keefe's attempts to order in high-ranking officers who would take command. Keefe hurriedly fudged this over, fearing Egan would see it as dangerous to himself. "I had the Precinct Commander phoned at home, for instance, and the Chief of Detectives, and the Chief of Operations. I made every effort to do it by the book before I went in there."

Egan, watching him, nodded.

"You could say that I also made every effort to talk my way out of that room," Keefe said, "that clearly I never considered shooting the man until the battering-ram hit the door."

Keefe had begun pacing, whereas Egan merely watched him.

"There are all kinds of testimony you might give that might help me."

Their eyes met and locked. Finally Egan looked away. "Why don't you let me think about it? Give me the name of your lawyer. I'll call your lawyer with my decision."

And that's how it ends, Keefe thought. Not one of them will stand up for me. He wanted to say to Egan: please help me, I am desperate. Instead he wrote out Bloom's phone number, handed it to Egan, and walked toward the door, where he said as calmly as he could: "Thank you very much for any consideration you can give my request."

As soon as the door had closed, Edna Egan came in from the kitchen. "What was that?"

Egan told her.

"He wants you to testify for him?" said Edna. "And what's he going to do for you, if I might ask?"

"It would mean giving the press another crack at me," Egan mused. "When I left I avoided seeing any of them, you know. They're no doubt still furious. They're looking for anything to make me look bad, you can count on that."

"Tim, you're out of it now. You're not going to do it. You're not, are you?"

"No," he reassured her. "No, of course not."

"You're well out of all that."

"Yes," Egan said.

"And you should stay out."

They walked back into the living room together. "He may go to jail," Egan said.

"That's not your fault."

Absently Egan put his arm around his wife's waist. "No, that's not my fault."

Keefe took the subway back into midtown and went directly to Bloom's apartment. "I struck out all three times," he blurted when Bloom had let him in.

"Would you like a drink?" inquired Bloom. "You look like you need it."

The lawyer busied himself mixing drinks at a sidebar. When he came forward he handed Keefe a glass.

"I say let's subpoena all three of them and make them testify."

"Have you ever heard the term 'hostile witness'? Do you know what a hostile witness is? If you subpoena them they'll be hostile, and whatever they might say won't help you, believe me."

Keefe sat down with his drink and stared at the rug.

Just then Bloom's phone rang. It was sitting on a table beside a lamp and he went to it.

"Oh yes," he said into the phone. "I see. Yes, of course. Thank you very much for calling."

Having hung up, Bloom turned to Keefe. "Did you give Chief Kilcoyne my home phone number?"

Keefe jumped to his feet.

"That was him. He says he'll testify for you."

Keefe moved back, and forth, talking volubly. He was very excited, and in his excitement suddenly hungry. "Let's go out and get something to eat," he told Bloom. "Maybe this thing is going to work out after all."

But the phone rang again almost at once. Bloom's end of the conversation was almost identical to last time. When he hung up he looked quizzically in the direction of Keefe. "You must be a very persuasive guy," he said. "That was the ex-Police Commissioner. He's willing to testify for you too."

Thirty-Six

THE FIRST OF THE FIRST DAY'S SURPRISES CAME WHEN Assistant District Attorney Christianson on behalf of the people of the State of New York filed a motion asking that the accused be remanded to jail for the duration of the trial.

At the defence table Keefe jumped to his feet. "What?" he cried. "What?"

The jury had not yet filed in but the courtroom was entirely filled and now buzzing. Two full rows had had to be given over to the press, and many reporters were already on their feet, ready to bolt for the telephones. Representatives of black civil rights groups had jumped up also, possibly to start cheering. There were five additional courtroom guards all of whom had jumped quickly into position to help preserve order.

Keefe stood rigid at the defence table, both fists clenched, as a conversation took place at the bench between the judge, Anne Christianson and Bloom.

Presently the judge declared a short recess to consider the State's motion. His name was Woodruff. He was in the eleventh year of his second fourteen-year term as a New York State Supreme Court justice.

A number of reporters ran to phone in the news, and as Anne Christianson too left the courtroom Keefe started after her, with Bloom, who grasped late what was happening, in hot pursuit.

The corridor outside was full of demonstrators. Anne Christianson had a headstart of about five paces on Keefe. Behind him came Bloom calling: "Phil, I beg of you. Phil –"

Keefe got in front of her, fists still clenched, his face red. "How dare you file such a motion?" he shouted.

She stared up at him, and for a moment seemed frightened.

"Why are you persecuting me?"

Bloom's shoulder hit him in the chest and almost knocked him down. By the time he had recovered his balance, the young woman was through into the ladies" room, and Bloom was shaking him.

"Are you crazy? Do you want to go to Rikers? Lay one hand on that woman and that's where you'll go. There's a rule in baseball," Bloom went on. "Touch the umpire and you're out of the game. Well, they have the same rule here. Touch that woman and you'll be remanded instantly. They'll bring you to court every morning in handcuffs. Is that what you want?"

A crowd surrounded them. Some may have been reporters. Strobe lights flashed.

Bloom said: "I would have made the same motion in her place. The object is to keep us so busy defending motions we'll have no time to defend our case. It's simple courtroom tactics and you better get used to it." Then he added a comment that chilled Keefe. "She's evidently a better lawyer than I thought."

When the trial resumed the judge denied the prosecution's motion without comment and signalled for the jury to be brought in. The opening arguments by both sides ensued. Miss Christianson, as she outlined the prosecution's case, portrayed the defendant as at worst a racist, and at best a mindless dilettante playing at being a cop, taking responsibility in a situation beyond his competence – with reckless disregard of the possible consequences. "Reckless disregard" were the key words. She asked the jury to see Keefe as the expression and embodiment of police reliance on force and violence. "Exonerate him," she concluded, "and you give your official benediction to the gunning down of unarmed citizens by policemen everywhere in the city and in the country."

Bloom leaned over to Keefe. "You sound like Jack the Ripper to me." As he rose to address the jury himself he was grinning at his joke. But Keefe behind him was not.

Bloom's own opening arguments were undramatic and very short. "Low key, all the way to the end," he said when he had returned to the defence table. "The opposite of her. The jury is in awe of her now because she's so good-looking. But just wait."

During the next weeks Assistant District Attorney Christianson called her witnesses and presented her case. The two investigating detectives each testified. The assistant medical examiner testified. Various exhibits were marked for identification and shown to the jury: the ballistics report, the autopsy report, the deceased's starter's pistol, photographs and various schematic drawings of Judge Baum's chambers. Assistant District Attorney Christianson made not a single mistake that Bloom could exploit, until she began to question the ballistics technician, Lieutenant Roche, about the deceased's starter's pistol.

"So with such a gun you can't shoot a man in the back, is that correct?"

"Not in the back or anywhere else."

"If you fired at someone with this weapon, nothing would happen to him, is that correct?"

"The noise might scare him."

Roche at this stage in his career had testified on ballistics questions hundreds of times, perhaps thousands, and it showed. He was what the legal profession calls an "expert witness", and no jury had ever disbelieved him.

"And would you say it is easy to recognize a starter's pistol, as opposed to one that you can shoot a man in the back with?"

Bloom objected and was sustained. The judge, high up on his dais, said: "We can do without the innuendo."

"A starter's pistol is easily recognizable, Lieutenant Roche, is that correct? There would be no excuse whatever for a trained police officer mistaking a starter's pistol for one that fired live bullets, is that correct?"

"I object, your honour," said Bloom. "I think the jury gets the point." To the agitated Keefe beside him he whispered: "Calm down. My turn comes on cross."

"All right," said the young woman. "Let us consider now the matter of the defendant's own gun. How many rounds were fired by Mr. Keefe?"

"All five."

"How many struck the deceased?"

"Only one. The others were in the wall or the ceiling."

"Would you characterize that as fairly inept shooting?"

"Well," said Roche with a smile, "at times some police officers have done better."

"In any case one shot was sufficient to cause the death of the victim, was it not?"

"Yes."

"Why then did the defendant fire all five?"

"I don't know."

"Was it recklessness?" said Anne Christianson. "Was it panic? Incompetence?"

"Objection," said Bloom.

"Sustained," said the judge.

Anne opened a new line of questioning. "How close to a starter's pistol would a competent police officer have to stand in order to recognize it for what it was, rather than a real gun?"

"Depends," answered Roche.

"Four or five feet?"

"At that distance a trained man could tell, I think."

"And how far during his captivity was the defendant from the deceased?"

"About four or five feet," answered Roche.

Bloom in his turn rose and approached the witness box. "Lieutenant Roche, two points," he said in a mild voice.

He gave the jury a moment to wonder what his two points might be, then proceeded to elicit certain facts from Roche. That the average shoot-out was over in under two seconds. That the average cop emptied his gun in that time, or tried to, as he had been taught, and often enough not only missed the perpetrator entirely but wounded or killed some innocent bystander. In most shoot-outs the cop was moving, and the perpetrator was also moving. In addition, as all cops confessed afterward, no man's hand was steady during a shoot-out.

"Would you say, Lieutenant Roche, that hitting the perpetrator with one bullet out of five was about average?"

"More or less," said Roche.

"In other words it's only on TV and in the movies where the hero fires only one shot, deliberately wounding his man in the shoulder."

Tension in the courtroom was so extreme that Bloom's remark brought down the house, so that the judge began hammering with his gavel.

Bloom, after a moment's thought, said: "Let's go on to point two. What exactly is a starter's pistol?"

"It's a revolver with its barrel plugged. It is usually of small calibre and it fires blank cartridges."

"I see. Does it look exactly like a real gun?"

"It's very close."

"Is it truly possible to recognize that a gun pointed at you is a starter's pistol, rather than the real thing?"

"It would depend how the light was," hedged Roche.

"Would it be possible to see that the barrel was plugged?"

"Oh no. Of course not. But you might be able to see that no bullets showed in the chambers beside the barrel."

"But even if one could see that the chambers beside the barrel were empty, still there might be a live round underneath the firing pin, is that not correct?"

"That is correct."

"In other words there was no way that Mr. Keefe could have known whether or not the deceased was capable at any moment of blowing his brains out."

"Probably not."

"There were in fact blank cartridges in that starter's pistol, were there not?"

"Yes, there were."

"And one of these blank cartridges had been fired?"

"That is true."

"In other words Mr. Keefe actually believed he had been fired upon?"

"That may have been the case."

Bloom was exceedingly tall, with thin shoulders and a long nose. He seemed to be enjoying himself. He came back to the defence table beaming and said to his client: "I really nailed her case there, didn't I?"

"I don't know," said Keefe.

"She's not in my league as a lawyer."

"Perhaps not," said Keefe, "but she's better-looking."

He was not being facetious. Despite her severe suits and tight bun of hair, his tormentor was a lovely young woman, eight of the twelve jurors were men, and certain of them could not take their eyes off her. He watched them ogle her now as she approached the witness box and began her redirect examination of Lieutenant Roche.

"From a distance of four or five feet, Lieutenant Roche, could you recognize a gun as a starter's pistol?"

"Yes, I could."

"Could other experienced police officers?"

"Many of them, yes."

"Would you say that a man who couldn't recognize a starter's pistol should not have been in that room in the first place?"

"Objection," shouted Bloom.

Keefe watched Anne walk calmly back to her table and sit down. How could a jury disbelieve her when she was so earnest and also so beautiful?

Lieutenant Craighead was sworn in. He testified that the defendant had spotted the load of stolen nose clips when driving his official car out of New York State on private business, which by law he was not allowed to do –

"Objection, your honour," said Bloom. "My client has never been charged with any misdismeanour of that kind."

"The comment will be stricken," said the judge. "The jury will disregard it."

But the jury had heard the charge. Keefe turned toward Anne Christianson, and saw she was smiling.

According to Craighead, Keefe had taken personal command and had continually interfered with Craighead's attempts to conduct the case according to standard procedure; Craighead had known the raid would go bad long before it did, and that he himself would be blamed for it.

Bloom got up to cross-examine. "Did Mr. Keefe not order you to conduct your investigation as you would any other investigation of that kind?"

"Whatever he said, I knew what he meant. These deputy commissioners are all alike."

"Oh?" said Bloom. "And as you looked into his mind what did you decide he meant?"

"Top priority."

"Did you bring the case to the attention of the Chief of Detectives? Did he question or countermand any of the decisions made during the course of the investigation?"

"No, he did not."

"In other words, the case was conducted in a manner best described as completely normal, is that not correct?"

"Bringing those reporters in there wasn't normal."

"But my understanding is that they were brought in only after the gates were knocked down and the arrests made. Is that not correct? So in what way could the reporters have had any bearing on the outcome of the case? And, in fact, the raid was successful, was it not? You arrested eight car thieves who have since been tried and convicted."

"We also arrested one innocent man."

Next Detective Dickinson, the man who had actually arrested Joshua Brown, was sworn in as a witness for the prosecution. He wore jeans, a heavy sweater and scuffed shoes. His hands were sweating and he could not keep them still. Detectives were ordinary police officers who served at the pleasure of the Police Commissioner. They could lose their prestige and their extra pay at a moment's notice.

"I didn't want to arrest the deceased," Dickinson testified. "The Deputy Commissioner made me do it."

He threw a furtive look in Keefe's direction. He was worried about himself, not Keefe. He wanted to seem as far removed from that arrest as possible.

Bloom rose to cross-examine. "You've raided a number of junkyards similar to this one in the past, is that not correct? And on each occasion you and your squad arrested every human being on the premises, is that not correct?"

The detective would not meet Bloom's eyes.

"The reason being that the law so stipulates, is that not correct? According to law every individual on the premises must be arrested, is that not correct?"

"Do you have to keep repeating: is that not correct?" said Keefe when Bloom returned to the defence table.

"What's that supposed to mean?"

"It grates on me."

"Don't tell me how to cross-examine witnesses," said Bloom testily. It was the first Keefe realized that Bloom was under strain too. Nonetheless, he was unable to apologize and for the rest of the day they did not speak to each other. Meanwhile, Keefe continued to listen to the testimony, continued to squirm. The direct examination of each of the witnesses – the accusations against him – lasted hours. Bloom's cross-examination each time lasted a much shorter time. Like advertising on television, it was all a matter of repetition. He was being damaged by repetition.

Sergeant Carmichael, former commander of the Stake-Out Squad, now a uniformed sergeant in the North Bronx, testified. Anne led him to describe the scene at the courthouse before the shooting. According to him Keefe had taken immediate command: "He was ordering everybody around." Keefe had approved the positioning of the snipers across the courtyard. He had then decided that he himself would substitute for the cleaning woman as hostage, even though Carmichael himself had volunteered to do it. "There were two of us volunteered, me and that sergeant that later killed himself in disgrace over this thing."

"Objection, your honour," said Bloom mildly. "The sergeant in question committed suicide many weeks after the alleged crime for which my client is on trial."

"The comment will be stricken," said the judge.

The prosecutor looked up from her notes. "And did there come a time when the defendant asked to borrow something of yours?"

"Right. My ankle holster."

"And what was the purpose of that?"

"So that he could bring his gun into the room with him. At the proper moment he planned to whip the gun up from his ankle and pop the guy."

"Thank you. No further questions." Anne sat down.

Looking pleased with himself, Sergeant Carmichael

waited in the witness box while Bloom came forward from the table for the defence.

"Now, Sergeant Carmichael," Bloom began, "you say Deputy Commissioner Keefe asked to borrow your ankle holster. How did he happen to know you carried your gun in an ankle holster? Were you wearing short pants?"

The courtroom broke into gales of laughter. Bloom looked toward Keefe and grinned.

"Are you sure you didn't force your ankle holster upon him?" Bloom said. "Are you sure the idea of 'popping' the deceased was not your suggestion, rather than the defendant's?"

"He's the one who shot the guy, not me."

"Did the defendant ever use the word 'pop' in your presence? In anybody's presence?"

"I don't recall."

"Did he use any other euphemism for shooting a man? Did you not, in fact, force your ankle holster upon him? Did he not all along insist that he had no intention of shooting anybody?"

"I don't recall," said Carmichael.

Bloom, pacing in front of the witness box, said: "You claim that the deceased did not invite Commissioner Keefe by name to enter the judge's chambers in exchange for the release of the hostage. Is that correct?"

"The judge. He wanted the judge. We were all running around looking for robes. Anyone could have impersonated the judge. It didn't have to be him."

Keefe was sure of nothing. Perhaps Carmichael was describing the events with absolute accuracy, and it was his own memory that was wrong. Perhaps he had dreamed about it all so much, had brooded about it so much, that he had created in his head a version that was both personal and fantastic – that had never happened.

"I see," said Bloom. "You were anxious to get in that room and pop somebody yourself. Is that correct?"

Anne Christianson rose to her feet to object, but Bloom plowed onward.

"What would you say if I were to bring witnesses in here to

testify that the deceased did request Commissioner Keefe by name?"

"Wait a minute," cried Carmichael. "I'm telling it the way I remember it. I have to admit I was out of the room part of the time and there was a lot of noise in there."

Anne Christianson was on her feet again. "Objection. Objection."

"You were out of the room a lot," said Bloom to Carmichael. "And there was a lot of noise in there. Wonderful."

"He's trying to intimidate the witness," Anne cried to the judge.

For all the ferocious drama taking place in his courtroom, Justice Woodruff seemed today, as always, half-asleep. "Calm down, Mr. Bloom," he said. He tilted back in his chair with his hands at his lips almost in a position of prayer, his eyes half-closed.

"Tell me about that Stakeout Squad of yours, Sergeant Carmichael," said Bloom. "Has that squad since been disbanded? Why was that? Was it because you popped too many people?" He turned away from Carmichael, walked past the jury box, and disgustedly sat down.

To Keefe it was overacting of the most unconvincing kind; but the jury seemed impressed, and Bloom turned toward him and gave a quick wink.

"Relax," he whispered to him. "We get to present our side soon."

For Keefe, the nights were very difficult. At least in court there were distractions. But the nights he had to get through alone, and darkness was his enemy. Each day the prosecutor attempted through her witnesses to paint him as an irresponsible killer, and when he was alone in bed each night trying to fall asleep, it always seemed to him that she had succeeded. The world would see him her way. The jury would convict him and he would go to jail.

At the end of the first week Sharon came, boarding the first flight after work on Friday evening. It left Los Angeles at ten P.M. and landed in New York at five-forty the next morning – two-forty A.M. Los Angeles time – the flight known in Hollywood as the Red-Eye. She caught a taxi to Keefe's apartment and let herself in. She had not warned him she was coming. It was not yet light outside. She looked down at him sleeping soundly as she undressed, then got into bed beside him.

He had fallen asleep only about two hours before, having tossed and turned till then, having got up to make himself innumerable cups of hot milk. Still, he woke at once. The emotion he felt was surprise mixed with joy. Before long the bedclothes were on the floor.

After that she arrived every Saturday morning, though he told her not to. The expense was frightful and each time she missed most of a night's sleep. But when she insisted he began to stay awake waiting for her. He would be at the airport when she landed and they would take a cab home through the empty pre-dawn streets. They would have breakfast in the kitchen and then go to bed and sleep until noon. Saturday nights they usually ate dinner in. Keefe could not bear to sit in restaurants, for inevitably someone would recognize him, and after that every patron in the restaurant would stand up to stare. He much preferred to eat alone with Sharon, and afterwards to sit on the sofa with her holding hands, watching television.

The following afternoon, Sunday, they would go out to the airport again. He would see her through security, and then watch her walk away from him. As soon as she had turned the corner in the corridor and was gone an emptiness descended on him like no other he'd ever known.

Carmichael's two snipers testified separately. They had been crouching in the window across the courtyard, they said. Deputy Commissioner Keefe had paid them a short visit, and at first had ordered them not to shoot, but later had changed his mind.

"How do you know he changed his mind?" Bloom asked first one of them, then the other on cross-examination.

"Sergeant Carmichael came back and told us it was okay with him," the first sniper testified. "If the guy showed himself, we were to pop him."

"There's that word again," sighed Bloom. It got another laugh.

The second sniper used slightly different wording. "The Sergeant came back and told us we now had the Boss's permission to whack the guy out if we got him in our sights."

"I'm not sure I understand," said Bloom mildly. "Does the term 'whack the guy out' mean the same as the term 'to pop him'?"

"Those words are interchangeable, you might say. Pop, or whack out, or hit. There are some other words too. I can't think of them right at the minute."

"Did you ever pop anyone, as you say?"

"All the guys that were on that squad did. That's what the squad was for."

"How many men had Sergeant Carmichael popped?"

"Four or five over a period of a couple of years. I'm not quite sure. They were stick-up men engaged in the commission of a felony."

"That made it all right?"

"That made it a legal shooting."

"And the deceased perpetrator in the case we are considering in this courtroom, was he engaged in the commission of a felony?"

"Of course."

"Then it would have been legal to whack him out too?"

"Yes, it would."

"Legal for you, but not for the defendant who is here on trial?"

The prosecutor rose to her feet: "Objection, your honour. The question has to do with an exact reading of the law and is beyond the competence of the witness to answer."

"Objection sustained," said Justice Woodruff. "Question and answer will be stricken."

On a Friday afternoon the prosecution rested its case. With the trial recessed until Monday morning, Keefe took a train out to the suburbs to visit his parents. He went into his old bedroom and to his amazement fell asleep with his clothes on almost as soon as he got there. He slept through dinner and his mother did not disturb him. When he woke up he saw that she had come in and put a blanket over him. He stood in his socks in the lamplight blinking. His trousers were all wrinkled. He was terrifically hungry. It was eleven o'clock at night and he went downstairs where his parents were sitting up waiting for him. His mother in her bathrobe reheated dinner for him and he ate at the kitchen table. His parents sat with him while he ate it.

"I guess you needed that nap," his mother said.

"You should have awakened me. I didn't come out here to make you fix dinner twice." His father drove him to the train. In New York he went into an all-night movie. When he came out he rode to the airport to pick up Sharon.

Later that day he went with Sharon to Bloom's office to discuss tactics. Next week his own witnesses would be called, and the trial would be won or lost – Bloom seemed to think of it as a kind of Super Bowl. You worked out your game plan, put in some trick plays and hoped for the best. If you lost, there was always next year. For Bloom, not for Keefe.

The lawyer intended to call only three witnesses, he said: Chief Kilcoyne, former Police Commissioner Egan and Lavinia Spencer. He added: "What about that cleaning woman? You've been in touch with her? She has her ticket? Are we sure she'll be on that plane?"

"I think so," Keefe said. "I did talk to her. I'm not sure of much anymore."

"I'll phone Kilcoyne and Egan in a few minutes," said Bloom. "I'll ask to meet with them to go over their testimony. You've told them I'd be calling?"

"Yes, of course."

Sharon and Keefe went back to Keefe's flat. They were eating dinner when the phone rang. It was Bloom. "We may have problems," he said.

There was no mistaking the gravity in Bloom's voice, and Keefe had responded to it with panic. "Problems?" he cried. "What kind of problems?"

Egan and Kilcoyne had both declined to be interviewed by Bloom prior to taking the stand.

He had telephoned them, he said. He had asked them to come either to his apartment or office, or he would go to their houses, whichever was more convenient. It was essential he meet with them to prepare their testimony. But both had refused.

"So what does it mean? What's going on?" said Bloom.

"How do I know?"

"Am I supposed to put them on the stand cold turkey? When we have no idea what they might say under oath?"

"Is that so bad?" said Keefe. He knew it was.

Bloom said: "Why are they behaving this way?"

"If you don't know, how should I know?"

"Are they in cahoots on this for some reason we don't know about? Don't get upset. Answer the first part of my question. Do you think they've been talking to each other?"

Keefe tried to think it out. "Kilcoyne called Gold right after I went to see him. But he didn't call Egan. At least, I don't think he did. My impression is Kilcoyne and Egan don't really like each other."

"So you don't think they talked to each other?"

"I don't know," said Keefe.

"Why do you think they've refused to be interviewed by me?"

Keefe's throat was constricted and he found it difficult to answer at all. "I don't know," he said once more.

"If they say the wrong thing, they can stitch you up faster than any prosecution witness could."

"I know that."

"It's a problem," said Bloom.

There was silence on the line.

Bloom said: "Would Kilcoyne agree to testify for you, then get on the stand and only justify himself? Would Egan?"

Keefe stood holding the receiver and blinking his eyes. He could feel sweat running down the middle of his backbone. "Kilcoyne was known at headquarters as Mr Straight Arrow," he told Bloom. "The most honourable man in the department." But Keefe was speaking mostly to himself. "It was a miracle he ever made it to four stars, everyone said. He wouldn't know how to dissimulate." His voice trailed off. "So everyone said."

"Do you believe it?"

Keefe's voice dropped almost to a whisper. "I don't know."

"How about the other guy?"

Keefe said nothing. There was nothing he felt he could say.

"All right," said Bloom thoughtfully. "You've answered one question for me anyway – the order in which I take them. I'll take Kilcoyne first, and we'll see what happens. If it goes wrong I won't take Egan at all."

"Fine," Keefe said.

"It worries me that they might want to use the witness stand as a forum. That they mean to justify their own conduct and to hell with what it does to you."

"I know it."

"Well," said Bloom, "you let me worry about this thing now. Try to relax over the weekend. I'll see you in court."

Keefe hung up, and as he turned toward Sharon tried to compose himself.

"What's the matter?"

His face was white, he supposed. "Trouble with a witness," he said.

"Kilcoyne or Egan?"

"Both. Bloom doesn't know whether to put them on or not. I don't know why he tries to make me worry about it too. Let's finish our dinner."

Keefe sat in front of his food which he was now unable to eat. After a moment Sharon got up and stood beside his chair and held his head against her body.

Monday morning. Kilcoyne was on the stand, being led back through the various stages of what Bloom at one point called his "illustrious" police career. Still unsure of Kilcoyne's intentions, Bloom treated him with extreme care. Why was he there? What did he plan to say? Was it safe to have put him on the stand at all? Finally, unable to delay any longer, Bloom asked him to describe the events leading up to the trial.

At first Kilcoyne was vague. It required precise questions to get details out of him.

Handing him a copy of the New York State Penal Law,

Bloom asked him to read aloud from Section Thirty-Five which dealt with the lawful use of force, and of deadly physical force.

Kilcoyne read the significant paragraphs in a loud clear voice.

There came a pause while Bloom's copy of the penal law was entered into evidence.

Next Bloom handed Kilcoyne a copy of New York Police Department regulations open to those pages covering the same subject, and again he asked him to read aloud.

Kilcoyne put his glasses back on and read in the same firm voice. A police officer was permitted to use deadly physical force when he reasonably believed its use was necessary to prevent or terminate deadly physical force from being used against himself or another.

"So the law is quite explicit on the use of deadly physical force, is that correct, sir?" said Bloom.

"Quite specific," said Kilcoyne.

"If you had been in Commissioner Keefe's shoes that night, locked inside the judge's chambers and a man was pointing a gun at you and threatening to kill you, would you have reasonably believed that you were justified in using deadly physical force against him?"

Here, following an objection by the prosecutor, there was a long interruption. Both lawyers approached the bench where Anne Christianson argued that Kilcoyne's opinions did not constitute evidence, while Bloom argued that Kilcoyne qualified as an expert witness: his opinions in his field were every bit as valid as those of the ballistics man or the medical examiner in their fields.

Justice Woodruff overruled the objection, and both lawyers returned to their places and the trial resumed. The court reporter was ordered to repeat Bloom's question.

It had not changed. Would Kilcoyne, in Keefe's shoes, have acted as Keefe had done?

Bloom had turned away from him. He was surveying the back of the room, as if in no doubt whatever as to what Kilcoyne's answer would be. The key question. Which way would Kilcoyne go on it? Bloom's heart was pounding. At the defence table, as he waited for Kilcoyne to speak, Keefe found it difficult to breathe.

"Yes, I would," said Kilcoyne. "The perpetrator had already kidnapped and held hostage one human being on that particular evening. Now he was holding Commissioner Keefe and threatening to kill him."

Bloom took a chance and plunged on.

"But the pistol he was holding was only a starter's pistol."

"Commissioner Keefe did not know that. I doubt I would have known it. Mr Keefe was dealing with what moral philosophers call an unjust aggressor. Morally as well as legally he had every right to fire."

Someone gasped. It was the only sound in the courtroom.

"Chief Kilcoyne, did you have a conversation with the defendant on the day following the incident?"

"Yes, I did."

"And what did you at that time say to him?"

This too was a risky question, but Bloom got the best response he might have hoped for.

"First I admonished him. I told him not to get himself in a scrape like that again. Then I told him I was proud of him."

"Thank you, Chief Kilcoyne." Bloom walked away from the witness box. "Your witness, Madam District Attorney."

She began to question Kilcoyne not about the testimony he had just given but about his decision to batter the door down, about its lack of wisdom, about current police strategies in hostage situations, about his sudden resignation from the department – was he, in fact, fired? She was attempting to discredit him as a witness but was able to complete very few of these questions, and there were virtually no answers from Kilcoyne at all, because Bloom continually objected, calling her line of questioning extraneous. Each time Justice Woodruff sustained him. Her cross-examination lasted most of the rest of the day, and another woman by the time it ended might have been reduced to tears of frustration. Anne Christianson shed no tears, but her bosom began to heave and her voice changed tone, rose to a higher pitch. By the time her questioning ended she had gone shrill. She asked the

490

judge for a recess, which was granted, and she disappeared from the courtroom. When the trial resumed twenty minutes later she seemed entirely composed.

"She's remarkable," said Bloom to Keefe.

"Is she?" said Keefe.

Bloom was gleeful. Keefe was not sure that that much had been gained.

Anne phoned Senator Buckner at Brutality Commission headquarters. First his secretary said he was in conference. When Anne insisted that she needed an appointment at once, the secretary put her on hold. When she came back on, the answer was that the Senator could not see her until the following week.

So Anne rode the Lexington Avenue subway downtown. It was light when she got on the train, dark when she came up the stairs on to the street, and she walked across to Buckner's office building. It was by then nearly six P.M. The offices were still emptying out. Each time an elevator came down, twenty or thirty people crowded out through the lobby past her. She waited.

Another elevator disgorged its load. Buckner strode purposefully toward the street doors, but she stepped in front of him.

"You've got to help me." She had intended to speak in a calm, measured way, to give him what amounted to a prepared speech, but her voice came out wrong.

Buckner peered this way and that, as if wondering who was watching, perhaps listening. "Lower your voice. There are people here."

"You promised me," insisted Anne.

Grabbing her arm, Buckner spun her toward the elevators. They rode up in silence. In his offices there were still people working. The corridor was narrow. Buckner was behind her, pushing her forward. He pushed her into his office and closed the door.

"Sit down," he invited. He gave her a false smile. "Now what seems to be the trouble? How can I help you?"

"I've done my part," Anne blurted. "I called you every night during the grand jury hearings."

"You shouldn't have done that," Buckner said. "In fact it's a crime. Grand jury hearings are secret, according to law."

Anne was taken aback. "You asked me to call you."

"That's quite a rash accusation, wouldn't you say?"

Anne bit her lower lip. "I need help," she said. "I might lose the case."

Buckner shrugged. "There's nothing I can do about that."

"You must have information that might help me," Anne said. "You did an investigation too."

"My staff. Not me personally."

"What have you found out that might help? You must have found something."

"I'll look into that as soon as I have time."

"I need it tonight. Anything."

"That won't be possible, I'm afraid."

"You've been having press conferences. You've been making statements to the press."

"That's what you do," said Buckner, "in a job like this." In her agitation Anne had begun to pace the room.

His feet up on his desk, Buckner watched her. "You're a very beautiful girl, you know that?"

"My career –"

"We've all got careers."

"You told the press you had new evidence."

"I hinted, my dear. There's a difference."

"Hinted?"

"I know a small French restaurant on the West Side."

A bargain was perhaps being suggested, but Anne rejected it. "I'm going to lose this case," she said again.

Buckner's face hardened. "Maybe you shouldn't have sought the indictment."

"You encouraged me to indict him." When Buckner did not reply, Anne added hastily: "He deserved to be indicted. It's what the evidence called for."

"That's what they taught you in law school?"

"Yes."

492

"The world is not the way they taught you in law school."

"No," said Anne.

"You better believe it."

Anne hesitated, then said: "Former Police Commissioner Egan is going to testify tomorrow."

Bucker's eyebrows rose. "For the defence?"

"For the defence. Do you have something on him?"

Buckner shook his head.

"Do you have anything on Kilcoyne? I could recall him to the stand."

"Not a thing, honey."

Anne was gnawing on her lower lip as she tried to come up with an idea to which this man would respond. "You could call Egan up. You could tell him not to testify."

"Did I hear you say 'tell him'?"

"Advise. Advise him that it wouldn't be wise. He'll listen to you."

Buckner's feet came down to the floor and he started to rise.

"Call my Boss for me, then. Tell him you think it was right that I sought the indictment. Tell him you advised me to do it."

Bucker stood up. "There's nothing I can do for you, honey. You're on your own."

It was as if Anne hadn't heard him. "You've got to help me."

After staring at her a moment, Buckner said: "Why don't you take a seat in that chair there? Try to compose yourself. I'm just going to talk to somebody in the next office."

While Anne paced the rug in front of his desk, Buckner went out through his anteroom and down the corridor to the elevators. He boarded the down car, descended to street level, crossed the sidewalk to the curb, hailed a taxi, and had himself driven home.

Thirty-Seven

BLOOM HAD DUG UP MATERIAL ON EGAN, AND HE HAD studied it. Now, exercising great care, he took him back through his police career, moved with him out of New York, and then from city to city, and then back to New York as PC.

"In every city in which you served, you put in reforms, is that correct? Entire departments began to function better, and in some cases the crime statistics went down, is that correct?"

"In some cases, yes."

Egan, returning to New York, had seemed the saviour of the city, according to the material Bloom had studied. The local news media had so described him. He had begun implementing the same reforms that had worked elsewhere, and the city took heart and began to believe the police mess could be cleaned up. But Egan had not stayed the course. He had not lasted.

It was not in Bloom's interest to go into this part of it.

"May I direct your attention now to a raid on a certain junkyard in which were found stolen cars. A number of arrests were made. Can you tell us who authorized this raid?"

It was the first hard question. Which way did Egan intend to go? At the defence table Keefe leaned forward tensely. If Egan laid the raid to Keefe's orders, or Craighead's, then the risk to Keefe's case suddenly became enormous. Bloom would have to break off his examination and hope the proseuctor when she rose to cross-examine, would not exploit the opening.

Some seconds passed. The former Police Commissioner seemed to be considering a number of possible responses. Finally he said: "I did."

At the defence table Keefe sat back relieved.

"And did Commissioner Keefe lead this raid on his own authority, or at your orders?"

"At my orders. It seemed an entirely routine affair. If he brought it off, the department would profit because of the increased stature that would accrue to this deputy commissioner, and he would profit personally through increased confidence and experience as a police official."

"And on what authority did Commissioner Keefe take command of the hostage situation that developed later?"

"It is my understanding that he attempted to contact various field commanders to take over operations at the site, but none of them arrived in time."

"In their absence, Commissioner Keefe took command. Is that correct?"

"That is apparently what happened."

"On whose authority?"

"The authority of the Police Commissioner, in his absence, devolves to the deputy commissioners in descending order of seniority. That's according to the city charter."

Keefe at the defence table was gleeful. Bloom appeared gleeful too, though he was trying to hide it. He now came forward with the penal code and asked the Police Commissioner to read the relevant paragraphs from Section Thirty-Five having to do with the use of deadly physical force. Egan did so.

"And would you say that Commissioner Keefe's conduct – the shooting of an apparently armed man who was threatening his life – was justified under that statute?"

"Absolutely," said Egan.

"Objection, your honour." Anne Christianson was on her feet. She advanced rapidly toward the bench. "We are not dealing with opinion here, but with fact."

It was the same argument that had failed before. Justice Woodruff appeared to rouse himself, then to become angry. The transition was so sudden as to catch the entire courtroom by surprise. "May I remind the District Attorney of the difference between ordinary witnesses and expert witnesses? As I explained to you during our last colloquy, we have all listened during this trial to the medical examiner, and to the ballistics technician. Both gave their expert opinion. In the case of Mr. Kilcoyne and Mr. Egan, we are dealing with a total of over sixty years of police experience. They are giving their expert opinion. The court is listening to their expert opinion. Objection denied."

"But, your honor –"

"Denied. Denied. Denied. How many times do I have to say it? Please sit down."

Anne Christianson did not sit down. She stood as if stupefied halfway between the prosecution table and the bench until Bloom's questioning finished.

Her cross-examination began. Egan's answers became ever more mild. Once the judge had to admonish him to speak louder. Again she tried to call into question the decision to batter the door down. Was this not contrary to all modern police thinking, and therefore a mistake, a disgrace, a callous disregard for human life, a demonstration of police stupidity and incompetence? But at nearly every question Bloom objected, and usually he was sustained by Justice Woodruff. Her unanswered questions fell like weights to the floor. Finally she stormed out of the courtroom crying over her shoulder: "Why don't you cross-examine the witness yourself, your honor, and see how many of those objections you'll sustain?"

The courtroom was in an uproar. The reporters were on their feet grinning, most of them already in the aisles and trying to get out to the corridor phones.

Woodruff meanwhile was banging his gavel, and when he had succeeded in establishing some order he thanked ex-Commissioner Egan and recessed the trial until the following morning.

Back in his chambers he sat behind his desk for a while, brooding. He was an old man and disinclined to meddle, but finally he telephoned the District Attorney of Bronx County.

"You'd better talk to that girl," he advised him, "before she has a crack-up in my courtroom."

The District Attorney too hesitated, then sent for her, but Anne had already left the building. He had people trying to contact her throughout the evening, and messages were left on her answering machine and in various places, but she did not respond to any of them.

She was at home. She cooked herself dinner, spent several hours studying transcripts of the testimony, then put on pyjamas and a bathrobe, and tried to figure out what to do. She was alone. No one was going to help her. Her quarry was getting away from her, and this could not happen. The next day in court her mind would have to be twice as acute, her cross-examination even more incisive. In this city the people in power were all in cahoots with each other, protected each other, and the worst were the police. They were untouchable. Now she saw that her hoped-for victory might be taken away from her, and she could not figure out what mistake she had made, what she might have done differently. The defendant was guilty – and so were the witnesses protecting him.

Bloom meanwhile had received a call at home, and he telephoned Keefe about it at once. It was late and the next day's newspapers were already on the street.

"Guess what?" Bloom said jubilantly. "A friend of yours wants to testify in your behalf."

"Who?"

"I just had this very peculiar call from Police Commissioner Gold."

"I don't believe it."

"He must have been watching the news broadcasts. Maybe he read tomorrow morning's papers. Or talked to a few people. He can see which way this is going. He wants to join the winning side."

"Tell him no."

"Why? He used you, didn't he? Why shouldn't you use him?"

"I want nothing to do with him."

"I already told him yes. I thanked him profusely."

"Why, for God's sake?"

"Because we need him."

Keefe's hard-won confidence evaporated in an instant. His hold on the real world was extremely fragile. If Gold's testimony were really that important, then his acquittal was far from sure. "Need him? I still don't see why."

"Get a good night's sleep," said Bloom. "And try not to worry."

The following morning Gold took the stand. A heavyset figure in a sharkskin suit, he looked self-assured and at ease.

Bloom treated him with extreme deference. It was a manner Gold was now used to and seemed to like. In any case, his testimony was relaxed, expansive. In Keefe's position, Gold said, any reasonable man would believe it necessary to use deadly physical force to save his own life. He added that if Keefe were not acquitted by the jury it would be a gross miscarriage of justice.

An instant after this statement, the prosecutor was on her feet. "I object, I object. Witnesses are not allowed to tell the jury what the verdict should be."

In the witness box Gold, smiling, studied his fingernails. Later, when the prosecutor attempted to cross-examine him, he refused to answer nearly all her questions on the grounds that he had not been present at the courthouse until moments before the siege ended. He could not be expected to discuss events about which he had little knowledge. Meanwhile Bloom's secretary had just reported that the plane from Birmingham was in the air and Lavinia Spencer was on it.

Bloom requested a two-hour lunchtime adjournment which was granted over the prosecutor's protest. Bloom had a car standing by. He and Keefe drove to LaGuardia Airport. They were waiting at the arrivals gate when Lavinia Spencer came off the plane. Bloom interviewed her in the back of the car as they returned to the courthouse, and as soon as the trial resumed she was sworn in. Bloom was gentle with her. In response to his questions she described how she had been taken hostage, how she had been dragged into Judge Baum's chambers with a gun pressed to her ear, how terribly frightened she had been. As she spoke the events must have become increasingly real to her for tears came to her eyes, and presently she began to sob.

"I know this is hard for you," said Bloom gently. "Would

you like me to ask for a recess so that you can compose yourself?"

Lavinia Spencer shook her head. "I's here to do my duty as a citizen," she said with great dignity, "and I mean to do it. And I mean to help that man there if I can."

Once again Keefe at the defence table was amazed by the force of character she projected. A barely literate cleaning woman from the Deep South held the entire courtroom in thrall.

She hadn't known who Keefe was that night, she testified, had never seen him before, had never even heard his name, but through the door she heard him pleading with the gunman to let her go.

"The man with the gun, he knowed him, though. He say: 'You the Commissioner, I knows you'."

"And at that point," said Bloom, "he offered to let you go if Commissioner Keefe would come into the room in your place, is that correct?"

"That is correct, sir."

"And he asked for Commissioner Keefe by name?"

"I don't rightly recollect if he asked for him by name, or only called him the Commissioner. He knowed who he was. He say, I want you. I don't want nobody else. I don't want no judge, I don't want no lawyer, I want you."

"And then what happened?"

Lavinia Spencer said: "There seems to be some question about this gun the man had. Seems like it wasn't even loaded. I didn't know it wasn't loaded, and neither did Mr. Keefe over there when he come through that door. His knees was shaking he was so scared. He come through the door to save me. I didn't notice nobody else coming through the door to save me."

Bloom knew when to stop. "Your witness," he said in the direction of the prosecution's table.

For more than a minute there was no sound or movement in the courtroom. The stout, middle-aged black cleaning woman occupied the witness box and the prosecutor stared across at her and did not move or speak.

"No questions," said Anne suddenly, and got up and

499

walked out of the courtroom. Justice Woodruff had no choice but to call a recess.

The summations began. For more than four hours Bloom went through the testimony of the witnesses. He was both thorough and eloquent, unlike his adversary who in her turn seemed unable to concentrate on the facts of the case, rarely focusing in on any points that the witnesses had made. When she finally sat down it was so late in the day that Justice Woodruff recessed the trial until the following morning.

Keefe phoned Sharon in California. "It goes to the jury tomorrow."

"All right," she said, "I better come right away."

"You just got back there."

"That doesn't matter."

"You can't even get the time off."

"I'll just take it. I'll come tonight."

Keefe met the plane before dawn. They reached the courtroom on two hours" sleep and in their separate places listened to Justice Woodruff explaining the law to the jury. The key words in the statute, he said, were "reasonable" and "necessary". It was up to the jury to decide whether Keefe had acted "reasonably", whether the use of deadly physical force had been "necessary." Finally Woodruff stopped, and the jury trooped out to begin deliberations. The rest of the courtroom emptied out quickly.

Anne Christianson went back to her office where she began smashing the potted plants on her windowsill.

Keefe sat on at the defence table for some minutes alone. His palms were sweating, and he had begun to tremble. Twelve men and women now had his life in their hands, and he could be sure of nothing. Bloom tapped him on the shoulder.

"Let's go get a bite to eat," he said amiably.

"I'm not hungry."

"They're liable to be out for days."

"How long do you think they'll be out?"

"Who can say? They may not even start to deliberate right away. They may send for lunch."

"While I wait for them."

Bloom laughed. "I never saw a jury that worried about the defendant suffering."

Sharon had come through into the well of the courtroom. She stood with her arm around Keefe's waist. She was wearing a red cloth coat and black high-heeled shoes. She looked pale.

"All right," Keefe said.

They walked out of the courthouse and found a restaurant about two blocks away. They went in and were seated. Sharon excused herself, and a minute later the beeper at Bloom's belt went off.

He got up from the table. "I'll call up. It's not the verdict, though. Juries don't reach verdicts in fifteen minutes."

But it was indeed the verdict. Bloom was told by the clerk to return to the courtroom instantly.

They reclaimed all three coats and waited for Sharon.

"Where is she?" said Bloom.

"We've got to wait for her," said Keefe.

"Come on, come on," said Bloom.

Sharon's red coat hung over Keefe's arm. He wanted to sprint for the courthouse.

"Go in the ladies' room and get her," said Bloom.

But Keefe, a prisoner of convention, could not.

"The woman at the cash desk can send her when she comes out," cried Bloom.

They left Sharon's coat at the cash desk, and ran down the street toward the courthouse.

The cashier, who was also the owner, was used to people running out of her restaurant to get back to court, and she kept her eye on the ladies" room door. When Sharon still did not come out, she went in after her.

She found her on her knees in a toilet stall retching into the bowl.

The owner was immediately alarmed. "It's not something you ate hére," she said.

"Of course not," said Sharon, wiping her mouth on a tissue.

"You hadn't even been served yet. There are people who sue."

"It's not something I ate anywhere." Sharon said, and pulled the handle and got to her feet. She went to the sink and began washing her face. In the mirror she watched her color begin to come back.

"Your husband has gone back to the courthouse," the woman told her. "He says you should go right on over."

"All right," said Sharon. "Just give me a minute."

The verdict had come so quickly that the courtroom was virtually empty.

"Ladies and gentlemen of the jury," Justice Woodruff said, "have you reached a verdict?"

Keefe wanted only to know what that verdict might be. First, however, the entire formula had to be acted out.

"We have, your honor."

"And what is that verdict?"

"We find the defendant not guilty."

There were seven spectators in the courtroom, only one of whom was a newsman. Nevertheless Woodruff decided to make a speech. He said he agreed wholeheartedly with the verdict, and that the defendant, far from being a criminal, was a hero who never should have been brought to trial. He felt so strongly about this, he said, that if the jury had brought in a verdict of guilty he had intended to set it aside.

"Maybe he would have," muttered Bloom to Keefe. "These guys all sound very brave afterwards but there aren't many with enough nerve to overrule a jury."

Keefe found that the initial surge of relief was already gone. He said to Bloom: "What do I have to do now?"

"Nothing. You're free to go."

"I don't have to sign out, or anything?"

"You're acquitted," said Bloom. "It's as if it never happened. You simply go out that door there. And when you get outside the building you can walk in any direction you want."

Sharon had entered the courtroom only moments before, just as the jury foreman sang out: "We find the defendant not guilty." Therefore there was for her no moment of suspense, only a sensation of disorientation and confusion. The judge now was making a speech. From the back of the courtroom she could barely hear the words and she was having even more difficulty deciding what they meant. She was afraid to move as if the verdict were in some way reversible; the judge might still change his mind.

Keefe came up the aisle toward her. "It's over," he said.

"That's good," said Sharon, and she nodded, as if to prove she understood.

"That's all there is to it."

She stood in her red coat still nodding. "I guess we can go."

What made her suddenly burst into tears? Keefe had his arms around her and she was weeping into his neck.

"Nothing to cry about now," he said.

It was over and he would not go to jail. "You have no idea how relieved I feel."

"Yes, I do," she said.

They reached the elevator bank just as the doors opened – both elevators at once, both full. Reporters and TV crews spilled out into the hall, and as Keefe, Sharon and Bloom stepped into one of the elevators the entire mob attempted to join them.

Both elevators descended to the ground floor again, and in the rotunda an impromptu press conference began. Keefe was bathed in light. Eight or ten microphones were thrust towards his face.

How did Keefe feel, they kept demanding.

The trial had been over for ten minutes, perhaps less, and the emotions that beset him were violent enough, but he couldn't pin them down. He was alternately giddy and still terrified. He wanted to giggle; one second later came another onrush of terror. The back of his undershirt was soaked with sweat.

He wanted to brag. I found the cleaning woman, he wanted to say, and I convinced Kilcoyne and Egan to testify in my behalf. This proves that, whatever the problem, if you do the work you can get out of it. More or less. You can avoid the guillotine. Then he thought bleakly: until next time.

503

The cameras were turning. The lights were giving him a sunburn. He had still not spoken a word. A thought occurred to him. He could give them a lecture. Acts have no objective value, he could tell them, only subjective ones. It depends how people decide to view an act – at first by how a few persons decide to view it, and then by how everybody does – and everybody will most likely be conditioned by the few, not by the act itself. It was not something that could be fought against or even explained. Like the universe itself, it just was. I mean to say, he could say, that instead of putting me on trial for what I did, you could just as easily have given me the keys to the city.

He wished they had.

Though the questions kept coming, he only licked his lips. He was not an astronaut. The moon was not coming closer. He had not spent 240,000 miles thinking up apt words for the history books. He could not think what to say at all. If he praised the jury system he would sound like every crooked politician that ever got off; or he could credit Bloom's brilliant defence. And it had been brilliant. But this too would sound like an admission of guilt; if you were not guilty, what did you need a brilliant defence for?

He tried to smile, but could not even do that. He turned to Bloom.

"Please set up a press conference. Tell them I'll talk to them tomorrow."

Taking Sharon's arm, he pushed through the crowd.

"The judge called my client a hero," Bloom said. "Upon refection, perhaps all of you will too." Keefe heard this when almost out of earshot and thought: I'm glad he said that. If they put it in their stories it might possibly help me. People might remember me as something other than some kind of vicious killer. He had no illusions, however. Vicious killer was the only notion raw enough, once these events had grown distant, to stick in people's minds at all. He could expect the whispers to travel through every cocktail party he attended for the rest of his life.

He had Sharon by the arm and dragged her along the sidewalk. He knew he ought to be feeling joyous, but already he was worried about the future. He was heavily in debt, he had no job, and it was no sure thing that anyone would rush to give him one. Sharon tried to talk to him, but the long ordeal had bred an immense loneliness. In the aftermath he was locked within himself, unable to make a connection with anyone. Sharon seemed to sense this. After a while she ceased any effort at conversation. She disengaged her arm, and they walked along separately.

"I'm very tired," she told him. "I'd like to go home and take a nap."

That night there was a dinner celebration hosted by Bloom. "I'm paying the tab myself," he announced loudly, raising his champagne in a toast. Everyone at the table laughed. Keefe's brother and sister-in-law were there, as were his parents, Bloom's girlfriend, and, of course, Sharon. Keefe smiled as broadly as he could.

When he woke up in the morning he could hear Sharon in the bathroom retching. As he lay awake he realized among other things that she was trying to retch as silently as she could. Then he heard her washing her face. When she came out and saw that he was awake, she said guiltily: "I must have had too much to drink last night."

They watched each other. She was wearing a flannel nightgown that stopped at her knees.

"You hardly drank anything."

"Oh yes I did."

He lay against the headboard. "I have something I want to say to you. Come here."

She took half a step closer.

He said: "I'm getting married. If you won't marry me, I'll marry somebody else."

It made her sigh. "I certainly am awfully glad to hear that."

Keefe laughed. "Come over here."

When she approached the bed he took her hands and asked: "Are you sure?"

"Oh yes," she said. "I bought one of those test kits."

"How did it happen?"

"The usual way, I assume."

Keefe laughed.

"You don't have to make an honest woman out of me, you know. It's my own fault; I'm not from your mother's generation."

"I've been wanting to marry you for weeks."

"You could have fooled me."

"I had nothing to offer you. I still don't."

"You'd be surprised."

"I didn't dare ask you."

Having pulled her down onto his lap, Keefe began kissing her. "Let's get married today."

"People can't get married in one day."

"As soon as possible, then. Today I'm going to see about getting married, and tomorrow I'm going to see about getting a job."

"What is it that you're seeing about right now, if I might ask?"

"We're about to have a little preliminary marriage right now. Then we'll go out and see about the rest of it. Take that thing off. There, that's better. You know something, I've never made love to a pregnant woman before."

"Now you're being kinky."

"It's all right, isn't it? You don't feel sick, do you? I'll stop if you want me to."

"If you stop I won't marry you. Please don't stop."

A little later Sharon gave another long sigh and said: "We can't see about getting married today. We have to go to Bloom's for your press conference."

It made Keefe thoughtful.

"Will there be a lot of newsmen there?"

"Probably. I have no idea what I should say to them."

"Tell them you knocked up your girl friend, and now you have to marry her."

"Okay," said Keefe. "That will give them something to think about. Can you see the headlines?"

"Accused man impregnates actress during trial."

"Mistress expecting; not raped, defendant avers."

Each headline was sillier than the one before it, and made them giggle.

"Soap star conceives in real life soap."

506

"Sounds like we did it in the bathtub."

They were laughing.

But Sharon became serious again. "If you had been convicted, I didn't know how I was going to tell you."

"Why didn't you tell me as soon as you knew?"

"You had enough to worry about. You didn't need to worry about your child being born while you were in jail. And then yesterday after the verdict you were so distant to me. Your life had just changed and mine was still the same. I was afraid you'd gone off someplace by yourself where I couldn't follow. So I couldn't tell you then either. I didn't know if you'd ever come back to me."

"No," said Keefe, holding her.

"So what will you tell the press?"

Sharon lay in the crook of his arm. His hand lay flat on her still flat stomach.

Many things were over, he could tell the press. Others were just starting. What more was there to say?

Thirty-Eight

FOUR MONTHS LATER, AT A PRESS CONFERENCE OVER which Senator Buckner presided, the results of his commission's long and supposedly profound investigation into alleged police brutality were made public, and a report signed by Buckner was distributed. The report was 108 pages in length. The assembled journalists saw at once that, although it recounted a number of past cases of police misconduct, most of them already notorious, it documented no recent ones. No one presently in power either at police headquarters or City Hall could be discomforted by any part of it.

No public hearings, though promised, had been held. No public testimony either by cops or alleged victims had been taken.

Buckner on the dais behind the microphones was flanked by the mayor on one side and Police Commissioner Gold on the other. He praised the mayor for his support, and for appointing the commission in the first place. He praised Gold for the controls the police department had already put in practice, thereby making any public hearings by him unnecessary.

The mayor and Gold, when questioned, spoke glowingly of the work of the commission, and they praised Buckner for his selfless and "brilliant" leadership throughout. They wished him well in the future.

The next day the White House announced the appointment of ex-Senator Buckner as ambassador to the United Nations with cabinet rank.

Among the accounts of all this was one that appeared in the *Chicago Tribune*, and in the 167 newspapers, most of them in the Middle West, that subscribed to the *Tribune* News Service. It was especially detailed and incisive, and afterwards was submitted by the *Tribune*'s editors for a number of prizes. It ran under the byline of Philip T. Keefe.